IS IT RAGS OR RICHES?

Also by Kevin M. Weeks

The Street Life Series:
Is It Suicide or Murder?

The Street Life Series:
Is It Passion or Revenge?

IS IT RAGS OR RICHES?

Kevin M. Weeks

With Book Cover Artwork by
Matt Brumelow

Book Cover Design by
Marion Designs

This book was printed in the United States of America.

To order additional copies of this book, contact:
Xlibris Corporation
1-888-795-4274
www.Xlibris.com
Orders@Xlibris.com

DEDICATION

"Our dreams push us towards making them reality."

OTIS TYE

Author Note's

Adult Fiction

Parental Advisory: Contains Adult Situations

SPECIAL ACKNOWLEDGEMENTS

God, I thank you for the gift of writing and the readers who continue to patronize *The Street Life Series*. *René*, all the words which I've come across could never define how grateful I am for your support. I'm your biggest fan. *Mr. and Mrs. Tony Rose and the African American Pavilion at BookExpo America*, thanks for endorsing the direction of my book series. *Ms. R. Wilson and family*, I appreciate your believing in Teco Jackson to do the right things in the series. There is more to come. I give a huge shout out to *The Literary Community* for embracing *The Street Life Series*. *Attorney Rodney Zell*, because of you, liberty is personified.

Thomas Weeks, I thank you for taking an active role in my publishing career. *Anita Weeks*, little cousin, I want to wish you the best as you move on to college to reach your goals in life. I know that the sky has no limit. *To other family members*, we will have a great family reunion. *Cary Eaglin*, I thank you for encouraging me through my periods of writer's block. *Billy Bullard* (*a.k.a Cheeseburger*), *DiAnthony Butler*, *Marcus* "Corey Jackson" *Feldman*, *James Fulks* (*a.k.a. Boogie*), *Daniel Hargrove, and William Mathis* (*a.k.a. Knowledge*), I am appreciative for the book reviews. Special thanks to the *Author's Club* at LASP for being an advocate of my work. Thanks to the **United States Postal Service** for delivering my manuscript safely.

A king will arise in his time. See you on the freedom side.

Chapter 1

THE BRILLIANT SUN beamed 96 degrees on the sizzling black asphalt streets of downtown Atlanta, Georgia. Looking from a right angle, everyone could see the heat waves rising. Some called Atlanta the Black Mecca of the South while others nicknamed it "The Phoenix City." Eventually, the world renowned rappers dubbed Atlanta the epicenter of the Dirty South. However, this was where Gail Indigo Que, a.k.a. GQ, named home to her famous Indigo Signature Collection by Frontino Lefébvre, a remarkable clothing designer out of Paris France.

Every fashion critic knows that New York City is the fashion capital of the world; however, GQ tired of the city that never sleeps and found Atlanta to be an economical location to make a name in the fashion business. She lived a picturesque life in a stupendous condominium at Park Place South in the Maple Walk Circle area of town. Her important stint in Paris was all she needed to finalize the terms and conditions of the contract with Mr. Lefébvre.

Just in an instance, the clouds held a place in front of the sun and cast down a shadow upon the bronze female sculpture whose outstretched arms release a phoenix in Woodruff Park. GQ's corporate headquarters was on the northeast side of Peachtree Street and 9 floors above her clothing store which was at ground level. She chose this area of town because it symbolized new beginnings.

GQ looked down to the park from her all glass corner office and watched the Atlantans, as they were called, playing chess and checkers at 10 separate stone game tables. Vagrants took the time to steal a nap on the cast iron benches in the park while tourists stopped at the vendor kiosks along the sidewalk. Upon the green grass, couples sat on Georgia State University blankets while teenagers gave the crowd a mock performance on the provisional stage, which was erected a week prior to Sunday's hip hop talent search concert. GQ laughed at 3 toddlers chasing rock doves and took amusement in two gray squirrels chasing each other from treetop to treetop.

She reached for her small black Kahles 10x42 binoculars which put her right upon the chessboard of two mature men. With brunet and gray hair, one man looked to be down on his luck. With a short temple faded afro haircut, his male opponent was dressed in Brooks Brother's black pants and a white shirt with the sleeves rolled up. To GQ, the only thing they appeared to have in common was a passion for the game.

GQ pushed a few chess pieces with Tommy Richardson, the fifty-year old man with the peppered color hair and mesmerizing brown eyes. She recalled that their last game ended in a stalemate. Thinking he was homeless, GQ treated him to lunch at The Varsity which is a historic burger and fries spot in Atlanta. Several games later, Tommy told GQ that he was a retired executive from Coca Cola Enterprises and teased that he no longer desired to impress women with his handsome looks but rather with his healthy bank account. Together, they laughed.

She disagreed with him because GQ was impressed by Tommy's rugged appearance the day she met him. His broad shoulders gave him a distinguished look. Easily, he could have been a fashion model in his earlier years. GQ even imagined that Tommy would look attractive without a shirt because he did not have a beer belly. She constantly scouted talent for her upscale fashion shows. He didn't know it, but Tommy possessed a player's swagger that would entice her middle-aged female clients to purchase a lot of clothes from her Indigo Signature Collection.

He became fond of GQ and treated her to dinner at Ruth Chris Steakhouse. GQ remembered that the ambiance of the building made her feel as if she were walking into an elegant country club. The oscar style petite filet mignon melted in her mouth and the crème brulee dessert tasted divine. They talked for hours about GQ's new fashion contract; and it finally dawned on her that it would take a powerful team and connections to succeed in the business world. She also recalled that her heart weighted down in fear and a grim look came across her face. At that moment, the glass in her hand fell and red wine splattered across the floor. That's when Tommy said, "Be encouraged Gail. Even when winning is illogical, losing is still far from optional." As the waiter rushed to the table, GQ did not feel comforted but rather overwhelmed by the entire evening.

GQ leaned against the smoke tinted window in her office and refocused by looking for the best game played. After narrowing it down to 5, she went back to Tommy's board. "Umm, let's see. . . . What do we have here? Umm . . . Okay," GQ said out loud to herself, "view the whole board because life is just like chess."

GQ recalled the time she served at the Philadelphia Women's Penitentiary for a crime that she did not commit. This was where her former cell mate, Chi Chi, taught her that there are major chess pieces which only move in certain directions; and there are those sacrificial pieces. Then GQ reflected back on her past street life in Philly and decided that she, true indeed, narrowly escaped being a pawn as the only female member of the Strictly Business (SB) crew. With her fashion career, she was positioned to win a new game.

She continued to speak which caused the window to fog up with her sweet breath. "Okay buddy boy, it's your move." Tommy was clueless that GQ was watching the game from approximately 100 feet up in the sky. As she studied his chess moves, GQ heard the loud sirens of Fire Engine 4 approaching the park in the distance.

"Let's see how you . . . Come on. I know you see that move!" She shifted her weight to her left leg. "Come on Tommy. You do that same move every time. If you push your queen to E7, he'll take your bishop." Her tone was that of a disappointed protégé. Just as Tommy was about to move his chess piece, she saw Fire Engine 4's coruscating red and silver lights. Then the long red truck blocked her view from the game. "Shoot!" she exclaimed and stomped her right foot.

By the time the fire truck navigated around traffic, it was too late. The game was over. Tommy was setting up the chess board to play another game. Then there was a knock on the door. Knock! Knock! Knock!

"Come in!" GQ shouted knowing the door knock of her hired assistant, Janet Carroll, from Manpower, Incorporated. Before GQ turned away from the window, she noticed the rock doves flying away at the sound of the loud sirens. As they flew closer in her direction, the rock doves reminded her of the pigeons in Center City Philadelphia. She could barely tell them apart.

"Ms. Que, I tried calling you. You have a call on line one. She says that she is your sister," Janet said in a strong southern drawl.

GQ lowered the binoculars, took a deep breath, exhaled slowly, and said, "Okay, thank you Janet." GQ picked up her favorite Philadelphia Eagles coffee mug and took a sip of the vanilla latte coffee which was an acquired taste. After placing the mug on her desk, GQ put on the telephone headset.

Janet admired GQ's twenty-something aristocratic posture because GQ looked like the tall and powerful women from Somalia, Africa. The wrap around cotton and purple dress complimented her figure. In addition, GQ's eyes were an ophthalmological mystery. Depending on the lighting, her eyes appeared hazel, light blue, or almond-blue.

After Janet left the room, GQ walked over to her black crystal chess set with a matching board that she purchased in Paris.

"Hello, this is Gail Que." She sat down on the peanut butter colored leather sofa.

"What's up sis?" asked her twin sister Gwen Que who was standing in the kitchen of a row house on 56th street and Thomas Avenue in West Philadelphia.

"Hello to you. Is everything alright?" GQ asked while allowing her left spiked shoe heel to dangle off of her left foot.

"Of course, why would you ask?"

"Well, I haven't heard from you since I wired you $7,000, which you—"

"Can we just talk and leave the mother role aside for once? Dang!" Gwen plopped down on the dinette wooden chair and put her left hand on her forehead.

As GQ practiced moving her black glass queen piece defensively, she allowed herself to relax. "Okay, I'm sorry. I do miss you. Is everything really okay?" GQ asked with a more concerned tone.

"Well, to be honest, I'm ready to leave the street life alone; and this city of brotherly don't love nobody."

"About time girl . . . But tell me, why all of a sudden?" GQ asked in a Philly accent trying to get her sister to open up. Gwen for some reason fell silent as a church mouse. "Gwen, are you still there?"

"Ah, yes. I'm here. I was robbed twice in West Philly. I . . . I . . . I hate to admit it, but I think your old man Travis had something to do with it."

GQ leaned forward from her reclining position and exclaimed, "He did what!"

"Well, he and I were the only ones who knew that the stash was here at the house. But, he didn't know about the loot you sent me. I kept that over nana's, and—"

"Are you okay?" GQ felt her heart racing.

"Yes, I'm fine. They just tied me up—"

"What? Where is Travis now!" screamed GQ who was now standing.

"He moved out the last time I was jacked. He's claiming that I had the stash stolen because I was able to re-up. I think he moved back to the house in North Philly."

As Gwen stood up and paced the kitchen floor, she couldn't believe that she was telling her sister about having to restock the drug supply. Would GQ realize this was a contradiction to her earlier statement about leaving the street life?

"Gwen, I told you to get rid of that house in the strawberry mansion side of town! Damn! Do you even have a gun?"

"Yes, I do."

"Are you still dealing?" She already knew the answer.

"Have you been listening? I just told you that I had to re-up." Catching herself again, Gwen said, "But, I'm about to stop right after—"

"Look, I'm sorry that happened to you. . . . I don't want you to end up like—"

"I got this. Trust me."

GQ's face turned somber because she was worried about her twin sister. "Okay, I guess you know what you are doing. When you think you're ready to better yourself and clean up your life, call me."

Moving back towards the window, GQ saw that the group of teenagers were now sitting on the steps by the water fountain that curved around the wall on the park's edge. When she saw Tommy and the black gentleman laughing, GQ sighed. Then she reached for the coffee; and the steam met her nose with an aromatic pleasure. She hoped this would provide a calming effect.

"I saw you in *USA Today* and on the cover of *XXL Magazine* with your new clothing line," said Gwen.

GQ turned to the glass trophy case which was suspended from the ceiling because she liked all her accolades at eye level.

Gwen continued, "Is Atlanta all that?"

GQ thought about it before she answered because she didn't want her sister to up and rush to Atlanta without any plans. GQ was now living a drama free life and planned to continue to project a positive image.

"Well, when you get the time and have yourself together, you can come see for yourself what it's like living in the Dirty South."

"You must be crazy. I'm not moving down there. You should have done your research. Georgia has one of the highest penitentiary rates in the United States of America. They will lock your ass up in Georgia. No sir. I'm not moving."

"If you live right, you don't have to worry about the penitentiary rate. Like I said, you will have to come and see for yourself that Atlanta is the happening place to be." Then GQ picked up the Atlanta Journal Constitution newspaper. The headlines stated "African American Church Unites with the Sons of the Confederacy at Ten Commandments Rally."

Chapter 2

. . . THE LIGHTS IN THE BEDROOM were out. She walked into the bathroom and turned the dimmer switch. Now he could see that she was only wearing a Victoria Secret's hot pink chiffon ruffle thong, which complimented her sienna smooth skin and accented her long supple legs. He observed her nice round hips.

She turned around and said, "Teco, is it okay if I take a shower?"

He didn't know if she could see him because of the darkness in the bedroom; however, he nodded as he became aroused at the thought of the water from the hand-held shower head pulsating against every curve of her body. Goose bumps formed on his large biceps. *Oooh . . . so tight and round.* The sounds from the shower flowed in his mind like a waterfall; and he soon fell asleep.

When he awoke the next morning, he reached to embrace her; however, she was gone. So, Teco got up, stretched, and walked into the kitchen. He smiled when he saw that she was wearing his favorite blue Nike t-shirt and eating his favorite cereal, Cocoa Puffs. Her long silky brown hair was tied back into a pony tail; and her face basked in the sunlight which peeked into the white mini-blinds. He froze right there taking in every moment. His heart skipped a beat; and he tried to mask his boyish expression.

She turned to him and said, "Good morning Teco." After noticing his mannish stare, she seductively asked, "What are you thinking about?"

Teco, Mr. Don Juan, just stuttered. The last time this happened was when he was in the fourth grade. "I was . . . I was . . . I was checking to see if we needed anymore milk." Walking over to the Whirlpool stainless steel refrigerator, Teco pulled the door and looked inside. "Nope, looks like we're good."

He immediately turned around and walked out of the kitchen. In the living room, Teco caught his breath. Then he remembered that he was standing in the exact same spot where she revealed to him the pink thong last night. *Damn, did I hit it?*

His heart began to flutter, so he ran up the stairs to take a cold shower. Teco turned the shower knob. *Man . . . I need a chill pill, 'cause I'm trippin'.* While the water heated up, he walked into his bedroom. He stumbled over the ottoman. When he looked down, there it was, laying in all of its glory . . . the hot pink thong.

Just pick it up. Did I hit it? Teco rubbed his sweaty fingers together and inched towards the thong. He felt his ears burning and a fire igniting within his stomach. He began to grow weaker in seconds. He touched the thong and felt its soft smooth texture. Its intricate chiffon fabric on the top rim was exquisite. Upon closer inspection, there was neither a stain to be seen, nor a weave out of place. It was magnificent.

Damn, did I hit it? Teco was intoxicated by the thong. Finally, he picked it up in order to place it gently against his nose.

"What are you doing Teco?" GQ asked standing right behind him. At this point, he decided to deny what he was thinking. The thong glided to the floor like a feather.

"I . . . I . . . I . . . was checking to see if it was clean."

"No you weren't," she said as her hand slid up and down his huge dark chocolate arm. GQ pushed him onto the bed and Teco tried to say something. He searched for words to make sense out of all of this.

Suddenly, she kissed him softly on the lips as he attempted to speak. Then she untied her natural curly hair which flowed gently to her shoulders. GQ said, "I'm not wearing a G-string." Teco reached underneath the t-shirt and moaned passionately.

Beside Teco's bed was GQ's purse which she reached inside. Hiding an object behind her back, she kissed him all over. Teco waited with bated breath for her to reveal an adult toy. As he looked into her hazel eyes, GQ climbed on top of him. From behind her back she pulled out her good old friend, Glock 17, and pointed it at Teco's head. . . .

POW resounded throughout the room as Teco's physical therapist slapped her hands together in order to rub the sweet almond oil into the palm of her hands. This startled Teco, which caused his entire buff body to jump underneath the white terry body towel. Sweat poured down Teco's face; and his left shoulder twitched. Stepping back 3 feet away from a cushioned therapeutic massage table, the therapist allowed Teco to regain his composure.

This was a facility that specialized in both physical and psychological recovery. Teco's psychologist wanted to know how often Teco was having what the team of doctors thought to be flashbacks. Therefore, the therapist made a mental note to jot this event down into Teco's chart.

Shortly after Teco was admitted into therapy, Washington, D.C. Homicide Detective Hanae Troop briefed the medical team about Teco's case file. Therefore, the therapist was given specific instructions on the questions to ask him if this episode happened again.

Teco's muscles needed to relax.

"Are you alright? Do you know where you are? What is your name?"

Teco looked around the room and then at the middle-aged woman with bright blue eyes. She was wearing a SpongeBob medical uniform. "Yes, Mrs. Cooper, I'm fine. Umm . . . My name is Teco Jackson," he said somewhat disoriented.

"Tell me again. What is your name?" She was concerned that he didn't remember that he was in an outpatient physical therapy session in Bethesda, Maryland. However, Mrs. Cooper continued with the prescribed method to coax Teco back into reality.

Teco did not respond.

She continued, "Teco, tell me what happened the night the doctors believed they almost lost you, after you flat lined, and the EKG machine began to beep again."

Teco said, "I saw a light that seemed to be much brighter than the sun. Each minute seemed to represent one year of my life. There were vivid gardens; and music I'd never heard before played softly. Then out of nowhere there was darkness and a voice whispered in my ear, 'Take this SB ring with you to the grave and give it to Bashi, you sorry ass mutha—.'"

"Who is Bashi?" asked Ms. Cooper.

"Bashi was the Strictly Business crew's crime boss from Mount Airy in Philly. GQ killed him," said Teco in a weak voice.

"Who is GQ?"

Mrs. Cooper touched the scar on his left pectoral. This was the physical location that still housed one of the slugs from the gun which almost killed Teco. The bullet was lodged near his spinal cord; therefore, doctors did not want to operate in order to prevent paralysis.

Then she motioned for Teco to turn on his back so that she could massage his upper left shoulder. Carefully gripping the towel, he turned over but did not answer her question.

"Were you a member of SB?" she asked.

"Yes." Slightly confused, Teco wondered if he were still in the Philadelphia courtroom testifying against GQ.

"Who was the person to last have the SB ring?"

Teco didn't answer.

"When you moved from West Philly to D.C., what was your occupation?" She always enjoyed hearing his response.

"I was Rising Sun, D.C.'s #1 male exotic dancer," he said with pride.

As her hips swayed, she said, "You can rise on me anytime."

They laughed simultaneously.

"Do you remember what happened the night you were shot?"

"After my nightclub performance, I . . . I thought I saw GQ. So, I ran out of the club. I can hardly remember anything else." His voice was getting stronger.

"Who is GQ?" Mrs. Cooper felt a muscle in a tight knot and applied more pressure to the spot.

"GQ was also a member of the SB crew. I still need to talk with her. Was I dreaming that I saw her at The Mirage club? Is she out of prison?" He tried to get up; however, Mrs. Cooper held him at bay.

Even with the light subdued and the earthly music sounds playing, he still was tense. For some reason the aromatherapy candles and oils seemed to do nothing for Teco in this setting. However at home, they worked wonders for him.

"Just relax now." She realized that Teco was coherent again and needed his muscles to stop contracting. Mrs. Cooper continued, "What do you want to talk about?"

"I have questions that you can't answer. How will talking to you help?"

"Well, just tell me what's bothering you. I see you like talking about your days as a male exotic dancer. Who was Teco before Rising Sun, the dancer?"

"Mrs. Cooper, that's a part of my life that . . . I . . . I . . . don't think you'd understand."

"What? You think that I can't relate?" She reached for more warm oil, rubbed her hands together, and placed them gently on Teco's upper back. Finally, he started to relax. "Well Teco, I've seen a lot and heard a lot."

"There are terms that you wouldn't understand. It will take too long to explain."

"Well, try me."

"What's a skimmie?"

"Oh dear, I haven't heard that one." She chuckled.

"A skimmie is a female. That's what we used to call them back in the day. At one point in my life I was transient. I found refuge in the homes of women." Teco was silent. "Bashi Fiten took me off the streets. He gave me an important job."

"Which was?"

"I was the enforcer for SB. My nickname was Homicide." At this moment, he realized he was sharing too much with her.

"Go on."

"Bashi was murdered. Man! I knew I should have dealt with her. GQ was the one that did Bashi in and I found his dead body. A CSI lady once asked, 'The street life, is it suicide or murder?' I couldn't get that out of my mind. I decided for me it was suicide to continue running the streets."

"I think you made the right decision."

"Yeah, but I'm still lying down on this table. The streets still came after me."

"I disagree. You're on this table because you were shot. You didn't do anything illegal."

No words passed between them for a few minutes. Then Teco said, "Mrs. Cooper, that's the funny part about all of this. After I was shot, the last face I remember seeing and the voice I recall hearing was a dude from the streets of Philly. I beat his ass for stealing drugs from the SB crew years before. I swear this was a vendetta."

"Did they ever find him?"

"I have no idea."

Detective Hanae Troop didn't know about Teco's apparitions or his theory of who shot him that night at The Mirage nightclub. Teco couldn't piece together the relevance of this vital information.

"Can you tell me why you said that your name was Teco Jackson?"

"No, I can't. Maybe I was dreaming. . . . Ummm . . . That feels real good," he said as she loosened a tight muscle in his neck.

"You like that?" Her caring voice was soothing.

"Yes," he said closing his eyes.

"Good." Mrs. Cooper remembered to report Teco's psychotic episode on his chart. After she noted the facts, she flipped back 3 pages and read the emergency contact sheet which outlined the name Hanae Troop in red ink. The patient's name at the top of the chart read: TECO TROOP.

Chapter 3

"TROOPER'S P.I., HOW MAY I help you?" asked Hanae Troop while reading a news article on her laptop about today's Ten Commandments Protest.

"Yes ma'am, my son has been missing for six weeks."

"Have you filed a missing person's report with the D.C. Metropolitan Police Department?" Trooper glanced at the caller-id which displayed Margaret Davis.

"I did all of that and the Philadelphia police would only take a report from me. Only after I threatened to go see the mayor did they go over to my son's apartment. They said there was no foul play." The caller's elderly voice became high pitched. "So, I took it upon myself to go over there. However, the landlord wouldn't let me in until I got authority from a judge. I went back and forth and back and forth." Then Trooper heard the frustration and determination in Mrs. Davis' voice. "When I did get into his apartment, I found one of those things them fast girls wear."

"What? A corset?" asked Trooper wondering why the woman just didn't call the Philadelphia Police Department.

"No, one of them G-Strings . . ." Mrs. Davis said in embarrassment.

Hearing the word "G-String" caused Trooper to stop scanning the news article. The hairs on Trooper's arms and neck felt like the rosette on a dandelion. "How did you get my number? What is strange about your son having women's lingerie in his room?" Trooper leaned back in her office chair to give the concerned mother her undivided attention.

"I received a letter today that says, 'If you want to find your son, contact Hanae Troop, D.C. Homicide Division.'" Mrs. Davis heard the rapid sound of a computer keyboard as Trooper frantically pulled up a nationwide search for G-String murders in the past 6 months. There were none. "So, I called the D.C. Homicide Division and a police lieutenant gave me your number. By the way, my son is gay."

Trooper raised her right eyebrow. *There are people who don't want their families to know about their sexual orientation, and some even move to another state.* Then she asked, "Is the letter signed?"

Holding her breath and closing her eyes, Trooper recalled that her last assignment with the department was on the G-String murder case. The killer went by the name of The Paradox. At their last encounter, she stared at the shadow of his trench coat and tear drop hat as he got away and she lay there on the ground with a bullet wound.

Mrs. Davis said, "No, but the note says 'Ignorance is strength.'"

Baffled by the statement, Trooper asked, "Are you sure?"

"I'm sitting here looking at it right now."

Relieved, Trooper asked, "Ma'am, can I have your number? I'll get back with you by Wednesday. What does it say again?" This time Trooper wrote down the quote and contact information.

After hanging up the phone, she holstered her weapon. Typing on the keyboard, Trooper did a quick search. Within seconds, the first line item stated: "Ignorance is strength, quote by George Orwell, 1984. (Also a paradox)."

Trooper's heart rate accelerated as she closed the silver laptop. Then she picked up her royal blue flip cell phone and the new black Dolce & Gabbana (D&G) sunglasses that Teco Jackson gave her as a gift. When she opened the office door, the sun hit her face at full blast. Shielding her eyes while putting on her shades, Trooper scoped out the area cautiously.

Standing at the front of an old automobile repair garage that her dad willed to her, Trooper locked the all glass door. Her father's sudden death at 69 years old shocked the entire community because he was in perfect health. After she turned the garage into her P.I. office, several of her father's friends continued to drop by in order to check up on her.

Then, Trooper jumped into the classic 1968 Mustang Shelby GT which she also inherited. Under the hood was a chrome 429 Cobra turbo jet engine with air scoops on top of the hood. By the rear quarter panels were side air scoops. The gray Shelby sparkled like quicksilver as the hot sun gleamed upon the northeast side of 10th Street.

On her way over to the D.C. Homicide Division, which was her old stomping ground, she thought deeply about the possibility of her archenemy resurfacing. Trooper's drive was reignited to snag The Paradox because he vanished like a thief in the night during their last encounter in the alleyway not too far from a nightclub called The Mirage.

When she pulled up into the police parking lot, she felt as if she swallowed a bullet. Walking into the building, the familiar pine scent quickly hit her nose. She removed her sunglasses and scaled the marble stairs as if this were her daily routine. With her head held high, Trooper put her right hand on the doorknob of the 19th century cherry oak twelve foot door. She entered the Washington, D.C. Homicide Division and headed towards the cubicle of Marcus Brown, a.k.a. Swoosh; however, he was not there.

Someone walked up from behind her and asked, "Trooper, is that you?"

Her milk chocolate skin was still flawless. With her bone straight black hair pulled back into a ponytail, Trooper wore a beautiful blue and pink silk scarf tied around her head. The white dress shirt and khaki pants that she wore made her look like she was ready to go on a stakeout. In her right hand was a Snickers candy bar.

Turning around towards the familiar voice, she asked, "Ronald, how are you doing?" Looking at his silver Homicide Division badge, Trooper asked, "When did you—"

"When Swoosh was promoted to lieutenant..." With a blond buzz-cut hairstyle, Ronald Heard showed his pearly white teeth as he held the badge with pride. Noticing that the room was exactly the same, Trooper searched for her old partner.

"Trooper, what can I help you with?" When Trooper blushed, Ronald guessed that she recalled the time when he had a crush on her. He continued, "You know, you still owe me that cup of coffee."

"Yeah, I do. Don't I? Well, when you're ready just call me."

He looked at her for a few seconds and said, "Is there anything else that I can help you with?"

Finally recognizing her, a few officers waved hello. "Where is Swoosh?"

"In the office next to the captain's," he said with a nod of the head and eyebrows raised. She understood the warning of his facial expressions but was willing to take the risk of running into Captain Wicker.

"Thanks Ronald."

Trooper didn't bother to knock but bombarded her way into the office. Swoosh was seated at his desk speaking on the phone. The manly office chair fit his tall and muscular basketball player frame. She immediately noticed that his brunet hair was thinning; and the blond highlights were now gray at the roots.

Swoosh looked up disapprovingly. "Excuse me, but let me call you back. Someone just flew into my office." He put the phone down and stood up rushing to the door. Before he closed it, he peeked into the bullpen area and scanned the hallway. When he turned around, Swoosh and Trooper locked eyes. "You have some gall to barge into my office like this. Are you crazy?" he asked reaching into his pocket and pulling out his Albuterol inhaler.

"No, but I will be if I don't catch that son of a—"

"Trooper, you know I can't help you. It's against department procedure without approval from—"

"I need your help," she said walking around the office touching the novelties on his desk. "How long have you had this office?"

Lieutenant Marcus Brown flopped down into his chair resting his elbow on the armrest while placing his hand on the side of his forehead. "If you came by more often, you would know how long I've been here. I can't help you."

"Like hell you can't! Don't give me that department bull." Before either could speak another word, Captain Wicker barged into the office.

"Damn, does anybody knock anymore?" asked Swoosh with his hands raised.

"Hanae Troop! Ronald told me that you were here. I want you in my office now!" shouted Captain Wicker, a stately black man who looked like he had too many beers over the years.

When she turned around to speak, Captain Wicker was no longer there. Then she looked back at Swoosh. Trooper knew that she didn't have to do anything the captain commanded because she was no longer on the payroll. However, she knew that respecting his demands would yield faster results.

"Did some lady call you about her son?" Swoosh asked playfully snapping his hands in the air and putting his hand on his hip.

Trooper laughed at his gestures and said, "Yeah, that's why I'm here."

As Trooper entered Captain Wicker's office, she saw that the picture of Captain Wicker and her was missing from the wall. She wondered if the empty space was a way to make an example out of her to the department. "Yes, sir," she said acting the employee role.

"What the hell do you think you're doing? You know that this is a restricted area."

"Yes sir, I do know that." Trooper put her hands behind her back as if she were chastised by a big brother.

"I knew you would be strolling your ass in here after you got that phone call."

Swoosh walked into the office and Trooper sighed.

Captain Wicker continued, "After a major stakeout on the biggest case this nation's capital has seen in years, you walk your little heinie into my office and put your shield and weapon on my desk. Then, you walk out of here without an explanation. Now, here, over a year and some six odd months, you show up as if it's all good. . . . Well, for God's sake, it's not!" he shouted and wiped the sweat from his brow with a dull white handkerchief.

"Captain, my fight is not with you," she said and took a deep breath.

"Trooper, what you did was unethical and you humiliated our entire team. And for the record, it had nothing to do with Mr. Jackson as to why I gave you a write up."

Trooper was fed up with his scolding her. "Like hell you didn't! Your main focus was to look good for the blue suits. No one was concerned for Mr. Jackson's life. I left the force to protect the department, who I thought—"

"You kidnapped Mr. Jackson! At that point, you took the law into your own hands." Captain Wicker was now pacing around the office.

Standing closer to his desk with her arms folded across her chest, she said, "As I recall, some sick individual calling himself The Paradox tried to kill Mr. Jackson. Plus, Mr. Jackson left the crime scene by ambulance. I would hardly call that kidnapping!"

"Trooper, he's a federal witness! You moved him from the hospital."

"Sir, that he may be . . . and if I didn't move him when I did . . . we . . . or he wouldn't be alive today. Now would he?" she asked, as if she just scored a touchdown.

Captain Wicker inhaled and said, "I had to go all the way to the mayor's office. . . ." He exhaled. ". . . Then, I pleaded with the D.A. for them not to arrest you for kidnapping. You can thank me for the Chief of Police approving your private eye license. You owe me. Now, where is Mr. Jackson located?" he asked as if he blocked her field goal.

Trooper looked at him with a formidable expression. "Sir, I'm sorry, but I cannot tell you that."

"Young lady, you are in direct violation of D.C. Code 47-2839." Then, Captain Wicker pushed an intercom button on his phone and commanded, "Ronald, bring me The Paradox file." Within seconds, Ronald walked in with a huge stack of manila folders and placed them on the desk.

"Trooper, sit down." Captain Wicker gestured with his right hand. After thumbing through the file, he pulled out 5 large black and white photos and passed them to her. Each photo showed a group of young black men, who appeared to be selling drugs on a corner. At closer examination, she noticed Teco, who was wearing a Gucci sweat suit. He continued, "This picture was taken in Conshohocken, Pennsylvania. See the guy to the right of Mr. Jackson? His real name is Robert Edwards. He has several alias names and one of them is Bobby Stephens, who you know as The Paradox."

As she gazed at the pictures, a blank expression came upon her face. *I wish I could remember the description of his face from that night in the alley. I only remember his eyes.*

"Are you okay? Is something wrong?" asked Captain Wicker, when he saw Trooper's countenance change.

"Where did you get these from sir?"

"We did a more extensive investigation on Teco Jackson, a.k.a Homicide, a.k.a. Rising Sun. FBI Agent Rozier came up with these surveillance shots from Conshohocken and Norristown, thanks to the Norristown Narcotics Unit." Trooper looked totally bored as he spoke. Captain Wicker added, "Back then, they ran a sting called Operation SB. The entire SB crew was about to go down. For some mysterious reason, the crew dispersed when the female crew member, Gail Que, a.k.a. GQ, got arrested. But, the funny thing is that Robert Edwards, a.k.a. The Paradox, files are sealed." Captain Wicker paused to see if there were any questions. "This was done by someone in extremely high rank." Looking out his office window, he said, "Get this. It was sealed by a federal agency right here in

D.C. The Paradox knows somebody or somebody knows him." Then, Captain Wicker turned towards her and sarcastically said, "Other than that, you know the rest; I'm sure."

Trooper shot him a sharp look. "These pictures prove nothing. As far as I'm concerned, they are simply a snapshot into Mr. Jackson's past. What else do you know about this guy, Robert Edwards?" she asked.

Captain Wicker looked sternly into Trooper's eyes, "Mr. Jackson and Miss Que are the only two people who can identify The Paradox. Trooper, where is Teco Jackson?"

She stood up and tossed the photos onto his desk. The pictures slid towards the captain. "Sir, I can't tell you that."

"Don't make me—"

With one hand on the brass door knob, Trooper asked, "Make you what sir?"

He shuffled the papers on his desk and authoritatively read out loud D.C. Code 47-2839. "All laws which govern the Metropolitan Police force of the District of Columbia in the matters of persons, property, or money shall be applicable to ALL PRIVATE DETECTIVES . . ." he said as he tossed the sheet of paper up in the air towards her.

"Captain, you need me. I know the criminal mindset of The Paradox. I was the only one on the force to smell his foul breath!" she exclaimed as he dared to insinuate that she was not following the law.

Captain Wicker waved his hands toward her, as if he were fanning away flies and said, "Trooper, just go . . . just go."

While she stormed out of the office, Ronald high stepped to walk with her.

Captain Wicker looked at Swoosh and said, "Put a tail on her. We need to find Teco Jackson."

"Are you serious?" asked Swoosh.

"Yes, and do it now!"

Swoosh knew that Trooper was too witty for this tactic.

As Trooper and Ronald exited through the huge cherry oak doors and descended down the marble steps, her voice echoed, "Ronald, be careful. I'll call you."

"So Troop, why did you leave the department?" he asked as he continued to walk by her side.

Trooper let Ronald's question dangle in the air. After The Paradox shot her in the alley, a few days later her father died in his sleep. Death gave her a new lease on life. Protecting and preserving what she shared with Teco Jackson became all she desired. Therefore, she left the police department; and she and Teco moved to an undisclosed location.

When Ronald and Trooper stepped outside, the protest against displaying The Ten Commandments at federal and state buildings was underway. On the right side of the street, the signs for the First Commandment read: "No other gods beside me." On the left side of the street, the opponent's signs for the First Amendment read: "Freedom of religion."

The original intent of erecting the Ten Commandments as the founding principles of United States law was shredding right before their eyes. News reporters shoved through the crowd as both sides chanted words which pierced through the heavens directly to George Washington and the Founding Fathers of the United States Constitution.

Ronald asked Trooper, "What do you think of this protest?"

After getting into the car, Trooper turned the ignition. Ronald backed away because he was startled by the rumbling sound which came from under the sporty hood. She replied, "Ignorance is strength."

Chapter 4

"THIS IS 11 ALIVE NEWS. You've just heard a report from our sister station, NBC Channel 4 on the Ten Commandments protest currently underway on 14th Street in the District of Columbia. Now, we turn to live coverage of a fire at the Highland Woods apartments in College Park . . ."

Tracey Edmond, a.k.a. Goldfinger, turned off the television. His index finger was severed during a fishing trip when he was 10 years old. On his 21st birthday, he purchased a prosthetic 14 karat gold finger for his right hand. This was over four years ago. Sitting in the wooden duplex house on Simpson Road in northwest Atlanta, Goldfinger stood in his small cramped bedroom. Still liking the flexibility that his finger gave him, he reached into the secret compartment of the dingy white walls and pulled out three kilos of pure fish scale cocaine. Goldfinger knew that he was embarking on a $66,000 deal which was his biggest ever.

The clock on his nightstand stated 10am; and he opened the makeshift curtains to reveal a beautiful Thursday. Goldfinger looked out of the second story window and thought about his older brother Tim. He never noticed the brown Mazda 626 across the street, where a man was taking pictures of him. Goldfinger did see two red cardinals mating in flight as they flew off into the northern skies. Time seemed to also fly since

Tim was first incarcerated in Fulton County. Goldfinger wanted to make sure that all legal matters were handled correctly for Tim because Goldfinger felt culpable for Tim going to prison. Suddenly, Goldfinger heard heavy footsteps in the house, which meant his boys, who called him Trey, were getting ready to go to work.

T-Sand, Squeaky and Pie were downstairs loading up their tools, just in case they needed to hold street court as the judges with their own laws. Each of them had roles to play when Goldfinger made deals. This was hot Atlanta's (Hotlanta's) toughest clique known for pushing drugs throughout the area. The Edmond family had southwest Atlanta (SWATS) on lock. The dealers, who sold Meth in Atlanta's Fourth Ward, were their only competition.

Terry Sand, a.k.a. T-Sand, was the lookout man for the crew because he was alert and sharp on his feet. He was the only member in the clique who had a full beard at a 5 o'clock shadow. At the local clubs, women ran up to him for autographs because they thought he was Gerald Levert. T-Sand was the one who never talked much; however, when he was around, there seemed to be a lot of action.

T-Sand observed Goldfinger coming down the stairs with a black duffle bag in his hand. Once downstairs in the purple living room, Goldfinger placed a 9mm weapon inside the bag with the drugs.

Putting on a double shoulder holster, Goldfinger said, "Shawty, get your chrome pistol grip pump and the Desert Eagle .44." T-Sand laughed because someone not from the area would have heard, "Shawty, git yo chrome pistol grip pump and da Desert Eagle forty-fo."

T-Sand was a transplant from Brooklyn, New York. When he moved down to Georgia, he found it very difficult to understand the locals. Each section of metro-Atlanta appeared to have a different dialect.

The people of the Dirty South culture slurred their speech. In the hoods up north, "shorty" or "skimmie" meant a female. In the Dirty South, "shorty" was stated as "shawty" which translated simply as friend.

Ultimately, when T-Sand heard the dialect of the Dirty South, he translated the words in his mind or on paper like a foreign interpreter translated French to English. Sometimes he simply asked, "What did you say?" And out of nowhere, the person would start to speak proper English.

T-Sand reached into the floor chest with his huge hands to get the pistol grip pump and the Desert Eagle .44 gun. He laughed when Curtis Walker, a.k.a. Pie, turned sideways with his back against the wall so that Goldfinger could pass through the narrow hallway on the way to the kitchen. They looked like two sumo wrestlers warming up for a fight.

Pie was the crew's driver and a damn good one. Known also as a car thief, he jetted through rush hour with ease. T-Sand observed that Pie was carrying a 9mm, which Pie placed between his legs, ready for access, when he drove cars. Pie was a tall guy with big ears. T-Sand never understood why the ladies found Pie's ears so attractive.

Runyard Mindigal, a.k.a. Squeaky, was Goldfinger's right-hand man and the pit-bull of them all. "What's wrong with you shawty?" asked Goldfinger.

"Man, my wisdom tooth is killing me," said Squeaky in the same Dirty South dialect. Coming out of the bathroom, he held his left hand tightly against his left jaw.

"See, I told you last week to go holler at Doctor Jaffe. He'll pull it for the low-low."

"Show you right. Man, I'm in pain. That's why I didn't go with y'all to the Station last night. Trey, you look like you spinning. You up for this?" Squeaky asked putting on his bulletproof vest.

"Eating them skittles is the only way that I can buck back. I'm trying to touch the rainbow," Goldfinger said turning up the water bottle.

"Trey, you need to stop popping that E," said Squeaky speaking of the drug Ecstasy, which Trey, a.k.a. Goldfinger, felt relieved his anxiety before each drug deal.

T-Sand looked at Squeaky and said in his Brooklyn accent, "Yo son, get your Mini Mac-10 and the Chopper. We pulling out soon."

These were a fraction of Squeaky's toys. Squeaky was known not to ask questions. If something didn't seem right he shot first and dared anyone to question his actions. No one on the streets challenged Squeaky because of his mean temper and Bruce Lee physique.

Firing up a blunt, Pie went into the kitchen with Goldfinger and pulled a slice of pizza from out of the refrigerator.

"Y'all ready to do this?" asked Goldfinger. As they all looked at each other, everyone shook their heads in agreement.

The air seemed to heat up as Pie went outside to the 1997 silver Chevy Suburban. A few minutes later the rest of the crew came out of the house with rustic quilts which camouflaged the Mini Mac-10 and the Chopper. Before T-Sand got into the Suburban, he stood by the door looking around.

"T-Sand, what's up?" asked Squeaky.

"I don't know, son. Something don't smell right."

Across the street was a team of undercover Georgia Bureau of Investigation (GBI) and Bureau of Alcohol, Tobacco, and

Firearms (BATF) agents who were clocking Goldfinger's every move on film with the assistance of the local drug task force. GBI even placed a GPS tracking device on the Suburban the previous night at Central Station to ensure they wouldn't lose them.

There was a static screech over the radio. "Wait, nobody move. One of them is getting out of the Suburban. Everyone stand down."

Squeaky got into his red Honda Accord LX and drove away cutting a sharp right off of Simpson road.

"Alpha Team, Bravo Team, Charlie Team, stay on the silver Suburban. I repeat; stay on the silver Suburban."

"Where do you think Mister Mindigal is on his way to?" asked Atlanta Homicide Detective Paul Yeomans.

"He's the one we want for a double murder," said the squad leader for the Charlie Team.

In the car with Detective Yeomans was GBI Agent Fred Franklin, who said, "Detective, we need to get them all at one time. You'll get your man."

Yeomans cut a sharp eye at Franklin because he never liked working with other law enforcement agencies.

Franklin thought Yeomans was a little too young and inexperienced. With a perfectly chiselled chin, short Ivy League haircut, and Hollywood Beach, California suntanned complexion, Yeomans' handsome presence brought too much attention to any stakeout or undercover operation. Therefore, Yeomans was on the line to prove that he was more than good looks.

The undercover surveillance team waited for an additional 15 minutes; however, the silver Suburban never moved.

"What do you think they're waiting for?" asked Yeomans, as he grew impatient.

"Who knows? We have them covered for 2 city blocks and the 2 monitors on the house are all clear," said Franklin.

"Checkpoint one, this is Mac. They are on the move."

"Roger that. Checkpoint one has them in sight."

Tony McLoughlin, a.k.a. Mac and the lead GBI agent, came back over the air and said, "All units, this is not a take-down. Just watch and assist. I repeat, watch and assist."

"Checkpoint one, copy."

"Checkpoint two, copy."

"Checkpoint three, we copy."

Agent McLoughlin sat in the unmarked black Suburban and watched as well. His worst habit was twirling his Irish Claddagh ring on his right hand, especially as he worked in the field. The symbol on the ring included two hands, which meant friendship, holding a crowned heart, which represented loyalty.

As Goldfinger and his crew hit Martin Luther King Drive, a red and black 848 Ducati Superbike pulled up beside them. The rider glanced at Pie, shifted gears, and touched the throttle a little, which made the front end of the Ducati rise up. When the wheels came down the Ducati took off in full speed.

"Yo son, look at that fool," said T-Sand, as he put on his brown Gucci shades.

Pie pulled up to the intersection of Martin Luther King Drive and H.E. Holmes Drive. Then they backed the Suburban into a parking space in a lot across the street from McDonalds.

"Checkpoint two, one of them is out of the Suburban and is walking towards the McDonald's. You copy?"

T-Sand checked out a white van as he opened the McDonald's door. Then he heard an annoying sound, which drew his attention to a homeless man crushing soda cans by the Allied Waste garbage dumpster.

Things appeared to be going normal for this side of town. A muffler roared and the fumes filled the air when a green Nissan Stanza pulled into the McDonald's parking lot. T-Sand stood in a defensive posture, ready to fire down on anyone who was in the wrong.

First, a blond bony dude got out of the car and posted up by a light pole and lit a cigarette. Then a brunette female about 6 feet tall emerged from the same Nissan and slammed the door.

"Check point two, copy."

T-Sand was starting to get a little hungry as he smelled the French fries. Then he turned around when he heard a sexy voice say, "Hi there handsome."

He saw this brunette woman with a little tight tush coming in his direction and licking her bubblegum colored gloss with the fullest set of lips he ever saw. T-Sand imagined that he was biting softly on her bottom lip. *Man, she fine.* Her tight black body dress displayed every curve; and he could feel his pants filling with desire.

"Damn ma, where'd you come from?"

She looked out of the window and said, "I was at the gas station and saw your fine self crossing the street going into McDonald's. So, I told my brother to pull over quickly so that I could holler at you."

T-Sand sat down in an empty booth in order to blend in with customers. When she leaned forward, he could see her cleavage. "Is that right?" asked T-Sand.

"Sure is," she said as she licked her lips and moved her right hand from her hip to her inner thigh.

Confident that the restaurant was clear, T-Sand said, "Hold up ma."

Goldfinger walked into the McDonald's with a black duffle bag and took a seat in the booth with T-Sand.

Then twenty-minutes later, two guys came in with an identical bag, which was weighted. Goldfinger told them to follow him towards the back by the exit and out of sight from the Thursday mid-morning customers.

Once everyone was positioned to block the patrons view, Goldfinger asked, "All the money there?"

"Yeah, it's all there. What about the girl?" asked East Point Black, who was speaking of the cocaine while his look out man, Sun Valley Slim, kept post.

"She straight," said Goldfinger as he unzipped the bag showing the bricks of fish scale cocaine. Sun Valley Slim reached inside his pocket, which prompted Goldfinger to reveal the 9mm gun that was on top of the cocaine. "Yo, be careful; and move slow."

Sun Valley Slim looked at Goldfinger, smiled, and said, "I'm just getting my pocket knife. I heard that you were a bit keyed up."

"Naw, I'm just on the qui vive."

"Yeah, I feel you." Then, Sun Valley Slim pulled out a Scott Tester. With his pocket knife, he broke the seal of the cocaine and put a little on the tip of the knife. When the powder went into the tester, he shook it up.

The cocaine turned blue after the thiocyanate dispersed. Then, the contents changed to pink when the hydrochloric acid hit it. After the chloroform mixed in, the contents turned blue again. Sun Valley Slim felt like he was teaching a chemistry class.

Goldfinger smiled at the purity of his product. *They will be repeat customers for sure.*

East Point Black said, "Wow, we got some of that Yankee Blue here." Thinking the best cocaine came from up north, East Point Black placed the black duffle bag full of money on the table. Goldfinger unzipped it and reached to the bottom in order to insure the money wasn't counterfeit bills.

T-Sand stood up and asked the brunette woman, "Look ma, do you got a number where I can hit you up?" While she wrote her number on a napkin, T-Sand witnessed Goldfinger and Sun Valley Slim exchanging bags.

As Goldfinger looked out of the window, he saw the Ducati at the gas station. Then T-Sand's eyes locked on two men getting into the white van which he observed earlier. When the van drove off towards the I-285 loop, Pie pulled up beside the back entrance of McDonald's. T-Sand and Goldfinger got into the Suburban; and they jetted back towards the house on Simpson Road.

In the SUV, Goldfinger picked up his cell phone, dialed, and said, "Yo shawty, were we followed?"

"Naw, I'm still watching them. . . . Wait, hold up."

"What's up?" asked Goldfinger as Pie checked the rear-view mirrors.

"Man! The whole parking lot is full of police. . . . Hold up. . . . They going in the Micky Dee's. . . . They doing something in the back where you were. . . . Oh shit!"

As Pie got closer to the house, Goldfinger asked, "What's up?"

"They came out with some camera equipment. . . . Ah man, that chick T-Sand was talking to . . . she talking to them."

"Yo, follow them," said Goldfinger.

"What's up son?" asked T-Sand.

"Get the trash bag from the glove box and put the money inside. We was just caught on tape by that snow bunny. She the po-po."

After he exchanged the money from the black bag to the heavy duty Glad bag, T-Sand pulled out the napkin and looked at it.

"Pie, pull over right here," said T-Sand pointing to a gas station on West Lake Road. When T-Sand got out, he tossed the black duffle bag into a Waste Management (WM) dumpster.

Then he walked over to the pay phone and dialed the number. The phone rang three times. The recording stated, "You have reached the GBI drug task force unit—" T-Sand slammed the phone down on the cradle almost breaking the ear piece off. "Shit!" he exclaimed.

Once he was back in the Suburban, T-Sand commanded, "Give the call."

Goldfinger dialed Squeaky, who answered a cell phone that was attached to a Velcro pad.

"Yo, what's up?" Squeaky asked. Goldfinger heard the roaring sound of the Ducati's engine.

"Where are you?"

"I'm five cars behind them, about to hit I-285. What's up?"

"What about the snow bunny?"

"That's who I'm following."

"Good. Take her out. She's the po-po."

"Check." The phone went dead.

On the interstate, the Ducati broke down into third gear and pulled directly behind the green Nissan Stanza. Squeaky unzipped his red and black leather suit. Then he pulled out the Mini Mac-10 and sprayed the Nissan as if it were raining. The Nissan swerved off to the right and hit a concrete noise isolating barrier wall. Almost decapitated by the debris, Squeaky ducked and took off around the I-285 loop.

Chapter 5

GQ WALKED OVER to her desk and pushed the intercom button. "Linda, go ahead."

"Your afternoon interview has arrived."

"Okay Linda, give me three," GQ said as she squirted a dab of her Palmer's Coca Butter lotion in the palm of her right hand and rubbed both hands together. GQ pulled out the portfolio and resumé for her early afternoon appointment. After putting on her taupe jacket which matched the pant suit from her Indigo Signature Collection, she pushed the intercom button again and said, "Okay, send him in please."

Jerome Love walked into her office wearing a charcoal grey sharkskin suit from the Sean John Tailored Collection with a pink dress shirt and charcoal grey silk tie. He marvelled over the oil paintings which graced the walls. "I recognize Coretta Scott King, Winnie Mandela, Maya Angelou, and Cicely Tyson. I've never seen this lady," he said pointing to the portrait in the middle.

"I found out about her recently over dinner. As it turns out, I have something in common with her."

"How so?" he asked tilting his head to the right and tapping his left index finger against his left cheek.

"Just like Frontino Lefébvre asked to see my work at The Art Institute of Philadelphia, a travelling book editor asked to read her manuscript. Once you recall who she is, you'll know that the rest is history."

"Ummm . . . so she is an author?"

"She was an Atlanta author. Her book was based on the Civil War and sold over 30 million copies . . . 30 million copies," said GQ.

"Let me think. She was discovered out of the blue like you. She wrote about the Civil War . . ."

"Here is another hint. 'Frankly my dear, I don't give a damn,'" said GQ faking a southern accent.

"What!" he exclaimed putting his right hand on his right hip. Mr. Love added, "Gone with the Wind is the movie!"

"Yep, this is a portrait of Margaret Mitchell Marsh, the author of Gone with the Wind. One of my chess partners told me about her."

Then he turned and walked over to GQ's black crystal chess set.

She asked, "Do you play the game?"

"No, I've never seen pieces like this. They are as big as one of those small glass Coca Cola bottles."

GQ extended her hand and said, "I'm Gail Que. You can call me Gail."

His androgynous handshake caused her to pause. Upon closer inspection, she noticed that he was wearing a hint of makeup which evened out his honey colored skin tone. There was something about him that she couldn't quite figure out.

"Nice to meet you. You can call me Love."

"Please take a seat and tell me about yourself."

Looking over his credentials, GQ knew that she would hire him from the day she set the interview. This meeting would confirm her gut feeling about him. He spoke for 15 minutes. She interrupted and said, "If I hired you today, how would you better the image of my business here in Atlanta?"

He smiled at her as if she were his very own science project and said, "Well first, I would like to do you over. Girl, who does your natural curly hair?"

Taken aback, GQ said, "Why would I let you do that?"

"You want people to see you and see fashion. Your magazine cover ads were okay. They just didn't come across as Ann Klein material."

"Oh really?"

"You didn't get this fancy office and that line of clothes on the first floor without someone backing you. Word on the Manhattan catwalk is that Karlyn Fashion Recruiters on 7th Avenue said you weren't ready to be a designer. If I was you, I would have stayed in New York and studied under the likes of legendary Andre Leon Tally," he said snapping his fingers.

"Are you serious?" GQ's temperature was rising.

He jumped at the sound of her authoritative voice. Speaking quickly he said, "Frontino Lefébvre knows talent. I agree with him. Your designs are extremely unique. I have worked in the New York Garment District for 15 years. I've worked with Ann Klein and Giorgio Armani. How did you find me?"

Trying to take back control of the interview, GQ said emphatically, "Let me be very clear. I graduated with honors from the Art Institute of Philadelphia. I worked my ass off travelling between Philly and Paris earning my degree and learning the ropes from Frontino Lefébvre. You didn't answer my question. How can you better the image of my fashion line?"

He looked at her sternly and said, "It's going to take more than education to win in this cut throat business. You are working in high fashion now my dear. What will it be for you? Rags or Riches?"

GQ remembered what Tommy told her. *Even when winning is illogical, losing is still far from optional.* Then she smiled and said, "I'm listening."

"I'll show you how to build the Indigo brand. You hire me and you will be invited to private parties with the top buyers of Macys, Saks, Nordstrom . . . Shall I continue?"

She stood and extended her hand again. "You are hired. Can you do lunch?"

"No, not today. As your Fashion Director, I'm prepared to line up a ton of people I need you to meet. Will I have an office?"

"Yes, Linda will show you the way."

"Let me go get my case out of my car. When you get back from lunch, I'll show you Atlanta fashion."

GQ looked at him with an intense expression and said, "Okay, let's see what you can do. Know that your job is on the line."

He didn't even respond. Instead, he sashayed out of the door.

Turning back to the window, she glanced to see if Tommy was still playing chess. Though Tommy was gone, a man was staring at her window through a pair of binoculars. *Pervert.* He looked like a 6 foot tall body builder straight out of Muscle & Fitness Magazine. His pecan tan skin complimented his gray eyes. If GQ wasn't mistaken, he was one of the guys who ran the streets in Conshohocken, Pennsylvania back in the day.

Putting the binoculars into his messenger bag, The Paradox stood there analyzing why his brilliant plan to cut off the head members of the Strictly Business crew failed. First, Bashi was killed. Then GQ was not only framed for Bashi's murder and sentenced to life in prison but also presumed killed in a fatal car accident after she was released. Then Teco Jackson was gunned down in the streets of D.C. How was it possible that GQ was in that office, living and breathing?

The Paradox looked around at all of the business people before he took out his cell phone. He wanted to make sure that he wasn't being followed.

"What are you doing calling this line? You know to report on a more secure line. This isn't safe!"

An Atlanta police car approached and turned on the siren. The Paradox cuffed the phone with his hand to block out the noise and said, "I need your help again."

"Look, you've already jeopardized the whole team. You need to face the facts. If you know it or not, the FBI and the D.C. Homicide Division are trying to bring you in for murder."

"But, I have one last mission, Gail Que," he said looking around to see if anyone was watching him.

"Soldier, you listen to me and hear me good! There is no funding for your mission."

"I'm trying to raise awareness now."

"You are going about it the wrong way. Won't you just come in and let them do what they need to do. Your mission is over."

Click.

"Hello, Hello."

The Paradox didn't want to hear anymore. Finding GQ was a difficult task because she narrowly escaped death after the explosive car accident in Philadelphia approximately two years ago. In the totaled automobile, there was only one burned corpse, which the Philadelphia Crime Scene Investigation (CSI) anthropologist determined through DNA to be male. The Paradox searched high and low for GQ until her picture hit the cover of *XXL Magazine.* Even though he was surprised to locate her in Atlanta, she still needed to be eradicated and posed a threat to his identification to the FBI.

Think Soulja! Think! The Paradox's alter ego exclaimed as he walked towards Underground Atlanta, a well known spot to shop, eat and party.

"Not now sir, not now," said The Paradox softly. All alone, he found his black Lincoln Navigator and drove down the ramp towards the cashier's booth. He slowed down to see if anyone was watching him. It was time for The Paradox to take action. "Will they send the team on another mission? If they do, I need to finish my last personal mission first."

Soulja, there is never a personal mission.

"Shut up! Just shut the hell up!" The Paradox shouted out loud as he reached for the valiums in the center console. When he saw only one valium pill left, he banged his fist on the dashboard. "No one will live to I.D. me to the police." Then he turned onto Northside Drive and passed the Georgia Dome.

He saw a silver Honda Civic pull up next to him. When a little boy with long braided hair made a funny face, The Paradox pretended to cut his throat with his right index finger. The little boy clammed up and his bright eyes widened.

The Paradox came to the intersection of Bankhead and Northside Drive, made a left turn, and passed the Boys and Girls Club. Driving down Bankhead Highway wasn't much different from the streets of Philly. People stood on the corners as a homeless man pushed a shopping cart filled with trash bags full of cans. This alerted The Paradox that he was indeed in the right area of the all brick apartments called Overlook Atlanta.

When he stopped at the traffic light of Bankhead Highway and Ashby Street, the police seemed to be waiting for him. The

Fulton County Sheriff cop cars came out of nowhere with their sirens in full blast and blocked the streets. Instinctively, The Paradox put his right hand on his century AK-47 rifle banana clip, which was on the passenger side floorboard. Within seconds, a motorcade came from his right carrying a bus full of county jail prisoners. Then he put the AK-47 out of sight.

He was in real deep thought when the car behind him tooted its horn because the light changed to green. The Paradox pulled off slowly. Then he saw the entrance sign that read "Overlook Atlanta" and turned into the apartment complex. He never expected to stop at a security booth.

"May I see your driver's license, sir?"

The Paradox double checked to ensure the rifle was out of sight. Instead of pulling out his license, The Paradox pulled out a fake CNN press pass. "I'm here to cover a feature story for tomorrow's paper."

As the security guard flagged him through, The Paradox headed in the direction of a few teenagers, who were playing tag football.

The Paradox said, "Excuse me." The teenagers turned around. "Can you tell me where building EE is?"

"Right over there, that's where I live." One of the boys pointed in the direction of the building and added, "You need to back up and go around that way."

"Thanks," The Paradox said with a smile. He passed a playground and the maintenance office, where two old white refrigerators were lined up on the side of the building. The dents were the size of stones; and The Paradox wondered if the neighborhood children used the refrigerator for target practice. He backed up into a parking spot to stakeout the apartment of Lisa Turner, who once dated the Strictly Business crew boss, Bashi Mujaheed Fiten.

While sitting in the Navigator, The Paradox noticed a silver Chevy Suburban because the audio system in the Suburban made the Navigator's rear-view mirrors vibrate to every beat of the bass. As the four guys got out of the SUV, he observed that all of the men were wearing different colored sweat suits and tan Timberland boots. The gold teeth and gold finger of one of the men sparkled in the sunlight.

Squeaky was the first to notice the man sitting in the Navigator. "Yo, T-Sand . . ."

T-Sand turned in Squeaky's direction.

Squeaky continued, "Who is that over there?"

Goldfinger's crew showed no fear, as The Paradox and Squeaky locked eyes. A major deal was about to go down, and no one was going to screw it up. Goldfinger walked over to the driver's side of the Navigator, pulled out his Desert Eagle, and tapped on the window with the shining steel barrel.

Chapter 6

2 Days Later

A BLACK HUMMER H2 LIMOUSINE pulled up to the gate at Johnson State Prison. Upon arrival, the first thing in sight was the silver wire fencing with razor wire at the top. An adjacent fence served as a wall with razor wire from the top to bottom. The limousine driver placed his hand over his brow to shield the sun in order to see the officer, who was holding a rifle in the tower. A black raven glided in the blue skies overhead. Goldfinger stepped out of the limousine and put on his shiny havana brown Ray Ban shades.

With head held high, a debonair man, who resembled Issac Hayes without the beard, strutted out of the red brick prison gatehouse. Before he reached the limousine, Tim Edmond turned around to look at "Smurfville," which was the name the inmates gave the prison due to the blue interior.

"Shawty, you ready to do this or what?" asked Goldfinger displaying his mouth full of gold.

As Tim sat down in the black Hummer, he was amazed at the fully equipped 20 passenger setup with a hardwood floor and fiber optic lighting. "You come to pick up the entire B building?" Tim asked laughing.

"Nothing but the best for you, man," said Goldfinger, who still couldn't believe that his brother was finally going home after serving ten years for murder. "So big bro, what's up with the funny hat?"

Tim pulled it off and held it in his hand. "This is my kufi. Some people called it a beanie."

"I know what a beanie is. You out now. You don't need that," said Goldfinger while Tim put the white knit kufi back on his bald head.

"See lil' brother, that's where you're wrong."

"Man, we can't pull no shorties with you having that on," he said pointing to the kufi.

"You want to know what it means?"

"No."

"Well, I'm going to tell you. In Islam, wearing a kufi is the way we separate the men from the women. Women cover their heads with scarves. We men wear a kufi."

"Give me a break."

As the limousine turned onto Highway 15, Tim closed his eyes and took a very deep breath because his younger brother Tracey Edmond hadn't learned anything from all of those talks during visitation. The twist in the matter was that Tim didn't kill anyone; however, he went down for the crime.

When they reached Atlanta at 2pm, Goldfinger said, "You think you can handle being in a crowd? I heard that guys getting out of prison don't like to be out and about after getting released from the joint."

"Man, who told you that? They crazy. I'm ready to be with people."

"Good. I'm taking you on a shopping spree. Then we will get some real grub."

The limousine driver took them to Lenox Mall in the Buckhead area which is known for luxury, style and the nightlife. After shopping for five hours and having clothes altered, the limousine driver took them down Peachtree Street.

They saw the ESPN Zone and shopping centers galore. Tim asked, "Yo, ain't that P. Diddy's restaurant right there?"

"Yeah, that's Justin's. I'm trying to find out when he's going to be in town; and I'll take you there." Goldfinger smiled as he saw the freedom in his brother's eyes.

As the limousine driver made a left turn into Benihana's parking lot. Tim was so accustomed to seeing women fully clothed during prison visitation that he just sat there for a few minutes looking out the window. *What is the world coming to?* Some of the women had on halter tops with shorts while others sported miniskirts with stiletto heels. For a man out of the penitentiary, it seemed as if the women lost respect for themselves; and the men whom they were with obviously didn't care either.

The Edmond brothers stepped out of the limousine dressed in Ralph Lauren black suits with lavender shirts. They were ready to play the game like the big boys. As a matter of fact, Goldfinger had the bank account to back it all up. This was Tim's first time at a Japanese steakhouse. Benihana's menu selection included a wide range of food, such as hibachi steak, hibachi shrimp and sushi to name a few.

Wearing a colorful kimono, a short and beautiful Japanese woman walked up to them and asked in a blended Japanese-English accent, "Do you have reservations?"

"No," said Goldfinger as Tim looked into the tropical fish tank.

"Follow me," she said. The smell of real meat and vegetables filled the room. Chefs were flipping knives atop of glistening steel grills and chopping food while making volcanoes out of onions. Once they took their seats, Tim began to enjoy the beautiful pictures on the walls.

"Excuse me," he said while pointing to a painting. "What type of flower is that?"

"That is a Japanese quince. You like?" she asked passing them each a menu.

"Yes, I like how the scarlet flower is shaped like a pear." He looked around. "And that one?"

"That is a Japanese Iris. That plant has flowers in a variety of colors."

"What does it smell like?"

"It smells very sweet. Bees like a lot," she said. After taking their order, she gave a graceful bow and departed with an endearing smile.

Tim continued to check out the place as she walked away. Minutes later, the chef came out and put their fish on the sparkling grill. Every time he chopped into the fish, he would exclaim, "Uhht! Uhht!"

"What are your plans?" asked Goldfinger.

Tim looked at his brother knowing that he wasn't ready to hear the proposition of getting caught into the game.

"Living in prison showed me that the things I did ten years ago ruined both our lives. I'm not doing anything to go back."

"I need another hand. About 2 days ago, some punk ass dude parked his Navigator on our turf and I had to check him."

"See, that's what I'm talking about. Your nemeses are those streets that you so love."

"Neme what?" asked Goldfinger.

Tim laughed and said, "How are you ever going to get a legit job if you refuse to educate yourself."

"A job!" exclaimed Goldfinger while throwing himself back into the chair. "Man, I don't need no job. I got 3 cars and 2 SUVs along with 2 houses, not including the one I bought for you. All of them are paid in full. What the hell do I need a job for?"

At that moment, Tim realized that his brother didn't know him. Family and friends only know the person you were before you went to prison. It's difficult for them to visualize the new man. "Tracey, 'the love of the world is the root of all evil.' This is wisdom from the Prophet Muhammad, peace and blessings be upon him."

"Man, who is this prophet that you talking about?" asked Goldfinger, who was getting annoyed.

A smile came across Tim's face; and he said, "The Prophet Muhammad, peace and blessings upon him, was sent to humanity to explain the way of Allah."

"So that means you will be putting your face to the floor kicking it like a jay geekin' for a hit?" he asked in a joking manner by referencing someone fiendishly craving a hit of crack.

Tim gave him a sharp look and didn't think it was funny at all. "You have jokes? You mean offering Salah which are my prayers. For that matter yes, I will be putting my face to the floor like a "J," because I'm obligated to offer Salah five times a day. The Prophet showed mankind how to do it properly."

"Bro, I'm telling you. You don't have to do that religion gig no more. Besides, you didn't commit that murder. I did."

"Shh! Shh! Do you have to tell everyone in the entire restaurant?" Tim asked throwing his hands up in the air.

While he was trying to school Goldfinger, Tim noticed a very beautiful sister who was sitting in another section of the restaurant.

Goldfinger turned in the direction and realized his brother's interest in her. "Yo, you like shawty over there?"

Because they both were looking at her, she responded with a soft smile.

Goldfinger looked at Tim and said, "You act as if you are scared of her."

"Tracey, I'm not afraid of her. When you've been told not to say anything to a woman flirtatiously for so long, it's not easy to open up like that. I can't go around and sleep with just any woman that I want." Tim liked the way the woman crossed her long supple legs. He continued, "As a Muslim, I have to get me a zauj, which means a mate. A wife keeps a man in check. When you both are striving in the same direction, it's a true blessing."

Goldfinger said, "Get married? Man, you tripping. Rashid got 2 baby mamas and he messing with a girl in The Deck."

"The Deck?"

"Decatur, Georgia. I guess Muslims ain't supposed to sell that hard either. Huh? Well, if you shaking your head no, something's wrong because Rashid got a whole crew of Muslims: Hamza, Abdul and Rafia. They all slinging weight."

"Trey, that's the reason why each Muslim's Islam is personal. If he or she doesn't learn the real way and live it, they will go astray. See, I'm only trying to make myself better." He looked at Goldfinger and leaned forward. "Can you blame me for that? You'll have to get to know this about me. Islam changes people; and I've changed."

Goldfinger looked at Tim as if he spoke some unknown language. Just to get Tim to calm down, Goldfinger said, "Yeah, I feel you. I'll be right back."

Tim watched as his brother approached the lady he was admiring. She was sitting with a man who exhibited feminine gestures.

"Excuse me. My name is Tracey and that's my brother Tim over there. He is on this Muslim kick and won't come over and holler at you. But, he digging you. What your name is?"

She scrutinized Goldfinger and wondered if he was for real or crazy.

Then she glanced over to Tim. *I wouldn't mind meeting him. He's kind of cute.*

Tim couldn't believe that his brother was doing this. Did he not hear a word he said?

"I tell you what. Meet me at The Loft on West Peachtree Street in Midtown. He will talk to you then." Goldfinger went back to the table with a smile on his face and a swagger in his step that labelled him a street thug. By the time he returned to the table the food was cooked.

Tim asked, "Man, what did you just do over there?"

"Chill bro, I got you hooked up for tonight."

"Woe, woe, woe, you did what?" asked Tim who was leaning all in Goldfinger's personal space.

"I got you," said Goldfinger flagging him off with his right hand.

"Have you not heard anything that I said to you?"

"Yeah, I heard you. Why you talking all proper like you ain't from the hood?" Goldfinger asked while Tim just shook his head.

"Can we just eat?" Tim figured if his brother's mouth was full that Goldfinger would say less. Tim was becoming ticked off by the minute and added, "And my name is Mustafa."

"Mu what?"

"Mustafa Muhammad," said Tim getting it all out on the table.

"Whatever big bro," said Goldfinger after taking a bite of his hibachi shrimp.

Tim Edmond, a.k.a. Mustafa, couldn't believe that his brother set him up with a female, which is forbidden in Islam. Mustafa loved his brother, who was trying to show him a nice time but knew that things wouldn't get any easier. He focused on the new taste in his mouth which took his mind off of what Goldfinger just did. "Man, this hibachi stuff is good."

Goldfinger smiled because he was pleased that his brother enjoyed the meal. They sat there for 2 hours trying different foods before they were ready to leave.

Walking out of Benihana's, the brothers could tell that the temperature dropped and there was a nice Georgia breeze. Mustafa reflected back to a message from his prison Imam Leader. *"My brothers, always remember that you'll forever be faced with decisions in life; and your decisions can better your life or destroy your life. So choose wisely."* Mustafa slightly bit down on his bottom lip because he was very upset with himself for not telling Goldfinger that he had no need to party.

The limousine driver opened the door for them.

Goldfinger said, "Thanks Mark."

"Yes, no problem."

Mustafa looked at the big television screen and asked, "Where are we going?"

"To a club called The Loft."

Mustafa knew that clubs were out of the question.

"Man, don't tell me you ain't going?" asked Goldfinger.

"I'll go, but I'm not sure how long I'll stay."

Flashing all of his gold, Goldfinger looked at him with a huge grin. "That's cool too." Then he pulled out a small shoe box.

"What's this?" asked Mustafa.

"Just check it out."

Mustafa pulled the lid off and stared at the contents for a few seconds. Then he reached in the box for the money. Knowing that nothing in life is free, he said, "Tracey, I told you that I don't want to be around any drugs. How much is this?"

"Twenty thousand . . . At the bottom is an envelope with the deed and the keys to your new crib in College Park."

"Well, I don't even want to know where you got the money. Thanks bro."

"Don't thank me now. You can thank me later."

This statement didn't sit right with Mustafa. Nonetheless, he knew that he needed to get his feet on the ground. Mustafa reached in his jacket and pulled out a Georgia Department of Corrections (GDC) check for $24,000. He saved all the money that Tracey sent him over the last 2 years. After placing the check in the box, Mustafa peeled off $300.

There was a line all the way around the building. The neon pink and green sign read "The Loft." Goldfinger rubbed his hands together like a mad scientist. "Okay bro, it's party time."

Mustafa watched as Goldfinger pulled out some pills and popped them in his mouth.

"Trey, I'm not here long. Trust me."

The limousine driver walked up to the club bouncer and gave him $100. After he returned to the limousine and opened the door, The Edmond brothers received VIP treatment as they entered the club.

They walked through what appeared to be a tunnel because the walls were round with neon lights flashing. The floor even flashed with lights. Mixed with different perfumes and colognes, the smell of tobacco was all in the air. Several women wore little to nothing with thong straps revealed at the waistline. Tim shook his head. *This must be something new because of that 'Thong Song' by Sisqo.*

Women were packed onto both floors of the 2-level club and outnumbered the men 5 to 1. This is what the men at Smurfville talked and bragged about, which was nothing to Mustafa.

Following his brother to the first level, Mustafa heard house music playing. The second level's serene crowd jammed to Rhythm and Blues (R&B) music with a touch of funk. Mustafa could smell the sweaty bodies. The atmosphere of the club did nothing but enhance their moods. Mustafa watched how the hypnotic lights danced around the ceiling while shining down on the party animals.

Entertaining Goldfinger were 2 Spanish females. Seeing Mustafa's overwhelmed expression, Goldfinger asked, "You alright?"

"I'm gone. I'll take a cab."

Goldfinger pulled his arms from around the 2 women in order to talk with his brother. "No, no, take the limo. He knows where the crib is. I'll be fine." He raised an eyebrow as he looked back at the women who appeared to be getting impatient.

"Yeah, yeah, I'll call you Trey," said Mustafa.

Mustafa was almost out of the door when someone grabbed him on his left arm. When he turned, she asked, "Leaving so soon?"

Close up and personal she was pure eye candy. "As a matter of fact, I am."

Looking into his sexy brown eyes and admiring his rock hard frame, she asked, "Can we talk for a brief moment before you leave?"

"If it's okay with you, can we talk in the limo? This noise is kind of bothersome."

"Sure we can. I'm Gail, but everyone calls me GQ."

She liked his bald head and wondered if he played basketball.

"I'm Tim, but I'd rather be called Mustafa," he said with his hand extended towards the door as he guided her respectfully to the limousine.

Chapter 7

CLUB NIKKI'S ON METROPOLITAN AVENUE was the hottest night spot because of the low-level drug dealers who thought they had it going on in southeast Atlanta. The Disc Jockey began to play "I Like Dem Girlz" by Lil' Jon and The Eastside Boyz as the crowd of men gathered outside of the club waiting to go inside. At that moment, a white stretch limousine pulled up to the entrance. The hip hop celebrity of the hour stepped out of the limousine with his signature gold pimp goblet studded with flawless diamonds. The female dancers who were outside entertaining the men in line went wild because they knew that the lap dance tips would be nice tonight.

Dead on the couple who was coming out of the club, The Paradox was ready to make his move; however, hindsight taught him to wait for the right moment. The Paradox knew that these were the correct targets.

The dark chocolate brother, who opened the club door, seemed to be a lot more intoxicated than the cocoa brown female who was laughing by his side. Because she was sweating, the cool night air caused a light vapor to flow from her short shiny hair. Her plump breast enveloped the cups of the Victoria's Secret black lace-up halter baby doll corset-style mini-dress. The seamed thigh-high stockings and 8-inch hot pink spaghetti strapped heels accented every curve in her dancer legs. The Paradox dreamed that she was giving him a lap dance, until the man took off his navy suit jacket and placed it around her shoulders.

The couple walked over to a red Lexus LS400 with custom tags that read "KEITH1." While standing by the trunk and holding a brief conversation, the couple did not notice The Paradox as he put on his wireless surveillance earpiece because the bouncer was clearing the path of the guest celebrity.

"So are you going to let me cut tonight?" Keith asked in a slurred tone. The bass to the music resounded throughout the neighborhood.

Smelling the beer coming off of his breath, she said, "You're drunk. You need to carry your ass home."

He loved her southern accent and said, "Cotton Candy, you know I got you. How much?"

Straddling between his legs, she swayed left and right, which caused him to become aroused. As he pulled her closer, she arched her back; and the gold glitter on her neck appeared to dance from the street lights. When she leaned back forward, he nibbled passionately on her ear. Just as his hand reached her inner thigh, she grabbed his hand and shook her head "no."

He whispered, "I can pay you good, slim." Pulling out a wad of cash from his left front pocket, she could smell ten fresh hundred dollar bills while he counted. Keith continued, "I got a G."

"Boy, put that money away. I need my job. The police might be around here." She scanned the parking lot but only saw a man sitting in a black Lincoln Navigator. She continued, "Alright, meet me up the street at Metropolitan Inn in five minutes. Bring a condom."

The Paradox started up the Navigator as the female dancer went to an old silver Honda Accord with Laurens County tags. There were hardly any other cars on the road. Keith drove ahead of the dancer while The Paradox remained two cars behind the Accord.

Glancing at the radio clock that read "3:00," the dancer pulled into the hourly rate motel. Looking up in the starry sky, she felt uneasy about this night. Then Keith gave her a bright smile and winked as he walked into the hotel. She sighed.

Moments later, the Navigator parked several spaces down from the Lexus. The Paradox located only one motion camera, which was directed at the lobby's entrance. To the left, one white and green Old Dominion 18 wheeler entered the truck parking lot. To the right, The Paradox watched Keith open the car door for the dancer.

Getting out of the SUV, The Paradox followed the couple to Room 202. As Keith struggled to put the key card in the slot, The Paradox continued to survey the area and walked pass them as if he were going to another room. The area reeked of hard liquor and the lights flickered.

When The Paradox heard the door to Room 202 close, he rushed down to the Navigator. Opening the SUV back door, he reached for the silver case that was on the floorboard. Pulling out the blue polymer Ruger P95 9mm pistol, The Paradox laid it on the black leather seat.

Reaching in the cargo pocket on the passenger side backseat, he removed a black mini-bag. Unzipping it, there were six different types of suppressors and a deluxe double magazine case, which held ten magazines. He attached a small silencer to the barrel of the Ruger P95 and inserted 17 subsonic rounds which were made for short range military use.

After loading the P95, he put the silver and black weapon into his back waistband and shut the back door. The palms of his hands became sweaty as his mind flashed back to his previous work in the G-String murders at the hotels around the Washington, D.C. area.

Moving to the driver's seat, The Paradox rolled up his sleeve and pushed the button on his Swiss Army military watch causing the face to illuminate in the dark. *Soulja, it's time.* He reached in the glove box and slipped on a pair of black leather combat gloves filled with lead. Then he put on his black leather trench coat.

After sprinting up the metal staircase, he stood to the left of Room 202 and peeked into the window. The Paradox could not see any shadow movement through the curtains. Then he drew his right leg back and slammed it into the door as hard as he could. The door flew open. BOOM! The doorknob went into the wall, putting a hole into the thin sheetrock. Then The Paradox slammed the door close.

Barely able to stand up without leaning on the bathroom doorjamb, Keith stumbled into the bedroom in his birthday suit and exclaimed, "Yo, what the hell are you doing!"

The Paradox pulled out the P95. When Keith saw the gun, he tried to run back into the narrow bathroom as if there was another way to exit. Two shots rang out, which knocked Keith into the sink. One more shot threw Keith's body into the mirror, which broke and pierced through his forehead. Blood splattered everywhere.

Hearing cries, The Paradox threw the shower curtains back and saw the dancer, who was balled up in the fetal position in the bathtub. Looking at the pistol, she began to hyperventilate. When she screamed, he raised the gun in her direction and motioned for her to come out.

"Shut up! Come over here!" The Paradox pointed to the king-size bed with the dingy floral comforter. After taking a deep breath, he rolled his head around cracking his neck.

Her black mascara was under her eyes as tears flowed down her angelic face. She began to speak with her trembling hands over her mouth. "The . . . the . . . money is . . . over there." She pointed to her purse that was on the table. When The Paradox didn't respond, she yelled desperately, "What do you want!"

The Paradox reached in his back pocket and pulled out a beautiful blue G-String, with four gold chains on the right side and lace on the left. The dancer stared at the G-String, trying to figure what the hell was going to happen next.

As he walked towards her, The Paradox said, "See, there's always room for mistakes. However, this is not a mistake. There is a game and you've been chosen as a player."

She backpedalled her way up against the headboard and screamed frantically, "No, no, please, please, no, I don't want to play!"

As she kicked at him with her right leg, The Paradox grabbed her left ankle. Then she tried to grab hold of the headboard, but her grip was useless and weak because he still managed to pull her towards him. She smelled his foul breath.

Yanking her hair, The Paradox smiled at his image in the dresser mirror as he held the G-String tight around her neck. She continued to kick and tried to pull his hands away; however, she was too late because he applied just the right amount of pressure. Then her arms went limp to her sides.

First mission complete. Good job Soulja. Now get the hell out of here. You were too loud.

Placing her on the bed with her left arm hanging off the side, The Paradox admired this new twist because he didn't stage the other crime scenes in the Chocolate City murders. Pulling out a pocket knife, he fumbled with the carpet only a few inches below her left hand.

Finally, he rampaged through her purse and took money from Keith's pants pocket. As The Paradox ran down the stairs, he heard police sirens coming in the distance.

When he slammed the door to the Navigator and cranked up the engine, a crowd of good Samaritans tried to bum rush the vehicle. Looking in the rear-view mirror, he narrowly escaped and turned onto the street before the cop cars bent the curve. The Paradox laughed and slapped the steering wheel because he could hardly wait to see his masterpiece on the news.

◊◊◊◊◊

BACK IN WASHINGTON, D.C., Trooper sat at her home office desk when her cell phone vibrated. Still in her black camisole and yoga pants, she jumped up to remove the phone from the charger.

"Hello?" she asked waiting for someone to say something, but there was a brief pause before the familiar voice spoke up.

Clearing his throat first, he said, "Hello Trooper."

She picked up the note that was mailed to her from the concerned mother in Philadelphia. "Hello captain, what can I do for you?"

"Trooper, we need to talk—"

"If it's about Teco, we have nothing to discuss."

"He's at it again. We think. Look, can you just come in and we'll talk about it?"

"He who?"

"Let's put it this way. There was a G-String murder last night in Atlanta, Georgia."

"Atlanta's not in your jurisdiction. Besides captain, right now I don't trust anyone from the department."

"This is extremely important and time is of the essence."

"We'll meet where I say so."

"Okay Trooper," he said with a slight laugh, "still cautious I see."

"Yep, you taught me well. I'll call you in two hours and let you know where to meet."

"Trooper, before you hang up . . . we got THAT call a few days ago. You did good by hiding Teco under your last name. It's possible that Teco will be a target again."

Not knowing how to respond, she just said, "I'll call you."

After hanging up the cell phone, she leaned back into her mesh office swivel chair. *I have to let Teco know what's going on.*

She picked up the 4x6 picture frame of Teco at the firing range and ran her index finger across his face. Then she stood up.

The closer she got to the mint green bedroom she heard some mumbling sounds but didn't see anyone. Looking at the queen-size canopy bed, Trooper saw that the lavender 1000 count sheets, down comforter, and decorative pillows were untouched. However, she still heard the cries of forgiveness and then praises.

When she reached the walk-in closet, the noise became very clear. She just stood there listening with her eyes closed. Ten minutes passed when Teco came out wiping tears from his eyes.

He was shocked to see Trooper.

"Teco, how long have you been praying like that?" she asked with warmth in her heart.

He looked at her surprised that she would ask him. "Well, I've been praying like that since God gave me a second chance at life. Why you ask?"

"Because I've never heard you pray before . . ."

He walked over to her and held both of her hands. "Baby, I pray every day for both of us and for our protection." He kissed her on the forehead and walked over to the treadmill, which was in a separate section of the master suite. "I guess you figured out that note?"

"Yes and no, but we have even more important business to attend to," said Trooper watching Teco punch the controls on the treadmill's digital panel.

"Okay, I'm all ears," he said picking up his pace in a slow jog, ready to generate a good sweat.

She didn't know how else to say it but one way. Trooper looked at Teco as he was now running at full speed. "The Paradox!"

When he heard the name, Teco stopped and slid off the treadmill almost bumping his head on the floor.

Chapter 8

TECO GAINED his footing and turned the treadmill off. Walking over to the mini-refrigerator, he retrieved a bottle of Dasani water. Then he reached for his yellow Speedo sports towel to dab the sweat from his forehead. Turning the bottle top, Teco took a long swig and asked, "Now, what did you say about The Paradox?"

"I just received a call from Captain Wicker; and he said that The Paradox is at it again." Trooper sat on the side of the bed.

"So, what does Wicker want from you?" he asked knowing that he wouldn't like her response.

"Well, he never said exactly. He wants to meet with me and talk."

They looked at each other; and he knew that he couldn't talk her out of going after this killer.

"Do you trust Wicker after the club ordeal the night I got shot?"

"Baby, I walked out on the force. The love I have for you got in the way of my job. It almost cost me my life. I need you to watch my back when I go talk with Wicker though." Trooper reached into the nightstand and pulled out a bite-size Snickers bar.

"Where and when are you meeting him?" he asked while taking another swig.

"I told him I'd call in two hours. This will give us time to set up a good location in public."

Teco knew that she would one day settle the score with their number one enemy. If The Paradox was indeed Bobby Stephens, who Teco humiliated on the streets of Conshohocken, then Bobby was the perpetrator who put the bullet into Teco's chest at the Mirage nightclub. Not wanting to go back to jail, the best thing was for Teco to support Trooper's gut instinct and sound judgement.

An hour later, Teco walked outside, looked up to beautiful blue skies, and thought it to be a nice day for Trooper and him to ride anyways. They jumped into the Mustang Shelby GT in order to pick up some covert equipment from the office.

"So what's the plan?" he asked as she backed out of the driveway.

"Do you have a jacket with a hoodie in the trunk?" she asked.

"No, but I have one at the office. Why?"

"I've been thinking. I don't know if this is a trap to find you or if it's really about The Paradox. I need you to be close by just in case we need to escape."

"When we get to the office, we'll see where the best place is for us to meet in public," said Teco.

Trooper's cell phone vibrated. She pulled it off of her belt clip and flipped it open. "This is Trooper."

"Hello Detective Troop, Doctor Hasan here." Trooper nudged Teco and motioned with her lips to signal who was on the phone.

"Yes Doctor Hasan, how may I help you?"

"I received another visit. This time it was the FBI who asked about someone by the name of Teco Jackson. Well, I told them that I've never heard of anyone by that name."

Trooper became at ease that Doctor Hasan didn't turn her into the authorities. He added, "They showed me a photo. I told them that he's never been here before. God forgive me for lying."

"Doc, he will if you ask."

"They've been sitting outside watching the place. I'm not worried about that. Oh yeah, thank you for the check which came today. Please be careful."

"We will Doc." She disconnected the call and parked the Mustang in front of the office. Appearing deep in thought, Trooper said, "Teco, let's meet Wicker at the bridge by the Navy Yard."

Teco's eerie feeling re-emerged because this was the spot close in vicinity to where he was shot. "Let's meet him at Union Station."

After they walked into the office, Trooper picked up a hooded black windbreaker jacket with Velcro lining that hid both a microphone and mini spy camera stick.

Teco retrieved the battery pack and the receiver from a cabinet, so that they could hear and record the upcoming conversation with Captain Wicker. Union Station was chosen as a suitable location to set up shop first.

When they walked out of the office, Teco scoped the area to see if they were being watched.

An hour later, Teco and Trooper entered the entrance hall of Union Station. Teco gazed at the breathtaking vaulted ceiling and statues of Roman warriors. This caused Teco to visualize himself as an African warrior from the Zulu tribe. He was ready for battle.

After they set up the surveillance equipment and checked the area, Trooper called Captain Wicker. "Hello. Meet me by the Phoenix in thirty. No, make it twenty."

"Phoenix what?" asked Captain Wicker.

"Captain, don't play. You have nineteen minutes left or I'm leaving." Trooper hung up, pleased that she had the upper hand this time around.

The captain dialed her back.

"Yes?" she asked while winking at Teco.

"Trooper, you know I can't make it to the Union Station Phoenix Movie Theater in seventeen minutes."

"Sir, I strongly suggest that you use the lights on your car. There you go," said Trooper as she heard the whirling sound of his siren. Then she disconnected the call, not giving him the chance to say another word.

"Hanae, look at me," said Teco.

"We've talked about this before and you know how I feel." She knew that Teco was getting ready to lecture her about safety.

"Yes, I do know how you feel; and this is why I need you to promise me one thing."

"Teco, a promise is only good when it's kept." Trooper managed to give him a smile while she peeked over his shoulder to assess the traffic flow of the exits.

"Well, just tell me that you'll let me help you get this nut case."

"You know I'll do the best I can. Let's see what Captain Wicker wants first."

Teco just gazed into her sexy eyes. He couldn't argue with Trooper even if he tried. "Alright, that's fair enough." Pointing to where this homeless guy was panhandling, Teco added, "I'll be right over there with the hoodie over my head and ready if you need me. Here, put this on." He gave her the receiver.

"Teco, heads up. Wicker's coming our way."

"Copy that. I'm right here." The vagrant guy looked at Teco really hard as if Teco intruded into his private residence.

Captain Wicker walked into the atrium out of breath. "Trooper, let's walk and talk."

She looked around to see if Captain Wicker had any backup with him. Then she glanced to see what Teco was doing.

"I'm alone. So, it's okay." Captain Wicker said noticing that she was distracted. "Trooper, you can relax," he said.

Teco said on the mic, "I'm right behind you."

After getting the reassurance from Teco's voice, Trooper began to walk by Captain Wicker's side. Then Captain Wicker led Trooper outside to the location where his police car was parked at the curb. When she looked back, Teco was gone.

"Trooper, get in," said the captain.

"Baby, I'm on him if he tries anything," said Teco. Trooper didn't know where Teco was posted; however, she got into the police car.

Captain Wicker checked out his rear-view mirror and took a deep breath, as if to imply that this situation was a matter of life or death. The captain searched the area to see if anyone stood out of place. The only person around was a homeless man catching some sleep adjacent to the building.

"Captain, what's going on?"

"We . . . Well, I received a call from the FBI, who says they believe The Paradox is at it again but this time in Atlanta, Georgia. They've requested your help."

"You're telling me that they sent you after me so that I can help?"

"I must say, when you came into my office last week, I was glad to see you." The captain grabbed her hand and held it tightly. "I trained you personally. At the beginning of your career, I was there when you lost control of your patrol car which killed that family; and your partner died. I was the one who believed in you when you wanted to quit the force."

Teco heard details about Trooper's past that he never heard before. He wondered did this have anything to do with her failed marriage because he understood the toll of losing a partner. Because Teco wasn't in the car with her, he couldn't console her; therefore, he grew gravely concerned.

While Trooper and Captain Wicker sat in the car, Teco and Trooper finally locked eyes. Trooper shrugged her shoulders as she tilted her head to the right. Teco knew that she would explain everything with him after this meeting.

Trooper pulled her hand away from Captain Wicker, who said, "Some new agents from the William Green Federal Building out of Philadelphia stormed into my office trying to tell me what to do. You know how much I hate being pushed around in my own house." He looked at her and added, "They asked for you personally."

"And what did you tell them?"

"I told them that your father passed away and you took some extended time off."

"Why didn't you tell them the truth?"

"Honestly, I want you back. You're the best at what you do; and you know this guy. It seems as if you've gotten into his head and can figure out his next move. The FBI wants to set up a multi-jurisdiction operation, where Philly, D.C. and Atlanta act as one large agency." His tone was persuasive.

"Captain, I have a business—"

"Before you say no, they've asked for a complete copy of our department file on The Paradox and the G-String murders." He reached on the dashboard to get a file that was four inches thick and laid it on her lap. Trooper looked at the folder as if it were a foreign object. "Oh yeah, I have something else for you."

The captain reached under the driver's seat, pulled out a black canvas bag, and said, "I think she's been in the dark long enough and could use some sunshine." Trooper unzipped the bag and pulled out her pistol, which she affectionately named "Sunshine." Captain Wicker confiscated the gun from Trooper shortly after he reprimanded her for not following police procedure the night that Teco was shot at the Mirage nightclub.

With the gun was a badge with the word "Lieutenant" in gold letters. She stared at Sunshine and the badge. "I'm sorry. I . . . I can't."

"Just take everything with you and think about it. If you say no, I'll understand and come to pick up the badge myself. By the way, tell Teco that I said thank you," said Captain Wicker with a sharp eye spotting Teco in the Mustang.

When Trooper walked up to the Mustang, Teco's arms were folded across the steering wheel; and his head was down. She put the file on the backseat and reclined the passenger side seat all the way back. Taking a cleansing breath, she removed the surveillance earpiece from her ear. Teco reached over and squeezed her hand tightly.

"Teco, I didn't mean for you to find out about my past this way. I wanted to tell you. Honestly, I did."

He kissed the back of Trooper's hand. "It's okay. When you're ready to sit down and talk about it, let me know." Teco tried his best to keep his eyes on the road due to the sunlight which cut through the woods as if the sun and trees were playing "hide and go seek."

Then in slow motion, a single triangular shaped tear fell down Trooper's left check.

After they arrived at the house, Trooper sat in the living room going through the file, hoping to come across something new. Even the FBI report showed nothing.

Instead, she noticed her own notes, which conjured up some painful memories. There was a note that read "Go visit dad tomorrow." She was so caught up into the case, that she never made that trip to visit him before he died. Trooper's priorities where all screwed up because her prime objective during that time was to find the whereabouts of The Paradox.

"Damn! Damn!" she exclaimed while shifting a part of the file onto the family room sofa and closing her eyes as tears streamed down.

Chapter 9

KNOWN FOR ITS HIGH TECH exercise equipment, the Washington Sports Club on K Street was packed with athletic enthusiasts. Because of the afternoon thunderstorm, the gym's indoor running trail provided a great alternative to getting drenched at Pope Branch Park. Teco grabbed his sports bag and walked towards the gym door.

His personal trainer asked, "Leaving early today?"

"Yeah Bruce, I am. I need to get to Baltimore," said Teco, who popped open a knockoff Burberry umbrella.

"Alright, B-more careful dude," Bruce said jokingly as he gave Teco a high five.

When Teco reached home, Trooper was upstairs in the bedroom putting her bulletproof vest into a khaki canvas utility bag.

"Hey, I have your taser," she said smiling at him.

"I've gone down to the District of Columbia Circuit ten times to get my gun permit. They keep telling me that it's in the mail."

"Well, at least you do have a permit to carry a taser."

"Yeah, I guess," said Teco putting his bag down in order to give her a tight hug.

"You smell good. I see you took a shower at the gym."

"I knew the time would be short," he said while nibbling on her ear.

"I'm proud of you."

"For what? Being back on time?"

"No, for completing your high level security training in order to become a professional bodyguard . . ." She nestled her head on his shoulder close to his neck.

"Oh really?"

"Yes, really. We are a force to be reckoned with. Don't you think?"

"The bad guys better watch out. Homicide's back," he said laughing at her disgusted expression.

Hitting his upper arm, she said, "Boy, you better stop. Your days as an enforcer are over. Read my lips. You are a bo-dy-guard."

Teco continued to laugh while he changed into a pair of black dress pants and a black Jockey t-shirt.

"Where's your vest?" asked Trooper.

"If it's not in my bag, then it's at the office."

Trooper stopped looking for his vest because she knew that they would pass by the office on the way to Baltimore.

"Where are we staying this time?" asked Teco. He didn't want to stay in a rundown hotel on the eastside of Baltimore again.

"Well, we have a celebrity client that's hot on the comedy circuit. His name is Mr. Thomas."

"Oh, that's the comedian who used to be on that hip hop news show called . . . called 'Yo MTV Raps.'"

"Yes, that's him. We're staying at the same hotel. He asked for you personally to be his bodyguard this weekend."

"I'm telling you baby. I was the one and only Homicide, the enforcer for the Strictly Business crew. My reputation precedes me. If I hadn't gotten locked up, Bashi would have been alive today. People recognize," said Teco proudly.

"Mr. Bad Ass, let it go. Mr. Thomas is also requesting that we get to the Crowne Plaza Hotel prior to his arrival. The show is at the Baltimore Comedy Factory."

Picking up the two bags, Teco stepped outside. He popped the trunk to a black Crown Victoria which they purchased from a government police auction for her P.I. business. Trooper surveyed the area for any potential stakeouts. The only thing she noticed was that the weather changed for the better because the sky was now nice and clear. This could turn out to be a perfect day for travelling on the Baltimore-Washington Parkway.

Within the hour, Trooper and Teco walked out of the office with Teco's vest. As the day got hotter by the minute, a mailman pulled up; and Trooper walked out to the postal Jeep.

"Hello, Ms. Troop," he said smiling.

"Hello to you. Have a nice day," she said as he handed her the mail.

"You do the same," he said and drove off.

Teco put the vest in the trunk and went to the driver's side of the car.

"And what are you doing, mister?"

"Baby, I'll drive, if it's alright with you?"

"I know a shortcut."

Teco opened the door for Trooper who sat down and adjusted the seats and the mirrors. Unconsciously, she put the mail between her thighs as Teco entered the car on the passenger's side.

She winked at Teco and said, "Ready partner?" Trooper noticed that his head was bowed as they pulled onto the northeast side of 10th Street.

When Trooper merged onto the Baltimore-Washington Parkway, traffic was flowing freely. Suddenly a pack of motorcyclists zoomed by startling Trooper. "Breathe" by Faith Hill was playing on the Magic 95.9 radio station.

She turned the music down and said, "Teco, I want you to know that you're good for me."

He liked hearing her talk like this because his past relationships were never open and honest. "Why you say that?" he asked wanting to hear more.

"I like the way you listen to me when I go on and on about things. You've grown extremely patient, and I love you for that. How do you do it?"

He rubbed the back of her neck and ear. "I'm getting to know you better each day."

"You really excite me when you flirt with me like that. You are my everything." Leaning over to kiss Teco caused her to remember that the mail was between her thighs. She picked up the stack of envelopes and put them on her lap. "This one's for you."

Teco opened the letter in regards to his gun permit and began reading.

At that moment, the car veered towards the emergency lane; and Trooper slammed on the breaks. Cars in both lanes blew their horns and sharply swerved across the road. Teco braced himself for the impact and the inevitable road rage. He said, "Girl, what the hell is wrong with you?"

Trooper's eyes were affixed to a piece of mail.

When she didn't answer, he asked, "Hanae, are you alright?"

As she raised her head, a look of nervousness consumed Trooper; therefore, Teco began to look around for suspicious activity.

"Hanae, are you alright? You almost got us killed!" he exclaimed with a clenched jaw.

She picked up the envelope by the corner with her fingertips.

"Okay, why are you holding the envelope like that?" he asked as cars continued down the parkway again. Then he pressed the car's emergency blinker button.

"The return address says Frances Bacon. I came across that name when I was doing research on the G-String murders," said Trooper.

"I don't get it."

"Francis Bacon is a famous English philosopher, who once said, 'The most corrected copies are commonly the least correct.'"

Teco and Trooper said simultaneously, "A Paradox."

"How in the hell did you remember that?" asked Teco.

"I don't forget much. That's why I love being a detective."

Teco reached on the backseat to get a small black tackle box. He gave Trooper latex gloves. Then he pulled out a zip-lock bag.

She opened the letter and something fell into her lap. She jumped because she didn't want to contaminate any evidence. Trooper picked up a Georgia driver's license of a woman with a beautiful cocoa brown complexion.

"Teco, do you know her? She is from Dublin, Georgia."

"No, she doesn't look like anyone I know."

"Okay, put it in the bag," said Trooper as Teco placed the zip-lock bag into a white legal-sized envelope. He knew that if any prints were present, Trooper would lift them once they got back into D.C.

Trooper read the letter aloud.

Hello Detective Troop,

Mecca is deserted because the eternal flame is burning up.

The nectar of the fruit is sour because there was a mix-up.

So travel with MARTA; you no longer have to giddyup.

The Paradox

"What? Why is The Paradox sending my queen mail? If this is Bobby, wait until we catch his ass. If he thought the first beat down was something, I just got a gun permit. Hanae! Hanae!" exclaimed Teco as he slammed his fist into the car door panel. Then there was total silence. "Let me drive to Baltimore," said Teco when he saw the zoned-out look upon her face.

Without a word, she got out of the car so that they could trade places. For a moment, she gazed off into the woods. After she sat down, Teco checked to see if any cars were coming before he peeled off onto the parkway. The smell of rubber filled the air.

Trooper's hands were shaking as she picked up the cell phone.

"Washington, D.C. Homicide Division, how may I direct your call?" asked a soft spoken woman.

"Captain Wicker please," said Trooper.

"Sure, can you please hold?"

Just as Captain Wicker walked into his office, he heard a voice from the speaker phone. "Captain, you have a call on line 2."

Never sitting down, he picked up the phone and said, "This is Captain Wicker. How may I help you?"

With a fired up voice, she blurted out, "Captain, this is Trooper. I'm on my way to Baltimore; however, when I get back, I'm coming in to see you. I've just received contact from The Paradox."

Leaning on the headrest of his executive chair, Captain Wicker said, "I thought you would come to see me sooner or later."

"Is this why you want me back? Thorns up your ass, maybe?" she asked regaining her composure and speaking of the FBI agents who were leading the case.

Captain Wicker took all of this in because he had no choice. Wanting to advance his career, he needed Trooper's help. Wicker said firmly, "I'll have your team ready."

"What team sir?"

"I think it would be good if you have your old partner back."

"Sir, with all due respect, thank you but no thank you. I have a new partner, Mr. Jackson."

"Now Hanae, you know I can't allow a civilian to be part of our team."

"Sir, he can be hired as an expert consultant. I won't have it any other way."

"I don't know if I can do that. You are taking this too far. Teco Jackson will get in the way of our investigation."

"Let me remind you sir that Mr. Jackson saved my life after that massive house explosion. The department was defenseless against The Paradox's ruthless attack. Plus, Mr. Jackson came face to face in a heated battle with The Paradox back in Philly. Mr. Jackson can hold his own."

Teco looked at Trooper astonished. Perhaps she saw some good virtues emerge out of his past life after all.

"Are you insane?" asked Captain Wicker.

"Also, take into account that The Paradox believes that Teco is deceased," she said convincingly.

Captain Wicker paused. "What are you talking about Teco being deceased?" he asked as he raised his right eyebrow.

"When you find a way to hire Mr. Jackson to assist with the case, then we can talk."

The phone went dead.

Gripping the receiver to the phone tightly, Wicker hated her bull-headed drive; however, there was more to her attitude, as if she knew something else. He reached for the intercom button and demanded, "Deborah, get the Chief of Police on the line. And I want Lieutenant Brown and Detective Heard in my office pronto." Then he slammed the receiver down on the phone cradle.

Chapter **10**

CAPTAIN WICKER LEANED back into his chair wondering if Trooper could deliver. Swoosh and Ronald rolled into his office and took a seat, as Wicker said on the phone, "Yes sir, I understand Chief. I thank you for your support."

Looking up, Wicker said to Swoosh and Ronald, "Okay, we have a very important case on our hands." After briefing them on the Atlanta G-String murder investigation, Wicker said, "Hold on for one minute."

He picked up the phone, dialed a number, and pushed the speaker button.

"This is Trooper." Swoosh and Ronald's eyes lit up at the sound of her voice.

"Trooper, I have the green light for Mr. Jackson to be hired for the Atlanta case only; otherwise, it's unethical. Also, I have Swoosh and Ronald in the office with me. Now, tell me about Teco being deceased."

"Hello Swoosh."

"Hello to you," said Swoosh with a slight smile.

"Ronald, how are you?"

Ronald twirled a ballpoint pen in his hand and said, "I'm fine and you?"

"Not so bad. Okay captain, when Teco left the hospital, I put his name with a picture in *The Washington Times* obituary column because I knew that The Paradox would come looking for him."

"Hah, that was not documented in the FBI report," said Wicker who was becoming more encouraged to have Trooper on his side.

She asked, "What's the catch of having a team?"

"As I told you before, Swoosh and Ronald will help you with the legwork until we have cause to move."

"Sir, we have cause. I've just received a letter from this psycho asshole. He sent me some poor female's I.D. I need to verify if she is the same victim in the recent G-String murder in Atlanta. If not, she may very well need our help. The first thing I need is a flight to Georgia."

Taking out a dingy handkerchief and wiping it across his forehead, Wicker exclaimed, "Trooper! Listen to me, damn it!" Then he loosened his tie. "You are moving too fast. We need to see what was sent to you before we go on a wild goose chase. What if this guy is lying low and waiting for you?"

"You're right. I'll send you the letter with the I.D by express mail. Have the Atlanta Police Department see if the photo is a match with the victim."

"I will keep you apprised of every aspect of this investigation. Oh, I'll fax you the paperwork for Mr. Jackson to fill out. By the way, I need to know which hotel you're staying at in Baltimore."

"Yes sir," said Trooper as she watched Teco jamming to a song by Eric B. And Rakim called "Eric B. is President."

"Lieutenant, be careful," said Captain Wicker to Trooper; and then he hung up the telephone.

Trooper knew that something wasn't right, but she just couldn't put her finger on it. "Teco, we may need to drive to Georgia."

"What did Wicker say about us?" he asked while turning the volume of the music down.

"Well, he's going to hire you as an expert consultant. I think they're using us as bait to find The Paradox."

"What?" Teco shook his head. "Look, let's just focus on the job in Baltimore; and on our way to Georgia, you can fill me in."

"Who said that we are going to Georgia? I said we may."

"I know you. This is not Wicker you're talking to. When we do find The Paradox, let me deal with him because this is an old score he's trying to settle."

"To The Paradox, it's not a score. It's a game. It's not about you and him anymore. He has killed innocent people; so you and I are on this mission together."

"I love you and don't need anything happening to you like before."

She reached over and grasped his big hand. "He won't get away this time. Captain Wicker has assigned a top notch team and it includes Swoosh and Ronald."

"Who is Ronald?" he asked shifting his weight to his right leg on the car seat.

"He's a guy who started out in the property room. After completing the academy, he must have taken my place. I guess," said Trooper shrugging her shoulders.

While Teco continued to drive, they passed a sign that read "Welcome to Baltimore — Home of the Blue Shell Crab." As they approached the inner city limits, the stench of raw fish from the Baltimore harbour came through the car vent. Turning up the volume to sing "The Kissing Game" by Hi-Five to Trooper, Teco couldn't hold a musical note if he tried.

◊◊◊◊◊

FROM THE CHOCOLATE CITY TO the small town known as Georgia's Emerald City in Laurens County Georgia, the drive was tiresome. Shortly after they turned off the exit, Teco couldn't believe the sight of fields and fields of cotton to his left and right. Without thinking he blurted out, "So this is where my ancestors picked cotton?"

Trooper playfully smacked him on his right arm and said, "Boy, none of your kinfolk picked cotton in Georgia."

"They might as well have. The south is one land. Plus, I can feel their spirits."

Teco drove to Loves gas station, which looked more like a truck rest stop. After pulling up to pump 3, he said, "Go in and pay for the gas. See if they can recommend a hotel around here."

Adjacent to them, a driver of a white Ford Mustang convertible with the top down played "Black Magic Woman" by Fleetwood Mac on 107.5 The Buzz. As Teco unscrewed the fuel cap, the fumes went up his nose. While he pumped the gas, Teco checked out the area. Red dirt was on the tires and splattered across the door panels of every 4x4 pickup truck and SUV in the parking lot.

Everyone waved hello; and Teco wondered if he were on another planet. Up north, everyone was so consumed with their daily lives that there was no way a stranger was going to be invited into the day's activities. Then a Swift 18-wheeler truck pulled up and dust seemed to rule the air.

While Trooper paid for the gas, she picked up a Georgia map. Looking at the cashier, she asked, "Do you know of any hotels around here that I can stay at?"

"Ma'am, I'm sorry, but I'm not from around here. I'm from Macon. You'll have to ask that guy sitting on the tailgate of that red truck." Trooper followed the direction of the cashier's index finger and saw a blond man with a beautiful mahogany hand carved walking cane. He wore a straw cowboy hat, denim shirt and khaki pants. His belly popped out between red suspenders.

Trooper approached the big belly man as he was drawing something on the ground with his stick. She asked, "Excuse me sir. Can you recommend a hotel in the area?"

"Why hello little lady, where are you from? You don't sound like you are from around these parts."

"I'm from Washington, D.C."

When he smiled, she saw that one of his upper front teeth was missing. "You are a long way from home. What business you have here in Dublin?"

She was taken aback by the interrogation of a total stranger. "Pardon me? I'm not sure why you are questioning me."

In a friendly tone he said, "Hold on to your britches; we in the south just like a little small talk. You know; get to know each other."

"I'm sorry if I came across brash. I'm not used to anyone caring about who I am or where I'm from."

"Well, welcome to Georgia," he said as he extended a clean hand, with signs of gunpowder stains.

"Thank you. I'm a D.C. Homicide Detective."

"You shitting me," he said laughing. "This is the first time I've shook the hand of a female African-American Homicide Detective. It's an honor." Then he respectfully tipped his hat.

Trooper blushed and asked, "Can you give me an idea of where to start looking for a hotel? This trip was unexpected; and I didn't have much time to plan."

"You investigating a crime here in Dublin? I don't know of anyone who has been murdered in about a year, except for

Charlie's cousin on his mother's side. He was just drinking too much of that moonshine and—"

"I'm sure the story is entertaining; however, I've been on the road for over 10 hours and would like to get some rest."

"Well, I know the owners of a quaint place called the Page House. It's something we call a Bed and Breakfast. You ever stayed at one of them before?"

"No, I can't say that I have."

"Well, if you are going to stay in the south, you might as well get a taste of southern hospitality. It's on a street we call "Millionaire's Row." How long you going to be here for?"

"A few days."

"Okay, give me a second." As the man walked over to the pay phone, Trooper looked at Teco and shrugged her shoulders.

With a bright expression, the big belly man said, "You in luck. They have a room."

Trooper took a graceful step back and extended her hand. She said, "Thank you. I'm sorry; I didn't catch your name."

"I'm Mayor Lewis. Pardon the attire. My friends and I just came back from deer hunting."

"Mayor Lewis, you've been most kind. How do I get there?"

A young brunet gentleman, who was wearing blue Dickey overalls, walked up beside the mayor. On the inside of his mouth, there was a big bulge of chewing tobacco which he shifted from one jaw to the other. Then he shot a big glob of brown tobacco spit out onto the ground. The young man turned to Trooper and said in a southern accent, "Pardon my manners."

Trooper said, "No bother, I'm a fan of a Washington Nationals baseball player who chews."

"Well then, you want to dip?" he asked with a chuckle. When Trooper rolled her eyes, he asked, "Who is this here, Mayor?"

"She's a distinguished Homicide Detective from our fine District of Columbia. I just arranged for her to stay at the Page House. Why don't you show her the way?"

"I'd be obliged," said the young man as he wiped his mouth with a red, white and blue hanky and extended his hand.

Because she didn't want to seem ungrateful, Trooper reluctantly shook his hand. Then the young man gave her a sexy wink; and both men laughed.

Trooper walked quickly back over to Teco because the tobacco spitting gentleman looked as if he were about to give Trooper a southern "pick up line" which was known as a "player move" in the north.

Putting on the fuel cap, Teco asked, "So did you find out anything yet?"

"I sure did," said Trooper as she pointed to their escort. "This gentleman is going to show us the way to a place called the Page House. And check this out. It's on Millionaire's Row." The excitement in her voice was priceless.

"Millionaire's Row? I'm down. Let's go check-in."

The 1975 Ford F250 pickup truck did a tailspin in the dirt as the Ford Crown Victoria followed down the country road. Teco, who loved to jet through the streets, immediately felt a manly bond with their escort and wondered if there were any race tracks in the area.

Next door to the Page House, Teco saw the Laurens County Library on the left. Then he couldn't believe his eyes. In a high pitch voice, Teco asked, "We're staying here?"

As the witty and statuesque Detective Hanae Troop stepped out of the car, her visual of the building seemed to move in slow motion as she took in a panoramic view. The four round pillar columns on the front porch appeared to extend at least 24 feet in the air. Trooper's mind flashed back to the story of Samson and Delilah, when Samson pushed against the pillars and destroyed the temple. As she looked up at the swaying American Flag, the inn represented a place of power and strength to her. The manicured lawn and grand walkway to the entrance was all that was needed to invite them into this place of grandeur. Simply put, the Page House Bed and Breakfast was majestic.

Chapter 11

TECO STOOD there in amazement. Just a few years ago, he was sleeping in the back seat of a Johnny which was the name of a stolen car to the thugs in the hood. Turning his life around made a huge difference. He was now on a path to discover the world, not by watching the movies, but live and in person. This was a pivotal moment for him. Seeing Trooper walk up the colossal steps, Teco was exuberant to know that Trooper was a dear friend.

"Well, come on in," said Mrs. Canady who was dressed in a pink polo shirt and blue jean pants. "Mayor Lewis called and said you were on your way."

Immediately smelling fresh flowers, Teco walked inside and revelled at the sight of 12 foot ceilings and elegant chandeliers throughout the first level.

Then Trooper sneezed.

"Bless you," said Mrs. Canady who was much younger than Trooper imagined.

"Sometimes flowers cause my allergies to flare up," said Trooper.

"I think they smell wonderful," said Teco, who admired the live floral centerpieces on the tables. When Teco walked over to the black Baby Grand Piano, Trooper came over beside him; and they admired its beauty.

"Well, here is your room key. I've put you in the Lovett room. It has a Jacuzzi and a kitchenette," she said tucking her brunette hair behind her ear.

"Are you normally booked?"

"Indeed, we have people from all over the world who come and visit us. Oh, there is a breakfast menu in your room on the desk. When you have made a selection, press 0 and let me know your choice. I'll show you to your room upstairs."

When Trooper looked up, she imagined that many brides descended this grand staircase during intimate weddings. When she opened the door to the suite, the view was breathtaking. There was a cherry oak queen-size canopy bed with the largest headboard imaginable. On the opposite wall of the bed was an enchanting fireplace, which would put anyone under its spell. The tiffany window and the oil paintings on the walls were a touch of class; and the soft plush vintage chair matched the hunter green colors in the comforter and the toss pillows.

Just as Trooper pulled out the case file from her utility bag, her cell phone rang.

"Trooper! What the hell is this? And where are you? And why haven't you reported in as I've requested?" asked Captain Wicker.

"Sir, which question do you want me to answer first?"

"Try all of them!"

"I'm sorry. I couldn't allow you or anyone to use Teco . . . I mean Mr. Jackson as bait. The last time I was in your office, someone put a gumshoe on me. Well of course, they couldn't hang too tough."

"I don't know anything about anybody tailing you." Captain Wicker was stretching the truth and added, "Plus, no one is using Teco as—"

"Like hell you're not! If you're calling me, you must have received the letter and the I.D."

Captain Wicker put his right hand on his forehead and closed his eyes. After taking a deep breath, he remembered what Swoosh told him. *She's too witty for a police tail, captain.*

He said, "Okay, let's start over."

"Sir, I'm sorry, but you out of all people should know how I feel about this case."

"Yeah, I tried to tell them that."

"Who are you talking about, sir?" she asked inquisitively.

"Oh, no one important."

"Did they find any prints?"

"No we didn't. However, we think we can find out something from the paper type or the printer used. We can't overlook anything this time. Remember, we didn't think the charred sewing machine was important after The Paradox booby trapped that house. Turns out he used the sewing machine to make the G-Strings." There was silence between them. "Trooper, where are you?"

"I'm in Georgia." Then she pulled the phone away from her right ear.

"What the hell are you doing in Georgia?"

"Sir, The Paradox wants me to chase him. He enjoys being hunted because the hunted becomes the hunter before it's over . . . the game that is. Without me, there is no game for him. You don't have to use me as bait because I'm already a target. Besides, he thinks Mr. Jackson is deceased."

"Yeah, yeah, you told me that already."

"I've been monitoring murder cases across the country to see if his M.O. came up; and there was nothing until now."

"The Paradox's modus operandi started in D.C. How is your parading down to Georgia without your team going to help? We've been here before Trooper."

Wicker couldn't deny that Trooper knew the profile of The Paradox and that she wouldn't stop until she captured this guy. However, Wicker's next career move was Chief of Police and dependent upon Trooper acting as an employee of the department versus a P.I. She needed to be a team player because it was imperative that they play ball with the Feds.

"Okay, what are your plans, since you're there already?" he asked rocking in his executive chair.

She wondered why he said "there already," as if he knew that she was in Dublin. She only said that she was in Georgia.

"My plans sir . . ." She watched Teco shake his head no. ". . . Well sir, we're not sure just yet. We need to find out what we can about this young female. We've just gotten here; and we're going to get some sleep before we set out in the morning."

"I want to know everything about this female and none of that poppycock!"

"Sir, just approve the travel paperwork for me being in Georgia."

"Yeah, Yeah, I'm on it already. Don't you need the rest of the team?" Just as he said this, two FBI agents walked into his office. "Hold that thought. I've got two blues in my face." He watched as they sat down and nothing more needed to be said.

FBI Agent Rozier said, "Captain, we received your email. Good job of pulling the old team back together."

Wicker breathed a sigh of relief.

◊◊◊◊◊

THE NEXT MORNING at the Page House, Trooper and Teco awakened to the smell of bacon and eggs flowing through the ventilation system. While Trooper showered, Teco went out to the sitting area and watched the freshwater fish in the 45 gallon tank. The neon tetras were swimming with ease.

"Teco, are you ready?"

When he looked up at Trooper, he stood to give her a morning kiss. Then they heard glasses "cling" as if someone were delivering a toast. Going down the grand staircase, Teco held Trooper's arm.

A man with a dirty blond crew cut stood in the dining room wearing a blue shirt and khaki pants. When they sat down, Mr. Canady placed their breakfast on the table, and said, "Good morning, I'm sorry I missed you when you checked in last night. I was at the grand opening of my friend's coffee shop."

"Good morning," said Teco.

"Which one of you is the detective?" he asked with a genuine interest.

Thinking he already knew the answer, Trooper said, "That would be me."

"Well, we are glad that you found us. How long will you be here?"

"We aren't quite sure yet," said Teco.

"Welcome to Dublin. We don't have dinner in the evenings; however, there are quite a few restaurants in the area."

"I'll let you two eat your breakfast. Do you want any grits?"

Trooper asked, "What's that?"

"Don't tell me you have never had grits before?" asked Mr. Canady with a little chuckle.

"It's a southern dish made from corn. I think," said Teco.

"You have got to try some," said Mr. Canady as he left for the kitchen.

Trooper asked Teco, "We are having corn for breakfast?"

"No, it's made from corn. Sort of like ice cream is made from milk. My grandmother used to make grits for me when I was little," explained Teco. "Try it. You never know."

Mr. Canady came back with two small china bowls with grits. The presentation was so nice that Trooper hated to disturb the contents. Teco and Mr. Canady watched as she took her first bite.

"Ummm. This is good. Better than I thought."

"Well, here is some butter and pepper. Some people add cheese; however, I thought we'd start you out with the basics." Mr. Canady and Teco laughed.

Trooper asked, "Can you tell me where the nearest police station is?"

"Sure, there is one down the street."

After Mr. Canady gave her directions, Trooper and Teco set out to solve the case of the woman who crossed paths with a deranged serial killer.

At the police station, Teco counted 7 police cars which told him that there wasn't much crime in Dublin.

"Is the Sheriff available?" Trooper asked the young receptionist.

When the Sheriff waved Trooper into his office, Teco remained in the lobby and observed the recently renovated police building. He sat down beside a new desk still covered with plastic.

To her surprise, the Sheriff's office was very similar to that of Captain Wicker's office in D.C.

"How may I help you?" he asked leaning back in his chair. Trooper thought that the Sheriff looked to be around 60 years old.

"I'm Lieutenant Hanae Troop from the D.C. Homicide Division. I'm here investigating a murder that maybe tied to a suspect that goes by the name of The Paradox. He uses G-Strings as a weapon."

The Sheriff's head tilted back in surprise. "Well lieutenant, we don't have much action such as that in these parts of Georgia. The only out of town visitors have been you and that fellow out there. I saw your car at the Page House yesterday."

"What can you tell me about Missy—"

"Lil' Missy Green?"

"Yes, how did you guess her last name?"

Taking a sip of his black coffee, he said, "There's not one soul here in Dublin that I don't know."

Passing him a photocopy of Missy Green's driver's license, Trooper asked, "Are we talking about the same girl?"

"She's the Green's older daughter. As far as I know, she's still alive and kicking. . . . We last placed her in the city of Atlanta."

"So, she's not living here in Dublin?"

"She hasn't lived here since she went to college in Atlanta. Hmmm, let's see." His eyes shifted to the ceiling. "She must have lived there about 2 years, maybe 3 now."

"Can you take us to the Green's residence?"

"Gladly, you can ride with me," said the Sheriff as he escorted them to the new police cruiser.

Trooper could not believe how peaceful it was living in the country. The Green's house was almost 3 miles away from the main road. When the Green family saw the Sherriff's car, they greeted him and his guests on the front porch of a large southern colonial style home.

"How are you, Sheriff?" asked Mr. Green. From the driver's license, Trooper noticed that Missy looked liked her father.

"I'm fine Marty." He took off his hat and added, "This is Lieutenant Troop and her partner, Mr. Jackson. They are from Washington, D.C. and have a few questions for you."

"Has something happened to our Missy?" Mrs. Green's maternal instincts emerged from the depths of her soul; and she put her hands over her mouth. Upon a second glance, Trooper decided that Missy inherited her beautiful cocoa brown skin from her mother.

"Ma'am, I'm not sure. Can you tell me where in Atlanta does she stay?" Trooper didn't want to reveal too much to the Greens until there was a positive I.D. Parents tend to overreact when premature information is fed to them.

"She is staying at a place called Metro. It's like a dormitory for students from different Atlanta universities," said Mrs. Green as Missy's younger sister held her mother around the waist.

What surprised Trooper the most was that the Atlanta Police Department did not get in contact with the family. This meant that Trooper was further along in the investigation than any other law enforcement agency. *Did Captain Wicker send the I.D. to Atlanta as he committed?*

Mr. Green appeared as though he wanted to say something; therefore, Teco walked over to him and said, "May I speak with you alone?"

They walked to the backyard which revealed acres of cotton.

"I'm not sure how you knew I wanted to speak with you in private. You must be a fine detective," said Mr. Green.

"Well sir, I'm not a detective. However, I know when a man has something to say." Teco's stance was regal.

With a serious expression, Mr. Green said, "My girls don't want for nothing. However, Missy tired of the simple country life." His head hung low as a tear streamed down his cheek. "Missy thinks she can become rich dancing in those lust houses in Atlanta."

"Is she a dancer?" asked Teco, who was very familiar with the lifestyle.

"If that's what you want to call it."

"Do you know where she dances?"

"Some place called Nikki."

"Do you have a recent picture of Missy?"

"When we go back up to the house, I'll get one for you."

Teco patted Mr. Green on the back of his shoulder; and Mr. Green's head hung high as he looked out across his 40 acres of land.

"Have you picked cotton before?" Mr. Green asked looking out into the horizon.

"No sir, I can't say that I have."

They walked deeper into the field of cotton. "Go ahead. Reach over and grab some."

Teco did as he requested and immediately snatched his hand back. "Damn!" exclaimed Teco because his finger was bleeding.

"I'm sorry. I meant to tell you about the sharp edges. You okay?"

After Teco sucked on his finger, he pulled out a handkerchief from his back pocket, wrapped his finger, and squeezed. "Yes, I'm fine. I'm fine."

"Just touch the white part."

This time Teco was able to extract a single ball of cotton.

"Now, you can say that you have picked cotton." With a serious face, Mr. Green added, "I'm able to take really good care of my family because of this white soft stuff. This land has been in our family for generations, since my great-grandfather fought in the Civil War."

Chapter **12**

PROVING TO BE A PLACE where people looked out for each other, the south offered refuge from the hustle and bustle of life in the City of Brotherly Love. GQ wondered why this was never reported on television. Even as she travelled to work on this cloudy day, drivers on I-75 waved at her as a way of signalling that she could move across several lanes to take the next exit. Sure there was the occasional individual who gave her the middle finger, but not on today.

When she arrived at her office, GQ realized that she was beginning to enjoy the company of her new employee, Jerome Love, who liked to be called "Love." She described Love as metrosexual because he treasured fashion and the city lifestyle more than he cherished anyone else in the world. Frequenting the hottest establishments was a part of his self imposed job description; and as a result, he brushed elbows with the top fashion industry executives on the east coast. Love turned out to have the skills GQ needed to take her business to the next level.

Going over her paperwork, GQ skimmed through reports of her line-up for the upcoming production in November. She knew that her company needed to showcase major gear for this immense show. However, her immediate commitment was to a few smaller shows. Finding new models was of the utmost importance.

Before she put the papers in her top drawer, there was a knock on the door. With a runway walk, Love entered the room with his Dick Blick sketch pad under his right arm and said, "Boss lady, I've been working on something for the fall show. I would like for you to take a peek."

GQ examined Love over the rim of her school teacher styled reading glasses. The only objects missing on her desk were a pointing stick and a big red apple. "Let's see what you have."

"No, let me work the design for you."

While GQ leaned back in her chair and picked up her Philadelphia Eagles cup, Love placed the Dick Blick pad on an easel. Then he flipped to a page with a very beautiful model wearing a colorful outfit.

He said, "This is a G. I. Q. empire halter dress."

Determined not to show any emotions, she smiled slightly.

Flipping the pad again, he said, "This is a Grand G. I. Q. halter dress with a neck collar that can be removed."

Shifting in her seat, GQ loved his work because halters were sure enough in style. "This will definitely be the dernier cri. Do you have more?"

Love said, "You are right. This will be the newest fashion in halter dresses to hit the runway. I do have more."

"Well, let's see." Gail stood to her feet and walked around to the front of her desk.

As they talked about the prospects of these outfits for future shows, Love knew that the halter dresses would do well. After they discussed the designs for over 20 minutes, Love said, "Boss lady, let me take you to lunch today."

Just as she was about to reply, Linda said, "Ms. Que, you have a call on line one from a Mr. Muhammad."

"I'll take the call." GQ walked behind her desk and picked up the telephone headset as she motioned for Love to leave her office. Walking over to the window to look at the chess games being played down below, she said, "Hello, this is Gail Que."

"GQ!" Mustafa exclaimed with a chuckle.

"Yes, this is she," she said acting as if she didn't know who was on the phone.

"I'm sorry that it has taken me this long to call you. I've been tending to my new house. Look, I won't beat around the bush."

"I like that."

"Can we do lunch?" he asked hoping that she would say yes.

"When might that be?"

"Today would be fine if—"

"Mustafa, I'm sorry, but I have a lunch appointment planned with my fashion director."

"Well, is it possible for us to get together later this week?"

"Let me check my schedule because I know that I have a trip to New York soon."

"If you don't mind, how long will you be gone?"

"I'm not sure, but I will get back with you on that."

"Okay, if you're not busy tomorrow, call me."

"I most definitely will. Okay, bye."

Hanging up the phone, Mustafa really enjoyed having his own place in College Park and knew that things would work out for him in the long run. The 3 bedroom house beat living in a 7 by 11 prison cell. The only thing he didn't care for was the familiar smell of fresh paint on the living room walls because a coat of blue paint was the only renovations allowed at Johnson State Prison.

Hearing a car door close drew him out of his daze. He stood up from sitting on the floor, which felt wonderful compared to the steel bench he sat on for ten years.

Before he could get to the door, a visitor entered the house and asked, "Yo, Tim you in here?"

Walking from the living room through the kitchen to the foyer, he asked, "Yo bro, who are you?" Upon another look, Mustafa couldn't believe his eyes. The visitor was his Italian foster brother, Bernardo. They hadn't seen each other since high school.

When they embraced, they locked like two pit bulls. As tears filled their eyes, they didn't hear several guests coming in behind them.

"Awww . . . look at this," stated Goldfinger.

When they let go and turned around, Bernardo waved to a woman who was carrying a tray of food.

They all gathered in the living room. Some sat on the white leather L-shaped sectional while others stood in various places around the room.

"Tim, this is my wife Karyan," said Bernardo.

She said, "Hello Tim—"

"Please call me Mustafa. What does Karyan mean?"

"It means 'dark one,' Tim. Oh, I mean Mustafa. I've heard so much about you."

Goldfinger scanned the room until he found a charming young lady and said, "Everybody, I want you to meet a new friend of mine. Her name is Lisa."

Lisa blushed and said, "Hello, I'm glad Tracey invited me to join you for the cookout."

As everyone greeted Lisa, Mustafa said, "You have a funny accent."

Lisa said, "I'm from West Philly. I've lived in Atlanta for a few years now."

"We don't have any people from Philadelphia. Do we?" Mustafa asked Goldfinger.

"No, but Lisa and I have made plans to go back to her old hood in a few weeks. She used to kick it with this kingpin with the Strictly Business crew. They are down with Young Black Mafia," said Goldfinger.

"Shhh!" exclaimed Lisa.

As she elbowed him in his side, Goldfinger said, "I'm sorry shawty; I'm just telling it like it is."

"YBM? Man, haven't you learned anything?" asked Mustafa, who sounded disappointed.

"Don't worry. The kingpin, as Tracey calls him, is dead," said Lisa.

"Word?" asked Bernardo.

"Yeah, he was killed years ago. Can we talk about something else?" asked Lisa.

"I want to hear this story. There is a lesson in it for my brother," said Mustafa.

Lisa looked around; and everyone's eyes were affixed on her.

Goldfinger sat down on the end corner of the sectional sofa; with his elbow on his left leg, he put his left hand on his forehead.

"Go 'head girl," said Karyan, who placed the tray down on the coffee table which was in the center of the room. "We all want to hear your story."

Looking at Goldfinger, Lisa said, "I don't think that's a good idea."

"We got your back. Besides, I'm the older brother. Tracey will just have to listen," Mustafa said sternly.

"Yeah, but you all aren't going home with him tonight," said Lisa.

Goldfinger took Lisa by the hand and positioned her on his lap. "Go on. Tell them or I'll never hear the end of it."

"I used to date this guy named Bashi Mujaheed Fiten," said Lisa as if she were giving an oration on stage.

"He was a Muslim? There is no way a striving Muslim would be into crime," said Mustafa; and they all laughed because Mustafa just got out of prison.

"Well, he was murdered by Gail Que. You know, that bitch that's been on the cover of *XXL Magazine*," said Lisa.

"What!" exclaimed Bernardo.

Lisa added, "Yeah, I testified at her trial and everything. Word on the street is that she got off on some kind of technicality."

"So, where's the lesson bro?" Goldfinger sarcastically asked Mustafa.

"That's deep. That fine sister, Gail Que, was a hood rat?" asked Bernardo.

All the women guests in the room thought that this information was better than anything in the *National Enquirer.*

"She wasn't a hood rat, she was Bashi's right hand," said Lisa.

"Daammn!" exclaimed Bernardo.

"A sister running a man's show!" exclaimed Kayran; and all the women gave high fives across the room.

"So, how did Gail rise to the top of the clothing business so fast?" asked Bernardo.

"I don't have any idea, but I know that she didn't sleep her way to the top." The ladies in the room leaned forward. "GQ, as we called her, didn't give it up to nobody. I do know that her money is long," said Lisa.

"How do you know that?" asked Bernardo.

"Because money was her motive for killing Bashi . . ."

Mustafa looked shocked. *Oh Shit!* Then a frown came upon his face. *Astaghfirullah, Allah forgive me for cursing.*

"Yo Mustafa, ain't that the lady I hooked you up with? So, what's the lesson, bro?" asked Goldfinger.

Mustafa sat there dumbfounded. *This can't be true about GQ.*

In an effort to savage the rest of the evening, Bernardo looked at Karyan and asked, "So, what's up with the food?"

Noticing that Mustafa was still speechless, Karyan said, "Lisa, help me get started in the kitchen."

Goldfinger licked his lips and blew Lisa a thank you kiss for getting him off the hook with his brother.

Mustafa asked Bernardo, "Man what's up? When did you get married?"

Goldfinger said, "No, don't change the subject now. Let's talk about Philly and the lesson I'm supposed to learn."

Mustafa said, "Man, shut up." They all laughed. Then Goldfinger and the crowd dispersed in order to give the two brothers an opportunity to catch up.

"I got married two years ago in France," said Bernardo to Mustafa.

Looking his foster brother over once more, Mustafa said, "Damn, you look good bro."

"What happened to your waves?"

"I needed a new start all the way around. Man, we have a lot to talk about. How is the military and that RELLIK team?" asked Mustafa.

"Yo bro, I'm not allowed to speak about that team with civilians such as yourself."

"Man, we fam. You been on that team for eleven years now. I know you can tell me something."

"I said I can't talk about it."

"How come you can't talk about something that you told me was the 'dream job of your life.' Ain't it some secret special forces team that goes on missions that the military special ops team can't handle?"

"Are you a civilian or not?"

Mustafa laughed and said, "Okay, okay, that's cool. So, how's the military?"

There was a dead look upon Bernardo's face because he really wanted to tell the truth about the events which transpired while they were apart. Even though the Persian Gulf War occurred years ago, Bernardo could not shake the travesty he saw right before his eyes during and after the war. However, he was sworn to protect and defend at any cost.

"You alright bro?" asked Mustafa.

"Yeah, I'm fine. A lot of my friends are still messed up from that Gulf War."

"You know, I learned that prayer works even when it seems as if we're praying for nothing," said Mustafa. Bernardo looked at Mustafa baffled because he wasn't used to such positive vibes from him.

"Other than tonight, have you tried to talk to Trey about leaving those streets alone?" asked Bernardo.

"Some what, but not really . . . not really."

"Did he tell you that he got shot five months ago?"

Mustafa sat at the edge of the sofa and exclaimed, "What! I thought he was locked up when he was missing 5 months ago."

"Yeah right," Bernardo said sarcastically, "he was missing alright and in the hospital."

Rubbing his right index finger over his sharply cut mustache, Mustafa said, "You know what? I knew something was wrong. Look, I'll deal with that later. What's to eat?"

"We didn't know you were Muslim; however, we do have some boneless chicken breast."

Mustafa's eyes lit up. "That's what I'm talking about."

Goldfinger walked back into the living room and placed a black duffle bag onto the end table, and Mustafa said, "I need to talk with you."

"What's up?" asked Goldfinger.

"I need about $150 thousand," said Mustafa.

Goldfinger and Bernardo appeared to be shocked at his request.

"A hundred and fifty thou? For what?" asked Goldfinger.

"Look Bro, I have plans to never return to prison. I need the money to start my own business, so that I can harden my foundation."

Karyan came to the living room listening to their conversation. Bernardo said, "Stop being so damn nosey."

She said, "I'm not nosey. I have an inquisitive mind."

"I've finished my business management course in the joint. Plus, I have my business plan mapped out," said Mustafa.

Goldfinger shifted his eyes over to Bernardo, who just shrugged his shoulders. "Damn, don't say nothing. What do you think, Nardo?"

"Give it to him. It's not like you don't have it to give," said Bernardo.

"What type of business will you be opening?" asked Goldfinger.

"I want to start a self-publishing company called "Musa Publications.""

"Musa what?" Goldfinger, Bernardo and Karyan laughed.

"Hold up! Hold up! Listen," Mustafa said trying to get them to calm down. "In Arabic, Musa means 'taken from the water.'"

Karyan was laughing so hard that she was holding her stomach.

Thinking this was the most ridiculous idea he ever heard, Goldfinger was stomping his foot and wiping a tear from his eye.

"Stop laughing. Listen." After a minute, they looked at Mustafa, who added, "Musa symbolizes that everything which has life must have water to survive."

Bernardo said, "Damn, man that's deep." Then they burst out into laughter again.

"Don't laugh at my dream, man," said Mustafa.

"Does every person coming out of prison dream of owning his own publishing gig?" asked Goldfinger.

The room was silent.

"I'm serious. Are you going to help or what?" asked Mustafa.

"Yeah, I'll give you the money," said Goldfinger who reached in the bag and pulled at a wad of cash. In Goldfinger's mind, he was thinking of a way to launder his street flow and what a better way than through a family business. Things really were moving in the right direction for them, so they thought.

Chapter 13

WITH HIS ELBOWS on his knees and hands to his chin, The Paradox sat on the king-size bed in the Super 8 motel in Midtown. Thinking about his next mission, he knew that changing plans now would cause future problems.

The off white walls were drab; and the citrus air freshener barely covered the smoke stench of the non-smoking room. Trying his best to ignore the voice in his head, he looked to the right, and there he saw his reflection in the mirror. Then his eyes focused on the Gideon bible on the end table.

Soulja, what the hell are you looking at? There's nothing in that book for you. I have all you need. You are met with disaster. What happened to all of the training that I gave you? Your mission to kill Gail Que in Philadelphia was totally unacceptable. You Failed!

The Pardox held his hands over his ears trying not to hear the voice. Then he said aloud, "I'm going to take care of her this time."

I don't think you can handle this mission. I think you're getting weak.

"Oh!" He stood up looking into the mirror and added, "Is that what you think? I'll show you. I'll show you. You just shut up and stay out of the way!"

Reaching for the black briefcase, The Paradox pulled out a newspaper. Lowering his eyes, he turned to the Entertainment section and focused on the *USA Today* article, which read "Taking the Que from the Indigo Signature Collection." With his fist balled tightly at his side, his expression was grimacing. Then he flung the briefcase; and its contents spilled all over the dirty carpet.

With his left foot, he kicked the papers and the briefcase out of his path. Searching for the article, he tore the page off and put it in his black trench coat pocket. Putting on the black teardrop hat, The Paradox left the motel room.

Around eleven o'clock at night, the ride to the Overlook Atlanta apartments was uneventful. Even the guard booth was empty. Remembering the direction, he parked the Lincoln Navigator in front of the maintenance office. Scanning the area, he looked up into a dark blue sky and saw a half moon. The only movement in the complex was a few crackheads who were lurking in the dark chasing that white ghost. Also, a light glowed a deep yellow through the window of Lisa Turner's apartment.

Putting on his black leather gloves, he flexed his hands to make sure that the gloves fit nice and snug. He loaded his Ruger P95 9mm and snapped on the silencer. A set of car lights beamed through the trees just as he was about to open the door.

Pausing for a moment, he saw a Fulton County police car coming his way, so he ducked down. The police officer flashed a light through the Navigator window onto two old white refrigerators and four washing machines that were less than ten feet away against the wall of the maintenance building.

Hand held tightly on the P95, The Paradox was ready to do whatever was needed and by any means necessary. When he no longer heard the engine of the police car, he raised his head to make sure that the coast was clear. Then he heard voices.

The same guy with the gold finger who previously forced The Paradox off the apartment complex was walking out of Lisa's apartment. The couple kissed each other goodnight, and Lisa went back inside.

Always on point, Goldfinger immediately noticed the Navigator and put his hand on his gun holster. Recognizing the shining steel barrel of the Desert Eagle against the street light, The Paradox knew that he had to cooperate; therefore, he put his P95 between his thighs, just in case.

With a gangster stride, Goldfinger walked over to the SUV; and The Paradox rolled down the window. Goldfinger said, "You need to push on."

"Man, I'm over here for some work. I ain't dealing," said The Paradox as sweat beaded up on his brow.

Goldfinger drew the Desert Eagle and pulled back the slide.

Then they both heard a door open and Lisa yelled, "Everything alright? I looked out the window and noticed you were still here."

Holstering the gun, Goldfinger said, "Yeah, go back inside."

Because the Navigator windows were tinted, Lisa could not make out the driver. She blew Goldfinger a goodnight kiss. As Lisa went back inside once more and cut off the outside light, The Paradox was contemplating his next move.

Goldfinger said, "Nobody parks in this hood if they don't live around here. Who do you know in the Overlook?"

Getting impatient, The Paradox said, "I told you man; I got no beef with you and your boys."

Turning the curve, the police car passed slowly. The cop rolled down the window and said to Goldfinger, "I'm watching you."

With his thumbs in each blue jeans pant pocket, Goldfinger nodded; and the officer pulled off.

"Tonight is your lucky night," Goldfinger said to The Paradox. Then Pie drove up in the silver Chevy Suburban. After Goldfinger got into the car, they headed down the hill.

The Paradox waited in the car for about an hour. Then he rushed to Lisa's front door. Boom! Boom! Boom! Boom!

Lisa practically jumped out of bed when she heard someone banging on her front door as if they were crazy. The last time this happened, it was the police coming to the wrong apartment. Putting on her Baby Phat white terry robe, she yelled, "I'm coming! Hold your horses!" Just as she reached the door she asked, "Who is it?"

"It's the Atlanta P.D. ma'am."

"Who?"

"Atlanta police . . ."

"Just a minute . . ." The door opened three inches; and Lisa peered through the security chain of the door and asked, "How may I help you?"

Lisa looked the man up and down. When her eyes went to his feet, he pushed the door open forcefully with his shoulder. Lisa fell backwards on her ass. She tried to run, but the Baby Phat robe was so long that it tangled under her feet. As she gained her balance, he pushed her back to the ground with his foot.

"Stay down or it will be worst!"

"Please don't hurt me. I . . . I . . . I don't have any money."

She tried to talk with him as she lay face down on the worn beige carpet. He pulled the belt from her robe to tie her hands. He could smell her fear and saw a wet yellow spot on the carpet. Grabbing Lisa by the collar of the robe, he dragged her across the carpet to the sofa so that she would be out of sight from the living room window. After locking the front door, he saw that the security chain was broken and two screws were bent.

With tears streaming down her clean face, Lisa asked, "What do you want from—"

"Shut up! You know why I'm here."

"I don't know why." She was moving like an inch worm as she tried to untie the belt from around her wrists.

"Yes you do. Shut the hell up!" He looked at her as she cried out. Then The Paradox pulled out the *USA Today* clipping. He grabbed her by the hair, which caused her to lift off of the sofa. He placed the article against her face and exclaimed, "This is why!"

She tried to lift her head and said, "I don't know what it says. I can't see it."

He grabbed her by the hair again and pulled the clipping away so that she could see.

She asked, "Why are you showing me Gail Que?"

"You know why." He pushed her hard against the back of the sofa.

"I swear. I don't know why you are showing me her picture."

He pressed the silencer to the left side of her temple. "You mean to tell me that you don't know GQ from Philly?" he asked with clenched teeth.

She tried to think harder and said, "I didn't say I didn't know her. I'm saying that I don't know why you are asking me about her. What does she have to do with me?"

Pointing the P95 to the middle of her forehead, he said, "Do you see clear now?"

"I haven't seen her for years." She could feel her heart beating rapidly against her chest cavity. He got closer to her face and she could smell his foul breath. She continued, "Is this payback for me testifying against her?"

The Paradox said, "You are my bait."

"Bait?" asked Lisa.

"She will come when she finds out who you are. You are an important piece of the puzzle."

"She who? What puzzle?"

"Are you hard of hearing? Your next kiss will be with Bashi in hell." Then two shots sounded. Matter and blood sprayed all over the *USA Today* news clip.

Then he went from room to room looking for her bedroom. Walking over to her dresser, he pulled open a few drawers and threw clothes all on the floor until he saw a peach colored lace G-String with a red ribbon rose. When he found her purse, The Paradox put Lisa's Georgia driver's license in his pocket.

Having this mission completed felt good to him. On his way out, he remembered that he almost forgot something. He went back over to Lisa, moved the corpse, and put the G-String by her face. Before he went out the front door, he peered through the blinds to see if anyone was outside.

He saw Goldfinger stepping out of the silver Chevy Suburban.

See Soulja, you have done it now. How are you going to get out? Speaking aloud to himself, The Paradox said, "I got this. Leave me alone. I can make my escape."

The Paradox looked around the apartment and noticed that there was a back door in the kitchen. Through the window over the sink, he saw that the coast was clear. When he went to open the door, the deadbolt was locked; and there was no key. Out of anger, he almost kicked the door, but that wouldn't accomplish anything. So, he went back to the front door.

"Lisa! Lisa!" exclaimed Goldfinger. The doorbell rang and Goldfinger dialed her number on his cell phone.

As the house phone rang, The Paradox paced the floor.

"Lisa! Wake up!" exclaimed Goldfinger.

When Goldfinger tried to turn the knob, The Paradox didn't know if Goldfinger had a key to the apartment, so The Paradox drew his P95.

"Yo, what's up?" asked Pie from the Suburban.

"She ain't answering the door or the phone."

The Paradox stared at the front door.

Pie said, "Maybe she stepped out for a burger."

"Are you serious?" asked Goldfinger.

"We can come back later," said Pie.

As Goldfinger went back to the car, The Paradox stood there like a wax museum statue. When he heard the muffler of the car in a distance, The Paradox looked out of the window.

Soulja, get the hell out of here!

The Paradox slowly opened the front door. There was no one in sight. By the time The Paradox reached the Navigator, the police car pulled up. The officer said, "I received a report of someone disturbing the peace. Have you heard anything?"

"No officer," said The Paradox who looked down at his black boots and saw drops of blood.

Chapter 14

THE NEXT MORNING, GQ was putting the final touches on the G.I.Q. halter dress for a show at the Ferst Center for the Arts. Ebony Fashion Fair was a corporate sponsor because they loved her new line and positive marketing message. The Indigo Signature Collection brand was synonymous with the term "new beginnings." In her advertisement campaigns, GQ leveraged the history of Atlanta burning down to the ground after the Civil War and rising again just like a phoenix. The print ads were a huge success. As she reached for the hot pink pin cushion, her office phone rang.

"This is Gail Que. How may I help you?"

"Well, it all depends. Are you free for lunch today?"

"Hello Mustafa!" she exclaimed in a happy falsetto voice. Then GQ placed the dress on her desk and leaned back into her executive chair in order to take in Mustafa's virile voice.

"Hello to you. How have you been, beautiful?"

"Oh, I'm beautiful today? I've been fine. Swamped with work though."

"Take a break."

GQ thought for a brief moment really wanting to see him again. "Okay, we can do lunch. What time are you picking me up?"

"Well, I thought that—"

"I'm sorry, but I must take this call. Can you hold?"

She hoped that he wanted to continue their conversation without any interruptions; however, he said, "Sure."

While he waited, Mustafa watched Karyan put a few more books on the shelf in his bookstore. Doing a wonderful job, she was hired as his assistant. Things were coming together really well for him.

When the music stopped playing, he heard GQ ask, "You still there?"

"Yes, I am," said Mustafa.

"Okay, you were saying something."

"How about I meet you outside of your office in 15 minutes?"

"Okay, I have someone that I would like for you to meet. So see you then."

After helping Karyan put up a few more books, Mustafa arrived at GQ's store right on time.

As GQ took the elevator down to the lobby level, she contemplated cancelling the luncheon because she had a more crucial issue to solve. One of her top male models was recently in a car accident, which meant that she needed to find a replacement. As she walked out of the elevator, Mustafa stood by the security desk. His smile was brilliant, and his right hand was behind his back.

"Hello," said GQ. When his right hand displayed white roses, she asked, "For me?"

He gave her a slight hug and said, "For all of you. Who did you want me to meet?"

GQ said, "Over here. Come with me."

She escorted him to Woodruff Park. Every street vendor was servicing patrons. The sidewalks were packed with business people who were walking at a fast pace in order to grab lunch and get back to work. Mourning doves pecked at the grass while the clouds moonwalked under the bright afternoon sun.

Just as they approached ten stone game tables, Tommy, who was just finishing up a game of chess, looked up, and asked, "Gail, how are you? Who might this fine gentleman be?"

"This is a new friend of mine, Tim Edmond. Tim this is Tommy Richardson, a very wise friend." The two men shook hands.

Disguised as a tourist on a park bench, The Paradox was clocking GQ and the tall brother, who was wearing a white knit kufi. The Paradox's hidden camera clicked away as the couple turned to walk towards Underground Atlanta, which was a move that he did not anticipate.

"Where are we going?" asked GQ.

"I have a surprise for you," said Mustafa.

"Oh really?" GQ looked at Mustafa as they crossed the crowded street.

"Excuse me," said The Paradox, who brushed against Mustafa in order to get ahead of them so that he could get better pictures of the couple together.

When they descended the flight of stairs, Mustafa held the door open for GQ.

"Thank you," said GQ.

"Sure."

At noon, Underground Atlanta was busy with consumers. A lady passing by looked at GQ and said, "I like your roses."

GQ asked Mustafa again, "Where are we going?"

He did not reply and simply smiled. When they reached the front of the bookstore, he stopped and said, "Welcome to my new business called Musa Publications. It's been opened for 2 days now."

She gasped and asked, "Are you for real?"

"Sure I am. Come on in."

"Back so soon Mr. Muhammad?" asked the cashier, who was sitting behind the counter which was in the center of the bookstore.

He nodded and showed GQ around the store until they reached the back corner. On a work table were sketches of magazine covers. The title of the magazine read "Rags to Riches."

Mustafa said, "This is where you can help me."

"That's odd," said GQ.

"What?" asked Mustafa.

"My fashion director asked me a while back. Will it be rags or riches for me?"

"That's not odd. It's confirmation."

"I'm not sure I'm following you."

"When something is destined, everything falls into place. See, I need your help. I want to create a fashion magazine."

Upon closer inspection, GQ noticed that she was on the mock-up magazine cover that read "Limited Edition."

"This is remarkable. However, I have no intention of investing in a magazine publication right now. My hands are full with my own business."

"That's the best part. I'm not asking you to invest money. My offer is to highlight your line, free of charge. In return, I want to have your permission to highlight the Indigo Signature Collection brand throughout the magazine each month. You know, cover your story from rags to riches."

Taken aback, she said, "I don't know."

"Gail, I remember a quote from Milton Friedman, who said, 'The business of business is business.'"

Before she could think, she said, "He also said, 'there is no such thing as a free lunch.'"

When Mustafa chuckled, GQ looked at him not knowing what else to say because she couldn't understand why he would be offering her this great deal. Then she remembered Tommy's words of wisdom. *When winning is illogical; losing is still far from optional.*

As he escorted GQ into his office, they heard the cashier ask, "Excuse me sir. May I help you?"

The Paradox was taken off guard by the friendly customer service and said, "No, I'm fine. Thank you, I'm just browsing."

The cowbell on the door sounded. Immediately, The Paradox saw a gold finger and quickly picked up a book to cover his face.

Speaking to the cashier, Goldfinger asked, "What's up shawty? My brother in?"

"Yes. He just went to the back with some lady. I'll call his office and let him know that you're here."

Mustafa said to GQ, "Excuse me please." As he was talking on the phone, he noticed GQ's mystical eyes. "Tell him I'll be right out." Mustafa stood up and said, "My brother is here to see me. Can you please give me a few minutes with him? Then we can have lunch at Jamaica Jamaica."

Still not knowing what to say to a man whose mannerisms seemed so genuine, GQ slightly smiled.

"Gail, your eyes are so—"

"Meet with your brother. Then we'll talk about my eyes. I want to hear more about your business proposition."

"I'd like that."

When Goldfinger saw GQ coming from the office, his mouth almost dropped to the floor, gold teeth and all.

"You should close your mouth before a fly navigates its way in," said Mustafa.

"Isn't that the shawty from Benihana's and the one Lisa was talking about at the cookout?" asked Goldfinger.

"Yeah, she's a dimepiece. Isn't she? Come into my office."

The Paradox watched GQ as she perused the books. She walked around the store admiring how Mustafa strategically placed the track lighting as a spotlight on each bookcase. Then GQ noticed a man who was reading a travel book. As she moved around the store, there was something familiar about him. GQ surveyed the guy and came to the conclusion that he must be a tourist because of the camera around his neck.

Once Goldfinger was in the office, Mustafa motioned for him to have a seat in one of the black leather guest chairs.

"So what's up Trey?"

Goldfinger looked around the medium-sized office and checked out the cherry oak bowed desk with fixed silver pedestals. Behind Mustafa, the credenza hutch with lights shined on a picture of the Kabba, an Islamic holy site. Tapping his gold finger on the arm rest and slouching in the chair just like a thug, Goldfinger said, "I see that you've got things moving very well in a short period of time. That's good."

Mustafa knew his brother too well. Sitting in the black button tufted executive chair, he asked, "What's really on your mind Trey?"

Goldfinger put the black duffle bag on his brother's desk.

"What's this?" asked Mustafa.

"Look and see."

Mustafa reluctantly pulled the bag close to him, opened the zipper, and asked, "And what do you want me to do with this?"

"Don't act stupid. Clean it for me."

Leaning forward putting both elbows on the desk and squinting his eyes in repugnance, Mustafa asked, "And how do you expect for me to do that?"

Likewise, Goldfinger leaned forward and said, "Take the money and put it into your business account. Then cut me a check that I can put into my account."

"Are you serious?"

"Yeah, I'm dead for real."

Mustafa leaned back into his chair really trying to take in his brother's request. His eyes shifted to the right of his desk; and there was the Qur'an which he lived by since becoming a Muslim. "I'm sorry, but I can't do what you're asking of me."

Goldfinger jumped out of the seat. "What the hell do you mean that you can't do this?"

Trying to remain calm, Mustafa said, "When I opened this business, I vowed to Allah that I would do right by Him; therefore, I dedicated this business to God."

"Man, you better get off of that Muslim trip. If it wasn't for me, you wouldn't have this spot. This is the thanks I get?"

"I really thank you for what you've done for me; and I'll repay you in full next year."

"I don't want your damn money. This is a family business."

At this point, Mustafa stood up mad as hell; and his deep baritone voice could be heard beyond the office doors. This sparked The Paradox's full attention along with others in the store.

Mustafa exclaimed, "Listen to me and you better hear me good! When I went to that hell hole for your ass, I lost ten years of my life for family. You didn't do ten years; I did! If at any time I thought you'd given me that money—"

"You what? You what mister all righteous now? If you would think back big brother, you gave me my first package to sell. So when you see me and the crew, you're looking at your damn self. You know what?" Goldfinger walked closer to Mustafa and said, "Shawty, you're going to wish that you cleaned this loot for me."

Observing his younger brother as they stood toe to toe, Mustafa could feel the old man trying to ascend back up in him. He knew that he couldn't chance going back to prison by fooling with his brother. "Man, just leave my office and don't ever try me like that. Don't threaten me either. Take your money with you." Then Mustafa took the duffle bag and threw it into Goldfinger's hands.

"Oh, it was good enough for you to take right?" asked Goldfinger, who stormed out of the office.

Not far from the nearby food court, The Paradox waited for Goldfinger so that he could follow him.

Chapter 15

LATER THAT AFTERNOON, an Atlanta smog alert was issued for the entire metropolitan area. All outdoor evening sports activities were cancelled. Though people were constantly asked by the city mayor to carpool, Peachtree Street was jammed with cars. GQ looked out the window of her office and hated that the chess tables were empty.

She retrieved her planner from the top drawer of her desk and checked her schedule for the rest of the month. When she noticed her upcoming trip to New York was not far away, she made a note to call John Robert Powers International to solicit their help in scheduling the male model auditions for her fashion show.

"Ms. Que, you have a visitor," said Linda through the intercom system.

"Thank You, I'll be right out." GQ wondered who could be coming to see her without an appointment. She cleared her desk of the small mess. After she opened the door, a big smile came across her face.

"Tommy! What are you doing up here? How are you?"

"I'm fine. I went into the store looking for you; and I was told that you were up top with the big dogs." His brown eyes sparkled. "Why didn't you tell me that you're the division president of your own fashion line?"

"I didn't want to sound so egotistical. Have a seat." She observed that Tommy's hair was dyed completely brunet which made him look ten years younger. His Johnson Motors short sleeve fitted t-shirt revealed his large bicep muscles; and his DIESEL boot cut jeans were snug. This didn't look like the man she had met months ago.

"Wow! These are some very beautiful chess pieces." He marvelled at the board; however, he was hesitant to touch a single piece without her consent.

"Thank you. It's my pride and joy — other than my signature clothing line." She took a sip of her coffee. "Would you like a cup?"

"Yes, I would like that, but I don't want to hold you up from your work."

"No, no, you're fine," she said walking over to the mini-bar. "How do you like your coffee?"

"Black with a teaspoon of sugar. Thank you."

"Sure, how about a friendly game? You know I owe you."

"Gail my friend, be nice to an old man."

"The way you are sporting those jeans doesn't look like you feel old."

They laughed.

"What do you really know about chess?" he asked with an alluring look.

Tommy's body language was extremely attractive to her. "What do you mean?"

"Do you know the history of chess and how you can apply it to your life?" he asked taking a sip of his coffee. "Ummm, French Vanilla . . . Great choice I must say."

"I didn't know that chess had a history which mattered." Looking at the chess board intensely, GQ tried to figure out what life lesson could chess possibly teach her.

"By the way, once you know the history, you'll never see chess or life the same."

In his own way, Tommy commanded GQ's full attention to the point that she got up and went to her desk. "Linda, reschedule all of my calls. Something just came up; and I'll be in a meeting with Mr. Richardson until further notice." Then GQ walked back to the chess board. "Okay, let's see what moves you have today."

When she took off her heels to get comfortable, Tommy felt that their relationship was going to the next level. He said, "Here, first come help me clear the board and please be very careful."

"With that cologne you are wearing, you better be careful. How did you know that I like for my male models to wear Boss Number 6."

"Ah, by Hugo Boss." He smiled at his subtle way of winning her affection.

"How old are you again?"

They laughed.

"First, look at the way the board is made. You have 64 squares which I call the 64 decisions of business. You have 32 business grounds and so does your opponent," said Tommy who sounded like a college instructor.

"I never looked at it that way," GQ said.

"Neither did I until I was shown. See, chess was played many centuries ago in China, India . . ."

"I thought chess was an American game."

"Well, no one really knows for sure which country chess originated." Then he picked up a chess piece. "Like this pawn. On the chessboard it represents a common worker. In the business world, that would be an entry level employee or a sales person."

"Oh I see. Where I come from that would be a foot soldier or a street corner hustler. A foot soldier is expendable to the street life."

"Good, I see you catch on quickly. Pawns are often left unprotected while wars rage around them."

"I've never understood why a person would risk their life for another man who will just bury them and find another flunky — well, pawn to take his place."

"Then we have the castle. From a business perspective, it's like the Coca Cola headquarters' building down the street."

"Okay, that would be the head house for any street organization. You know, where the money is stashed," said GQ who was appreciative that Tommy was creative in teaching her things.

"Then you have the knight; and on a chessboard, the knight represents the professional solider whose job is to protect persons of rank. In the corporate world, lawyers and accountants protect the different parts of the company."

"Well in the streets a knight would be an enforcer or a bodyguard." GQ thought for a moment and added, "When I ran the streets, there was this guy named Teco Jackson. He was hired to be the enforcer of the crew that I was with. It was called Strictly Business or SB for short."

"Yes, I remember you telling me about him. Whenever you mention his name, I can see the pain in your eyes. Gail, that's when loyalty comes into the game of life. Now this next piece is very tricky because they say that business and religion don't mix. However, for me, I began to see religion differently."

"Why? You don't believe in God?" asked GQ.

"Gorgeous, I didn't say that."

GQ blushed because this was Tommy's first time winking at her.

Tommy continued, "The bishop is the piece that's tricky. In the eighteenth century, the bishop represented the church. Then it dawned on me. In the business world, the Human Resources or H.R. department is the bishop because they give the workers counsel; and if you think about it, that's one of the roles of the church. In addition, H.R.'s goal is to recruit, develop, and retain loyal employees."

"Tommy, I don't know about that role on the streets because there isn't much positive counselling going on." They laughed; and GQ added, "The sixty four squares on the streets are cut throat."

"That's a great way to put it. Well, that leaves us with two pieces left. Next, let's address the queen." Tommy looked at GQ and asked, "Why are you smiling at me? Oh I get it. Women rule. As you know, the queen is the only piece that represents a woman. If you ask me, women's liberation started way before the 1960's."

"Why do you say that?"

"Think about it. In eighteenth century chess, the queen was the most powerful piece."

"Oh, I see your point."

"Let me give you another example. Before I retired, I lost my executive vice president position to a woman."

"Oh Tommy, I'm so sorry to hear that," she said feeling sorry for him.

"No, no, Gail don't."

GQ was confused now.

"She was my protégé. So, my presence is still there; and she still comes to me for advice," he said with a proud smile.

"It don't go down like that in the hood because the queen is that female who sleeps with the head boss from the streets. The queen can be ruthless if she feels that anything threatens her position."

"You are wrong."

"What?"

"Yes, you are wrong. You told me a while back that you were the right hand to the SB boss. In his own way I suppose, he mentored you on how to deal in the streets. He watched you navigate in a predominantly male world. Gail, you were the queen. When you saw that guy Teco Jackson as a threat to the boss, you told me yourself that you quote unquote 'put that cigarette begging, car stealing, dick slinging bum in check.'" They laughed again; and Tommy looked deeply into her eyes. *Is this the right time to tell her?*

"Yeah, I guess you are right. I worked my ass off in those streets, like I do now. The only difference is that I get nervous in this corporate world. Tommy, you are the only person who will help me. It seems like every time I turn around it's a 'pay to play' culture."

"Take a deep breath. You do have someone. His name is Frontino Lefébvre. He is backing you with the marketing, sales, legal, accounting, and HR team." Tommy softly caressed the right side of GQ's face with the back of his right hand and added, "You are a phoenix."

GQ put her left hand over Tommy's right hand and asked, "What do you want from me?"

Tommy removed his hand and said, "Anyway, the last piece is the king. In the corporate world, there isn't just one king who runs everything because a corporation has board members. So, in corporate America every person at the hierarchy is his or her own king and governs his or her own castle. That is, until the other kings or rising kings vote him or her off the board of sixty four squares."

"In the streets, they are called kingpins. Rivalling kingpins take over drug turfs; and most of the time, the ruling kingpin is killed by someone on the inside because of no loyalty and a lot of jealousy," she said with a small tear in her left eye.

He wiped the tear away and said, "But you told me that you didn't kill the SB Boss. Why are you crying?"

"I still don't know who killed Bashi. It couldn't have been Teco Jackson because he was locked up in jail. I don't know who killed Bashi; and I was his right hand."

"Well, it couldn't have been an inside job."

She smiled and said, "You are right. What am I thinking?"

Tommy said, "Gail, the street life and the corporate life aren't that different. There are just very opposing rules." He was quiet for a moment. "Gail, do you have someone special in your life?"

This question caught her way off guard. In the free world, Tommy was the first person to ever hear intimate details about her past life. He was showing her unconditional love.

When she raised her head ready to answer him, a voice from the intercom said, "Ms. Que, I don't mean to bother you. Can you please come to my desk? Mr. Muhammad is here."

GQ looked at her timepiece and rushed to put her designer heels back onto her feet. As she stood, she said, "Tommy, excuse me for a second."

Then he stood and gave her an intimate hug. She could feel his desire filling up within his pants as his warm body gently pressed against hers. Cuffing her chin with his right hand, Tommy gave her their first kiss. Her breathing slowed; and she placed her hands on his waist. When they hugged once more, Tommy amorously placed his mouth against the side of her neck.

"I . . . I . . . I have to go," said GQ as space finally divided them. How was she going to walk out of the office without revealing the passion that consumed them?

"Wait right here," she said as she went into the adjourning bathroom. As GQ looked in the mirror, she knew that her life was going in the right direction. However, Tommy and Mustafa were two very different men.

"Gail, are you alright?" asked Tommy.

"Yes, I'm coming out." As she returned to join him, she saw that Tommy regained his composure.

When they walked into the lobby area, Mustafa extended his hand and said, "You are the man I met in the park, right?"

"Yes, how are you Tim?"

"Wow, you are better at remembering names than me."

"Well, it's something I learned in business," said Tommy who turned to GQ, kissed her on the cheek, and headed towards the elevator.

Chapter 16

THE ONLY THING SLOWER THAN sweet Georgia molasses is government bureaucracy. Deciding to wait until the travel and living expenses were approved by Washington, D.C., Trooper and Teco sat in a hotel dump on Fulton Industrial Boulevard in order to save their personal money. This was a far cry from Trooper's dreams of staying at the Ritz Carlton in downtown Atlanta. She couldn't believe that Teco wasn't fazed by these deplorable living conditions. Then the cell phone rang.

Captain Wicker said, "Trooper, we have another problem. Philadelphia District Attorney Brown called me and woke me out of my sleep last night with some disturbing news. Is Teco with you?"

"Yes sir," said Trooper who was looking at Teco out of the corner of her eye.

"Everything is approved. I'm sending the rest of your team to Atlanta today. You need to go to the Georgia Bureau of Investigation. Down there they call it GBI. Ask for Agent Tony McLoughlin. D.A. Brown informed me that he received a Georgia driver's license from Francis Bacon. Do you remember that name?"

"Yes, from the Missy Green case." Trooper's mind was racing.

"The envelope had the same type of postage stamp and same city post mark. The name on this license is Lisa Turner. D.A. Brown ran a check. There were no priors. Then someone on his staff did a newspaper search and found out that Lisa Turner also testified at the trial of Bashi Mujaheed Fiten."

Trooper's heart was pounding. How was she going to break the news to Teco? This was not good at all.

Captain Wicker continued, "I called the Atlanta Police Department and reported what the Philly D.A. said. Two hours later, I received a call from GBI that a body was found at Lisa Turner's apartment."

"Do you have a number for the GBI agent?" asked Trooper.

"Sure, hold on."

Trooper went over to Teco and hit him on his arm in order to get his attention so that he could write down the number. "Okay, nine-nine-seven-zero-two-six-zero . . . got it." Repeating the number again, Trooper double checked to make sure that Teco wrote it down correctly. She said, "I'm calling him right away to let him know that I'm on the way."

"Look out for the Feds to be on this one because a G-String was found on the scene," said Captain Wicker.

"Oh great, that's all we need."

With her mind still racing, Trooper put the cell phone down and retrieved a bite-size Snickers bar from her purse. She didn't know how to break the news to Teco who was on the computer searching online newspapers for any information on the Missy Green case.

"Teco."

"Yeah, what's up?" He never took his eyes off of the computer display.

"I need to talk with you about something," said Trooper while finishing her candy bar.

"Go ahead; I'm listening."

"No, I need you to focus on what I'm saying to you because—"

"Okay I'm all yours," said Teco as he closed the laptop.

"Lisa Turner, the one who testified—"

"Yeah, I know who she is. What about her?"

"Her name came up in the investigation. We need to head over to her apartment. Did you know that she lived in Atlanta?"

"Yeah, I knew that. She moved here shortly after Bashi's trial."

"Teco, if she is dead, you may have to I.D. the body."

A grim expression came across Teco's face. "What do you mean I.D. the body? You said her name came up in the case."

"Well, Captain Wicker said that GBI might have found her body."

"Might? Or did?"

"I don't know just yet. I will know once I make this call. Plus, there was a G-String at the crime scene."

Teco slammed his fist down on the desk.

"Where did you put that piece of paper with the number on it?' asked Trooper.

Teco found the paper and called out the numbers to her as she dialed. Then the phone rang six times before someone picked up.

"Make sure they tape this section off. . . . This is McLoughlin." The man said in a loud and commanding tone.

"Yes, this is Lieutenant Troop from the Washington D.C. Homicide Division."

"Oh yeah, I was informed about you. How can I help you?" asked Agent McLoughlin who was overlooking the onlookers.

"I'm in southwest Atlanta. Can you give me the directions to Lisa Turner's apartment?"

"No I can't, but hold on." He walked over to an officer.

Not believing that Lisa was dead, Teco's mind flashed back to the intimate evening that he and Lisa spent together during the criminal trial for Bashi's murder.

"Lieutenant Troop, you still there?"

"Yes."

"Here's one of the local officers. She'll give you directions." He gave the phone to the officer. Trooper overheard Agent McLoughlin say, "And bring me my phone when you're done."

GBI Agent McLoughlin ducked under the yellow crime tape in order to go up the back iron stairs to the location where two police officers stood posted.

"Hello Sir," muttered one of the officers.

Before McLoughlin went into the apartment, he put on blue shoe covers and a pair of latex gloves. From the doorway, he could smell the remains of a rotting corpse; then he saw where the decomposing body was lying on the floor.

"Can I see your log sheet Sutherland," asked McLoughlin, who smiled at Jenny Sutherland whose blonde bob haircut gently touched her chin.

"Yes," she said as she finished the papers.

"What can you tell me about the victim?" asked McLoughlin who knelt down beside the body. He added, "You've been working for the city what . . . 15 years now?"

"Yep, I started off as a patrol officer. Then I worked my way up to Head Medical Examiner. Why?" asked Jenny.

"You don't look old enough to have worked that many years."

"Save the southern charm. Listen, when I got here, the young lady was blown up like a tick; and I had to do my . . . Well you know, poke the body thing with—"

"Okay, okay, I get the picture," he said twirling his ring.

"Because the body had larvae that were about 5 millimeters long before reaching the prepupae stage, I'd say it's been about 2 days. I don't know about you, but I sure don't like having to swat after blow flies when they reach the final stage. Then the cycle continues. I've taken samples of the maggots and placed them in alcohol which will allow me to preserve them."

"Okay, okay, what's up with the G-String?" asked McLoughlin who picked the G-String up with an ink pen.

"Well, it's not my size," she said jokingly. When he just looked at her, she added, "I haven't figured that out. You know — come to think of it — we had a Jane Doe a few days ago; and there was a G-String placed near the body at that crime scene also."

"Who is the lead detective on the case?"

"You see that handsome young man in the blue shirt with his signature brown sports jacket coming through the door as we speak?"

"Are you serious? Damn."

"Why do you say that? Detective Yeomans is one of the best detectives on the force. He is admired by everyone on this site. So if I were you, I'd watch that tone."

"Well at GBI, he is known as a pretty boy."

"Why Mac, are you jealous?" she asked while looking at Yeomans' tight jeans.

"Hell no."

She thought that Mac's tamed auburn dreadlocks were over the top for such a conservative city. Because he looked to be multicultural, no one really knew his racial background; however, his name was Irish. This didn't matter to Jenny because his skills in the field were above reproach.

Knowing how to attract a crowd, Yeomans was surrounded by officers who wanted to update him on the case. As a CSI officer passed him the log book, Yeomans said, "Oh great, GBI is here."

McLoughlin noticed that Yeomans winked his left eye at Jenny. "Detective Yeomans!" exclaimed McLoughlin as if they were personal friends. Making sure his GBI badge was visible, McLoughlin added, "Do we have a problem?"

Yeomans said, "I would say that we do. We're at a murder crime scene."

"Remember me from the Tracey Edmond case? I'm Agent McLoughlin, GBI." They shook hands.

"Agent Mack . . . Law . . ." said Yeomans who was trying to pronounce the name.

"Everyone calls me Mac for short."

"Okay Agent Mac, how can I help you?"

"Well, we can start by leaving the agent off, just Mac. Let's go outside so that we can talk."

Knowing that there was going to be a major crime scene territory battle between agencies, Jenny winked her eye at Yeomans and said, "If you need me I'll be here."

Outside, Trooper pulled up to the scene which looked similar to the Chocolate City urban streets. Then she placed her D.C. lieutenant badge around her neck; and Teco pulled out a toothpick from his shirt pocket and put it into his mouth. As Trooper and Teco walked up to the apartment, news crews were interviewing neighborhood witnesses. Many of the neighbors still wore bath robes and slippers.

Trooper walked up to a female officer and said, "Excuse me. Who's the lead detective?"

The officer said authoritatively, "Ma'am, you need to step behind the yellow tape with the other news reporters."

"Where is GBI Agent McLoughlin?" asked Trooper who now held her badge in front of the officer's face.

When the officer looked at the badge, she apologetically said, "Lieutenant, he's standing over there."

While McLoughlin was talking to Yeomans, Trooper's stride was totally professional. Her black suit with white dress shirt gave her a distinguished look.

"Mac, I don't know who is responsible for this murder; however, the Edmond crew is still on our hot list. We are still investigating the car crash of your undercover agents on the I-285 loop. The Edmond crew hustles out of a few housing units over there," said Yeomans, who nodded in the direction of an apartment where two females were watching. "As you know, this is one of their number one locations."

"Well, somebody had to have seen something because what seems normal usually isn't. I want to see the Red Dogs Strike Force reports," said McLoughlin.

"Excuse us. Which one of you gentlemen happen to be Agent McLoughlin?" asked Trooper.

Admiring Trooper's beautiful appearance, Yeomans asked, "And you are?"

"I'm Lieutenant Troop from Washington, D.C.; and this is a consultant on the case, Mr. Jackson. Two more of our team members will be in Atlanta later."

"Oh great!" exclaimed Yeomans while McLoughlin quickly outstretched his right hand to Trooper and then to Teco.

"Lieutenant, I'm Agent McLoughlin. Call me Mac. We talked over the phone. I'm glad that you made it. We were just talking about the case."

"I see this is the crime scene," said Trooper.

"Yes, it is. As a matter of fact, let me show you inside," said Mac.

She searched the onlookers to see if The Paradox might be watching.

When they all walked into Lisa's apartment, the room's bad stench met them at the door. When Teco saw Lisa's face, he ran out of the apartment and down the back metal staircase. On the lawn, he threw up his morning breakfast. Holding his throat, he thought that he would collapse, right then and there.

Trooper stood there conflicted as how to respond. If she ran behind Teco, that reaction might give away her personal involvement with him. So, she asked, "Can someone go see if he is alright?"

Before Trooper said another word, Sutherland was already outside and asked Teco, "Is this your first crime scene?"

"Oh shit! Oh shit!" Teco exclaimed as he held his forehead with his left hand. When the world seemed to spin around, he began to hyperventilate.

"Someone, throw me a brown paper bag!" exclaimed Sutherland. "Here, breathe into this bag."

As Teco took the bag, Sutherland noticed the tiny scar under his right eye and his smooth dark chocolate skin. She was amazed that he didn't mess up his white polo shirt and black trousers. With her hand on his broad right shoulder, she said, "Inhale, exhale. That's it." Then she passed him a tissue to wipe his full-sized lips.

Teco said, "I'm alright. Give me a minute."

"Just breathe."

"Damn! Damn! Damn!" exclaimed Teco and tears streamed down his face.

Not understanding why he was so emotional, Sutherland said, "Let's walk over to the basketball court away from everybody."

The walk helped Teco pull things back together. The onlookers cleared a path and wondered was he a relative of the deceased.

At the basketball court, Teco said, "I'm sorry about that. I . . . I . . . I know her. Damn."

"Who is she?"

"She's from Philly. She dated a kingpin named Bashi Mujaheed Fiten and testified at his murder trial. Why the hell would someone do something like this? If it's Bobby, I'm going to beat his ass. Shit!"

"Calm down. Calm down. Is her real name Lisa Turner as it says on the report?"

"Yeah." As Teco took a deep breath, she pointed to a nearby bench.

"Who is Bobby?"

"We think he has a vendetta against anyone associated with the Philadelphia Strictly Business crew. He's calling himself The Paradox; and he's a contradictory son of a bitch."

"Have a seat over here."

"Who are you?" asked Teco, who didn't understand why she was so concerned.

"I'm the Head Medical Examiner. My name is Jenny Sutherland."

Teco didn't respond.

"What's your ties to Lisa Turner?"

"I also testified at the murder trial of Bashi. That's when Lisa and I became good friends. She encouraged me to get on with my life."

Sutherland added, "Confucius once said, 'Death and life have their determined appointments; riches and honors depend upon heaven.'"

"What does that mean?" asked Teco, who took offense to her unsolicited counsel.

Giving him an inquisitive stare, Sutherland simply walked away, pushed through the crowd, and went back under the crime scene tape.

Chapter 17

"THIS IS FOX 5 NEWS. We're here at the Overlook Atlanta apartment complex where a body of a woman was found. Our sources tell us that she was fatally shot multiple times. If you look beyond the crowd, you will see the Chief of Police coming to provide us with an update. . . ."

Sitting in the motel room, The Paradox jumped to his feet to get closer to the 27 inch Magnavox television. He commanded the cameraman to pan the perimeter because he just knew that Trooper would not let him down. Suddenly, the statuesque female detective of his dreams stood in the background behind two Atlanta police officers.

With his right hand, The Paradox rubbed the television screen as if he could really touch Trooper's soft face. He remembered that she smelled like the first day of spring. *Look at my baby in full swing. See you soon!*

The Fox 5 News reporter added, " . . . Tune in tonight at 11 for further updates. We now turn to coverage of a fire at the Timber Trace apartments in Stone Mountain."

Wearing a purple smoking jacket and black silk pajama pants, The Paradox sat down on the bed. From the nightstand, he retrieved his Congressional Medal of Honor and a military patch that read "RELLIK." He began to sob.

His entire military career was devoted to fighting the War on Drugs. The RELLIK strike unit was formed to eradicate the major sources of cannabis and coca production around the world. However, the RELLIK operation lost its government funding. In turn, The Paradox stole and trafficked weapons to affected countries so that the locals could continue to fight the drug cartels. As a result, The Paradox received a dishonorable discharge and was incarcerated at Fort Leavenworth Prison for 2 years. While serving time, he devised a plan to take out the strongest links in the drug supply chain, no matter how unorthodox.

Knowing that his ultimate goal was too complex for one man to accomplish, The Paradox sobbed until he grew tired and fell asleep.

. . . The Atlantic's ocean blue waves slammed against the starboard side and came back with a left hook on the port side of the huge iron monster named the U.S.S. Thunderbolt. No one on the ship knew that the RELLIK strike force unit was aboard but the tall and slender captain. Holding tightly to their AR-15 rifles, the team members sat in a room on the 4th deck in the pitch black while the scent of salt water filled the air.

To protect their identities, all six members of the RELLIK strike unit were identified by letters and numbers: R1 through R6. The Paradox's number was R-4. The entire unit was made up of the elite branches of the U.S. Military and subsidized by the Central Intelligence Agency (CIA). The team was trained on Improvised Explosive Devices (IED), military grade suppressors and booby traps in order to inflict deadly force. The covert operation was to cut off at the knees the producers of cannabis and coca leafs. Because RELLIK's tactics posed a threat to national security, the details did not fall under the Freedom of Information Act.

Their last assignment in India resulted in a total of 15 people being killed in order to get to one leader of a drug cartel. The real cataclysm was the 14 locals who died because their main purpose of growing cannabis and coca was to make a living by selling leafs for medicinal reasons. However, a drug cartel took over the fields in order to produce illegal marijuana and cocaine. This was happening worldwide; and tonight's mission to eliminate another leader of another drug cartel was no different.

When the ships red light came on, the team stood, but no words needed to be spoken because this was their drop off point.

Then the captain said, "Team RELLIK, we have twenty-four hours to get in and out."

There was a knock on the iron door. Cling! Cling! Cling! R-2, an Italian, was point man and opened the door. Then the captain, with two fingers, motioned for them to follow him.

Once on the main deck of the ship, R-4 pulled the deflator cord just before the black watercraft was lowered into the ocean with a 50 horsepower motor attached. As the unit started towards landfall, the night was so dark that they could barely see their hands in front of them, let alone the land.

R-3, who was the only female, looked at her watch to check the compass in order to ensure that they were going in the correct direction; and they were. She enjoyed the rampant water ride.

Once on land, they first hit the Namib Desert in South Africa. The moon's glory shone upon the sand which was so dark brown that it looked like an imperial topaz in the night. This route took them to the Namibia jungle in South Africa. As they emerged from the jungle into an open field of garbanzo vegetation, the team knew they would encounter arachnids as big as their hands. The day was about to break and according to the map, they were only half-way through the vegetation.

At sunrise, RELLIK finally travelled through the jungle a few yards from a small village. As their camouflaged suits harmonized with the jungle, R-4 crouched to the ground and suddenly looked up because he heard movement in the trees. He observed two monkeys jumping from treetop to treetop. Then his attention turned to the beautiful sounds of birds. In sight was an old military truck moving in RELLIK's direction. This caused the chickens to disperse out of the way of the vehicle. Little children, who were wearing goatskin clothes, played with the sheep. Baaa! Baaa! Baaa!

RELLIK emerged from the jungle in diamond formation, one facing north, one south, one east, one west as two held the center. Everything seemed to cease. Team RELLIK held their AR-15's with a 37mm M203 grenade launcher for possible guerrilla attackers.

Getting out of the truck, a native man, who was wearing khaki shorts and shirt, exclaimed, "Kom saam met my!"

R-2 asked, "Are you our contact?"

"Yes, that will be me. Salaam," he said in English with an Afrikaans accent while placing his right hand over the left side of his chest.

The native kids ran up to them; and the man said something in Afrikaans which caused the children to scatter back to their huts.

He looked at the RELLIK team in awe and said, "Come with me."

They loaded into the military truck and travelled for what seemed to be an hour to the northern part of Namibia by the Okavango River. When the Jeep pulled over beside the forest, their escort said, "This is as far as I take you. May Allah be with you."

RELLIK went through the coca field and covered a great deal of ground until they came to their mark. Unexpectedly, there was gunfire. POW! POW! POW! . . .

The Paradox woke up and realized that he was not in Africa. Even though the air conditioner was running full blast, he rubbed the sweat from his forehead. Thinking about the task at hand, he reached for the phone and left a message for a RELLIK member who was close to him. He needed to talk with someone but knew that they were forbidden to make any type of contact without permission.

Watching the phone for over an hour, The Paradox waited as if he were in the field on a mission. He became even more enraged at those who trained him. When the end came, his superiors would get the blame for all of his actions; he promised himself that they would.

His alter ego wouldn't let up. *Soulja, are you going to sit there like a deserter?*

The Paradox grabbed the side of his head to cover his ears. All alone, he knew that he needed to finish his mission and expose those who supplied the drug cartels state side.

Soulja, you have me. I'm with you for life and nothing can divorce us.

"Leave me the hell alone and get out of my head. I don't need you in my life!" exclaimed The Paradox as he stood up. This internal battle was causing him to have a migraine. "They told me, do this R-4, do that R-4, kill, kill, kill!"

You have abandoned the military book which was meant to guide you. You were supposed to treat it as your bible.

"Those African tribes' crops were to be used for medicine, not drugs. Why did the natives have to die?"

You are weak. After you were dishonorably discharged, you were supposed to fight the war on drugs on the streets of Conshohocken. I told you not to get hooked up in the game.

"Shut up! Shut the hell up! I kept seeing those innocent people die in the fields of the safari, just to take out a few men. I wasn't weak. I needed to escape."

So you got hooked on the very stuff you were fighting against? That was stupid.

"Shut up! I took the SB crew stash for evidence."

That's why Mr. Teco 'Homicide' Jackson whopped your ass on the streets. You went down like a baby.

"Baby my ass. One more hit and the SB crew will be totally history."

Because of you, RELLIK is disbanded. When you went on that crime spree in Washington, D.C., the mission was spoiled forever.

"No! No! I can pull it back together. I'm clean now. We can win the war on drugs. Detective Troop is going to help me."

You are an idiot. Detective Troop is going to take you down.

"I am not an idiot! I'm the bad ass Drug Czar now. The guy with the gold finger is also a target because his time for selling drugs must come to an end."

After gazing into the mirror for a few seconds, he put on his brown safariflage clothing. Then he sat down on the side of the bed to tie up his combat boots. The Paradox could see now that he was blinded by the truth and was told a bunch of lies by his former commanding officers.

Within the hour, The Paradox drove down Simpson Road to the home where he followed Goldfinger a few days ago. He knew that he couldn't make the same mistakes that were made when he went after the SB crew. Parking the Navigator five houses away gave him a good view. He reached in the center console and pulled out his binoculars to survey the wooden duplex house. He noticed a shadow passing in front of the living room window.

Looking out of the back window of the Navigator, he made sure that the coast was clear. On the back floorboard was a quilted blanket. Underneath, he grabbed the homemade pipe bomb. When he moved to get out of the Navigator, he paused because he saw the inner lights of a nearby car. Then two men stepped out. The man with dreadlocks carried a large weapon under his jacket.

Picking back up his binoculars again, The Paradox watched as the men walked over to a black van. When the van's door slid open, The Paradox saw the computer equipment and even more men.

"Shit!" The Paradox exclaimed.

Soulja, it's too hot. Find another approach.

For once the voice in his head said something meaningful. After carefully placing the pipe bomb back on the floorboard, The Paradox drove off into the night.

Chapter 18

THE NEXT DAY, Trooper took her hair and pulled it behind her head into a ponytail which was a sign that she was ready for work. She looked down on the lobby floor and saw a large symbol that looked to be covered in two inches of thick clear wax. There was a circle with the words "State of Georgia" at the top, "Bureau of Investigations" at the bottom, and at the center was the year "1776" with a colonial soldier dressed in blue.

"Trooper!" exclaimed Swoosh.

Without thinking, she ran and gave him a big hug.

This didn't set well with Teco because Swoosh's hands rested on Trooper's hips. Swoosh shook Teco's hand; and Ronald walked in the building holding a small black velvet pouch.

The security guard at the desk looked perturbed at all of the commotion going on in the lobby area and said, "Excuse me. Will you please wait for Agent McLoughlin over there?" Teco welcomed the interruption of Trooper and Swoosh's deep conversation.

Teco extended a hand and said, "Hi, I'm Teco."

"What's up? I'm Ronald."

"So, what's in the bag?"

Ronald untied the gold string and poured the contents of the bag into his right hand. "These are D&D dice."

"Why would you need D&D dice for a Doctor of Divinity?"

Ronald laughed at Teco's unfamiliarity of the dice. "No! I use them for a role playing game called Dungeons & Dragons, D&D for short. I even belong to a D&D club. The game was designed by two guys by the name of Gygax and Arneson in the 1970's."

"Role playing? Huh."

"Yeah, you know a good detective has to get into the mind of the perpetrator. During criminal profiling, I find it useful to act out the part of the bad guy and try to get into his or her mind. As a D&D player, the game has taught me to expect the unexpected."

"Okay," said Teco who thought this was a very strange strategy of fighting crime.

Teco outstretched his hand and asked, "Can I see them?"

"Sure, there's a total of seven dice. This is a D4. It's called that because it has four sides. This is a D6, and this one is—"

"Okay, I get the picture." Teco looked over at Trooper who was sitting on the lobby sofa talking to Swoosh. Teco added, "So how does the dice work in the game?"

"It's like this. D4, D6, D8 and D12 are rolled for weapons damage from a character in the game." Ronald picked up two more dice. "This is a D10 which you roll for a percentage chance. Then you have the D20, which is my favorite because it determines success or failure." Ronald put the dice in the pouch, except for the red D20 die which he put in his front right pocket.

"Well, has it helped you to improve your detective skills?"

"I think so. These criminals are always into their own fantasy. If I can second guess them and be there before they make their next move, it's all the better."

As Teco turned to lure Trooper away from Swoosh, Agent McLoughlin emerged from the elevators with a plastered smile on his face.

"Lieutenant Troop, hello," he said extending his hand.

"Hi Mac, I want you to meet the rest of our team. You have already met Teco. Lieutenant Marcus Brown and Ronald Heard just arrived from the airport."

"Call me Swoosh," said Lieutenant Brown.

"Just call me Ronald."

Mac said, "Let's go down to Atlanta police headquarters. Detective Yeomans is waiting on us as we speak."

"Before we leave, is there an office where we can get updated about the case first? I want to make sure we are all on the same page," said Swoosh.

Leading them to an office on the lobby level, Mac switched on the lights. Teco opened his computer backpack and pulled out the laptop. Then Mac attached Teco's laptop to the LCD projector and pulled down the screen.

Ronald asked, "Trooper, have you and Teco found out anything yet?"

Before she could answer, Swoosh chimed in and asked, "So partner, is this the work of The Paradox?"

"Well, yes and no to both questions," she said as Ronald and Swoosh looked at each other. "See, from what I can tell in Lisa Turner's case is that it doesn't look like his work; however, if it is, he is becoming more vicious and in a rage about something."

"He should be," said Ronald with a smile.

"Why is that?" asked Mac.

"Because he has Trooper back on his ass . . ." said Ronald who laughed.

Teco said, "Let me share a few things. This guy is far from weak. He will kill in a heartbeat. To him, this is a game; and I believe that we are the pieces."

"What is The Paradox doing in Atlanta?" asked Swoosh.

"That's a very good question which I haven't figured out just yet; however, I won't stop until he is in custody," said Trooper. They knew that she was serious as a heart attack. Without thinking, Trooper asked softly, "What does he want in Atlanta?"

"What did you say?" asked Swoosh.

"No, nothing, I was just thinking out loud."

"Yeah, I know. What did you say though?"

"I was asking myself, what does he want? There has to be something. Teco, pull up a search on Atlanta."

Within seconds a picture of the beautiful city skyline popped up on the large screen for everyone to see.

"There's a lot of history here to read," said Teco.

"The last words The Paradox said to me were 'you might find me in the Black Mecca of the South, Chi-town, the Big Apple, or the City of Syrup."

"City of Syrup?" asked Mac.

"Yeah, that's what they used to call Houston because in that city there was an abuse of cough syrup with codeine," said Teco.

"Well, they call Atlanta the Black Mecca of the South because of the high population of African Americans who come here in search of the American dream."

When Teco pulled out a piece of paper in a plastic bag, Swoosh said, "Let me see that." After a few minutes, Swoosh said, "It says, 'The nectar of its fruit is sour.'"

"Maybe, he was talking about the peaches in Georgia," said Mac, who was twirling his ring. Then he added, "Jenny, our

M.E. said that Lisa's body was moved to face the northwest direction?"

Teco did a search on Atlanta and northwest. "Look at this. In 1836, the state began to build the Western and Atlantic Railroad in the northwest part of the state."

"Don't start the history lesson. You are beginning to sound like Trooper," said Swoosh. Then Trooper corner eyed him.

"Let me finish. During the Civil War, Atlanta served as an arms supply deport for the Confederate Army. Union troops led by General Sherman captured the city and eventually burned Atlanta down to the ground. When it was rebuilt, Atlanta became known as 'The Phoenix City.' Doesn't the note say something about burning up?" asked Teco.

Swoosh held the plastic bag up and said, "It says 'the eternal flame is burning up.'"

"As you know the Olympic flame burned during the 1996 Summer Olympics here in Atlanta," said Mac.

"It says something about MARTA. What is that?" asked Swoosh.

Mac said, "It's the public transportation system in Atlanta. Some of the locals say it stands for 'moving African-Americans rapidly through Atlanta.'"

"That's racist," said Trooper.

"See it for what it is and see it for what it's worth," said Teco.

"The bottom-line is that he is confirming that he is in Atlanta," said Ronald, who tossed the red D20 die on the table. "He is drawing us into this fantasy world."

"Well team, let's head on over to see Yeomans," said Mac as Teco packed up his computer.

If Teco wasn't mistaken, Swoosh put his arm around Trooper's waist as they headed out the door.

Within the hour, they walked into the main lobby of the City Hall East building on Ponce de Leon Avenue. Mac walked over to the security desk and signed the team in for the day.

The elevator stopped on every floor until they reached the 9th floor. Teco observed that the officers were going about their normal day. This was the first time he ever worked on the right side of the law.

Mac approached a female receptionist who sat at a small desk. Every time she moved her head, the earring in her nose sparkled from the lights which were above her head. The weave hairdo the receptionist sported must have been styled at home by a relative or friend because it was not professionally done at all.

"Excuse me," said Mac.

The female had the audacity to put up her index finger as she continued to speak on the phone. Her demeanor to include her head movement told them that this wasn't a business call.

Growing impatient, Swoosh stepped forward, flashed his badge and said, "We need to see your supervisor or you can call Detective—" Turning to Mac he asked, "What's his name?"

"Yeomans," said Mac.

"Hey girl, let me call you back; these police flashing their badges. . . . I see badges all day. Okay?" She ended the call, rolled her eyes, and dialed a number. "Sir, you have a few guests. Yes sir, I sure will." She looked at the group; however, her eyes fell upon Teco. "He says he'll be right out. Y'all have a seat in those chairs over there." As Teco sat down on the brown and orange faux leather chair, the receptionist gawked at him.

When Detective Yeomans came out, Trooper stepped forward to shake his hand. She said, "Detective, this is the rest of my team, Detective Heard, Lieutenant Brown, but we call him Swoosh. You've already met Mr. Jackson."

Detective Yeomans shook their hands and said, "This is my partner, Detective Fordham."

"Gentlemen, ma'am," said Yeomans' female partner who hoped that Trooper wasn't territorial because Fordham had no time for disputes about who was the head vixen.

Because Detective Fordham held file folders in her hand, Trooper could tell that Fordham was very martinet; however, Trooper wondered how helpful she would be on the case.

"Come with me. I have a room for us to work out of down this hall," said Detective Fordham as they all followed.

The room was nice and cool with a large 64 inch screen, a huge conference table, great lighting, and a total of ten mesh office chairs. Detective Fordham placed the files on the table and took off her jacket which revealed a fitted blue shirt and a plump toffee cleavage.

The temperature of the room increased as Trooper saw Fordham lean towards Teco. *Oh hell no, she didn't.*

Seeing the tension between the two most beautiful women in the building, Yeomans cleared his throat and said, "Okay, this is the file from our Jane Doe."

Trooper pulled her chair closer to the table and opened the file. Her eyes widened when a picture fell onto the table. "The Jane Doe is no longer a Jane Doe; she's Missy Green from Laurens County." Then Teco pulled out the photo that Mr. Green gave to them.

Yeomans said, "We have determined that the bodies of the victims in the Jane Doe case and the Turner case were positioned with their heads in the northwest direction."

Reading the Medical Examiner's report, Trooper saw annotations that the position of the body at death did not match the position where the body was found.

Fordham displayed a crime photo of Missy Green on the projector screen.

Interrupting Trooper's concentration, Yeomans said, "These marks tell us a lot about the killer or killers' style." Trooper started to speak, but Yeomans continued, "There is the standard post-mortem hypostasis. See these purple areas here." The red laser pointer, which Yeomans was holding, displayed on the screen. "Missy Green was killed on the bed by ligature. We don't believe it was due to sexual or autoerotic pleasure."

"Excuse me, who found the body?"

"Shortly after the call to 911, my partner and I were on the scene. The body was still warm. The ligature appears to be soft and the markings are identical to the G-String that was found at the crime scene," said Yeomans.

Trooper made a mental note to call the Sheriff at Laurens County.

Detective Fordham went to the next photo, which displayed the G-String with a note attached.

Welcome to Atlanta Trooper!

Flippantly, Detective Fordham said to Trooper, "Sounds like this nutcase has a hard on for you."

Trooper's breathing became extremely short. At that moment, Yeomans knew that Fordham was picking the wrong fight.

Chapter 19

LATE EVENING, THE TEAM of detectives stood in gloomy Room 202 at the Metropolitan Inn. They methodically walked the grid from the first CSI investigation. Then they conducted their own zone search and divided the room into four quadrants. Trooper, Swoosh, Yeomans and Fordham each searched a section. Teco and Ronald stood by the door and observed. All crime evidence seemed to be located at point one in the room.

After the search, Ronald said, "Wait! Don't take off your gloves yet. We have one more thing to do. We are going to reconstruct this scene."

"What!" exclaimed Fordham.

"Great idea Ronald, let's look at the photos and get the layout," said Yeomans, who was fascinated by the thought.

"Why are we doing this?" asked Fordham.

"I must admit that I also find it very hard to believe that the G-String is all there is to this case," said Trooper.

"I'm not trying to undermine you all, but our Atlanta CSI team combed every inch of this place."

"Detective Fordham, if this is truly The Paradox, he is much more complex than you can imagine. It takes ingenuity and skill to come up with the solutions to his puzzles."

"So, all of this is a test?" asked Yeomans.

"Well, it's a test and a game. The test was to get me to Atlanta. Now the game begins. I understand that Ronald is an expert at reconstruction."

"Alright, we are going to do a little role playing," said Ronald.

Teco said, "Man, this is not Dungeon and Dragons. This is real life."

"Teco, you ran the streets. You are here as our consultant so we can get into the head of this guy. Your time will come. Like Trooper said, this is a game now; and it takes skills. Because of D&D, I'm the sharpest person in the D.C. Homicide Division in catching the bad guys."

"Okay, I'm listening," said Teco who didn't want to draw attention to his past life.

"Yeomans, you be the male victim and Fordham you play the female victim. Teco, you can be The Paradox. Let's see, Fordham, I need you to lie down on the bed," said Ronald.

With an adamant expression, Fordham said, "Oh hell no, I'm not lying on that bed where a dead woman was killed."

"Fordham, look in the trunk of our police car and get that folded clear plastic tarp," said Yeomans.

Scanning the room, Fordham noticed that everyone was serious about this re-enactment.

"Okay, from the reports and the photos, the male victim was shot here. So, Yeomans lie down on the floor in the northwest direction."

When Fordham came back into the room, she held the clear plastic covering. "What am I to do with this?"

"Teco, help her cover the bed so that we can act this out. Yeomans, I need you to stay right there. Okay Fordham, the victim's corpse was right here," said Trooper.

"Dang, do you have to use that word?" asked Fordham.

Because the Atlanta diva was starting to cave, the smirk on Troopers' face was priceless.

After Fordham reclined on the bed, Trooper positioned Fordham's body to match the picture.

Ronald said, "Okay, move your left arm over the edge of the bed and let it hang right there. Yeah, there you go." Thinking of what to do next, he added, "Teco, you are re-enacting The Paradox. What do you think he did next after he killed the two of them?"

Teco walked out of the room. Boom! Teco burst back into the hotel room giving the team his version of what most likely happened. Now standing beside the bed, Teco asked, "Why did he kill them?" No one responded so he continued, "The note said 'Welcome to Atlanta Trooper.' So, he knew she would come to the crime scene. It's got to be something near the bed. You guys did a thorough search of the room."

Trooper stepped back to get a clearer view. *What is he trying to tell me? Talk to me. Talk to me.*

"What's up?" asked Ronald.

When Trooper held up her right index finger, Ronald sighed deeply.

"Shhh!" Trooper hissed. As she knelt down, her knees popped. "I think I have something. This carpet looks plugged under Fordham's left hand. Let me see the Maglite flashlight."

Ronald handed the flashlight and a scalpel to Trooper.

Yeomans took photos of the four inch square slit in the carpet.

Swoosh said, "If I didn't know any better, I'd say that we've all worked together for years. Trooper, be careful that this is not a booby trap."

The entire room fell silent.

Trooper said, "It's clear."

After Trooper pulled up the carpet, Yeomans asked, "What the hell is that?"

Trooper revealed a blank sheet of paper. She turned the paper from the front to the back, still nothing. Then Trooper went into her bag, pulled out her blue ultraviolet light and flashed it onto the paper. Trooper read the message to the team.

Hello Detective Troop,

Now that there is no more rising sun, I want to see your body to the core.

When we meet again, remember, less is more.

The Paradox

Trooper said, "This guy is sick. Have you checked the other hotel rooms because he likes to leave secondary crime scenes."

"Yes, we already checked the entire premises," said Fordham getting up from the bed.

"What does that note mean?" asked Yeomans standing up from the floor.

"Rising Sun was a victim during the G-String murder investigation," said Trooper who cut her eyes over to Swoosh.

Swoosh, Ronald and Teco stood there waiting for Trooper to tell Yeomans and Fordham about the facts of the Washington

D.C. case. Just as Teco started to speak, Trooper signalled for him to keep quiet.

"So, do you think the killer knows that you are in Atlanta?" asked Yeomans.

"Trust me, he knows," said Trooper as she opened the motel room door and walked down the stairs towards the police car.

Within minutes, a lady was all up in Trooper's face and said, "This is Cindy Stepanofa with Fox 5 Atlanta. I've just received word that GBI has asked for help from the Washington, D.C. Homicide Division on the double homicide case. The officers tell me that you are Detective Troop. What is your role in the case?"

As his right toe touched the hot water in the bathtub, The Paradox stopped and headed back into the bedroom at the Super 8 motel in Midtown. He was hoping to see Trooper on television. Taking a seat on the edge of the bed, The Paradox was willing to risk his bath water getting cold just for a glimpse of her.

When the cameraman panned to the far right, The Paradox couldn't believe his eyes. Then Cindy Stepanofa ran up the stairs to the ban of detectives and said, "Sir, Detective Troop refuses to speak with us. Can you please tell us why Washington, D.C. detectives are working the case?"

The man with the wavy hair pushed the camera away, shielded his face, and said, "No comment."

Swoosh screamed, "Get these cameras out of here."

The Paradox grabbed the television with both hands and yelled, "No! No! No! This can't be! This can't be!"

Pacing the floor, The Paradox was so enraged that he threw the table lamp to the floor and it shattered into several pieces. He picked up his black briefcase and exclaimed, "Shit!"

He rummaged through the briefcase until he pulled out the clipping from *The Washington Times* newspaper. He scanned until he reached the section that read "Male Exotic Dancer Teco 'Rising Sun' Jackson Deceased."

Chapter 20

THE NEXT DAY, GQ FINALIZED the finishing touches on the runway at the Ferst Center for the Arts. Everything was going wonderfully. There was a great deal of hustle and bustle in the area. Everyone was accounted for except one male model. The ten female models from Paris were in the dressing room with Love, GQ's fashion director. The production crew was erecting the backdrop; and the light technicians were working from scaffolds while the sound technicians were completing the audio check.

Checking her timepiece, GQ knew that everyone would be in the ballroom practicing by now for the big show. She was expecting representatives from Dolce and Gabbana, Alice and Olivia, and Marc Jacobs. This show would be a pivotal point in determining if her signature collection would be accepted in the fashion world.

GQ walked across stage left when the stage manager walked up to her and said, "Excuse me. I would like to speak with you about security."

With her left hand over her forehead in order to block the bright stage lights, GQ asked, "What will be the cost?"

"Five-thousand added on to the balance."

GQ thought about the offer. Even though she had a partnership with another security company, this was a much better deal. "Sure, I'll approve. However, your security has to be in black tie attire."

"Oh, of course they will be. Can you sign here?" asked the stage manager who passed GQ a clipboard.

Just as GQ finished signing the papers, her cell phone vibrated. "Excuse me," said GQ turning her back to the woman. "Hello, this is GQ."

"Hello to you. How are you today?"

She smiled. "Mustafa hello, where are you?"

"I'm on my way."

"Okay, after practice I want to show you something."

Mustafa's mind began to drift off into his own dream world. He tried his best not to think of anything sexual because of his religious beliefs. However, he realized that he was biting down on his lower lip when he heard her voice.

"You still there?" asked GQ.

"Yes, yes, I'm here. I should be there in an hour or so. I'll see you then, In Shá Allah."

"In shá what?" GQ asked.

Mustafa laughed.

"What's so funny?"

"Nothing, In Shá Allah means if God wills."

"Okay." They both laughed, which GQ thought was a cute gesture. Then she put the phone back into her back pocket. As she walked to the front door of the center, The Paradox drove by and missed her by a hair's breadth.

Before The Paradox got out of the SUV, he checked his wig and fake eyebrows to make sure everything was in order. When he opened the car door, he checked out the area to see if anyone suspicious could be posing as an undercover agent. At the back of the SUV, the scent of fresh tar enveloped his nose. The Paradox didn't realize that he was standing in the fresh tar until the suction almost pulled his low cut boots off. This is when he noticed that half of the parking lot was resurfaced.

The Paradox retrieved a black duffle bag and put on a jacket with a County Inspector patch. Then he pulled out a pair of Ray Ban dark shades to add to his disguise. With the bag in one hand and a clipboard in the other, he walked up to the front door.

The outside lights were not on, which could only mean that the Ferst Center for the Arts was closed. However, to his surprise the door was open. "Hello? Anyone here?" he yelled out as he walked farther into the lobby which was dark. Therefore, he took off his shades.

"How may I help you?"

He blinked his eyes twice, maybe three times, to quicken his focus. "I'm with the County Building Inspectors Office. They sent me to inspect this district for building erosion. We ask—"

"Please follow me," she said turning around. They walked up more steps to a large open theatre.

"Wow! This is nice," he said with a huge smile.

"Yeah, it is. Isn't it? It's been here since 1992. Not many people know this, but it was originally named the Georgia Tech Theatre for the Arts . . ."

The Paradox really didn't give a flip about the history of this place. "Can you show me the cellar please?"

"Sure, it's this way." As they were walking, they came past the runway for the fashion show.

Looking at the elaborate layout, he said, "Doing some remodelling?"

"Oh no, not really . . . There is a fashion show coming up, and the stage is being extended.

"Oh I see. I'll need to inspect that stage before I leave."

Why would he want to inspect the stage? She opened the door to the dark vast area which went deep underground. Then she flipped the switch on the wall. Only parts of the entrance way were illuminated. "When you get to the bottom of these steps, there's another switch on the beam post to light the rest of the cellar."

"Thank you. I won't be down here long."

"Be careful of the rickety steps. When you are done, I'll be in the office by the lobby. Just knock on the door."

"I will."

When he descended the wooden steps, the soles of his boots still felt sticky. Reaching the bottom step, he cleared the way of some cobwebs out of his face. Then he heard mice making sharp squeaking noises, which explained the stench. Going down on one knee, he put the duffle bag on the damp concrete floor.

The Paradox reached into his pocket, retrieved driving gloves, and pulled out a 12 inch black plastic box from his duffle bag. After carefully placing the box on the floor, he looked inside and admired the newly designed masterpiece, a pipe bomb packed with a high velocity C-4 explosive.

Double checking his work, his eyes followed the blue, red and orange wires to make sure the connections were correct; they were. Tracing the yellow wire from the 6 volt heavy duty Rayovac battery to the two channel receiver, The Paradox inspected the Servo motor and cam lobe at the top which served as a remote controlled detonation switch. Then he checked the safety switch in order to make sure the safety was in the off position.

With ease, he reached into the duffle bag and pulled out two small brown paper bags. The bag with steel balls was placed beside the Servo motor; and the bag full of nails and bolts was positioned by the safety switch. Afterwards, The Paradox closed and placed the pipe bomb box back into the duffle bag.

Carrying the bag on his shoulder, he slowly ascended the stairs, entered the theatre, and looked around to see if anyone was watching him. There wasn't. With only the wall lights on, the whole theatre area was dim and gloomy. Walking up to the runway, he perpetrated the whole act as if he were inspecting the stage. He was able to navigate his way underneath the stage floor to the center.

His next moves were deadly. From his pocket, he retrieved a beige G2 Nitrolon compact flashlight, turned it on, and placed the flashlight into his mouth in order to free his hands. Reaching inside the duffle bag, he pulled out the pipe bomb and scattered the steel balls, nails and bolts all around the box. With dexterity, he did not disturb one wire. Taking a deep sigh, he flipped the safety switch.

BOOM went the sound of a stage light which crashed above him upon the stage floor. He heard people scurrying and voices yelling.

He held his breath thinking that the pipe bomb would blow any minute. However, nothing happened. Wiping the sweat from his forehead, The Paradox took a cleansing breath. Reaching inside the bag he grabbed the masking tape, self adhesive Velcro, and cutting pliers. Like a professional electrician, he attached the pipe bomb underneath the stage and made sure everything was intact.

People were still walking on the stage above. His heart raced wondering how he was going to escape without notice. Then he saw another way out and crawled until he was on the back side of the black drapes. Nearly bumping into a male model, The Paradox high stepped it for the closest exit door and never stopped by the front office.

When GQ walked back into the theatre, she heard Love say, "Okay girls work it! Work it! Yes! Mustafa give me a racier look. You're doing fine. Fine I say."

GQ couldn't believe her eyes.

Her effeminate fashion director had on a colorful ruffled shirt. He continued, "Okay, yes, Jevanta work it. . . . Turn . . . Turn . . . Now walk it out. Yes!"

The theatre was full of models and cameras taking shots from various angles. In the back right corner, a makeup artist from Paris set up a glamour station. In another area, hair was being styled. The Indigo Signature Collection clothes from suits, slacks, gowns and other pieces were being switched from rack to rack. The place was organized chaos.

GQ walked over to the photographer and said, "Hey Xavier."

When he felt her arms around his neck, he turned around to face her and said in a French accent, "It's so nice to see you. I must say that you have some flawless models here in America."

"How did the guy with the white thing on his head get recruited?"

"We were short one man; and Love couldn't resist having him in the show. For an amateur, he's a natural. Is he one of yours?"

"Yes, he's mine alright."

Xavier pulled his right hand away from the camera, looked at GQ and asked, "Have you been bad?"

She set her eyes on Mustafa and said, "No, not yet but I'm working on it." Her adrenaline peaked as she watched the models come down the catwalk. "Do you think he's photogenic?"

"Well, let's look at the fact that people in the industry love an oval shaped face. I think he has a rugged but smooth look that will work." Without thinking Xavier added, "He's fine too."

"Yeah, I think so too."

Making sure that everything was going well with the lineup, GQ turned around to chat with other members of her team. A few New York fashion agents, who were gathered sipping coffee, noticed her immediately. One of the agents captured GQ's attention by tapping on her upper arm. As she gave the agent additional information about the upcoming show, GQ realized the time. Two hours had passed since she arrived.

When she looked over her left shoulder the models were coming her way with bottles of water and thick hand towels while dabbing their faces from the sweat from the hot lights. She searched the room for Mustafa. When she found him, he seemed to be in deep conversation with two female models from Paris. He really seemed to be enjoying his modeling stint.

She was shocked by the emotional feelings she felt for him. It was quite natural for a person to become jealous of someone whom they liked; and she really liked Mustafa. GQ searched around the room to see if anyone was watching her because women are more inclined to detect vibes of jealousy.

When Mustafa cast an eye over the room towards the entrance, he noticed GQ to the left by the agents' station. Then he laid eyes on the convexity of her buttocks in fitted jeans. He didn't want to seem like a teenager; therefore, he gained his composure. "Excuse me ladies," he said and never gave them a chance to protest. Mustafa walked up behind GQ and said in a deep sexy voice, "Hello Ms. Que."

She spun around as if she were on the runway and hadn't seen him before now. "Mr. Muhammad, did you enjoy yourself today?"

"Yes I did. Were you surprised? Mr. Love doesn't take no for an answer. At first I didn't know what I was doing. What time are you leaving today?"

"It all depends on when you're done." Looking around he shrugged his shoulders with both hands turned upright.

"I believe I'm done now. They only have me on four slots."

"Okay, let's go; but first, let me speak with my photographer." She walked over to Xavier and told him that she wanted copies of Mustafa's shots in color as well as black and white.

Mustafa crossed his arms to enjoy the view of GQ's nice shape rocking from side to side. Not being allowed to touch a woman for ten years was one thing, but freedom to hold GQ in the flesh was another. Deep within, he wanted GQ. As she walked back in his direction, he noticed that she held her head high.

"Are you ready?" asked GQ. She never missed a beat in her sexy stride.

When they reached the door, he asked, "Where do you want to go?"

"I'm taking you to the Sundial Room."

Mustafa hailed a cab and within minutes, they were at the Westin Peachtree Plaza.

The elevator ride up was breathtaking and a jazz band could be heard once the doors opened. The candles filled the air with a lavender aromatic scent. In the lounge area, the leather couches were arranged in a spherical configuration with a round table in the middle.

"Let's have a seat," said GQ while grabbing Mustafa's hand. They walked over to an empty section.

"I want to look into your eyes; so I'm going to sit over here across from you," said Mustafa.

"Tonight, we're celebrating; and that calls for some good bubbly."

"What is bubbly?"

"You know, champagne."

"And what might this occasion be?" he asked.

She batted her long eyelashes and said, "You of course!"

"What do you mean?"

"You did so well today at the rehearsal."

He didn't recall seeing her there at any time until the end. Then he reached his hand into the mixed nuts dish on the table and shook them up in his hand as if he were about to roll some lucky dice. "Is that right?" he said popping the nuts into his mouth. "So, if you were not there, how would you know if I did well or—"

"Mustafa, you must remember that I'm the boss, and the crew works for me."

As Mustafa crossed his legs, the waitress walked over to their table wearing black tuxedo pants and a white shirt. She pulled out a pad from her black apron and asked, "May I take your order?"

"Yes, I would like a bottle of Chianti in the bucket please."

The waitress looked at GQ inquisitively. *Do you know how much that is?*

Continuing her conversation with Mustafa, GQ enjoyed seeing him squirm at her advances. "Do you have a girlfriend?"

He couldn't believe how forward GQ was about things. "No, as a matter of fact, I haven't been looking."

"Good, do you mind if I come sit next to you?"

"Sure, I would like that."

When GQ stood, a tall guy who looked like Steven Segal with long black hair in a ponytail approached the table.

"Good evening. I see that you ordered one of our finest champagnes."

GQ reached into her purse, pulled out a Platinum American Express card and said, "Please open the tab using this. You can take the tip percentage out as well." Then she sat beside Mustafa.

As he turned to face her, he looked outside the large restaurant windows. The panoramic view of the city was awesome. In addition, the jazz music was getting louder and louder, until he saw the entire jazz band. He held her hand and said, "Gail, we haven't had a drink yet, and this place is already spinning."

Chapter 21

JUST BEFORE THE BREAK OF DAWN, Squeaky, Goldfinger's right-hand man, walked out of a wooden 1950's ranch house on Center Hill Avenue wearing Perry Ellis black trousers and a black t-shirt. In the Navigator tailing Squeaky, The Paradox couldn't believe his eyes. *Who in their right mind would paint a house orange and yellow?*

Getting into a pearl white 1985 box Chevy Caprice Classic with 24 inch chrome rims, Squeaky drove to a 1940's red brick ranch house on Baker Street. There were two motorcycles, one blue and the other red, parked in the driveway. On the manicured centipede green grass, a weather-beaten pink Little Tikes Country Cottage Playhouse stood empty. Barking loudly was a red nose pit bull. The brown dog charged at Squeaky; however, the steel chain pulled the dog back just inches from Squeaky's black trousers.

After an hour, Squeaky came out of the house with one of Goldfinger's female runners who sported tattoo sleeved arms in her black G-Unit sleeveless tank top or wife beater as they say in the south. Wearing her black leather one-piece motorcycle suit down to her waist, she kissed Squeaky on the cheek as he helped her zip up. Then she waved goodbye as Squeaky revved the box Chevy engine.

Squeaky made eight other stops in a section of Atlanta known as a Disorderly Conduct (DC-6) zone for high drug traffic. Still following Squeaky, The Paradox noticed that Squeaky entered each house empty handed but came out with a brown paper bag under his arm. Descending the steps of each house on point, Squeaky held his right hand closely to his waist while gripping a Browning BDM 9mm pistol with a 15 round magazine.

Next, Squeaky headed to Delmar Lane. Looking into the driver side mirror, he noticed a black Navigator following him; therefore, he placed the gun between his legs. Protecting the crew's money was all that mattered.

As Squeaky made a right onto Linkwood Road and a quick left onto Delmar Lane, he no longer saw the SUV and parked in front of the sixth house on the right. When Squeaky went inside of the ranch home with white vinyl siding, The Paradox pulled into an empty field on the left and noticed that there were several cars down the block near the box Chevy.

Coming out of the house, Squeaky held another brown paper bag. That's when The Paradox decided to make his move on this madcap drug dealer. The Navigator came towards Squeaky at full speed. Just as the tires began to catch a good grip, Squeaky was quick. He fired five shots at the Navigator and rushed back into the front seat of the box Chevy. The gun play caused The Paradox to snatch the wheel to the left; and the Navigator rocked side to side after sliding sideways to a screeching halt.

When The Paradox heard the bullets hitting the doors of the Navigator, The Paradox jumped out of the SUV holding a Chinese Assault Rifle with an extended clip and came over the hood unloading while the brass catcher spiraled 15 spent casings into the bag with 20 still left in the extended clip.

Walking over to the box Chevy, The Paradox saw that Squeaky was spitting up blood onto the steering wheel. House doors slamming sounded throughout the neighborhood as Goldfinger's foot soldiers took to the streets. Someone from behind a raspberry Cutlass fired 3 shots that almost hit The Paradox on the right side of his shoulder.

With swiftness, The Paradox dropped to his knees, let off the rest of his clip and slapped in another. Retrieving two rapid-release smoke hand grenades from his trench coat, The Paradox threw the grenades towards the house. Sliding into the back seat of the box Chevy, he hated the graveolent smell of marijuana in the car. After grabbing a large unzipped gym bag with money inside, he placed an envelope on the back seat. As The Paradox got out of the box Chevy, the men shooting at The Paradox did not see him due to the smoke that lingered in the air for 3 minutes which made for a clean getaway.

Throwing everything onto the passenger front seat of the Navigator, The Paradox checked his rear-view mirror and did not see anyone following him. Driving down Delmar Lane, he made a quick left onto Harwell Road until he arrived at the Harwell Body Shop where he switched vehicles. After driving for a few minutes on I-285 in a red Jeep Cherokee, he heard a thumping sound and pulled over on the side of the road.

Soulja, move fast.

"Yes sir," he said to his alto ego as sweat fell from his brow. He could still smell the gun powder on his hands.

Then he heard footsteps. When he turned his head, The Paradox saw a man wearing a brown jacket, blue shirt and khaki pants.

In a southern drawl, Yeomans said, "You alright? I saw that your blinkers were on. It's hot huh? You are sweating up a storm."

Closing the trunk of the car, The Paradox said, "I thought I had a flat tire, but everything's okay."

On the handheld radio attached to Yeomans' hip, they heard the police dispatcher. "Calling all cars, calling all cars, we have a 10-17 at the 2900 Block on Delmar Lane." Then the dispatcher continued to call out several ten-codes which caused The Paradox to freeze in his tracks.

Yeomans said, "I have to respond to this call. Have a nice day." Turning on the police car lights, Yeomans did a quick u-turn which caused dust to fly up in the air.

When Yeomans arrived, the police cars' fulgurant lights danced on the front of the houses.

"We need the M.E. We have three victims with gunshot wounds. The scene appears to be a drive-by," said a Fulton County police officer to the dispatcher.

The dispatcher said, "That's a 10-4."

Before Yeomans got out of the car with one foot on the ground, he put a piece of spearmint gum in his mouth. Then he saw Detective Fordham. When their eyes met, they both knew that the media would have a field day once they arrived.

Jenny walked up to the officer and said, "I'm already here. What you got?"

"See this guy on the ground? It looks like he was trying to crawl back into the house. The white 1985 Chevy is positioned like a drive-by shooting was the cause—"

Fordham said, "I've been here a while. You can rule out that drive-by."

"Why's that?" asked Jenny who was surveying the scene.

"There is a witness who says that this was not the doings of a person in a car who sped away. There was a man who got out of a black SUV who created this warzone."

"That could be over 100,000 people in metro-Atlanta. Hell, the guy, whose car was broke down on the side of the road, could be the killer if that's the only description you got. Do you have any more details?" asked Yeomans.

Jenny knelt down next to one of the men on the ground as another CSI investigator performed a skid test on the tire marks near the box Chevy. Then Detective Fordham walked over to the house with so many holes that it looked like a piece of Swiss cheese.

As Emergency Medical Technicians (EMT) arrived, several residents said they could not breathe because of the smoke from the hand grenades.

Then Yeomans overheard someone say, "Damn, I can't believe they killed my boy! Shit! Them Fourth Ward boys violated big time. I got something for their ass." Unfortunately, Yeomans couldn't identify the person who made the remark in the crowd.

When Yeomans looked in the box Chevy, he exclaimed, "Son of a bitch!"

Everyone looked at Yeomans. The officer asked, "You know this one?"

"Yep, this is Runyard Mindigal, better known as Squeaky. He's one of Goldfinger's boys. We have a warrant out for his arrest in a double murder of two undercover agents. Ain't this some shit."

"What's the big deal if Goldfinger and the Fourth Ward crew are killing each other," asked the officer.

"Who do you work for? You sure are a dumb ass. The city of Atlanta doesn't need this type of publicity. Are there any more witnesses?"

"Just follow the line over there," the officer said pointing in the direction of the Swiss cheese looking house.

Assuming this was not the witness' first time seeing such a horrific scene, Yeomans walked over to him because he showed no visible signs of nervousness. Yeomans cleared his throat and said, "Excuse me."

"Yes sir," said the young man who was wearing a long white t-shirt and sagging baggy blue jeans.

"I'm Detective Yeomans. Do you know anyone by the name of Tracey Edmonds? His street name is Goldfinger. He wears a prosthetic gold finger."

"Should I?"

"That's why I'm asking Mr.—"

"Butler!" exclaimed Detective Fordham who was standing nearby.

"Do you have a first name Mr. Butler?" Yeomans glanced over at Fordham wondering how she knew the spectator.

"Yeah, it's Jerry."

Yeomans could have sworn that he saw a diamond or two when Jerry smiled. "Do you have any I.D. on you?"

"That chick over there got it."

"That chick has a name. It's Detective Fordham. Well, let me ask you a few more question about—"

"Yeomans Sir," said an Atlanta P.D. officer, "CSI needs you."

Turning to the officer, Yeomans said, "I'll be there after I interview this witness."

"Fordham had me run his I.D. He's clean sir," said the officer who passed to Yeomans the driver's license.

"Good, good, Mr. Jerry Butler, don't go far. I'm watching you." Then Yeomans turned to the officer. "Test him for gunshot residue. I'll hold on to this," said Yeomans putting the I.D. into the breast pocket of his signature brown sports jacket.

When Yeomans walked over to Jenny, he saw that she was holding a clear Ziploc plastic bag with a white envelope inside. "Have you viewed it yet?" he asked.

"No, not yet . . . I found it in the backseat of the Chevy," said Jenny passing him the bag.

Yeomans put on a pair of latex gloves while Jenny walked to the other side of the box Chevy. She leaned over to look through the car window and said, "Have you seen these bullet holes on this side?"

"Yes I did. That's why I told them to test that Butler guy for gun powder residue. One or both of the victims must have caught a bullet from someone who was shooting from inside of that house. . . . Damn!" exclaimed Yeomans.

"What is it?" asked Jenny who was taking measurements of the bullet holes.

Chapter 22

"THERE IS A SILVER THONG with a note attached inside of this envelope. Is there another female victim we don't know about? We need to lock this area down and make sure every person in this neighborhood is accounted for," said Yeomans.

After laying the envelope on a black cloth on the hood of the car, Yeomans looked at the note attached to the G-String and said to Jenny, "Look at this."

Hello Detective Troop,

Find the clock and do an about face because the name Cecil Selby is commonplace.

The Paradox

Yeomans walked over to his police car. Standing with the door open, his left elbow was on the door; and his right elbow was on the roof. He scanned the crowd and stopped when he noticed a familiar face. While dialing a number on his cell phone, he put his right foot on the threshold as he spit out a piece of chewing gum onto the ground.

There was Goldfinger; and their eyes locked. Yeomans looked down to terminate the call; however, when he raised his head, Goldfinger was no longer there. "Shit!" Yeomans exclaimed as he redialed the number again.

When he closed the car door to go after Goldfinger, Fordham walked up to Yeomans, bent over to pick up the gum with her ink pen and said, "This is a crime scene. That is a really bad habit of yours."

"Put it in the ashtray," he said pointing into the car while hearing the phone ring.

"Hello, this is Trooper," she said sitting in a junior suite at the Westin Perimeter Hotel.

"Detective Yeomans here."

"Hello Detective, how are you?"

"Well, I'm fine, but I can't speak for the two men kissing the dirt and the other one behind the steering wheel who will never drive again."

"I see. Busy day?" asked Trooper who hated when people didn't get to the point.

"Yes, I must say that it has been. And you?"

"Well, the team and I are here working the case. We've found out that Gail Que is doing business here in Atlanta under the name of Frontino Lefébvre. We are going to check it out tomorrow."

"That's great. However, I need you at this crime scene," he said without enthusiasm.

"Hold on, let me put you on the speaker phone. Okay, go ahead."

"Turn on the television. We have all the news stations in Atlanta down here, even CNN. We have what looks like a hit on one of the biggest drug crews in Atlanta."

Also in the Westin Perimeter Hotel suite, Swoosh looked at Ronald, Trooper and Teco before he said, "This is Swoosh. What does that have to do with us?"

There was a brief pause as Yeomans scanned the crowd for Goldfinger. "There was a note tied to a G-String left at the scene. Trooper, it's addressed to you."

"Where are you?" she asked picking up a Westin hotel ballpoint pen.

"Don't worry. I have an officer coming to pick you up as we speak."

Swoosh, Ronald and Trooper looked at each other in total disbelief. Ronald pulled out his red D20 die and was ready to reconstruct another crime scene.

"Don't look crazy. Let's get geared up," said Swoosh to Ronald and Trooper.

Back at the crime scene, the news crews were getting in the way of the investigation. Reporters were interviewing potential witnesses as police officers began to push them farther back from the crime scene tape in order to better secure the perimeter.

McLoughlin drove up. Following closely behind him was another vehicle with government tags.

Yeomans knew the second car could only be the Feds. *What are they doing here?*

Getting out of a black Ford Crown Victoria, McLoughlin stood in front of the car to assess the crime scene.

When McLoughlin walked over to the box Chevy, The Paradox stood next to a cameraman from Fox News. The

Paradox immediately noticed Mac twirling a ring around his finger. *That's the man that was on the news. I wonder who is in that government car. Where is Trooper?*

"I see you got some work on your hands," said Mac to Yeomans.

"Yeah, you can say that again. What are the G-men doing here?"

Mac turned to look at FBI Agents Rozier and Mullis, who were still sitting in the car. "They work out of D.C. and want to see Mr. Jackson."

"I wonder Mac. What are Swoosh and Trooper not telling us about this killer?" asked Yeomans.

"I know that it has something to do with the D.C. side of this investigation."

"Naw," said Yeomans shaking his head, "I think it's a little more than that. Look what Jenny found." Yeomans showed Mac the G-String with the note attached.

"Where'd you get that?" asked Mac.

"Right there, back seat," Yeomans said pointing.

"You've got to be kidding me. I guess the peach state isn't so sweet anymore. Well, you might be right. It just may be more to this than we know."

The Paradox watched two additional cars pull up to the crime scene. He immediately saw Swoosh on the front passenger's side. Everything seemed to move in slow motion when the D.C. Homicide Division lead detectives emerged from the car at the same time as if their movements were rehearsed.

The camera crews bum rushed the car; and Swoosh once more towered over the news crew while pushing them back. Swoosh, Ronald, Trooper and Teço never saw the Feds.

Still in the government car, Agent Rozier said, "Just as I suspected . . . look who is here. What is Rising Sun doing wearing a bulletproof vest with a quick draw holster?"

"Aw, ain't that cute. They all have on the same gear. What is Jackson doing with a weapon?" asked Mullis. Shifting his body to get a better view, he continued, "Yep, he's holstered."

"Who is the pretty boy looking all gung ho wearing the tactical leg holster?

"Good question. Let's go see," said Mullis.

As Trooper read the note, she shook her head. The Paradox could tell that she was trying to hold back her anger. As she searched the crowd to see if The Paradox was around, he ducked behind a cameraman. Trooper knew that she could never forget his gray eyes which seemed to turn as black as coal under the illuminated street lights. Then Trooper saw an officer brief Yeomans, who went into a house.

"Mr. Butler, I think we have something to talk about," said Yeomans.

"I haven't done anything wrong because—"

"Well, according to our gunshot residue test, you fired a weapon." He eyed the young man.

"I didn't do nothing wrong," he said defensively.

"I never said you did!" Pointing outside the window, Yeomans said, "See those two men in black suits getting out of that car? They are the FBI from Washington, D.C. I think you need to do some talking and quick."

The guy known as Jerry Butler looked at the agents and blurted out, "Okay! Okay!"

"First, where's the gun?" asked Yeomans.

Jerry Butler's eyes shifted to an old school floor model wooden stereo.

Yeomans walked over to the retro stereo and pulled the top open. There was nothing inside but a turntable and 8-track player. Then he pulled the entire piece of furniture away from the wall. The backing to the stereo was missing which exposed illegal guns galore.

"Detective Fordham, put cuffs on him," said Yeomans as he walked out of the house and headed toward Trooper. "I want you to know that the Fed's are here, and they're coming our way," Yeomans said to Trooper.

The Paradox smiled until he saw the two FBI Agents approaching him. Then they turned in the direction of Trooper; and The Paradox sighed. *See Soulja, you're cutting it closely. Get out of there and fast!*

"Listen to me. Leave me alone!" exclaimed The Paradox. The Fox News cameraman looked at The Paradox inquisitively.

The Paradox's jaw tightened in anger when he saw Teco. *Damn, he's walking as if I never shot him. I know I hit him at least 2 times.*

As Teco looked into the crowd, The Paradox ducked behind the cameraman again.

"Hello Lieutenant Troop!" exclaimed Rozier.

"What can I do for you today, gentlemen," she asked defensively.

"Mr. Jackson, is he licensed to carry that gun?"

"Yes he is," she said looking at Yeomans.

Teco was speaking with two officers when he heard, "Mr Jackson!"

Trooper followed behind Rozier and Mullis in full stride.

Turning to see where the deep voice came from, Teco stood toe to toe with Agent Rozier and Mullis. Ignoring the FBI agents, Teco hoped that he wasn't making a mistake by turning his back to them.

Grabbing Teco by the shoulder, Agent Mullis said, "First of all, it's good to see you are alive and kicking. Did you know that it's a federal offense to fake your own death?"

"I have no idea what you are talking about," said Teco.

Rozier grabbed Teco by the right arm. "Mr. Jackson, come with us."

Trooper pushed Mullis out of the way to get to Rozier. With her teeth clenched together, she said, "Agent Rozier, not here."

The news crews turned at the sound of the altercation and headed in the direction of Trooper. Before they could get too close, the Atlanta P.D. pushed the reporters back farther behind the crime scene tape.

"Detective, I mean Lieutenant Troop, this is a federal matter."

"What the hell are you talking about?" asked Trooper.

"It's a confidential matter in a federal investigation," said Mullis.

"I know damn well what this is about. It's some of your bullshit!"

Mullis licked his lips, rubbed his head, and grabbed Teco's left arm tightly.

"Man, if you don't' get your damn hands off of me!" exclaimed Teco.

Mac and Yeomans were trying to understand what was really happening.

"I said not here! I won't let you take him in as if he's some street punk or a criminal," said Trooper.

"Well, let's see what the evidence says about this matter," said Mullis smiling.

Swoosh came over quickly and grabbed Trooper by the arm. "There are too many cameras out here for this bull. You know that Teco has to go with them."

"Well, you better handle your friends before I do," said Trooper.

"I know but not here in front of all of these people."

Swoosh looked at all of the reporters who were watching, turned to Rozier, and said, "When this is over, we'll follow you."

Rozier turned to Trooper, smiled, and winked his left eye.

As Trooper walked away, a woman broke through the crime scene tape and said, "Ma'am, I'm from CNN, we would like to have you on our Larry King Live show. Call me." As Trooper put the business card in her pocket, two Atlanta P.D. officers hastily escorted the CNN reporter away.

Chapter 23

IN THE FBI Atlanta Field Office building on Century Center Parkway, Teco sat in the interrogation room alone. His posture looked strong and upright as he admired himself in the two-way mirror. Reaching in his top shirt pocket, he pulled out a toothpick and put it into his mouth.

"You know, when a person folds their arms across their chest like that it's a defensive gesture. So be prepared for his bullshit. Remember, he's an ex-drug dealer and knows the ropes," said Mullis looking through the interrogation window.

"Yeah, you're right," said Rozier.

Teco exhaled deeply because he was ready to get all of this behind him. *I wonder who is on the other side of that glass looking at me.* Just as Teco was about to get up, the door opened and Agent Mullis and Rozier walked into the room. Mullis carried a tape recorder while Rozier carried a thick folder. They both looked at Teco as if he were already guilty of a serious crime.

"Have a seat over here Mr. Jackson," said Rozier pointing to a chair across from them. "No, over there!"

Teco looked at the uncomfortable steel folding chair. *Well, there goes the good ass cushion.*

The two agents made unwelcomed grunting sounds that bounced off the starch white walls with a loud echo. As Mullis sat in the cushioned chair, Rozier continued to stand and paced the floor.

"Okay, Mr. Jackson. Do you know why you're here this afternoon?" asked Mullis as he placed the tape recorder on the table while he waited for Teco to respond.

Teco leaned forward with both elbows on the table. He pulled the toothpick out of his mouth and said, "Well, to be honest, I thought this was an interview to see if I can provide you guys with some form of training . . . possibly in the subject of entertaining your ladies in the bedroom." Then Teco leaned back into the chair.

They eyed Teco; and Rozier said, "Do you think this is a comedy club?"

"It must be if you are dragging me down here on some trumped-up charges."

"Let's see just how spurious these charges really are, Mr. Jackson," said Mullis.

"Huh?" said Teco.

"You heard me . . . spurious as in trumped-up. Or haven't you gotten your GED since you've been shacking up with Detective Troop?"

"See, I'm not going to play any of your bullshit mind games. I'm way smarter than you think I am, Mr. Spurious."

"Fine, before we begin, I'm going to tape our conversation," said Mullis as he pushed the record and play button.

"I haven't done a damn thing," said Teco putting the toothpick back into his mouth.

Rozier jumped the gun and said, "Good. Do you know—"

"This is Field Agent Mullis; and I'm in the room with Field Agent Rozier and suspect Teco Jackson. Today is—"

"Look, can we just get on with this mess!" exclaimed Teco.

Agent Mullis continued with his pre-interrogation recording and said, "Mr. Teco Jackson, do you know Bashi Fiten?"

Teco stared at Mullis not knowing what kind of tricks they were trying to play. "You know damn well I know who he is!"

"Mr. Jackson is that a yes?" asked Mullis.

Teco rolled his eyes and heavily sighed.

"Okay, then that is a yes. You know what? We're not going to beat around the bush with you. I want to take your mind back to when you escaped from the Georgetown University Medical Center. You left your personal belongings."

Throwing up his hands, Teco said, "I did not escape. What the hell are you talking about?"

Agent Rozier pulled a picture from the folder and slid it over to Teco. "We gained a warrant to possess your things because, at the time you were shot, you were also a federal witness. The hospital admissions office gave us a watch and a ring."

Teco picked up the picture; and he couldn't believe his eyes. There was Bashi's ring just as he remembered from his apparitions during physical therapy.

Rozier chimed in and said, "Our concern is just with the ring. When I examined the ring, it surprised me when I saw the initials SB as well as M.B. Fiten."

"Look, dig this; I don't know anything about that ring. When I left SB, I stopped wearing my Strictly Business ring."

Rozier threw a stack of pictures which slid to the edge of the table and stopped in front of Teco. Standing behind Teco and bending over to speak into his right ear, Rozier asked, "What about these?"

"What do these pictures have to do with—"

"You know what? I'm tired of playing games with you!" shouted Rozier, which caused Teco to sit up straight in his chair. "You think you can go from shit to sugar by partnering with a private eye agency?"

"What? Are you jealous?" asked Teco who smiled despite feeling indignation for the interrogation.

"I think you know something about Bashi," said Mullis.

A long screeching noise sounded throughout the room as Teco pushed the chair away from the table. This caused Rozier to almost fall backwards.

Hitting his chest, Teco said, "I protected Bashi. If I wasn't in jail at the time, Bashi would have never died. So, you can take this bullshit and stick it up your ass." Then Teco got up and paced the floor furiously because he couldn't imagine anyone accusing him of any wrongdoings to the very man who took him off the streets.

"Teco, just tell us where the ring came from. Did you have a hit on Bashi because he wouldn't bail you out of jail? Did you kill him for the money?"

Teco stopped pacing the floor. He came face to face with Rozier and said, "I don't know who planted that ring on me; and for the last time, I didn't kill Bashi!" At that moment, Teco heard a voice in his head. *Take this ring to the grave with you and give it to Bashi; you sorry ass mutha—.*

Now standing with his right foot in the seat of the chair, Mullis said, "Well, we have a serious problem. Gail Que, the one convicted of Bashi's murder, her case has been overturned. This means that the killer is still out here. The family and the citizens of Philadelphia want to see justice even if Bashi was a low life drug dealer. See our problem?"

Teco's mind was far from what they were saying because his previous flashback came in clearer as to who could have planted the ring on his finger. He needed to talk to GQ because she was at the same club the night he was shot. *Shit!*

"Rising Sun do you have your G-String on? I've got about twenty dollars to tip you. Or do your G-strings now have holsters?" asked Mullis who laughed cynically.

That was all Teco was willing to take. He was so close to Mullis that Mullis could feel the air coming from Teco's breath. In a challenging manner, Teco said, "Listen here man. I don't know what your problem is; but if you want to see my G-String, just tell me . . . you soft ass chump!"

"Mr. Jackson, think about what you're about to do and where you are. You are not in a win-win situation right now," said Mullis.

With a cup of hot tea in her hand, Trooper touched the doorknob to enter the interrogation room. Detective Yeomans walked hostilely towards her, which caught her off guard. Yeomans pushed Trooper hard up against the wall, which caused the hot tea to splash onto Yeomans' lower pant leg. However, he was too ticked off to concern himself with his appearance.

While he braced his hand on her shoulder, she tried to push back; however, he had the advantage with her up against the wall. Yeomans asked in his southern drawl, "What kind of shit you have me into? Who the hell is Teco 'Homicide, Rising Sun' Jackson?"

Trooper looked him square in the eyes with her hands gripped around his wrist as he held tightly to her shirt. "You have no fucking idea who you are talking to. Get your hands off of me!"

"No, you don't know who you are dealing with. You're in my damn city, and you better tell me everything right now Trooper."

Trooper did a martial arts move by twisting his wrist in the opposite direction of his body, which caused him to release her shirt. Then she pushed him away. When she heard footsteps running down the hall, she saw Swoosh and Ronald coming to her aid.

"Yo! What the hell are you doing?" Swoosh asked Yeomans. "Trooper, you alright?" If Swoosh wasn't mistaken, he thought he heard Trooper hiss.

"You should be asking him," she said as Yeomans rubbed his wrists.

"What's up with you two?" asked Ronald.

"Karate Jane over here is acting like she's in a Turner Classic Movie," said Yeomans nodding towards Trooper. "I just got off of the phone with my superior and he informed me that Teco Jackson used to be a drug dealer and possibly knows The Paradox. Then guess what he tells me next? The Paradox tried to kill Teco Jackson. Now this psycho son of a bitch is in my damn city reeling in the bait! And you want to ask me what's wrong?" The salty sweat from Yeomans' forehead stung his eyes; and he wiped his face with the arm of his brown jacket.

Guilt came across Swoosh's face for not coming clean. However, Trooper spoke up and said, "Teco Jackson is not a suspect in any of these investigations."

Swoosh gave Yeomans the rundown on what happened from Teco's days in Philadelphia until Teco was gunned down at the Mirage male exotic dance club.

Yeomans asked, "So Teco is not a consultant on this case?"

"He is officially hired by the Washington, D.C. Homicide Division to help us with the Atlanta case only," said Swoosh.

"Oh great, a vigilante stripper gone straight . . ."

Just as Trooper was about to speak, her cell phone rang. "Hello, this is Lieutenant Troop."

"Hello, this is Christa Hall from CNN," she said with southern charm.

Trooper paused for a moment and walked down the hall away from Yeomans, Swoosh and Ronald.

"Lieutenant, have you given any more thought about coming on the Larry King Live show?"

Not thinking about the repercussions, Trooper said, "Tell Mr. King that I'll give him a story never told about the person committing these murders."

"I'm listening."

"I must admit, your network can help us."

"How is that?"

"I think your show will help us draw the killer out."

"Correct me if my research is wrong, but his last victim was a male exotic dancer. He died right?"

"No, his last victim from the D.C. case didn't die; and I can get him on the show as well."

"You do know that this case is larger than the Atlanta Child Murders in the early 1980's right? I mean the media helped law enforcement back then. We here at CNN are all about civic duty. I know we can help on this case."

"I sure hope so."

"Well, let me get back with you on a date and time."

By the time the call ended, Swoosh and Ronald came running down the hall and said, "Trooper, a bomb just went off! We spoke to Yeomans. He wants us over there now. Let's go. Let me drive."

Within the hour, Swoosh, Ronald and Trooper pulled up to the Ferst Center for the Arts. The Paradox lurked in the crowd watching his entire masterpiece unfold like clockwork. He looked up to see if he could perch atop of a nearby roof so that he could bust a shot off in case Teco Jackson showed up, but then he noticed the Fox News helicopter circling the area. *Where is Teco?*

As Ronald emerged from the car, dark grey smoke poured out of the building, which caused the choppers flying above to scatter smoke in different directions. SWAT, fire teams, and rescue squads were all over the place. Because the firemen were bringing the blaze under control, he knew that re-enacting the crime scene would be difficult because the building's interior was pretty much demolished.

Trooper refused to ask how this episode involved the D.C. department because for some reason she knew that it did. Trooper saw Yeomans who was signalling for her to come his way.

Apologetically, Yeomans said, "Trooper—"

She said, "Forget it. Nothing happened. What's this place?"

Smiling because Trooper was showing the spirit of a true cop, Yeomans said, "It's a center for the performing arts. From what I know, someone was due to have a fashion show here. The place was full of models and fashion agents from New York and Paris."

"Who were the sponsors of the show?" asked Swoosh.

"That's why I need y'all here. It's that company Trooper mentioned."

"Frontino Lefébvre?" asked Trooper.

"Yes, that's it."

"You have got to be kidding me. That's Gail Que's company. Is she here?" she said scanning the crowd of onlookers.

Just before Trooper caught his eye, The Paradox smiled and headed for the red Jeep Cherokee, which he previously purchased at the chop shop listed under the business name of Harwell Body Shop.

"We need to find her," said Ronald.

As the police taped off the area, Trooper and the crew walked right past The Paradox, who was now sitting in the

SUV. Under his breath he said, "Trooperrr." Then there was a tap on the window.

When he rolled the window down, the Fulton County officer said, "Sir, you need to leave this area."

The Paradox held up his fake press pass.

"Well, you should be over there," said the officer pointing to the other news trucks.

Throwing up deuces, The Paradox drove away.

The center was in total pandemonium as emergency workers scrambled all over each other to save those who were determined to fight back death. As stretchers passed by with victims who were bleeding profusely, Trooper frantically searched to see if she recognized Gail Que with any of the EMT personnel.

Chapter 24

MUSTAFA'S RIGHT ARM was in a sling; and his head was in gauze. As he came out of the arts center, Mustafa saw a beautiful woman with a long ponytail putting a blue wool fire retardant blanket over GQ and rushing her off into a police car.

As the cameras flashed, the news reporters shouted, "Miss Que! Miss Que!" However, a few police officers formed a human barrier around her.

The Paradox followed them to where the vehicle was parked. *See Soulja, you have failed again.*

"Shut up and leave me alone!" The Paradox exclaimed. He took out a note pad and jotted something down. While keeping his eyes on the black Crown Victoria with Washington, D.C. license plates, The Paradox went back to the news press area. He began to panic and continued to talk to himself.

A young boy who was with his father turned to see who was talking to the big man. However, the boy didn't see anyone else around.

The Paradox looked down at the boy and said, "Hey kid, you want to make twenty bucks?"

"Sure, what do I have to do?"

"Take this note to that police woman right there," he said pointing to Trooper.

The boy said, "Dad, I'll be right back." However, his father didn't respond but kept filming for NBC's 5 o'clock news program. Then the boy walked over to Trooper who was talking to the woman from CNN. He waited patiently until Trooper finished her conversations and said, "Miss police lady."

Adjusting the colorful scarf on her head, she turned to face the young voice and asked, "Yes, how may I help you?"

Then he handed her the note. "That guy over there paid me to give you this note." He looked in the direction of The Paradox; however, The Paradox was now gone.

Trooper read the note. Her eyes darted back and forth in the crowd of bystanders. Then she turned to the young boy. "Where's the man? Can you point him out for me?"

"He's gone."

"Swoosh, we need to get GQ out of here. The Paradox is here. Look at this." Seeing a 20 dollar bill in the boy's hand, Trooper asked, "Is that the money he gave you?"

The boy nodded his head yes.

"Let me have that one and I'll give you this one," she said pulling out a fresh 20 dollar bill from her back pocket. As she pinched the corner of The Paradox's money, Swoosh passed her a clear plastic Ziploc bag.

GQ sat in Trooper's car by herself crying and trying to reconcile today's travesty. All she knew was that a bomb went off during the final rehearsal of her fashion show.

Can the Fiten posse be involved because they think I killed their brother Bashi? Why now? Does the Fiten posse have a Young Black Mafia crew in Atlanta? Who could be responsible for this? I was doing so well. I didn't come to Atlanta for any drama.

As GQ sobbed softly, Trooper, Swoosh and Ronald got into the car with her. "Please tell me. What's going on?" GQ wiped the tears away which smeared the makeup on her face.

"Ms. Que, when we get you to a safe place, we'll explain everything," said Trooper who saw that GQ was extremely frightened. Then Trooper dialed Teco.

"Hello," said Teco.

"This is me. Where are you?"

"I'm just leaving. Why? What's up?" Teco asked as he stood on the corner hoping to see a taxi coming.

"Meet me at the City Hall East building. There was a bombing. And . . . well . . . Let's just say it's very important."

"Alright, I'm flagging down a cab now. Is everyone alright?"

"Yes. Are you okay?" Trooper asked in a soft voice.

"Yes, baby I'm fine. You know they can't faze me. I'll tell you about it later once we're alone tonight."

"Good, let me go. I'll see you soon."

"Okay." Teco wondered why Trooper didn't say the normal lovey-dovey goodbye. Once Teco was in the cab, the driver turned up the radio and "Angel of Mine" by Monica played on Majic 97.5.

Within minutes, Teco arrived at City Hall East. He decided to wait in the lobby on a cherry oak bench. Suddenly, he heard helicopters in the air. Reporters were attempting to get into the building; however, police officers were now on the scene keeping the crowd at bay.

What the hell? Looking around, Teco saw uniformed and plain clothes officers who were escorting a man into the building. The person in custody could have gone for a physical trainer because his muscles were visible through the t-shirt. Then the man eyed Teco with a facial expression of shear hatred. *Who is that? Does he know me? Is he mad at me or the world?* Paranoia began to set within Teco.

Coming through the glass double doors was Swoosh, Ronald, Fordham and Yeomans. Trooper entered the lobby escorting someone. Teco couldn't I.D. the individual because there was a blanket over the person's head.

Yeomans yelled, "Get them back! Get those reporters out of here!"

Standing to his feet, Teco locked eyes with Trooper. Simultaneously, Trooper pulled the blanket from over the woman's head. Teco gasped.

When Gail Que noticed Teco standing there, she blinked her eyes twice to make sure she wasn't hallucinating. Then she slowed her stride as things seemed imperceptible to Teco.

GQ didn't know what to make of finally coming face to face with the man who was the cause for her spending all of those years in prison.

Teco's heart rate increased to the point where he was feeling faint. *Is that GQ?*

With both hands GQ pushed Teco hard in the chest which caused him to fall backwards onto the bench. "You cigarette begging, car stealing, dick slinging bum, stay away from me!"

Trooper grabbed GQ by the arm.

"No, don't hold me back. This dumb ass son of a bitch put me away for a crime I didn't commit!" exclaimed GQ.

As Teco whisked up from the bench like a black cat, he said, "Hold on you trifling wannabe fashion designer. You need to face the facts that Bashi chose me as the enforcer because things were getting too dangerous for you to handle on the streets. But no . . . you wanted to act like one of the boys. And the next time you put your hands on me . . ."

Close enough to kiss Teco, GQ said, "If you weren't always looking out for yourself, no one would have died. Now you drag my ass right back into your shit! I am not staying in this building with this good-for-nothing backstabber!" Then GQ punched Teco dead center in the nose and blood splattered onto his shirt. GQ added, "That's for snitching."

The paparazzi, behind the guarded glass doors, went into a yelling frenzy with cameras flashing.

Yeomans exclaimed, "Trooper and Fordham, get her the hell out of here . . . Now!"

Trooper said, "No, you take her with you. Let me catch up with you guys later. What floor?"

Fordham said, "The ninth floor in room 906."

Trying to stop the bleeding and the throbbing, Teco held the bridge of his nose and stood there in disbelief. However, because Teco didn't even flinch to hit GQ back, he gained a lot of respect from Yeomans and the officers in the lobby area.

Yeomans knew that this fiasco was going to be unwanted headline material for the front page of the morning Atlanta Journal Constitution newspaper.

"Somebody please tell me what's going on?" GQ asked Fordham.

"I'm sure they'll tell you what you need to know," Fordham said as she directed GQ toward the elevators.

Chapter 25

OUTSIDE OF THE City Hall East building, the flood lights cast a golden glow on the City Hall East tower. Circling the city block four times, The Paradox hoped that a car would exit out of the full parking lot.

Soulja, I told you that the police knew your plan. Detective Troop is too smart for you. Let me handle things.

"And what are you going to do? Just leave me alone. I told you that I can handle Detective Troop. I should just blow up this whole City Hall building and get them all in one shot," The Paradox said aloud.

Now you know damn well that won't work. It takes time to set things up; and you can't even find a parking spot.

"Sir, can you let me handle this mission on my own? I told you that I don't need your help."

Soulja, always remember that what you can't get in the wash, you can catch in the rinse. Don't screw up this mission.

Circling the building one more time, The Paradox searched for an alternate entrance in order to snatch up GQ.

Soulja, once inside, then where would you go?

Not wanting to come under suspicion of police security for staking out the area, The Paradox decided to formulate his next plan back at the boarding house, which was across the street from the Greyhound station and a few minutes away from Little Five Points.

On the 9th floor inside City Hall East, GQ sat in a small waiting area watching CNN on a 27" inch Magnavox television.

"This is Christa Hall. There was a massive explosion at the Ferst Arts Center where Atlanta's very own Gail Que was unveiling this season's fashion line in her Indigo Signature Collection by Frontino Lefébvre. Our sources tell us that it's too soon to tell the total number of fatalities. However, there were at least thirteen people who lost their lives. We will keep Ms. Que and her staff in our prayers. . . ."

Wiping the tears from her eyes, GQ's thoughts were on Mustafa, then Teco, and back to Mustafa. She wondered if Mustafa made it out alive; however, she was too afraid to ask. GQ reached over and turned off the television. Because it was cool in the room, she placed her legs on the soft black leather sofa and wrapped the blanket around her body making sure that she was covered. As she closed her eyes, she could taste the blood in her mouth from an open cut. Then her thoughts shifted back to Teco. *Why is he working with the police?*

On his way to the conference room with Trooper, Teco stopped for a split second in the waiting room. *Damn, GQ still looks gorgeous.*

Filing into the conference room behind Trooper, Teco believed that every person's eyes zoomed in on him off of the jump. Therefore, he displayed a mug face expression back at all of them.

Fordham chimed in to shatter the tension that loomed in the air. "I'm glad that you two could join us. We were just looking over the evidence on the screen. The last note and the $20 bill have been sent over to the lab for forensics testing.

The money showed droppings of blood. We want to see if the sample matches the blood type of any of our victims. You might remember that one victim was the guy who was killed in the box Chevy on Delmar Avenue."

"That's good detective," said Trooper.

"Okay, what are we working with?" Teco asked as he shifted the toothpick to the other side of his mouth.

"Well guys, we need to study these notes very well to see if there are any clues as to where The Paradox might hit next. Fordham, will you please display the note from the Ferst Arts Center?" asked Trooper.

Dear Detective Troop,

The six point star has several definitions.
So choose the five point star for premonitions.

You have 72 hours or Boom!
My train is coming; so stay out of the newsroom.

The Paradox.

"When I once served in the arm forces, we went on these field operations called a ten-one, ten men against one person. We were taught how to draw a person into a trap. Perhaps this is The Paradox's plan for GQ and Teco," said Yeomans.

"What if the location is not in the city of Atlanta? It may be what we call an offset which is a tactic to throw us off of his tail," Trooper said taking a bite of her Snickers.

"No, it's Atlanta alright. Remember that the bodies were facing the northwest direction," said Yeomans.

"Ronald, can your D&D role playing help us to solve these new clues?" asked Teco.

Ronald walked towards the screen and reached into his pocket. "Teco, it's not as simple as you may think."

"We have to find this damn clock," said Trooper.

"Okay, write these words down and put them in two columns on your legal pads." Ronald gave them the words from the Delmar Lane and Ferst Arts Center crime scenes with instructions for each column. Then he shook the red D20 die in his hand.

"You guys have got to be kidding me on this dice luck stuff," said Yeomans. Fordham threw up her hands and walked out of the room.

"Detective, in the Chocolate City we believe in hunches. You must admit that Ronald hasn't been wrong yet," said Swoosh.

Ronald released the red D20 die, which tumbled to the center of the table and landed on the number fifteen.

Yeomans stood there with his arms folded across his chest thinking about how childish the D&D crime investigative tactic looked.

Ronald said, "Alright, in this column look at these combination of words: six points, six point star, point six star, star point six, star six points. Do any of these names sound familiar Detective Yeomans?"

"No they don't, son," said Yeomans. Ronald gave Yeomans an evil eye for calling him son.

"What about five point star, point five star or star five points?" asked Ronald.

"Wait! Wait!" exclaimed Yeomans. "Say that last one again."

"Star five points."

"That's it. There is an area of town called Little Five Points. Are you saying he's playing D&D with us?" asked Yeomans.

Ronald said, "Well, we don't have enough information to say that he's playing D&D."

"Look right here. The note says "My train is coming. Maybe GQ rides the train to work," Ronald said as everyone focused on the projector screen.

"But is there a clock in either of these places?" asked Teco.

Swoosh said, "That's a good question."

"Let's talk with GQ now to find out what she knows about this guy," said Yeomans.

Fordham stormed back into the room and said, "We have a press conference in 5 minutes. The mayor is up for re-election and is breathing down the chief's neck to catch this killer."

Trooper rolled her eyes. "This is insane. You are trying to keep the Atlanta mayor in office while we are trying to save people's lives. For that matter, we might be preventing the whole damn city of Atlanta from going up in flames again."

Fordham looked at Trooper and said, "This is no different from the bullshit politics in D.C.; and you know it. Let's conduct a press conference that makes The Paradox sweat."

No one spoke while in the elevator to the lobby floor. Fordham directed the team to the platform where the mayor, her Chief of Staff and Press Aide were standing ready to brief the room. The brown lectern was full of microphones and displayed the Georgia Seal on the front panel. In the audience, news reporters from the major stations held mini-recorders in their hands.

Detective Fordham walked up to the lectern and said, "Ladies and gentlemen, members of the press, I present to you Atlanta's mayor."

As the mayor placed her right hand on the microphone, all kinds of questions flowed throughout the air. Knowing that she couldn't address the specifics, the mayor turned to Yeomans who walked up to the lectern.

Christa Hall asked, "Detective, is this the work of a lone wolf?"

Yeomans said, "As far as we know, it is the work of a single perp."

"Is it true that you have under protective custody a possible victim who may have been the target?" asked Christa as the other news agencies looked perturbed that Yeomans was only answering CNN's questions.

"I'm sorry, but we can't reveal that information."

"Our sources tell us that this is the work of a killer who goes by the name of The Paradox and is out of Washington, D.C."

Yeomans looked at the mayor.

Christa continued, "Is this why the detectives are here from D.C.?"

"I'm glad you asked that question," said Fordham who looked over to Trooper. "Here with me, I have some of Washington D.C.'s experts at profiling the person who has become known as The Paradox."

A man from way back in the crowd of reporters yelled out, "Detective Troop! Detective Troop!" The camera lights made it difficult for anyone to see who was talking.

Trooper walked up to the lectern, covered the microphone with the palm of her hand and asked Swoosh, "What the hell is he doing here?"

Swoosh shrugged his shoulders. Feeling like he was fading into the shadows of things, Teco watched the entire situation unfold.

"Lieutenant Troop, is it true that you're still trying to catch The Paradox?" asked the male reporter from The Washington Post.

"Yes it is."

"Is Detective Ronald Heard qualified to be on such a high profile case? He has a reputation of using very eccentric methods in solving crimes."

"Everyone on our team is qualified to handle and assist the Atlanta P.D. In fact, because of Detective Heard, we have made significant progress in the case," said Trooper.

"Lieutenant one more question. How are you and your team going to protect D.C. when you're here in Atlanta?"

This question caught Trooper off guard. Swoosh stepped to the microphone and said, "We have a major case here in Atlanta with evidence that ties back to the case in Washington D.C. Our mission is to protect every citizen regardless of jurisdiction."

As they walked away from the cameras, Yeomans said, "How in the hell does the press have this information?"

Fordham asked, "Is the Washington Post going to be a problem?"

"For you, no," said Swoosh rubbing his forehead.

As Trooper stepped off of the platform, the Washington Post reporter winked his eye at Trooper.

Leaving the press conference, Trooper decided to speak with GQ. However, when Trooper entered the waiting room, only the blanket was on the sofa. Trooper walked back down the bright white hallway at a quick pace. She searched several rooms. As Trooper passed other police officers, they looked at Trooper as if she were crazy; however, GQ could not be found. Trooper began to breathe frantically and rushed into the ladies room.

Chapter 26

AS TROOPER BURST out of the restroom, she turned in a complete circle with her hands on her hips.

Yeomans grabbed her by the arm and said, "Are you okay?"

Scoping out the large open cubical section, Trooper still didn't see any signs of GQ. "Excuse me!" exclaimed Trooper.

"Are you okay?"

"No, I'm looking for . . . I'm looking for Ms. Que."

"Oh, Fordham moved her out of the public waiting room. One of our officers is taking her statement in that cubicle," he said pointing a few feet away.

Trooper stepped into the cubicle, interrupted the conversation, and said, "Ms. Que, let's go."

GQ looked up but did not move. She was not going with anyone until they told her the whereabouts of Mustafa.

"Ms. Que, I said let's go."

GQ said, "I've been waiting almost three hours for some explanation as to what happened and why! And to top it off, I'm here with Mr. Teco "Homicide" Jackson who tried to destroy my life and now is hanging out with cops."

"Alright, alright, I understand," said Trooper patting GQ on the shoulder.

"Let's go find out what we can."

Trooper and GQ walked down the hall to the conference room, which was dark because the team had returned to review the evidence. When Trooper turned on the lights, GQ blinked twice so that her eyes could adjust to the sudden brightness in the room.

"Please have a seat," said Trooper to GQ who was now the center of attention.

Ronald was star struck as he sat across from GQ. *I wonder can I get her autograph. She is absolutely beautiful, even with smeared makeup.* Taking a deep breath, Ronald opened a folder.

Trooper said, "Okay Ms. Que—"

"You can call me Gail or GQ," she said cutting her eyes at Teco.

"Alright GQ, I'm going to try my best to fill you in on what has transpired. But first, let me introduce you to our team."

"Please do," she said batting her long black eyelashes.

"This is Detective Ronald Heard from D.C. Sitting beside him is Lieutenant Marcus Brown. We all call him Swoosh. He is also from D.C. Detective Yeomans and Detective Fordham are with the Atlanta P.D Homicide Unit. GBI Agent McLoughlin is not here. Teco Jackson is a consultant on the case."

GQ said, "You've got to be kidding me!"

"We believe the person of interest is from Conshohocken, Pennsylvania. You might know him by his street name of Bobby Stephens. We have reasonable cause to believe that he wants to kill both you and Mr. Jackson."

"But why? I haven't done anything to Bobby." As if a light bulb came on, GQ said, "This can't have anything to do with me, because Bobby had a beef with Teco . . . not me."

"Do you remember someone name Twyla Burke, who went by the alias of Candi in Philly?" asked Trooper.

GQ thought for a moment and said, "No."

Teco chimed in and said, "You know, the dope fiend who Bashi took off the streets. Her family owned a bunch of strip joints."

"Oh yeah, I remember. What does Candi have to do with this?"

"Well, Bobby is also a suspect in the murder of Twyla Burke. Before Twyla died, she told me that Bobby wanted to take out the Strictly Business crew," said Trooper.

"Bobby wasn't a dealer. Why would he care about Bashi pushing drugs on the streets of D.C.?"

"That's where you can help us. We still don't understand his motive. Was he killing D.C. male strippers because he was jealous of Twyla dating other men or was he killing D.C. male strippers to weed out Teco Jackson?" asked Trooper.

Yeomans couldn't believe how much information Trooper, Swoosh and Ronald were holding back until now.

"Do you have any more questions?" asked Swoosh.

"Yes I do," said GQ looking at Teco. "Why did you help the Philly police send me to prison?"

Teco stopped doodling on the piece of paper and raised his head. All eyes in the room locked on GQ's almond blue eyes.

Trooper cleared her throat and said, "Let's give these two some privacy."

Without hesitation, the others got up and left their papers along with their beverages on the table. Teco put his pen down and leaned back into the chair. Before he spoke, a female officer opened a side door and said, "Oops, excuse me."

"No, it's alright. How may I help you?" asked Teco.

"I have the results from the Ferst Arts Center explosion," she said holding a folder in her hand.

"You can put it right there. They will be right back," said Teco pointing to a stack of folders on the desk.

After the officer left, Teco leaned forward with both elbows on the table and smiled as he pulled the toothpick from under his tongue. "Well, to make it plain and simple for you, I thought you killed Bashi."

With anger GQ said, "Why would I do that? I loved Bashi. He saved me from being homeless. I wasn't going to be an addict like my mother."

"But you were being evasive when I questioned you about who killed Bashi. Plus, people on the streets kept telling me that you'd taken over the SB crew when I was locked up in jail. So, I thought you killed Bashi because you were jealous of my relationship with him." Talking with theatrical hand movements while stressing his case, Teco continued, "Once I got out of jail, your boy Travis kept acting as if he were about to buck on me. What was up with that?"

Everything GQ withheld for so many years emerged like a fire hose of water. "I was supposed to protect Bashi. I helped him build the crew; and then you got put down with us. Yes, I was jealous of your position. He acted like I couldn't handle things, but I wasn't going to kill him." Now standing with her arms across her chest, she said, "I thought it was Bashi's brothers that tried to kill me when Fatboy died."

"The Fiten posse? YBM?" he asked with a squinted left eye. Then what GQ said hit Teco like a ton of bricks. "Whoa, whoa, whoa, what did you say?" he asked with his hands up in a stopping gesture.

"Back in Philly, someone tried to kill me and Fatboy."

"You had my homeboy killed? Your beef was with me, not my peeps!" Teco walked around the conference table to confront GQ face to face, but she kept backing away from him.

"Homicide, it wasn't like that," GQ said in a pleading sob.

"Stop calling me Homicide; my name is Teco. Did you have my best friend Bernard Gordon killed?" he asked as a single tear fell down his face.

"No, it wasn't like that. Our relationship was personal."

Trooper walked in, assumed Teco was about to assault GQ, and said, "Teco, hold up. What are you doing? Please sit down."

Teco's lips were trembling for the life of his homeboy. "Teco, you have to stay focused on the mission. GQ is not the enemy. You have to protect her and clear both of your names."

GQ looked miffed. "I don't need any protection. I'm fine."

"Hanae, I can't do this anymore," said Teco.

Never witnessing this softer side of Teco, GQ looked at him in amazement.

"Look, this is what we'll do. We will go back to the hotel. Ronald and Swoosh can keep an eye on GQ in their suite until we sort all of this out."

"Wait," said GQ, "I have to see about the people who were hurt at the arts center. They need to know that this asshole is not going to win. My fashion line will continue."

"Listen here GQ. There is a crazed maniac out there trying to kill you and willing to kill others in order to get to you. If you want to live, I suggest you PTG!" exclaimed Trooper

"What?" asked GQ.

"Play the Game," said Trooper.

THE NEXT MORNING, Teco was still tired after sleeping for a few hours. He tossed and turned thinking about the last

time he spoke with his best friend, Fatboy. The last time Teco saw Fatboy was back in Philly. Teco was so busy chasing dead presidents by dancing at a Philly nightclub that he didn't take time to say goodbye before jetting off to his next gig.

Then he remembered that Fatboy was trying to tell him something over the cell phone, but the reception was poor. *Was Fatboy trying to tell me something in code? Shit!*

When Trooper walked in the room with a tray full of Danish pastries and orange juice, he sat up because he was very hungry.

"Baby, we need to go somewhere. Put on something nice for the camera," she said.

Teco really wasn't up for any type of interrogation. However, he knew Trooper needed this break in the case. After taking a bite of the apple Danish, he got out of bed, showered, and dressed in a black sports jacket with a red pull-over long sleeved shirt and black slacks. Then he put on his shoulder holster.

"Baby, why are you holstering?"

"You know just as well as I do. As long as Bobby is running the streets, I'll never be safe."

"Well, you do have a point there. Did you find out anything about your best friend last night?"

"Yes I did . . . but nothing that will help me find out the truth about what really happened. So, I guess I'll have to either take GQ's word for it or drill her some more."

Trooper backed up out of the bathroom wearing a blue Jockey sports bra and boy styled panties.

"Baby, please be careful not to upset GQ because we really need her on our side."

"I only want the truth from her," said Teco.

"I understand." Trooper looked at the clock on the nightstand. "Come on Teco; we need to go."

"Have you talked with Swoosh yet?"

"Of course I did. He and Ronald will hold her in their suite."

"Okay, let's ride out."

While Trooper drove on I-75, Teco turned up the radio and "U Got it Bad" by Usher played on 95.5 The Beat. He reached over to hold Trooper's hand and said, "I want you to know that you're everything I've ever wanted and desired in a woman."

"Why's that?"

"You've pulled the best out of me while showing me a new outlook on life and the important things that matter."

"So, are you ready to settle down? Is that what you're telling me?"

Teco rolled down the window so that air could flow through the car because it was getting a little stuffy after she asked him that question.

"Can we talk about this after the case is over?"

Trooper couldn't understand why he was being evasive. "Teco, either you do or you don't. I'm not getting any younger and neither are you."

"Isn't that our exit over there?" asked Teco.

Trooper put on the turn signal to change lanes. Taking the next exit, she followed the signs that read CNN.

Upon arrival, the mock news reporter stations were encased with thick glass all around the entrance area. Teco even thought about being an anchorman for a brief second; then he let the thought escape his mind.

Trooper said to the security guard, "We have an appointment with Christa Hall."

The man behind the desk scrolled down a list of names and then stopped. He picked up the phone, spoke to someone, and pulled out two CNN visitor passes. "Please sign here and wear these badges at all times while you are inside of the building. May I see a picture I.D.?" After verification, the security guard continued, "Thank you lieutenant. Ms. Hall will be right down."

"Thank you."

Teco looked around the lobby. Within a few minutes, they heard, "Hello Lieutenant Troop, sorry to keep you waiting." Then Christa looked at Teco and said, "And this is?"

Teco smiled at the professional woman who was wearing a black and pink pin-striped butterfly jacket with matching wide legged pants. The detail that set this pant suit off was the pink trim around the jacket and pockets. Her black curly hair hung right below the shoulders, and her smile made the entire room bright.

"This is Mr. Jackson," said Trooper.

"I'm happy to meet you."

"No, the pleasure is mine," Teco said with smoothness.

"Here, follow me. Before we do this interview, we need to go over a few things."

There was a strange expression that came upon Trooper's face.

"Lieutenant, are you alright?" asked Christa.

"Yes, I'm fine. What's that over there?" Trooper asked pointing out of the window.

Chapter 27

"OH THAT? THAT'S OUR FAMOUS Centennial Olympic Park."

Walking towards the large glass window, Trooper looked at the reporter not knowing what to say.

"Is there anything that you'd like to share with me before we go on the air?" asked Christa.

"The killer, who goes by the name of The Paradox, left me a note about a clock. We searched all over Atlanta for all known clocks, and we found nothing that seemed to make sense. However, we never came down here to this area," said Trooper.

"What makes you think that this is the clock you're searching for?" asked Christa.

"That's the thing. I don't know. However, I'm going to find out right now."

Without notice, Trooper headed toward the exit.

"You have to be back within the hour for the taping. Do you mind if I tag along?"

Stopping in her tracks, Trooper said, "That's on you, but please stay out of the way."

Christa rushed to keep up with Trooper. "I hope this will turn out to be an exclusive report."

They stood at the corner looking over into the park. Everything seemed to be normal. At the park's edge, Trooper looked left and right.

Then Trooper saw the CNN clock and noticed that everywhere they turned people were around them. Couples were playing with their children by the small waterfall. Others chilled out on their blankets. Then Teco and Trooper walked up to the clock and examined it very carefully. However, they found nothing of significance.

"Is this the right clock?" asked Teco.

"The note said 'Find the clock and do an about face,'" said Trooper who turned around.

A teenage boy tried to do a stunt on his skateboard; but instead, he fell. As business people walked on the sidewalk, Trooper noticed the names engraved on the bricks.

"Who are all of these people with their names on the ground?"

Christa said, "During the 1996 Summer Olympics, the committee sold bricks to everyday citizens in order to commemorate the event being held in the city of Atlanta."

Trooper turned to Teco and said, "Find the name Cecil Selby. I'll call the local police and tell them to clear this park as well as set up a secure perimeter. We don't know what is down here."

As officers arrived to clear the park, Yeomans said to Trooper, "I hope you're right about this. I don't like making the department look like a fool."

"Did you bring me that note?" asked Trooper.

"Yes," said Fordham who pulled the note from a folder.

"Okay, we need to find Cecil Selby."

They began to search the bricks. When Teco got halfway through the park, a loud horn sounded, which was an indication that the brick was located. This particular brick was raised a few inches above the ground while the others were not.

"Detective, can you get your CSI team down here?" asked Trooper.

"I'm already on it," said Yeomans.

As Teco studied the brick, he couldn't figure out what The Paradox was up to. *Why this park? Why this Cecil Selby guy? Who is he?* Teco knew that this would only get worse if they didn't catch The Paradox.

While the CSI team did their magic, the area was cleared for any explosive devices. However, when they lifted the brick, there was a white piece of paper. They called Trooper over to them. The note read as follows:

Dear Detective Troop,

You've kept Homicide alive, but tell him a final bonjour.

Back in 1497 Lenox Mall at E-4 was such grandeur.

The Paradox.

"Oh Shit!" exclaimed Yeomans, "We need to get to this mall A.S.A.P. I'll let Mac know."

"Wait, let me write this number down," said Trooper.

"Hurry, we might not have long," said Yeomans.

Trooper said, "Our car is at the CNN building. Give Teco the address to the mall."

Hanging in the balance, Christa Hall exclaimed, "Lieutenant Troop! Lieutenant Troop!"

However, Teco and Trooper rushed away to Lenox Mall. On the way, Trooper called Swoosh to give him an update.

"No Swoosh, you stay right there with GQ. We have enough protection."

"Is Teco with you?" asked Swoosh.

"Of course, why?"

"I've been talking to Wicker, and there's something going on that we—"

"It will have to wait. We've pulled up to Lenox Mall."

As Trooper entered the mall, she couldn't believe the lavish style with white marble floors and walls. *What could The Paradox possibly be doing here?* She thought she knew The Paradox's preferences which did not fit the millionaire lifestyle.

"1497, 1497, what's up with 1497?" Trooper asked Teco.

As Trooper walked through the mall, she followed the signs to the food court. Her high heels were clacking against the marble floor making their own music. She slowed down to look at the patrons who were eating to see if The Paradox was in the crowd.

"Teco, do you see Bobby Stephens?"

"No, but if I do, you'll be the first to know because I'll be shooting and asking questions later. He threatened me in that note. I can't get that out of my mind."

Trooper smelled the food being served and watched people with their shopping bags in their hands smiling and laughing. Everyone was having a wonderful time, not knowing that their lives could be in danger.

"Yeomans, we need to find the Lenox Mall police to update them on why we're here," said Trooper.

"Trooper," Yeomans said, "we are the police."

She ignored Yeomans until she found two police officers who were patrolling the mall. As she briefed the officers,

Trooper asked them to explain the addresses of each store.

"The stores are numbered by letters on the public mall map. I have the stores' suite addresses."

"May I see the suite numbers?" asked Trooper. After she found suite address 1497, Trooper sprinted by Fordham and a lot of civilians on the escalator. As she straightened her jacket while checking her gun called Sunshine, Trooper looked like she was doing some quick window shopping to those who passed her down the aisle.

Teco jogged to catch up with her and said, "Where's everybody?"

"I don't know. Yeomans doesn't believe me." She looked at the map and said, "Here's suite 1495, our store has to be next door."

Then Trooper heard footsteps coming up behind her.

"Did you find 1497 yet?" asked Mac who was breathing a little heavy.

"I'm glad to see you join us," said Trooper smiling.

"I wouldn't miss it for the world."

"I'm not sure if this is the store. I'm also not sure what we're looking for." She walked into a boutique with shoes galore.

"May I help you all?" asked the store owner.

"I'm looking for a message from . . . a friend. I think he left me something valuable in this store." Trooper stood upright hoping that she sounded convincing.

"I'm sorry. We don't have a lost and found department. That would be at the mall customer service kiosk downstairs," the owner said in an aristocratic tone.

"This is a matter of life and death," said Trooper.

"I'm sorry. If you can afford Italian leather shoes I am more than happy to help you," the owner said sarcastically.

Just as Trooper was about to give the woman a piece of her mind, one of the mall policemen came into the store and asked, "Any luck?"

"No, I'm looking for a note."

"Wasn't the H&M store founded in 1497?" asked Mac.

"I don't know, let's go downstairs and see."

Mac said, "Trooper, I have an idea."

As they walked into the H&M store, Mac approached the checkout counter and said, "My mother ordered my wife a package from the H&M store in New York. I asked them to forward it to this store. My wife's name is Hanae Troop."

Trooper held in her laughter. This was the funniest thing that she heard since being in Atlanta.

"Let me check our shipping list," said the store manager. She picked up a clipboard looking for the name and flipped the page. "Oh here's the name Hanae Troop. Let me get the package for you."

"Wait, do you mind if I go with you?" asked Mac who showed the lady his GBI badge.

"Oh my," she said looking astonished, "this way."

"How did you know this store was founded in 1497?" asked Trooper.

"When Yeomans read me the note over the phone, I looked it up on the internet. However, I didn't understand the connection until now," said Mac.

In the back of the store, Trooper placed the package into a plastic bag.

Out of nowhere, she heard POP! POP! POP! POP!

Mac, Trooper and the store manager hit the floor.

Yeomans said, "Hey guys, I'm sorry about that; I stepped on some bubble wrap. Did you find anything?"

Mac said, "Man, you almost got shot. Here, take the evidence back to City Hall East."

As Trooper dusted off her clothes, she concluded that The Paradox was playing a game; and they were experiencing his warped world for real.

Chapter 28

BACK AT CITY HALL EAST, Detective Yeomans stood in front of the big projector screen with his hands folded atop his head, which showed the wet spots under his armpits. He kept looking at the note from the H&M store from Lenox Mall. He couldn't figure out how all of these notes were related.

Fordham walked into the room with a cup of cowboy coffee. Then she sat in front of the other six empty cups on the conference table. "Don't you think you need to rest?" she asked seeing Yeomans becoming more and more flustered that he couldn't put the pieces together.

"You know how I get; and believe me, I have my analeptic pills. Do you think I need to get some D&D dice like Ronald?"

They laughed and Fordham said, "I'm not knocking him, no matter how crazy his methods seem. He's helped us get to this point in the case."

"You can help me by getting back on the computer," said Yeomans who never took his eyes off of the projector screen.

"Tell me something Paul. What is E-4 about?"

"Well, the only E-4 that I know about is a rank in the military. E-4 is a specialist."

"Maybe he's trying to tell us something about the military."

"Didn't the report say that this guy is ex-military?" asked Yeomans.

"You were in the armed forces. Won't you start thinking like The Paradox. Why don't you do some D&D role playing?"

They laughed again.

"Damn! What is this showing us? Put a map of Atlanta on the screen please," said Yeomans

"Sure." She pushed a few keys.

Yeomans picked up a pen and walked to the board; and Fordham followed him. There was nothing that tied any of the locations together.

"So what now?" asked Fordham.

"That's a good question." He went to the computer to red dot the locations. However, he realized that something was wrong. "Some of these locations are in other counties. Give me a scope of metro-Atlanta within a fifty mile radius."

Yeomans took a seat while looking at the board; and out of nowhere, it seemed as if something went off in his head. "Well, in the military when they give you a coordinate, it's given in latitude and longitude with lines north, south, east and west directions. E-4 could be east. However, the number 4 doesn't add up."

"What about the bodies being placed in the northwest direction?"

"Now you might have something."

After entering all of the locations from the crime scenes and notes into the computer, Yeomans started connecting the dots with vertical and horizontal lines. Small squares began to form. He couldn't believe what he was starting to see. "I'll be damned. It's a grid, Fordham, it's a grid of metro-Atlanta."

"Holy shit! So the question now is, how long has this guy been here?"

"I have no idea, but one thing is certain. He has our city mapped out into a battle field just like the damn military. Now I need to figure out what the hell he's planning. Pull up the last note that was retrieved at the H&M store."

Dear Detective Troop,

The rank is filed from E-1 to E-8.
Don't try your luck; play for a small stake.

During this game drink water, not wine.
Time, space and matter are important; you have seen the time.

The Paradox.

"What is the stake?" asked Fordham.

"I'm not sure. Now that we know what the playing field is, we have to figure out if we need to play defensively or offensively."

"Does it matter? Our main objective is to catch The Paradox. Right?" asked Fordham.

"Yep, you're right. But, what damage will he do in the mean time to stop us? Remember, he has killed people in broad daylight."

"You are making a good point. What do you think the water relates to? Could it be the Sweetwater Creek or the Chattahoochee River?" asked Fordham.

"We have Berkeley Lake too. It says 'during this game drink water.' Now which one of these places would you drink from if you were in battle? That's the question."

"Me, I'm a country girl. I would drink from a creek."

"I see. What's the deal on that Cecil name found at Centennial Park?"

"Cecil Selby? When I entered the name on the computer, nothing came up. I have a few more things to try," said Fordham.

He took a swig of his coffee while looking at the note posted on the big screen.

Fordham looked up, shook her head and said, "Those pills and that coffee are making you sweat. You need me to go get a fan?"

"No, I'm fine thanks."

"Do you think we should call in the D.C. crew to help us?"

Yeomans gave her a hard look, which translated to mean that she wasn't asking the right questions.

◊◊◊◊◊

WORKING WITH THE WESTIN Perimeter Hotel maintenance staff, Teco placed square mini-cameras around the hotel in different locations. The wireless cameras were designed for a 1000 yard range with the pickup of a FM AVT 900 megahertz receiver which was programmed into his computer.

In the hotel suite, Ronald was posted outside of GQ's bedroom. He was watching a rerun of the Martin Lawrence show. Every time Martin would say "wazzup," Ronald would burst out into laughter. He thought Martin Lawrence to be the funniest comedian to hit the stage.

When GQ came out of the room with just a white terry cloth towel around her body, her beautiful physique captured

Ronald's full attention. Standing in the doorway, GQ looked radiant as her eyes seemed to fade from hazel to almond-blue in a blink or two.

"Yes Ms. Que, how may I help you?" he asked cutting through the chase trying his best not to glance at the opening just above her left thigh.

"I need a change of clothes. My clothes from yesterday smell like smoke and my underwear . . . well, you know."

A lump formed in Ronald's throat. "Let me call the lieutenant to see what he wants me to do." He reached for the phone as GQ moved towards the couch where he was seated.

"Can you not make decisions on your own?" asked GQ as he dialed.

"No, I can't because I have to follow protocol." Then he pushed the last number.

Swoosh picked up as he was taking his last swig of beer in the hotel bar. Ronald explained GQ's request and Swoosh said, "I'll be right up in a few minutes."

Ronald watched as GQ walked back into the bedroom. When he hung up the telephone, he turned the television volume up.

When Swoosh called Trooper, Swoosh was unaware that Trooper and Teco were already at the hotel.

Teco was taking a hot shower when Trooper knocked on the door. When she went into the bathroom, the steam hit her instantly causing moisture to form on her beautiful skin. Sliding the shower curtain back, she saw Teco on his knees as the hot water lashed against his back. The water cascaded down his chin and flowed to the bottom of the tub as if he were a statue.

Feeling the draft envelope his body, he raised his head with bright eyes opened. Trooper couldn't discern whether the water cascading down Teco's face were tears. However, the look on his face was undeniable. He was grieving for his best friend, Fatboy.

"Baby, are you alright?" she asked.

"Yeah, I'm fine. What's up?"

"We have a job to do. I need you to check the perimeter."

Teco just put his head back under the water.

"Did you hear me? I need you to check the perimeter."

"Shit! I mean snap! Alright, give me a minute," he said turning the water off. When he did get out of the shower and dried off, Teco went to the laptop and entered in a code. Within minutes an image of the hotel lobby appeared on the screen.

"What does it look like?" she asked while putting on her shoulder holster.

He said, "We're clear there." Teco tapped more keys; and the outside hallway appeared on the screen.

As Teco and Trooper walked down the hallway to Ronald's room, they proceeded with caution with their hands on their side arms, ready to do damage if necessary.

Teco knocked on the door twice; and Swoosh opened the door. GQ was sitting on the couch wearing a white robe.

"What's the job?" asked Trooper sitting down at a chair on the far right of GQ.

"I need to go get some of my clothes if I'm going to be away like this," said GQ.

Teco looked at Swoosh and sighed deeply because he knew if GQ didn't get what she wanted that GQ would start ranting as she did when they lived together with Bashi. Back in the day, she was a gangster prima donna. He also knew that

Trooper would prefer GQ staying inside and out of sight from The Paradox.

On cue, Trooper said, "I don't want you parading in the streets."

"How long do you want me to sit here without any clothes? Do you guys have a budget to buy me more clothes?" asked GQ.

"Okay! Okay! I'll take her," said Teco.

"The hell you will!" GQ shouted. "I want Detective Heard to take me."

Ronald blushed.

"I tell you what. We only have one car; so if you want your clothes, you'll be protected by me and me only," said Teco.

"And who the hell are you? A cop?" asked GQ.

"No, consider me your personal bodyguard. You're going with me!" Teco said authoritatively.

Chapter 29

"WELL, IT'S SETTLED," Swoosh said stretching. "Trooper, after we powwow about our plan, I'm going to catch me some zees."

Turning to GQ, Trooper said, "You can get dressed."

"In what?" asked GQ. "Haven't you heard a word I've said? My clothes are dirty."

"Ronald, give her one of your t-shirts, a pair of your sweat pants, and a cap. That should keep her disguised. Go to housekeeping and ask for a broom. She can enter her house as if she is the cleaning lady or something. I suspect that The Paradox doesn't know where she lives or she would be toast by now."

GQ said, "Do you not see me standing right here? I am not invisible you know."

Trooper didn't respond and walked back to the other suite with the surveillance equipment.

After GQ left the room to get dressed, Teco put in an earpiece and said, "Testing, testing one, two, three."

Ronald said, "I hear you loud and clear."

Teco smiled while loading his Browning BDM 9mm pistol and slipped the gun into his adjustable holster.

Ronald turned on the flashlight which was mounted to his pump to see if the batteries were low.

When GQ came out of the room, she asked, "Is all of this called for just to pick up some clothes?"

Then Teco motioned for GQ to come over to him.

"I'm not putting on that vest," GQ said in a very challenging manner.

"Don't act as if you're new to this. This Teflon vest is for your own protection," said Teco.

GQ snatched the vest out of his hand and put it on with ease.

Teco put his right hand to his right ear and said, "RS-one to SS-one."

"RS-one go ahead," said Trooper.

"Check perimeter, we're ready to move."

Looking at the surveillance cameras, Trooper said, "Roger that RS-one. On my cue . . ."

GQ asked Teco, "What the hell is SS-one? If you are protecting me at least I should know the code."

"If you tell a soul, you will jeopardize this entire operation."

"Boy, I ain't stupid. What's the damn code?"

"RS-one is Rising Sun-one. SS-one is Sunshine-one. Sunshine is Trooper's weapon."

"RS-one, you're clear to move," said Trooper.

"SS-one, give the front desk a call. Tell them we're moving the sheep, and we'll be exiting the emergency door just in case they forgot to cut off the alarm."

"Copy that RS-one."

"Why do I have to be a sheep?" asked GQ. "Can't I be Cinderella or Snow White?"

"Girl, shut up," said Teco. "Ronald, go pull the car around to the east side of the building and wait there until we have clearance from the front desk," said Teco.

"I'm on it." As Ronald left, he pulled his badge out so it could be seen. Teco stood by the door checking everything out and giving Ronald enough time to get to an exit.

"RS-one, come in."

"SS-one go ahead."

"You're clear to move the sheep. Be careful."

"Roger that." Teco looked at GQ and said, "When we leave, I want you to stay on my ass."

"Yeah, yeah, whatever. Can we go?"

Checking both directions as he exited the room, Teco said, "Let's move."

Going down the hallway, GQ stayed close to Teco as instructed.

She said, "This vest is very uncomfortable."

"Yeah, but protecting you is even more uncomfortable. Whether you realize it or not, it's important for both of us to stay alive and get the person who really killed Bashi. So stay close to me."

When they hit the bottom steps in the emergency exit, Ronald was just pulling up the car.

Teco hopped in the front passenger's seat, and GQ got into the back.

"RS-one to SS-one."

"Go ahead RS-one."

"We're headed towards GQ's residence."

"Yes, I've entered you into the GPS. Got you."

"That's a 10-4."

Teco turned up the radio to better hear "So Fresh, So Clean" by Outkast on V103. A SUV pulled up behind them, and Teco said, "Heads up."

Ronald automatically placed his hand on his pump as Teco watched the SUV for a few miles in the side mirror. When the black vehicle took the exit ramp, Teco heard GQ sigh.

"Do you have something to say?"

GQ gazed out of the window for a moment and said, "As a matter of fact I do."

Teco turned the music down.

"How and why? The Homicide I knew was a hater of the police. Now you're teaming with them? Have I missed something?"

Teco cleared his throat and said, "To be honest, it's not that I didn't like the police. I had no respect for the ones that you paid money to so that the runners could sell drugs hand to hand on the streets."

"We're not talking about me. I'm talking about you," she said.

Teco said, "When Bashi was murdered, I decided to get off of the streets, and the first job that paid decent money was male exotic dancing."

"By the way, you did put on a good show that night back in D.C.," said GQ.

"Anyway, when I got shot, I almost died."

GQ said, "When I heard the bullets ring out that night, I told the driver of my car to take me straight to the airport. I was headed to Paris to start my fashion career."

"I decided to give up male exotic dancing. With all of those men dead, and me almost killed as well, I did some research and decided to become a professional bodyguard. Now that I know you didn't kill Bashi, let's find out who did. Okay?"

"So, you're fighting crime now?" asked GQ.

"Well, let's say that I'm leaving that up to the police. My new ambition is to protect people from criminal acts. I mainly want to help the police find out who killed Bashi and Lisa."

GQ gasped. "Lisa is dead?"

"Yeah she is. I believe you were next."

Looking back to see if anyone was following them, GQ said, "Why do you think that I'm next? I'm not down with SB or YBM anymore."

"The killer had the *USA Today* news article about you in Lisa's apartment."

The car fell completely silent.

Knowing that he needed to clear the air, Teco said, "So tell me. How did Fatboy die?"

"He and I were in Philly about to celebrate my new fashion contract."

Hearing her voice tremble, Teco didn't want to put her through this; however, he wanted to know how his best friend died.

"I'll never forget it. Fatboy was driving, and I heard thumping sounds hitting the side of his car. He pushed my head down, and something hit the car extremely hard. The car flipped several times. I was able to climb out through the sun roof before the car blew up in flames."

"Damn!" exclaimed Teco. When he banged his hand on the dashboard of the car, GQ jumped. "I wonder was it The Paradox. How could he be in D.C. and Philly at the same time?"

"Take this exit coming up," GQ said to Ronald.

"One thing I will promise. He won't get you," said Teco.

"No Scrubs" by TLC played on V103 as Ronald pulled onto GQ's block.

"GQ point to your house for me," said Teco.

"Right there."

"SS-one, we are at the location copy?"

"10-4," said Trooper over the radio.

Ronald turned the Crown Victoria around and parked five condominiums away. He pulled out his Simmons 10x47 binoculars and scanned the area.

The Paradox noticed the Crown Victoria but couldn't determine who was in the car. So, he just chilled. Then he immediately saw a tall slender guy with a blond buzz-cut hairstyle emerging from the car. *Okay, who else is in that car buddy boy?*

Then he saw Teco come out of the car and someone wearing sweat pants with a cap and holding a broom.

Soulja, now you can catch them in the rinse. I told you that you'd get the upper hand.

"Yes, you did. Now let me handle this mission," said The Paradox while reaching in the back seat of the Jeep Cherokee for the Ruger 10/22 with a 50 round drum magazine and a M079 LF Launcher attached. Then he put in a 37mm smoke generator and started the engine of the SUV.

GQ, Teco and Ronald walked into GQ's Park Place South residence. Teco felt like he was on the MTV Cribs television show. The white modern furniture with the 12 foot vaulted ceilings in the living room took him by surprise. When he looked at the adjourning kitchen with granite countertops and a chef's island, Teco's stomach began to growl.

GQ ascended a spiral marble staircase to the bedroom floor.

Teco said, "Don't take long." Then he heard his echo. "Yo Ronald . . ."

"What's up?"

"Man, I've never been in a house this large that wasn't purchased with drug money. Can you believe this place? And it's all legit."

"Yeah, I know what you mean. I guess some of us don't work as hard to get to this level. Word in the homicide unit is that Gail Que worked her ass off in prison. While others were sleeping on their bunks, she was studying fashion design. Her grandmother shipped her all kinds of fashion courses; so I've been told. We investigated GQ after she became a target. Ms. Hazel Eyes is all clear."

"Wow, you say it like you admire her or something."

"I actually envy her. Wouldn't you just love to live in a place like this?"

"So work your ass off," Teco said; and they laughed.

Ronald posted by the front living room window. For some reason, he felt as if he left something in the car. He reached for his red D20 die in his pocket. "Damn-it!"

Teco turned towards Ronald and asked, "What did you say?"

"Nothing man, nothing." Ronald was so focused on not having his red D&D die that he didn't see The Paradox driving by GQ's residence in the red Jeep Cherokee.

Chapter 30

GQ CAME DOWNSTAIRS holding an engraved tote bag. Her Indigo Signature Collection sweat suit was a touch of class. Even while wearing the bulletproof vest, she looked as if she were going to the country club to watch a game of tennis.

"I'm ready to go," she said.

Ronald left the house first. He checked the car and turned the ignition.

Teco said, "SS-one come in."

"RS-one, go ahead I'm here," said Trooper who was tapping her nails on the hotel table. She wanted to be there. Moments like this made her very uneasy.

"We're on the move leaving the location. Copy."

"10-4." On the computer screen, she followed the red dot on the GPS map. Then she heard a knock at the door. "RS-one, hold on I need to go check the door."

"10-4," said Teco.

Back at the hotel, Swoosh was standing at the door with his hands behind his back.

"What's up?" Trooper asked.

"I got something for you," said Swoosh.

"Oh really?" she asked as she blushed. Her eyes lit up when Swoosh pulled out the king-size Snickers. "Come in. I was just checking their location."

"I really need to speak with you."

"What? You want to play a game of basketball with the Atlanta boys?" she asked.

"Oh I see you've got jokes."

"No, I know you play ball at least three times a week. It's difficult when you are on the road like this."

"I didn't come here to talk about me," said Swoosh who didn't really know how to step to her with his inner feelings.

"What's up?"

"Umm . . ."

"I'm listening."

"What do you possibly see in Teco Jackson? I mean, you two are from two different worlds."

Trooper was about to take the first bite out of her Snickers, but pushed it back into the wrapper. "What he and I have is really none of your business."

"I'm not trying to get into your business—"

"Yes you are. We've had this conversation before," said Trooper snatching the earpiece out of her ear.

"I've known you since we've been in blues. I've seen you go from a soft beat cop to a strong detective. I don't think you took enough time to get over the death of your partner, your divorce, and then your father's death after that."

"Marcus, this is my life; and it's my decision as to whom I see. You have no damn right."

"You don't get it do you?" Swoosh wanted to tell her everything but didn't want to drive her away. "What makes you think that Teco is going to stay with you?"

"Marcus, shut up!"

"Trooper, have you seen the way that Teco and GQ look at each other?"

"Sure, I've noticed it. But, he has assured me that they have never been anything more than friends."

"And you believe him?" asked Swoosh cutting deeply into her spirit.

"Yes, I believe him!"

Trooper and Swoosh continued to argue as Teco tried to reach her.

"RS-one to SS-one, you copy? RS-one to SS-one, you copy?" asked Teco. However, there was no response.

When Teco and GQ also got into the Crown Victoria, Ronald thought that he saw a car out of the corner of his right eye. However, he didn't see anything out of the ordinary.

Just as they pulled out of the neighborhood, there was a loud thud and white smoke followed. Teco's eyes widened because he feared the worst. Smoke fogged around the car.

"GQ, get down!" shouted Teco.

Ronald couldn't get a good visual. He put the car in drive and mashed down on the pedal; however, they didn't get far. The Crown Victoria collided into the SUV's side like a cannon.

"Oh Shit!" exclaimed Teco.

The Paradox jumped out with the Ruger 10/22 in his hand while firing down into the huge cloud of smoke. Teco didn't have time to retaliate with his own fire power. Having bulletproof windows in the Crown Victoria was a major benefit. Teco tried to think while the sounds of bullets hit the body of the car and window shield like hailstones.

GQ screamed her head off. "Oh no! Teco, this is how Fatboy died. We are going to die. Bobby is going to kill us!"

"Gail, shut up!" exclaimed Ronald who hit the gas and cut the wheel of the car to the left as the bullets came towards them at full blast.

"Trooper! We're under fire!" exclaimed Teco. However, there was no response. "I repeat. We're under fire!"

"SS-one repeat?" asked Trooper who put back in the earpiece as Swoosh left the room.

"I repeat. We're under fire!"

Trooper ran down the hall and banged on Swoosh's hotel room door. She screamed, "They are in trouble! They need backup!"

Swoosh picked up his cell and called Yeomans.

"Tell them that help is on the way," said Swoosh.

"RS-one, backup is on the way," said Trooper to Teco.

Ronald, Teco and GQ were choking on the smoke. Ronald drove on several residences' well manicured lawns trying to elude the rain of bullets. As they crashed into a mailbox, GQ's head hit the side of the window.

"This can't be happening again!" exclaimed GQ.

Teco asked, "Ronald, have you driven in high speed chases before?"

"No, not really. Only in training."

"Let me drive." Teco held the wheel as Ronald slid under him. Bullets were hitting the back windshield of the car.

Once Teco hit the road, the car almost lost control and fishtailed into the woods. However, he was too good of a driver for that to happen. Teco knew when to let off of the gas as he maneuvered the car. This was a technique he learned when he used to boost cars. Then Teco put a great deal of distance between the Crown Victoria and the red Jeep Cherokee.

"Is everybody alright!" exclaimed Teco.

No one answered.

"Is everybody alright! Is anybody hit?"

Chapter 31

GQ CHECKED her head and didn't see any blood. Ronald patted himself down.

"Teco, are you okay?" asked Ronald.

"Yes, I'm fine." Teco put his hand up to his ear and realized that the earpiece came out. He searched the front seat until he found the earpiece and put it back into his ear.

That's when he heard Trooper say, "RS-one, are you alright?"

"SS-one, we're fine. I see the police headed in the direction of GQ's neighborhood. Tell Yeomans to make sure that they check each condo. It's possible that others may have gotten hurt."

"That's a 10-4 RS-one. Come to command post two."

"That's a 10-4 SS-one."

Teco accidentally pushed the talk button in the lock position on the earpiece, which meant that Trooper could still hear the conversation in the car.

"GQ, are you alright?" Teco asked.

She looked at Teco and asked, "Am I going to die Homicide?"

"No, just like old times baby girl, just like old times, I can't allow that to happen to you."

"Homicide, I need you. Don't let me die."

"I got this. Do you want Ronald to drive so that I can come back there to sit with you?"

As Trooper and Swoosh walked into the City Hall East building, Trooper pulled the earpiece out of her ear.

"Is everything alright?" asked Fordham who was waiting in the lobby for Swoosh and Trooper's arrival.

"Yeah, Teco's fine," said Trooper.

"No, I'm talking about you," said Fordham.

Trooper didn't respond.

Within 30 minutes, Teco, GQ and Ronald walked into the City Hall East building.

When Detective Fordham stepped out of the elevator, she was glad that they were alive. "Hey there, security called to tell me that you were down here."

As they exited the elevator on the ninth floor, a group of Detectives stood clapping as they walked down the hall to the conference room. Ronald held his head high because he was able to get everyone back safely to the Atlanta Police Department Homicide Unit.

Swoosh, Trooper and Yeomans were looking at the projector screen when Teco, GQ and Ronald walked into the room. Trooper walked over to Teco and threw her arms around him. Ronald walked around the table to sit in the first available seat.

"What's up with the grid?" asked Ronald.

"We don't know yet. We think The Paradox is using it to play his war games."

Ronald began to read the notes beside the grid. Without knowing that he was thinking aloud, Ronald said, "Damn, he's good."

"What do you mean, he's good?" asked Swoosh.

"Look at this. You have an eight by eight grid, which is a total of 64 squares. Does anyone know how to play chess?"

Everybody glanced up at the screen.

"Are you sure?" asked Yeomans.

"Let's view the clues. The Paradox wrote in this note that 'rank is filed from E-1 to E-8. What he didn't say is that the files in chess are from A to H, which is a total of eight letters," said Ronald.

"Umm, I see what you mean," said Trooper.

"Now the ranks are 1 through 8. Put a number 1 to the side of the bottom left square, then at the top of that the number 2, then the number 3 all the way to 8. Now underneath the bottom left square put a letter A, then beside it the letter B, all the way across to the letter H."

"The Paradox is playing chess using algebraic expressions. We need to be on point. He's made the first move," said Teco.

"Then that means that any move we make can cost us dearly," said Swoosh.

"Yeah, you're right," said Ronald.

"So what would be our move?" asked Trooper.

"The object of chess is to capture the king. Let's move this pawn that way so that we can get to his king quicker," said Ronald.

"I wouldn't make that move," said GQ. Her unexpected comment caused everyone to look directly at her.

"Do you play chess Ms. Que?" asked Yeomans.

"As a matter of fact, I do; and I'm quite good at it." GQ stood up and walked towards the big screen. "Let's understand chess. Whoever opens up with the first initial move has control over the game. Everything in rank 2 and 7 are all pawns, which are known to be the sacrificial pieces."

"Can you tell us what that means in layman's terms?" asked Fordham.

"Bobby has set up Atlanta as the chessboard. I believe he has already picked out a game. If I were you guys, I'd be trying to find out which game he is playing."

"Huh?" asked Yeomans.

"What do you mean that he's already picked the game?" asked Fordham.

"There are over a billion games that have been played and recorded professionally. He may be using one of those recorded games. So if I were playing this game, I would counter move by pushing my pawn from E-7 to E-5."

"So how do we know what his next move is?" asked Trooper.

"Let's go with GQ's advice. Based on the map, the location of E-5 is Mercer University. That's where we will go next," said Yeomans looking at the location.

"What about that Little Five Points place? Shouldn't we start there?"

"You know, you might be right Ronald," said Swoosh.

Mac walked in the room and said, "Guys, this is beginning to look really bad. Three of Ms. Que's neighbors were hit with strays, but we have no casualties. CSI counted 41 casings from a Ruger 10/22 and 7 casings from a 40 calibre. I hope the 40 cal belongs to you Ronald."

Ronald nodded his head yes.

Mac continued, "Plus, there was a 37 millimeter smoke generator just like the one used on Squeaky, Goldfinger's boy. This is military type stuff, and my GBI supervisor will be calling the Feds."

"Shit!" exclaimed Trooper.

Teco walked over to Trooper and directed her to the back of the room. He whispered, "I'm very sorry, but I think it's best that I leave tonight."

Trooper looked deeply into his eyes and said, "You know that I know you didn't murder Bashi. That ring came from somewhere else."

"This isn't just about what the Fed's think. Keeping GQ alive is beyond an option. There is no other choice. Your priority right now is to catch Bobby."

Trooper leaned on the back credenza as she studied his face to see if there was more to what he was really saying to her. "Well, you know that I will call Mullis and Rozier to inform them of what happened. When they hear about all that occurred over the last few days that will help clear your name for sure. We need them on our side."

"Trooper, I need to go to the hotel so that we can pack." Teco was ready to give her a goodbye kiss right there. "I understand that you can't come with us, and I wish—"

"Hold that thought. Let me go talk to Swoosh." Trooper walked over to Swoosh and told him about Teco's plan.

"How long will he be gone?" asked Swoosh in a low tone.

"How ever long it takes to keep GQ safe and alive until we find Bobby." Swoosh didn't like her answer but knew that she was right.

"Where's he taking her?" asked Swoosh.

"I don't know. Let me ask him." Trooper walked over to Teco and they chatted for a while.

Walking back over to Swoosh, Trooper said, "He's taking her to New York."

Within the hour, Teco, Trooper, Ronald and GQ returned to the Westin Perimeter hotel. In his suite, Teco threw his tactical vest on the center of the bed and went into the closet to get his suitcase. Trooper turned to face him.

"Why New York?" asked Trooper.

"You have no idea what we just experienced on the streets of Atlanta. GQ has to get back to some since of normalcy. I think it's best for her to lay low for a few days and work on her fashion line in an undisclosed location."

"Ummm, hummm," said Trooper, "I see how beautiful GQ is and how she responds when you talk to her. She is Gail Indigo Que, the CEO of her own clothing line."

"That may be true, but she is not my Trooper," said Teco.

"I know you are turned on by an intelligent woman. Plus, you and she have a past together."

"You are turning me on with this jealousy bit."

"I'm not jealous. I'm being realistic," said Trooper.

"Let's go talk with Ronald," said Teco.

Teco picked up his surveillance equipment and checked the perimeter to make sure it was clear for them to move. On the way down the hall, Teco pinched Trooper on the butt.

"Alright now, don't start what you can't finish," she said in a low sexy tone.

Once in Ronald's suite, Trooper saw that GQ was typing an email on Ronald's laptop. "GQ stop! Don't tell anyone where you're going. I don't think you should be using a laptop at all," said Trooper.

"I rather you use mine," said Teco.

Trooper looked at Teco. *No, he didn't.* She knew that Teco wouldn't allow anyone to touch his laptop.

GQ sighed and closed the computer top.

Ronald retrieved the red D20 die from his pocket and rolled it around in his right hand.

"Okay Ms. Que, if you're going to New York, we need all of your emergency contact information."

GQ reached for Ronald's laptop, but Teco put his huge warm hand over hers to stop her. Trooper observed that Teco and GQ's unspoken words seemed to carry a great deal of weight.

Ronald said, "Teco, by the time you reach the Big Apple, you'll have the information on which hotel you'll—"

"I have already made online reservations at a four star hotel," said GQ.

"Ms. Que, four star hotels are not in your vocabulary until Bobby is caught. Sorry," said Ronald.

There was a knock on the door which startled GQ.

Teco reached for his sidearm.

"Who is it?" asked Ronald with his gun out.

"It's Detective Yeomans and Swoosh."

Teco gave Ronald the okay to open the door. Swoosh walked in first with Yeomans following him holding a digital camera in his hand.

"I want you guys to see what this asshole did to four of our city cruisers." Yeomans turned on the camera to show them the crime scene.

"Did you catch The Paradox?" asked Teco.

"No," said Yeomans.

Teco grabbed Trooper's hand and guided her out of the door.

"What's up with those two?" asked Yeomans.

"I think you need to ask them," said Ronald.

Trooper wasn't in their suite all the way before Teco turned her around and kissed her erotically. Her response was everything that he desired.

However, her arms were blocking him from pulling her shirt up. "Baby! Baby!" she exclaimed while breathing heavily.

"Yes, yes, yes baby!" Teco never ceased from kissing her.

"We don't have time to do . . . ummm . . . ummm . . . this." She didn't want Teco to stop.

He was not going to leave Atlanta without making love to his queen. When she realized that he wasn't stopping, she pulled off his shirt and kissed his chest. As he caressed her soft butt, Teco picked her up and carried her to the bed. Once on the bed, she pushed his tactical vest to the floor. Unsnapping her jeans, Trooper revealed her pink and blue boy cut panties.

Seeing Teco undress turned her on the more. Then he climbed onto the bed as her legs parted. She was ready to receive him with pleasure.

Though her lingerie hid her Egyptian treasures, he still wanted to go down and taste the sweet aroma of her sex. However, he knew that time was limited. He reclined on his back to allow her to lie on top of him because this gave her more control to navigate him to the center of her wet ebony soft spot. To his delight, Trooper let out a deep passionate moan.

Then the hotel phone rang.

"Shoot!" exclaimed Trooper.

"Baby, you have a job to do," he said holding her at her slim waistline.

Listening to his heartbeat, which sang a special song just for her, Trooper refused to move.

Therefore, Teco reached over to pick up the phone. "Hello."

"Your flight leaves in less than two hours. There is a cab waiting for you and GQ downstairs," said Swoosh who immediately hung up.

"Baby, get up. I'm on the next flight to New York," Teco said to Trooper while tapping her gently on her side.

"Hmmm, do I have to?"

He looked at the clock. With one of his male exotic dancer moves, Teco stole a few moments to move his hips in a manner that drove Trooper wild. When she reached her peak, he let loose inside her ebony world.

Chapter 32

AS THE PLANE pulled into gate A21 at the Hartsfield-Jackson Atlanta International Airport, the lead flight attendant said on the intercom system, "Attention all passengers, I thank you for flying Delta Airlines. If you have another flight, the gate agent can direct you to your flight. If this is your final destination, we hope you enjoy your stay in Atlanta, Georgia."

Gwen was very excited about seeing her sister. She knew that GQ would show her a good time around the Black Mecca of the South. For some reason, she felt nervous. She constantly looked over her shoulder as if she were being followed.

After pulling down the only RollAboard luggage that she owned, she held a second smaller bag very closely to her side. Once she was off the plane, she began to look for directions. She followed the crowd until she saw the Ground Transportation sign. When she was almost hit by an electric airport cart that was transporting four passengers with their luggage, she said, "Hey, why can't I get a ride?"

Going down an escalator, she stepped onto a moving sidewalk. Gwen never saw a moving sidewalk before, let alone stood on one. Continuing to follow the signs, Gwen walked on the south side and passed baggage claim. People were everywhere as far as she could see. She felt very happy that she didn't have any bags because the people waiting at the baggage carousel looked like ants crowded around a feeding hole.

When she walked through the sliding doors, the loud sound of jet engines pierced her ears; and the smell of jet fuel and exhaust fumes consumed the air. Then she heard the chants of transportation drivers.

"Need a safe ride? Hey lady, didn't I just see you go into the airport? Wait, did you change clothes?" asked a limousine driver.

What a lame pickup line. Gwen went to the taxi line. As the cab driver took her bags, she pulled out a small piece of paper and gave it to him. "Do you know where this address is?" she asked in a Philly accent.

"Sure, it's about thirty minutes away," he said in a Somali accent. "Is that all the luggage you have Miss Lady?"

"Yes, it is."

"A lot of women come to Atlanta for a fresh start. Are you a dancer?"

"Hell no," she said wondering why he was all in her business.

"Then you must be a college student."

As Gwen got into the car, she didn't know if she should just take another car. "Welcome to Atlanta" by Jermaine Dupri played on HOT 107.9 as the driver made a left onto I-85 north.

"Can you please turn that up some? That's my jam!" exclaimed Gwen.

"Sure, you like that?" he asked looking into the rear-view mirror.

Would I have asked you to turn it up if I didn't like the song?

He still was trying to make small talk with her. "Did you know that this city has turned out to be known as the gay capital of the United States?"

She totally ignored his ignorant comments.

"First time in Atlanta?"

"Yes it is."

She is so beautiful, just like the women from my home country of Somalia. As "U Remind Me" by Usher played, he turned up the radio and began to sing the song. "I can dig this jam. This is my kind of music."

He thinks he's slick talking about this is his kind of music. How much longer is it going to take?

When the high rise buildings were in sight, he said, "Welcome to the Black Mecca of the South."

"Thank you. Are there any nice clubs here?"

He looked at her through his rear-view mirror wondering if her eyes would tell him if she was on the other side of the rainbow.

"What type of clubs are you looking for? Same sex, social life, or straight?"

She decided to ignore him again.

"This city is full of a lot of clubs. You no worry about the nightlife. As a matter of fact, the hotel you are staying at isn't too far from where a lot of people hangout. Yes, there are a lot of clubs here."

"Is there a club at the hotel where I'm staying?"

"Oh, I know a real nice place called the Westin Peachtree Plaza. My sister works there. If you'd like, I can give her a call so you can see if she can book you at the better hotel. The hotel where you are staying is not safe."

Gwen thought about it as he was checking his messages on his cell phone. "Well ma'am."

"Okay, only if you let me talk with her."

"Alright cool. If you don't like what you hear. I'll take you wherever you would like to go, free of charge."

He dialed a number and passed Gwen the cell phone. "Hello." The ladies voice was soft spoken. She told Gwen about Westin Peachtree Plaza and offered her a discounted rate. Gwen loved all of what she was hearing. After hanging up, she gave the phone back to the driver.

"So what will it be? Are you changing hotels?"

"Sure, why not?"

When they pulled up to the Westin Peachtree Plaza, the bellhop, who was dressed in a nice red bandit collar jacket, opened the door for Gwen. The yellow trimming on his jacket set the entire uniform off. He said, "Welcome to the Westin Peachtree Plaza."

After Gwen paid the taxi, he gave her a business card and said, "My sister will take very good care of you. Her name is Samone Adams. If you need to go anywhere, call me."

As Gwen walked through the revolving door of the flamboyant Westin Peachtree Plaza, a huge smile came on her face. *This place reminds me of the Radisson Plaza Warwick on 17th and Locust in Philly. The only difference with this hotel is all the glass and mirrors they have around. It looks like a crystal palace. That's what I would have named it.*

She walked up to the red ropes that led to the front desk, and she couldn't believe the beautiful decor. The brass countertop appeared to be worth a fortune.

"Ma'am, may I help you?" asked the front desk clerk, who looked Gwen up and down as if Gwen didn't belong at the Westin.

"Yes, Ms. Adams, please."

The clerk pushed a button on the phone as she picked up the receiver. "She'll be right out ma'am. Can you please stand to the side?"

A beautiful woman came out from the office door, which looked like it was a part of the wood panel wall.

"Ms Que?" she asked with a smile. Gwen walked forward to the desk. "How are you today?" asked Ms. Adams hoping that Gwen knew how to play the game.

"I'm fine. Thank you for asking."

"Your suite is ready," Ms. Adams said pulling out some paperwork for Gwen to sign. "May I see your I.D. please?"

Gwen removed the bag from her shoulder and put it on the desk. When she did, Ms. Adams saw all the cash money.

"I take it that you will be paying with cash?"

Gwen looked into her bag. Then she looked at Ms. Adams. "Yes, that will be cash."

When she saw the name Gwen Que, Ms. Adams asked, "Ms Que, forgive me if I'm wrong. Are you the GQ of the Indigo Signature Collection?"

"No, I'm not. She is my sister."

The woman became very excited. "I thought you looked like her. I'm wearing your sister's lingerie line, the cami with the matching G-String."

Gwen thought that this was a little too much information; so she just smiled to play the part.

"Is your sister coming here? I would love to meet her."

"I've been trying to reach her myself. Where can I get some nice shoes?" Gwen asked ready to get out.

"Have you ever been to Lenox Mall?"

"No, this is my first time to Atlanta, what time does it close?"

Ms. Adams looked at her watch. "About nine o'clock. I'm off at six. How about I call you? We can meet in the lobby. I'll take you there to shop. It's very nice."

Gwen checked her out. "Sure, we can go, only if this mall has some fine brothers."

"Well, that would be Greenbriar Mall," Ms. Adams said. So what do you want, the brothers or the shoes?"

"For sure, the brothers," Gwen said; and they laughed.

Gwen was tense about entering the suite. However, she couldn't wait to see inside. Standing in front of the door on her cell phone trying to reach GQ, she used the key card to open the door. As she turned the knob, GQ's voicemail came on, so Gwen left a message. The door clicked and she opened the door to luxury.

◊◊◊◊◊

BOARDING A DELTA FLIGHT at the B7 gate at the Hartsfield-Jackson Atlanta International Airport, Teco escorted Gail Que to the window seat on the plane, which allowed him to know her every move.

"GQ, I'll be right back," said Teco.

She wondered where he was going. Then she saw that he was talking to a flight attendant. *What is he up to?* Just as Teco took a seat, the plane pulled away from the gate. GQ asked, "What was that all about?"

"GBI Agent McLoughlin made arrangements for me to get the passengers list to determine if we might have an unwanted guest aboard. Now get some sleep. It's late."

"Yes master," she said with sarcasm.

While the plane rumbled and shook as it took off into the air, Teco also took a long deep breath and closed his eyes.

Man, what in the hell is going on? How did she get back into my life? Teco hit his left fist into the palm of his right hand. *I've got to figure this shit out.* Then he looked over to GQ to see if she was faking to be asleep. She wasn't.

The flight attendant walked up to Teco with a tray in her hand. "Would you like something to drink?"

"A coke with a little ice. Thank you."

There was a woman sitting in the seat diagonal from him. When she kept staring at him, Teco didn't know if he knew the woman. Therefore, he just smiled. When she showed him her law enforcement badge, his smile dropped. His life appeared to be spiralling out of control.

Bashi told me not to start a beef with Bobby. I should have listened. No, I had to be a bad ass. Now look at me.

GQ was sleeping like a baby, safe and sound.

He said to GQ, "I have to keep you alive. The Feds are not going to rest until they pin Bashi's death on somebody. It wasn't me. Damn! I pray you don't flip the script on me and try to put me in the joint to teach me a lesson."

GQ didn't hear a word. She continued to sleep and turned her back away from Teco.

His mind drifted back to the days when he ran with the SB crew. Now he was a bodyguard for the woman who probably despised him the most.

Closing his eyes, Teco joined GQ in sleep.

. . . At the SB crib, there was a hard knock on the door. Teco knew that it was his best friend, Fatboy, who was coming to pick him up. When Teco opened the door, no one was standing there.

The red sun caused Teco to block his eyes from the rays with his left hand. He knew that something wasn't right as he walked out to the middle of the lawn. His world appeared to be drifting as he walked half of a mile.

When he turned in a complete circle, there was only darkness. Then every twenty yards a lamp post lit up a side street. Therefore he set out on his journey.

Hearing footsteps behind him, Teco stopped to see if anyone was following him. There wasn't. So, he went on his way once more. He heard the sound again. He stopped, turned around, and said, "Bring it on."

The street before him morphed into a street reaper with no mouth and no eyes. Before Teco could run, the street reaper enveloped his entire body and shook him. . . .

The turbulence from the airplane caused Teco to awaken with bright open eyes. Showing him her badge again, the police officer diagonal from him asked, "Bad dream?"

Chapter 33

IN THE BATHROOM at the boarding house, The Paradox stood in front of a white metal medicine cabinet thinking about what transpired at Mercer University. He was really stupefied when he overheard the SWAT team congratulating the detective with the blond buzz-cut for figuring out his grand plan by using a role playing technique. This really ticked The Paradox off. In fact, the other detective with the brown jacket almost caught The Paradox dropping the next letter off in Mercer University's campus mail. As luck would have it, there was a row of shrubbery that gave The Paradox cover.

Admiring his looks in the mirror, he smiled as he rubbed his fingers through his soft hair.

See Soulja, you didn't think that the police could safeguard Gail Que and Teco Jackson. Did you?

He grabbed the sides of his head with both hands and said, "Leave me alone."

The Paradox reached for the razor on the sink, ran the razor under the hot water, and pulled the razor from the front of his head to the nape of his neck. Completing the finishing touches to his baldhead, he applied baby oil in order to create a sparkling glow.

Dressed in black cargo pants and a black t-shirt, he put on a green army field jacket which he knew would be hot. However, how else was he to hide the bulletproof vest? So to him, the jacket really served its purpose. He believed that the Atlantans would simply pass him off as a war veteran.

Opening the closet door, he retrieved the gym bag that he stole from the Goldfinger crew. The money inside totalled over $18,000.

When he left the boarding house, a half moon was in the dark navy blue skies. A bus pulled into the Greyhound station parking lot. Standing there in the dark for a moment while watching the taxi drivers who were huddled around, The Paradox thought the cabbies were African. However, on closer observation, he could tell that they were indeed Haitian.

There is too much damage to the Jeep Cherokee; I need a new ride.

At the nearby Magic City nightclub, music could be heard very clearly. "Get Low" by Lil Jon, The Eastside Boyz and the Ying Yang Twins blasted through the open windows which served as a way for the women dancers to get cool air. Outside, there were fancy cars and a few guys who The Paradox surmised to be drug dealers.

I wonder what really goes on in that joint.

Walking past the bus station, the scent of diesel fuel attacked his nose with no warning. However, this did not bother The Paradox because he was a soldier.

Halfway down the street, he heard a voice say, "Hey Red." The female leaned against a diamond blue 1968 Cadillac Deville convertible, which looked black due to the darkened sky. She smiled and showed The Paradox her thighs.

Scoping the lot, The Paradox noticed a man who was wearing a black suit with thick gold chains that glistened underneath the street lights.

The Paradox said, "I'm on a mission Tiny." Amazed at how street walkers put their lives in danger, The Paradox thought this to be her lucky day because he didn't need any additional bait for the detectives on his case.

Until the break of dawn, he walked for miles.

"How are you doing today sir? Nice morning to buy a car," said a used car salesman. "See anything that you'd like to drive away in?"

The Paradox looked at the salesman and then to a row of cars that were lined up with neon green price tags. Walking over to another section, The Paradox's interest was drawn to a black commercial utility minivan.

"You like this for your business?" asked the salesman.

"If I give you cash now, will you take four?" asked The Paradox.

The salesman's eyes lit up as if he had hit the jackpot for the minivan. "Let me go see my manager. I'll be right back." The salesman spun around and took off like a rocket.

The Paradox pulled the van driver side door open and looked inside. He surmised the minivan to be fitting for his next mission.

Coming over to The Paradox with a clipboard and a big Kool-Aid smile, the salesman said, "Sir, my manager said that would be a good deal if you're indeed paying in cash. Here are the keys. Go ahead and start her up."

On the first try, the engine hummed. However, the inside of the van smelled like motor oil; therefore, The Paradox concluded that the van might have been used as an auto parts van.

"I'll take it for a spin," said The Paradox.

"Sure, may I have your license? Also, you'll have to sign that you are taking it for a test drive."

"If I buy this today, can you throw in thirty day tags?"

The salesman looked at the license and said, "Mr. Ransom, for that, you'll have to pay for temporary insurance." Through the driver side rear-view mirror, The Paradox watched the salesman go into the dealership building.

When the salesman came back with the tag, The Paradox heard a loud noise on the rear door and pressed the gas pedal without getting his fake driver's license back. Driving three blocks down, he entered onto I-285 to see if the van was fit to fulfill his mission. After passing a few exits, he took the Memorial Drive exit. Being very pleased with the minivan, The Paradox made a u-turn and headed back to the car dealership.

When the minivan pulled back into the lot, the salesman said, "You gave me a scare there because I thought you weren't coming back. I decided to give you a few minutes though. Do you like the way she rides?" The salesman held the clipboard to his side with his right hand; and with his other hand extended, he passed the driver's license to The Paradox.

"Yes, the van will do."

They walked towards the dealership office. For a brief moment, the salesman started to get nervous as The Paradox reached under his shirt and pulled out a gold money clip.

"What's the total?" asked The Paradox.

"Six thousand, three hundred and fifty nine dollars and that includes the tag."

The Paradox knew that the salesman was taking advantage of him with all of the underhanded surcharges; however, he said, "I'll take it."

"Great, let's go inside to finish the paperwork."

"Sure," said The Paradox, "can you please do me a favor and mail this letter off with your mail today?"

"Yes, Mr. Ransom. The mail carrier should be on her way around noon."

"Thank you kindly."

Within the hour, The Paradox pulled up to the security gate of Overlook Atlanta. After displaying the fake CNN press pass to the guard, The Paradox waved to a grounds worker who was emptying the trash by the basketball court. He parked the minivan to observe the traffic flow from one of Goldfinger's dope apartments. Getting out of the car with his gun, that he called Body Rocker, concealed in the back waistband of his pants, he walked up to the front door.

Before The Paradox could knock, a small slot in the door came open. "What you need?" asked a young man with a southern accent and a gangster attitude.

In a Philly accent, The Paradox said, "I'm looking for the dude with the gold finger." Hearing footsteps, The Paradox did a quick turn; however, the person passing by was a resident in an adjourning apartment.

The small slot in the door slammed shut and opened back up again. "You got the wrong spot, big dude."

"Look, it's about business. Somebody from the Magic City nightclub sent me here."

"You got the wrong door." Then the small slot closed again.

Maybe I do have the wrong apartment. As The Paradox walked back to the van, two guys approached him from the end apartment unit. Unfortunately, The Paradox couldn't get his hand on the P95 pistol fast enough.

"Big dude, who you looking for?" asked Pie while he and T-Sand blocked The Paradox's path.

"What's it to you?" The Paradox asked while mugging them up and down.

"Yo son, because you be asking for our folk . . . Where you from? What's your name shawty?" asked T-Sand in a Brooklyn accent.

"You can call me Body Rocker; and I ain't your shawty. I was looking for some work. Feel me?" The Paradox asked raising his left eyebrow.

"What kind of work you need, Body Rocker?" asked Pie.

"See, it's nothing like that." The Paradox stepped to the right side of Pie and T-Sand; however, T-Sand blocked his path again. This time The Paradox swiftly pulled out his P95 pistol.

Pie and T-Sand did not notice until it was too late to react. All they heard was a bullet injecting into the chamber.

Knowing that he had the upper hand, The Paradox pressed the big pistol into Pie's left side.

Raising his hands, Pie said, "Yo shawty, we don't want no trouble."

As T-Sand reached for his pistol, there were footsteps coming in their direction from one of the apartment units. With both hands up, Goldfinger yelled, "Yo! Yo! Chill man. We just protecting ours."

Seeing the gold finger, The Paradox smiled.

"You better get that burner out of my peeps side," said Goldfinger in his Dirty South accent.

Out of nowhere, The Paradox felt the barrel of Goldfinger's 9mm weapon against his right side.

Goldfinger said, "Look over there and there."

From an apartment window to The Paradox's left was an AK-47 assault rifle pointed at him, and to the right in another apartment window was a pump shotgun.

"Yo, I was just trying to get some help," said The Paradox who didn't even budge to put his P95 pistol away.

"We got what you need man. I already told you that," said Pie who didn't break a sweat.

"Goldfinger, let me holler at you man to man," said The Paradox.

Giving the directive nod, Goldfinger put his 9mm down and everyone, including The Paradox, followed suit.

"Come with me over by the basketball court," said Goldfinger.

The Paradox was on point and realized that Pie and T-Sand were in shooting range.

"So what type of work you looking for?" asked Goldfinger who pulled out a pack of Newport cigarettes.

"I need your help in snatching this chick up," said The Paradox who saw teenage boys entering the basketball court area.

While lighting up the Newport, Goldfinger thought about The Paradox's request and chuckled. "You joking right?" asked Goldfinger who blew out the first mass of smoke. The sun made the gold finger sparkle as he took another hit of the Newport cigarette.

"I'm very serious. Would you think that I'd go through all of this for a laughing joke?" asked The Paradox.

"Who is she before I agree to anything?"

"That's none of your business. The less you know the better. So, can you help me out or what?"

"You must be the po po or the Red Dogs trying to set me up."

"The red who?" asked The Paradox.

"Don't act like you don't know the Red Dogs. Some bullshit about 'running every drug dealer out of Georgia.'"

"Look man; I am not the police. Either you can take the job or you can't." Becoming impatient, The Paradox pulled out the keys to the minivan. *I'm not impressed by these Red Dogs. When are they going to wake up and catch these dealers? I will have to continue to take matters into my own hands.*

Goldfinger asked, "Wait, why you rushing? We just had some unwanted dealings with the police. I'm not trying to let that happen again. So just chill out so we can talk this out. To do the job, I'll need half now and the rest when the job is done."

"What's it going to cost me?"

"Ten stacks. I need five now and the rest later. Let's go inside to do this," said Goldfinger who tossed the half lit Newport to the ground and stepped on the cigarette butt.

The smell of strawberry incense filled the apartment. There were no visible signs of drugs or drug paraphernalia. The Paradox was shocked because the apartment was well furnished in a modern decor and looked like a high tech computer lab. A police scanner sounded out ten codes; and Goldfinger's surveillance equipment was state of the art. When The Paradox saw his minivan on one of the monitors, he now understood how Goldfinger knew everything that transpired outside.

Sitting in the dining room under a colorful tiffany chandelier, The Paradox counted the money and pushed the loot that he previously stole from Goldfinger halfway across the table.

As Goldfinger reached for the stack of $100 bills, The Paradox placed his hand over the money and said, "Not so fast partner." Goldfinger and The Paradox locked eyes. The Paradox added, "I need to know who is going to do the work."

Goldfinger said, "Well, that depends on what you need done."

"I need a man that knows how to navigate the streets of Atlanta at high speeds."

"I got just the man for the job. When is it going down?"

"In a few days I'll need him ready when I call."

They sealed the deal over a gentleman's handshake. When The Paradox and Goldfinger stood up, Goldfinger's posse entered the dining room with their side arms in clear view.

Chapter 34

IN A BRIEFING ROOM at City Hall East, Trooper summarized the details of the current assessment on the case. The list of law enforcement agencies involved sounded like alphabet soup. The task force included the Explosive Projectile Nuclear Unit (EPNU), Atlanta Special Weapons Assault Team (ASWAT), Bureau of Alcohol Tobacco and Firearms (BATF), Georgia Bureau of Investigation (GBI), Federal Bureau of Investigation (FBI), the Fulton County Sheriff's Department and other local law enforcement department heads.

After Trooper finished speaking, Swoosh asked the audience, "Does anyone have any questions?"

A few seconds passed, then an officer raised his hand and asked, "Can you please tell us The Paradox's motive?"

"We have reason to believe that the person of interest, Bobby Stephens, wants to kill everyone who was once associated with the Strictly Business crew out of Mt Airy, Pennsylvania. Once a member of SB, Gail Indigo Que now lives in Atlanta. Also, we have been informed by the Philadelphia Police Department that Lisa Turner, who also lived in Atlanta, was a close friend of the deceased SB crew boss. These may be reasons why Bobby Stephens, a.k.a. The Paradox, was drawn to the Atlanta area. However, we don't know why he would continue to go after former SB crew affiliates since the crew has been disbanded for several years," said Trooper.

Swoosh stood up and added, "Look guys. Sorry to the ladies in the room; you know when I say guys that I'm including you all too. I believe that The Paradox is fascinated with Detective Troop. He writes her notes with clues. Let me add that Detective Troop is known to be the best in the field. So, The Paradox wants to prove that he can outsmart her. That's my take on things."

Trooper added, "There is a gag order on the information we are about to share. Nothing leaves this room." She pulled up the grid of metro-Atlanta to explain the chess game to the taskforce. "Now we will brief you on what we believe to be The Paradox's next move."

The EPNU commander came to the platform and said, "We have consulted with a chess expert from the United States Chess Federation (USCF). Detective Heard and Detective Yeomans are at Mercer University, which we believe to be the location of our move in this twisted chess game." The commander took out a laser pointer and moved towards the overhead screen. "Based on the information gathered and the metro-Atlanta grid, the Inman Park MARTA station near Little Five Points may be The Paradox's next move. We have four bomb sniffing dogs and a computerized robot named TRASH at the train station now. We are taking every precaution to keep our teams and the citizens of Atlanta safe." He paused to make sure there weren't any questions. Then he continued, "The local police unit has closed a total of five exits, of which two are emergency exits, here and here. Once we reach the site, EPNU has full control of the mission. After this briefing, I'm expecting everyone in this room to be in full tactical gear before we deploy. God bless and may we all return unharmed."

Everyone in the room emerged from the briefing room headed to the parking lot. Rolling up a map of the Inman Park MARTA station near Little Five Points, the commander of the EPNU slid the map into a long cylinder tube which he capped off.

As Trooper walked in the parking lot looking for her car, she phoned Teco. When she received his voicemail, she said, "Hello baby, I missed you this morning. We're getting ready to storm the Little Five Points area. Be careful. I promise I'll be careful as well. Love you."

When Trooper arrived at the Inman Park MARTA station near Little Five Points, Ronald and Yeomans were getting out of a police car. Christa from CNN ran over to Yeomans and asked, "Detective, can you tell us if this is related to the same suspect who bombed the Ferst Center for the Arts?"

"Crystal, we don't know whom we're dealing with at this point."

When he mispronounced her name, she rolled her eyes because Yeomans knew her name. Christa asked, "Is there a bomb? The Inman Park MARTA station has been closed all morning."

"Will you just let us do our jobs?" asked Yeomans who walked away annoyed.

Running behind him, she said, "But Detective, we the people—"

"Somebody move these cameras back!" exclaimed Yeomans who pointed to a uniform Atlanta police officer.

From Moreland Avenue to DeKalb Avenue, everything was blocked off. Nearby the bomb detection dogs canvassed the outside perimeter of the station. In addition, the EPNU's huge black truck was parked on the sidewalk by the Brewhouse Cafe and served as the command post. The smell of coffee made the technicians mouth water; so Yeomans told one of the MARTA police officers to get coffee for everyone on duty.

Trooper walked up to the truck and watched four men lift a man-sized machine out of the truck. The human like upper body of the computerized robot was similar to that of a punching Body Opponent Bag (BOB) with a lower body made of steel and mechanical fingers capable of crushing a metal pipe.

Just as the robot was on solid ground, a computer technician punched a few codes onto a laptop keyboard. After surveying the desolated area, Trooper heard a whirring sound and saw red and green lights. TRASH was fully powered.

"Lieutenant, meet TRASH," said the technician.

In a computerized voice, TRASH stated, "Hello lieutenant."

Walking around the machine, Trooper said, "Oh, he's cute. Why do you call it trash?"

"TRASH stands for The Recovery Automated Search Human-dynamo. Plus, if anything goes wrong, he's really trash," said the technician with a chuckle. Then he put on a black outfit with attached gloves. The wires from the gloves connected to the computer. When the technician's hands moved so did the mechanical fingers on TRASH.

"Wow! We have to get one of these!" exclaimed Trooper.

The technician put on a pair of dark glasses with ear buds protruding from the side.

"TRASH, shake the detective's hand."

The robot complied.

"Nice to meet you TRASH," she said with a smile.

"TRASH, whose hand did you just shake?"

As Trooper stared at the robot, the computerized voice stated, "Lieutenant Hanae Troop, Washington, D.C. Homicide Division, age—"

"Okay, TRASH that's enough," said the technician. Looking at Trooper, he continued, "TRASH has a database connection to NIST, AFIS and NCIC in West Virginia."

Only witnessing technology like this on television, Trooper was shocked at the technological advancement of TRASH.

"TRASH, let's go to work. Move forward."

"Does it go up steps?" asked Trooper.

"Sure, you'll see," he said while moving the joy stick.

TRASH's robotic lenses were PC-79XP color covert pinhole cameras. From over 400 feet, TRASH could see in total darkness. The attached infrared illuminators captured a crystal clear picture at 1200 lines of resolution from up to 1 mile away. The robot was ready for action.

"Since the 1996 Summer Olympics bombing, we've come up with the best techniques like TRASH to detect black powder, smokeless gun powder, and any combination of sugar and potassium chlorate residue." The technician looked at Trooper to see if she was paying attention. "See, bombers need not be very sophisticated these days."

Biting down on her lip, Trooper said, "Yeah, that's what scares me about The Paradox."

"Well lieutenant, The Paradox hasn't met TRASH. If there's a bomb in the MARTA station, TRASH will find it. Its database picks up explosive substances like trinitrotoluene also known as TNT, pentaerythritol tetranitrate also known as PETN, and cyclotrimethylenetrinitramine also known as RDX. Although criminals still use dynamite, other nitro-glycerine based explosives have been replaced by ammonium nitrate based explosives or ANFO as we call it. At the Ferst Center of the Arts, the residue discovered was consistent with C-4. . . . Okay, it's show time."

TRASH reached the Inman Park MARTA station gate. The computer technician stretched the robot's arm forward as if the technician were reaching for something in the air.

Trooper, Swoosh and Ronald watched as the human-dynamo's arms reached up to the train station keypad on the wall and inserted a key.

The gate rolled upward. Looking like the Michelin Tire man, each of the six GBI officers who were dressed in black bomb protective gear moved forward staying ten feet behind TRASH.

"Ronald, what did you guys get from Mercer?" asked Swoosh while watching the robot as the technician recorded the findings.

Ronald said, "There was another message. I don't remember what it said, but it was another chess move. When we took it to the lab, the move on the metro-Atlanta map was knight to F-3. Atlanta PD believes the location to be the World Congress Center. I think the best thing to do is to mimic The Paradox's move to make the game complicated."

Swoosh rubbed his head and asked, "What if we make the wrong move, then what?"

"How would we know where to go? Will it be his move or our move?" asked Trooper as she took a bite of her Snickers bar.

"If we counter with a mimic move, our knight to C-6, then that would put us at a location called Johnson Ferry Road," said Yeomans who joined them.

Trooper asked, "What's on Johnson Ferry Road?"

"That's the question," said Ronald.

"That is a good question. Choosing the perfect move has me uneasy," Trooper said in a low tone.

"Trooper, let's just do what we do," said Swoosh.

"Stop!" exclaimed the computer technician.

TRASH came to a complete stop as did the officers following the robot.

Ronald felt as if he was on a movie studio set and the only person missing was John Travolta.

"TRASH is moving five feet northeast," said the technician.

Around the corner on Dekalb Avenue, The Paradox stopped at the roadblock in the commercial utility minivan which was now covered with white temporary vehicle paint.

Cautiously approaching the white van with the words "Black Bird Security" on the sides, a SWAT officer said, "This road is closed sir."

"Atlanta PD called me in to secure Little Five Points because your guys are stretched on resources. They want to ensure that there's no looting while y'all do whatever it is that you do," said The Paradox.

"Can you step out of the van sir and open the back door?"

"Sure, I'm just doing my job."

"We understand and we're doing our job as well. Just open the back door."

The Paradox did as the officer instructed; and the back of the minivan was empty. Speaking on the handheld radio, the officer said to his commander, "All Clear." Motioning for the barrier to be lifted so that the van could pass through, the officer turned back to The Paradox and said, "You can pass and be careful."

Off of Moreland Avenue, The Paradox turned into a back alley. In about 5 minutes, he peeled off the white temporary vehicle paint from the black minivan. After tossing the wig into the dumpster, he dressed in an all black jumpsuit, a cap and leather gloves.

Surveying the area, The Paradox realized that the coast was clear. Then he walked backwards until he reached a nearby fire escape which led to the roof of the Front Page News building. Once atop of the roof, he military crawled to the edge with his Leupold RX-3 laser rangefinder to scope out the area. Immediately, he saw a large black truck on the sidewalk on Moreland Avenue.

That must be the police command post. . . . ummm . . . There's my girl.

Beside an air conditioning unit, a black Homeland Security covert gun case was stashed. Leaning against the unit, The Paradox never saw the piece of metal sticking out which snagged his jumpsuit. He wanted to mutter out curse words; however, he knew the officers would hear him.

When he unsnapped the loop straps which released the AR-15 rifle, The Paradox attached the 39 x 40 rubber armored scope. After taking a deep breath to slow down his heart rate, he sighed heavily and pulled out the custom silencer. Six holes were drilled in the AR-15 barrel. Sliding the makeshift silencer over the entire barrel, he turned the silencer clockwise until it tightened. The special design was made to muffle the crackling sound which misdirected the noise through the airwaves. This feature would give him enough time to escape or so he hoped.

The Paradox retrieved the collapsible carbine stock and let down the feather weight bipods where he placed a white envelope under one of the legs. Pulling a black roof top camouflage cover over his body, he inserted the 30-round magazine. When he pulled the bolt back, the .223 round jumped into the chamber ready for action. The Paradox crawled back to the edge and placed his chin on the carbine cheek rest while easing his eye to the scope. Then he switched the reticle to green and waited for the right moment.

Soulja, one shot one kill.

While the rifle scope was focused on the MARTA station's front entrance, The Paradox noticed a robot rolling out of the gate; and bomb squad team members were taking off their helmets. He could see the sigh of relief on their faces.

It's not over just yet guys.

On Moreland Avenue, Ronald reached into his pocket and shook the D20 red die in his hands as he walked in the direction of the MARTA station entrance. The Paradox gripped down on the hand guards and peered through the scope just as Trooper and Swoosh entered the station flanked with other officers.

POW! Rock doves on the roof's edge scattered as the bullet penetrated the air. On Moreland Avenue below, there was a piercing scream as every officer hit the pavement.

Chapter 35

"NOOO!" SHE RAN over to him and attempted to lift him up; however, he was too heavy. So, another officer helped as the Atlanta SWAT team surveyed the area for the location of the security breech.

She grabbed the radio and said, "Officer down! I repeat, officer down! We need medical over here stat!" The blood was gushing out of his chest as if someone shook up a soda can. With trembling hands, she pushed down on his chest to apply pressure.

Swoosh said, "Ronald, breathe! Breathe, don't leave us like this. You hear me!"

Trooper cried out with blood on her hands, "Oh my God! God no! Please no!" Blood came from the corner of Ronald's mouth and ran down to his neck.

Ronald looked at Trooper as she tried to visually focus on him through her teary eyes. She felt that this would be his last breath.

As he coughed, Ronald said, "Trooper, don't cry." His head slowly leaned to the left. With muscles now relaxed, so did his hands. When his fingers opened up, his D20 die rolled to the ground. After it stopped spinning, the red die landed on the number 1 which represented death in Ronald's role playing game.

Trooper scooped the D20 die up and held it tightly in her palm. She was too emotional to handle Ronald lying lifelessly on the ground. Therefore, she walked away from the entrance of the MARTA station.

Unseen by the police, The Paradox knew that he needed to desert his tools in order to get past the roadblocks. When he jumped down, The Paradox quickly changed clothes and got into the minivan which was now the original color of black with CNN News on each side.

"Excuse me sir, how did you get in this secure area?" asked a foot patrol officer.

The Paradox flashed his fake press pass and said, "The mayor asked CNN News to film the city's officers in action. After shots were fired, I was commanded to leave the premises."

After looking deeply into The Paradox's eyes, the foot patrol officer removed the temporary red and white striped roadside barrier to let the minivan through. As helicopters hovered above, The Paradox felt good about his accomplishment. *One down, two more to go.*

◊◊◊◊◊

THE NEXT MORNING, Teco and GQ were about to leave the Harlem YMCA Hotel in New York when GQ was bombarded by the media at the door.

"Miss Que! Miss Que! Is it true that you were the murder target during your fashion show back in Atlanta, Georgia?"

GQ lifted her Kate Spade Clinton street purse to block the flashing cameras from her face.

Teco stepped in front of her and said, "She has no comment. How did you guys find out she was in New York anyway?"

"Hello? We are the media. Who's that guy?" asked the CBS cameramen who took pictures of Teco. Walking towards the limousine which was parked in front of the YMCA, he almost knocked Teco to the ground. Roughly pushing the cameraman aside, Teco opened the limousine door for GQ.

However, the CBS reporter blocked the doorway and asked, "Miss Que, do you think that the Washington, D.C. detective who died yesterday in Atlanta was murdered by the same person who attempted to kill you?"

This unexpected news caused Teco's heart to drop to his stomach. He felt bad about making GQ stay isolated from all of civilization. "What detective are you talking about?" asked Teco who reached for his cell phone to call Trooper.

"The Associated Press reports that the detective's name is Ronald Heard," said the CBS reporter.

"Shit!" exclaimed Teco who practically shoved GQ into the limousine.

Through the closed limousine door, Teco could hear the reporter ask, "Did you know him?"

As he signalled for the limousine driver to take off, Teco flipped open his cell phone. When Trooper's phone rang three times before going into voicemail, Teco exclaimed, "Shit!" He tried once more and received the same machine voice recording. His eyes focused on GQ who sat there speechless.

"Can you cancel your meeting today?" asked Teco.

"No, not today. There is nothing we can do to bring Detective Heard back. I have to keep moving."

"Don't you think you are putting yourself before others?"

"This is Bobby's twisted way of slowing me down long enough for him to win, and I won't let him have any power over my life. My mentor told me, 'When winning is illogical, losing is still far from optional.' We have to keep moving forward and put this street shit behind us Teco."

"Well, after you finish with your meeting, we are going to Philly."

"Why? I have deadlines to meet and people who depend on me for their livelihood."

"The less you know the better." Teco kept getting Trooper's voicemail recording, so he put his right elbow on the armrest of the door and stared off into the clear blue sky. GQ noticed that Teco's bottom lip was moving yet he never said a word.

Teco sat there feeling really ill about not being able to contact Trooper. He didn't know what to think of the matter in Atlanta. As he held his cell phone in his hand waiting for it to ring, a single drop or water rolled down his right cheek. He couldn't figure out why the tear appeared in the first place. Did he really care for Ronald or was he worried sick about his woman?

Opening the cell phone, Teco tried to call Trooper again; however, he received the same voicemail recording. *Who can I call? Think. Think.* He tapped the cell phone on his bottom lip as his mind raced to and fro.

The limousine pulled up to a tall white marble building with gold trim doors on Broadway. When Teco looked up, the words on the awning read: Bad Boy Entertainment Worldwide. Turning around to check out the area, Teco couldn't see well because of the tinted windows. He stepped out of the car first, not giving the driver a chance to do his job. "GQ, it's clear," he said slipping on his shades while observing the street crowd at the same time. Out of nowhere it dawned on him who he could call.

When they were safely inside the building, GQ took Teco to the top floor. The receptionist escorted GQ into a large boardroom. Standing outside the room by the door, Teco dialed a number on his cell phone.

"Captain Wicker speaking, how may I help you?"

"Captain Wicker, this is Teco!" he said loudly because he was relieved to hear a familiar voice. "Have you heard from Trooper?"

There was a long pause.

"Yes I have. Where are you Teco? Isn't she with you?"

"No, I'm in New York."

"What!" shouted Wicker who jumped to his feet in disbelief, "New York? What the hell are you doing in New York? You're being paid to be in Atlanta."

Teco held the phone away from his ear and walked towards the seating area by the receptionist. "I'm protecting my ass. What does that matter to you as long as I'm on the job? What happened to Detective Heard?"

Just hearing Ronald's name slammed Wicker back down to earth. Flopping down into the worn out black executive office chair, Wicker didn't know what to say. "Teco, there was never a bomb at that Little Five Points place. It was a staged plot to, ummm, draw the team and possibly you out." Pulling out the second note, Wicker added, "According to the note faxed to me—"

"Yeah, yeah, I know about the notes. Is Trooper alright?" Teco held the phone closer to his ear awaiting Wicker's answer; but instead, he heard the sound of computer keys tapping. "Captain, are you there? Did you hear me?"

"I'm sorry Teco. What did you say?" asked Wicker who was sending an email informing Agent Rozier that Teco was in New York. "Yeah, I heard you. What hotel did you say you're staying in?"

Teco paused and hung up the cell phone without notice. *Oh hell no. For some reason, I'm really having second thoughts about trusting the captain.* Walking to the elevator, Teco headed downstairs.

"Excuse me," Teco said to the limousine driver while scoping out the area at the same time.

"Yes sir, how may I help you?" he asked in a Mid-eastern accent.

"Do you know where a rental car place is, preferably Hertz?"

"Yes I do. As a matter of fact, there's one not far from here. Do you need to go now?"

Leaning on the door, Teco scanned the streets. "As a matter of fact, I do."

"Okay, hop in." The limousine driver moved to open the door for Teco.

"Since Miss Que isn't with us, I'll ride shotgun," said Teco with a slight frown.

"Sure sir," said the driver who pulled off into the Broadway traffic.

In less than 2 minutes, the limousine pulled up to Hertz on West 55th Street.

"Excuse me sir," said the driver. Teco turned around with one hand on the door handle. The driver continued, "Do I need to pick Miss Que up?"

"No, you can take the rest of the day off."

While waiting at the Hertz counter, Teco thought about calling Trooper; however, he decided to call Swoosh. The only problem was that he didn't have Swoosh's cell phone number. So, he dialed the Washington, D.C. Homicide Division; and the voice response unit prompted him through the directory names.

"This is Linda Hubbard, Lead Crime Scene Investigator."

"Linda, this is Teco. I've been trying to contact Hanae all day, but her cell phone keeps going to voicemail. Do you have Swoosh's digits?"

"Teco?" asked Linda.

"Yeah, Teco Jackson."

"Oh yeah, how are you doing?"

"My bad. I'm fine. How are you doing Linda?"

"I'm fine. I just can't believe Trooper and Swoosh are working this multi-jurisdiction operation. Did you hear about Ronald? I wish I could go down there and—"

"Linda, I would love to talk, but it's important that I speak with Swoosh."

"We're not supposed to give out any numbers. You didn't get it from me," she said looking around her work area as if she were being watched. She fingered through her phone book and gave him the number.

Back in Atlanta, everything appeared back to normal, except for the police tape around the front of the Inman Park MARTA station. Swoosh's cell phone vibrated, which startled him. Swoosh was zoned out as he stared at the white chalk line. He tried to really pull himself together as he answered the phone. "Hello . . . Hello."

Teco couldn't really hear Swoosh because there was so much static on the line. "Swoosh, hello, Swoosh!"

Swoosh recognized Teco's voice and disconnected the call.

Taking a deep breath and then exhaling slowly, Trooper slid on her black Dolce & Gabbana shades. "Who was that on the phone?" she asked analyzing the possible bullet trajectory.

"Oh, that was a call that I missed," Swoosh said.

"According to CSI, the shot came from here to here, but I know better. The perpetrator was somewhere close where he couldn't be seen." Down the street, Trooper heard a bass line thumping. As the brown 1962 Chevy Impala got closer, the song "Rollout" by Ludacris could be heard for an entire block.

Swoosh watched Trooper write down a geometric expression in order to calculate the possible angle. Thinking that she might ask to use the calculator on his cell phone, he cleared Teco's number.

Trooper walked over to the white chalk line on the ground and took a few steps backwards. As she turned around to face the street, she said, "I need you to do something."

"Sure."

"Ronald is two inches shorter than me." Trooper pulled out the Medical Examiner's report with the details about the gunshot wound. Then she continued, "Take this chalk and mark six inches below the neck and one third inches across from the left armpit."

As he tried to figure out Trooper's method of madness, Swoosh rubbed his forehead. He couldn't understand how she remained so calm after Ronald's death. Then at a fast pace, Trooper dashed towards the Front Page News building.

Chapter 36

"HOLD UP. SLOW DOWN ALREADY," he said pulling out his inhaler.

"No, Swoosh you stay by the chalk line." Standing in front of the Front Page News building, Trooper took off her shades. Her eyes followed the roofline of the building.

Swoosh walked over to her and asked, "You think?"

"Yep, I do. This must be the location where the shot was fired." Trooper thought it to be very odd that a newspaper building would have a 5-tier fountain and a patio full of tables with umbrellas. Once inside the Front Page News building, Trooper said, "Well, I'll be . . ."

There was a long bar with empty wooden high chairs and a blue neon sign trimmed in yellow that read "Hot Crawfish Now!"

Swoosh asked, "Do you get the feeling we stepped out of Atlanta straight into a restaurant in New Orleans?"

Trooper said, "You read my mind. Is The Paradox trying to tell us that we are cooked?"

A brunette female bartender came from around the corner and said in a southern accent, "We don't open until eleven."

"We're Detectives from Washington D.C. working with the Atlanta P.D. and we need to get on top of the roof." By the time Swoosh finished the sentence, his shiny badge was back in his black belt badge holder.

The manager greeted Trooper and Swoosh. After he led them to the fire escape, Trooper called over the radio and said, "I'd like to check out the top of the roof of the Front Page News building."

Yeomans said, "Red One, provide cover."

"10-4, Red One is moving."

Within seconds, Trooper heard the black and red police helicopter hover over the roof top. As she backed away from the building to get a better view, she saw a black rope drop from the helicopter; and a SWAT officer said, "I'm on the roof sweeping for devices."

The multi-jurisdiction team waited with baited breath for what surprise was coming next.

"SWAT to command."

"Go ahead," said Yeomans.

"Sir, the roof is clear, there's a top cover and under it is a sniper's rifle on a bipod."

Trooper and Swoosh climbed the fire escape. Within minutes, Trooper, Swoosh, Yeomans and a CSI team were also sweeping the engagement zone.

"Trooper, it's hot up here," said Swoosh.

"It's not called Hotlanta for nothing," said Yeomans.

When Trooper reached the air conditioner unit, there was a piece of metal protruding out of the roof. "It appears that something snagged this," said Trooper who bagged the small piece of cloth as evidence.

As Yeomans lifted the tarp, Trooper's cell phone vibrated.

"Hello, this is Trooper." No one said anything. "Hello!" There still was no answer, but the sound of music was in the background and the sound of men making cat calls in the distance.

Just as she was about to hang up, she heard a voice say, "Trooooperrr! You know I miss seeing you."

She froze, gripped the cell phone with both hands, and said, "You sick son of a bitch! Where are you?"

The SWAT team turned to face her.

The Paradox said, "Detective Troop, do you have to be so venomous?"

"You didn't have to kill Detective Heard. He didn't do shit to you. Won't you come face me like a real man and stop acting like a pussy."

"I will in due time. Just let me explain."

"What in the hell do you have to explain to me? I think you need to be explaining your actions to your maker."

"That also will be done in due time. Everybody wants answers, but no one wants to listen." There was a long pause; and he knew that he had her attention. "I don't have long to talk before they trace my call; so I will be quick. You still there?"

"Yeah, I'm still here," she said with her left hand held high in order to stop the SWAT team from coming any closer to her.

"Are you still on the roof?"

"Why the hell would I tell you that?"

"I will assume that is a yes. That means you've found one of my toys."

"That means you are getting sloppy, Bobby."

"First, I want you to hang up and go down to the ground level. Wait for my next call."

"I never said I was on the roof. You will have to do better than that."

"Detective Troop, if I wanted to kill you, I could have done so at the Ferst Center. Wait, maybe I could get you now," he said with a cynical laugh.

The SWAT team leader assumed that The Paradox was on the phone line with Trooper because she started to look around.

"Hello? Hello?" The line went dead.

Looking off the side of the building, Trooper watched the CSI team process the crime scene by the MARTA station. Then she climbed down the fire escape and saw a white substance by the trash dumpster. She approached the closest CSI officer who was dusting for prints and asked, "Can you get a sample of that white material over there?"

As the CSI officer nodded, Trooper's cell phone vibrated. "This is Trooper," she said ready to hear The Paradox's explanation.

"Trooper, why is Teco Jackson in New York and not with you?"

She was shocked to hear Captain Wicker's voice. *Damn he has bad timing. How did he find out that Teco is no longer in Atlanta?*

"Sir, now is not a good time, let me call you right back." She never gave him a chance to protest and ended the call.

As she waited for The Paradox to call back, she held the cell phone tightly in her hand until it vibrated. "Hello!"

"Are you alone?"

"You must think I'm an idiot."

"Detective Troop, this all started when I joined the military years ago. I was trained to do what I'm doing."

"What does killing innocent people have to do with the military?" She thought to tell him that she knew about the chess game but decided against it.

Unexpectedly, The Paradox went berserk on the phone. "I never wanted to kill those people. They are enablers of drug usage. This is about fighting the war on drugs. Will you help me?"

"You need some mental help."

"In the end, you will see that I'm the one who's sane. These people dealing drugs need to die."

"You are an idiot. It is not your job to decide the best approach for fighting the war on drugs. That's why there is a United States Drug Czar."

"Don't listen to the bureaucrats because their hands are tied. Why do you believe Teco Jackson? He and GQ have been promoted in the drug trade. Why are you protecting them when you're supposed to be on my side to annihilate their asses?"

"No, no Bobby, you have it all wrong about them. They have changed their lives."

"Bullshit! Don't play with me or I will kill you."

Deciding to fabricate a story, The Paradox said, "So why is Teco Jackson in Philadelphia as we speak? He has you fooled Detective Troop. He is no longer a runner. Teco Jackson is a Drug Lord."

This can't be. Teco is in New York?

"Are you going to help me now that your lover is sleeping with GQ?"

He is lying.

"Did I hit a nerve Detective Troop?"

"I thought you needed me? Why would you want to kill me?" asked Trooper.

"Because the game is almost over . . . You need to make your next move."

"Hello? Hello?" She stood there sick of his roller coaster ride. Then her cell phone vibrated again.

"Hello."

"Trooper, what are you trying to pull over on me?"

"Sir, we needed to protect Gail Que and keeping her in Atlanta was not a good idea."

"Says who? Teco Jackson has Gail Que in custody?" asked Captain Wicker.

"Yes sir."

"Trooper! What the hell are you running down there? This doesn't sound professional at all."

"Captain, can you save me the bullshit? Have you forgotten about Ronald?" A SWAT officer watched Trooper as she vented. "It's about time that you tell me what's really going on. I warned you before I agreed to come back to the force."

"Trooper, you get Teco Jackson back to Atlanta."

"Be up front. What does Teco really have to do with any of this?"

"What I'm about to share must stay between us only. The Paradox is not your average soldier."

"Huh? What do you mean by that? Don't hold back," she said as she paced around the 5-tier water fountain.

"He's from a special government unit called RELLIK. We don't know if he's working alone or with others from his old unit. He is out to make the United States government look bad. And when I say bad, I mean really bad."

"Captain, I have to go. I'll call you later on my decision to bring Teco back to Atlanta." Trooper observed the Atlanta PD officers working by the Marta station and the SWAT team on the roof of the Front Page News building. Glancing over to Yeomans and Swoosh who were reading a map, Trooper tried to process the magnitude of the situation. *Teco and GQ, drug lords?*

Chapter 37

AS TECO READ *The New York Times,* he waited for GQ in the lobby area of Bad Boy Entertainment Worldwide. When he looked up, GQ walked out of the elevator with an accomplished smile.

"So things must have gone well for you."

"I would say so Mr. Bodyguard," she said flirtatiously batting her eyes.

As she headed towards the exit, Teco grabbed her hand. "No, this way . . ."

She followed him out of the back door and was flummoxed because there was no limousine waiting for them. On Teco's heels, her shoes clattered against the pavement.

"Teco wait. Where is my limousine?"

Stopping in front of a black Range Rover, Teco said "I'm your driver. Now, get in."

"You could at least open my door Homicide."

As he reluctantly opened the car door for her, he said, "I told you not to call me that."

Within a few minutes, they pulled behind the Harlem YMCA where there were still a few reporters lingering around. However, Teco emerged from the car alone.

"Sir, is Miss Que in hiding? Why isn't she with you?" asked the CBS reporter.

"Sorry, no comment." Teco walked into the hotel and within a few minutes, he returned. He was extremely pleased that the reporters were gone. Opening up the back door of the Range Rover, he said, "Let's go GQ."

As they walked into the building, GQ's mind was elsewhere because Teco confiscated her cell phone. *Damn, I need to find out if Mustafa is alright. They rushed me off so fast that I didn't have time to check on him. Plus, I need to talk to Tommy; and let him know that I'm fine.*

"GQ, you have 15 minutes to pack so we can leave. I'll be right outside of your door."

She walked into the cramped hotel room with bare white walls. Putting her Kate Spade purse on the twin-size bed, she searched under the blue and pink flowery bedspread for the television remote. Upon second thought, she decided to just manually turn on the television. When she realized that none of the New York stations were carrying the Atlanta story, she decided to change into something more comfortable.

Once GQ packed, she picked up the beige hotel phone and said, "I would like to make a call to Atlanta, Georgia."

The hotel operator said, "The number please."

The phone rang three times; and GQ left Mustafa a voicemail. Then the operator dialed the second number for GQ.

"Tommy Richardson."

"How are you?"

"Gail, how are you? I've been to the office, but Linda refuses to give me any information," said Tommy sitting on a black leather loveseat in the master bedroom of his Buckhead Place townhouse.

"Tommy, I'm fine."

"Are you hurt? I've been watching CNN and hearing about this Paradox guy. None of this sits well with me. Let me fly you to my private beach house in Maui. It will be safe there." He placed his Cohiba cigar on the side of a rosewood ashtray.

"I promise; I'm fine. The Atlanta PD hired the most capable bodyguard in the world to protect me. I'm in New York," she said twirling the telephone cord between her fingers.

"Well, I can come out to visit you? I miss you Gail. I've wanted to talk with you about your fashion business. I have a sponsorship idea to pass by you. And you being my protégé not to mention my . . . well, you know—"

"Tommy . . . that's what I want to talk with you about. My feelings for you aren't tied to money or the contacts you have. I am accustomed to doing things all by myself. So, let's just focus on . . . us."

"Okay, you're making an old man feel like a teenager. What about that Mustafa guy? I don't want any trouble," he said sitting at the edge of the loveseat.

"I'm going to take care of all of that. Trust me."

"When will I see you again?"

"Soon, I'll call you later. I shouldn't be here long."

"Ciao Bella," he said in an alluring deep voice.

"What?"

"Ciao Bella means goodbye beautiful in Italian."

"So, what would I say to you?"

"You would simply say 'Ciao.'"

"Ciao," she said with her hand on her hip.

Beating on the door, Teco exclaimed, "GQ! Let's ride! We have things to do; plus, you better not be on that phone."

GQ reached for her suitcase. *Teco and I lived together too long at the SB crib back in Philly. He thinks he knows me.*

When she walked out in a pink sweat suit, he was taken off guard with how attractive she looked. That was what he liked about GQ. Her body could be totally covered, and she appeared to be wearing nothing at all.

Once they reached the lobby, Teco went to the front desk while GQ waited by the back exit.

"Checking out?" asked the female desk clerk.

Teco passed her a credit card and peered over his left and right shoulder. "Ma'am, may I have a copy of the phone bill?"

"The telephone charges are right on your receipt with your room charges," she said with a bright smile. "Please sign here."

As he walked towards the exit, Teco sucked his teeth when he saw the two long distance calls to Atlanta, Georgia.

He unlocked the black Range Rover and put their bags in the back seat. "Get in and get down like before."

As they traveled on the Jersey Turnpike, Teco said nothing. GQ felt the tension between them. So, she climbed up to the front seat to see if she could read his facial expressions. "What's wrong with you?"

"If you really must know," he said gripping his left hand tighter around the steering wheel. "I was praying for a safe trip to Philly."

"You? Praying?" she asked in disbelief. "When did you get religious?"

"When you look in the eyes of the Grim Reaper who's holding a large scythe and wearing a black hooded cloak, you learn to pray real fast."

"Boy, you ain't seen no Grim Reaper, but I feel you on the fact that prayer changes things."

"Listen, I asked you not to make any calls to Atlanta, period," he said sternly while tossing the hotel bill into her lap. Then his cell phone vibrated. "Hello."

"Teco baby, I've been trying to reach you. Are you okay?" asked Trooper sitting at the patio table outside of the Front Page News building.

"I'm better now that I'm talking to you."

There was silence. Then Trooper said, "Teco, he killed Ronald. He killed Ronald. He was just starting his career."

"I know baby, I know. Some news reporter asked me about the Detective who was killed in Atlanta. So, I called Captain Wicker."

"Are you by yourself?"

Teco cut his eyes over at GQ.

Trooper added, " . . . because we have a lot to talk about. Where are you now, baby?"

Glancing at the colorful GPS on the dashboard, Teco said, "I'm right outside of Philly."

Trooper couldn't find the words. She didn't understand how The Paradox knew that Teco was in Philadelphia. At that moment, doubt consumed Trooper's entire being.

Chapter 38

THE FOLLOWING AFTERNOON, The Paradox was ready to drop another note. This target he didn't want to kill because it was more of a souvenir for him. Goldfinger was aware that The Paradox was on his way to pick up the hired help.

When The Paradox pulled into the Overlook Atlanta apartment complex, the security guard in the booth waved him through the entrance. While sitting in the parking lot watching the fiends come and go, The Paradox dialed the number.

"Yo, this Goldfinger. Talk to me."

"Send your boy out," said The Paradox who immediately disconnected the call.

Two men wearing black sweat suits and tan Timberland boots emerged from one of the housing units. The Paradox noted that the one with the big ears carried a 9mm in his waistband.

Standing by the driver's side window of the minivan, Pie said in a Dirty South accent, "Shawty, you the big dude that put that gun to my ribs."

"My bad, it wasn't personal. What's your name?" asked The Paradox in a West Philly accent.

"They call me Pie."

"Body Rocker, what's up?" asked Goldfinger.

"Listen, no disrespect, but I don't allow any guns around when I'm on a mission," said The Paradox to Goldfinger.

Goldfinger pulled Pie to the side. The Paradox could tell that they were talking about the situation because of the hand gestures. Then Pie pulled out the 9mm and gave it to Goldfinger. After passing Pie a cell phone, Goldfinger went back into the apartment.

"Pie, I need you to put this bulletproof vest on. You drive," said The Paradox.

"So where are we going?" Pie asked as he got into the minivan.

"Do you know where Peachtree Street and Decatur intersect?"

"I know just about every street in Atlanta. I get my kicks at Lucky Shoes near Decatur Street. You hired me because I'm the best damn driver in the ATL, right?"

"Yeah, I guess."

"So what's the plan once we're there? I'm asking so I can have my escape route in mind."

"Well, it's like this. I don't know if or when my target will arrive."

"So we going to sit and wait until shawty show up?"

The Paradox offered no additional information and reached into the glove box to pull out a brown medical bottle with a clear fluid inside. Smiling as if he were a mad scientist, The Paradox put the bottle in his side pocket. Then he took out a handkerchief which he folded and placed in his shirt pocket.

As Pie turned onto Martin Luther King Drive, they headed towards downtown Atlanta. When they were on Peachtree Street, The Paradox said, "Pie, we need to park in front of the Indigo Signature Collection store in that building."

Pie did as instructed; and The Paradox went inside of the Indigo Signature Collection store hoping to get a glimpse of GQ. On his way out, The Paradox noted the security monitors behind the counter and saw that one camera was directed at the front entrance with a clear shot of the minivan where they were parked.

As The Paradox looked across the street, he saw a woman exiting out of a Lucky Shoes & Bags store.

Gwen Que took out her cell phone and dialed a number.

"Indigo Signature Collection by Frontino Lefébvre, how may I help you?"

"May I speak to Gail Que?" asked Gwen.

"I'm sorry, but Miss Que is not in the office," said Linda.

"Listen, I have been trying to reach Gail for several days and she doesn't answer her cell phone." The sun beamed down on her silky smooth skin, so Gwen leaned up against the Lucky Shoes & Bags building in order to be in the shade.

"My apologies that you can't reach Miss Que . . . She will be out of the office for an extended period of time. Do you want to speak with her Fashion Director Jerome Love?"

"Hell no, he won't tell me any information either. I'm her sister and I want some answers."

"I'm sorry, but I have strict orders not to provide any information on her whereabouts. I can assure you that your sister is doing well . . . Hello? . . . Hello?"

Gwen closed her flip phone, put it in her purse, and gathered her shopping bags. She decided to go up to GQ's office in order to speak with someone in person. *How is GQ going to invite me to come to see her and she ain't even in Atlanta? I need something to drink. It's hot as a mug out here.*

As she crossed the street, The Paradox was standing beside the minivan perpetrating as if he were enjoying the generic brand cigarette. Then he pulled out the bottle and handkerchief.

Gwen's hair bounced upon her shoulders; and she moved gracefully in hot pink sandals with each stride. The brown and pink tie dye halter dress stopped just above her knee.

GQ, yesss! It's time for you to meet your maker.

The Paradox tapped on the side of the van to alert Pie.

When The Paradox nodded in her direction, Pie smiled. *Damn, she fine.*

"Pie, start the van."

"I got it! I got it!" exclaimed Pie who turned the engine over.

Gwen didn't feel well. She didn't know if it was because she couldn't reach GQ or if she was coming down with a summer cold.

A few feet from the clothing store and in front of the bank, Gwen noticed an attractive man who looked like Issac Hayes. When she kept walking, he waved and yelled, "Gail! Gail!"

Simultaneously, Gwen felt someone grab her by the waist and press a cloth over her mouth and nose. Before she could fend off her attacker, the muscles in her body were uncontrollable as she lost all consciousness.

The Paradox hopped in the back of the minivan with his victim and shut the door; and Pie took off.

Mustafa ran after the minivan yelling "Hey! Stop that van! Hey!"

Bystanders were looking at Mustafa as if he were crazy. Mustafa almost tripped over the Lucky Shoes & Bags shopping bags that were left on the ground. He continued to run in the middle of the street until a yellow Corvette almost hit him. Then he realized that the minivan's driver was too fast.

Pie looked in the side view mirror and thought that he saw Goldfinger's brother, but he wasn't too sure who was standing in the middle of the street stopping traffic.

Mustafa patted his pants pockets and realized that he didn't have his cell phone. So, he ran over to a blond haired man who was driving a candy apple red BMW.

"Yo man, help me. Some dude just snatched up my girl!" exclaimed Mustafa.

The BMW driver wanted no dealings with what he just witnessed and rolled up his window. However, Mustafa was too quick and opened the car door. Forcefully, Mustafa pulled the man out of the BMW. As the car began to roll forward, Mustafa jumped in and gave chase after the minivan.

At the next intersection, the red BMW was cut off by a police road block before Mustafa could reach Pryor Street.

Banging on the steering wheel and the dashboard, Mustafa exclaimed, "Shit! Shit!"

The police drew their weapons on Mustafa, commanded him to exit the vehicle and lie down on the ground. By the time, Mustafa realized what transpired; there was no time for recourse. Atlanta PD handcuffed him quickly.

Damn, I don't want to go back to the chain gang. What was I thinking?

While sitting in the back of the police car, Mustafa saw that the shopping bags were still scattered on the ground. A crowd of onlookers gathered around. One of them was Tommy Richardson who shook his head from side to side.

Pulling out a pad, the police officer opened the door and said, "Son, what is your name?"

"Mustafa Muhammad. I own the new bookstore in Underground Atlanta."

The officer closed the car door and walked over to a female detective who looked over at Mustafa.

The detective passed the officer a memo pad, opened the door to the police car and said, "Hello, I'm Detective Fordham. Let me get those cuffs off of you."

Mustafa was in a daze as he emerged from the back seat of the police car.

"Mr. Muhammad, can you tell me what happened? I was passing by and saw the crowd. Several have stated that you witnessed a woman being abducted; and you were trying to go after a van. Is this true?"

"Yes, I thought I saw my girlfriend, Gail Que, being abducted."

Fordham gave him an inquisitive stare. *Why would he think Gail Que was in Atlanta? I can't reveal her true whereabouts.*

"Sir, are you sure it was her?"

Mustafa said, "Yes ma'am. This big dude who looked like a wrestler put something over her face and shoved her into a black minivan." After Mustafa completed his statement, Detective Fordham explained the situation to the owner of the BMW.

Several miles away, Pie turned off of Route 66 onto a bumpy red clay country road. The fields were barren; and three black ravens circled the clear blue skies. Coming closer to the dilapidated red barn, Pie noticed that the doors where barely attached to the hinges.

The Paradox said "Drive to the back."

"Big dude, do you need some help?"

"I'm going to open the barn door. You get the girl and bring her to me."

When Pie opened the minivan back door, he asked, "What the fuck?" The female moved around a little as she began to come out of her comatose state. Pie continued, "Man, this is that fashion chick that Goldfinger's brother keeps talking about. I ain't down with this shit." Pie reached for his piece; however, he remembered that Goldfinger confiscated it back at Overlook Atlanta apartments.

Scanning the area, Pie could not find anything to subdue The Paradox. Two shots were fired. Pow! Pow! Then The Paradox reached into the back of the minivan and retrieved from his pocket the brown medical bottle. Within minutes, Gwen was out again.

The Paradox stood there with his hands on his hips. When he grabbed Pie by the ankles, The Paradox almost forgot what it was like to drag a dead frame. At the edge of the woods, he kicked Pie's body into a ditch. Then he trotted back to the minivan and drove off while leaving a cloud of red dust in the distance.

Chapter **39**

AS "83" BY JOHN MAYER played on Q100, Yeomans knew time was of the essence in catching The Paradox before there was another tragic death. He didn't know Detective Heard that well, but it was wrong that he died in search of a mad man.

After Yeomans drove around I-285 at eight o'clock in the evening, he pulled the police car over to the emergency lane and tapped his fingers on the wheel. As the cars sped past him, the car rocked from the gust of wind. At times, Yeomans would drive around I-285 for hours just to iron out his next move on a case.

Yeomans reached in the backseat and retrieved his briefcase to look over the D.C. files because he felt there was something missing from the murder case. He pulled his brown jacket off, threw it on the passenger front seat, and rolled up the sleeves of his blue shirt. This was a normal ritual for him when he needed time to himself.

Deciding to check his messages, Yeomans flipped open his cell phone. The first message stated, "Detective Yeomans, this is Beth, GBI Forensics Firearms Examiner. Mac told me to give you a call regarding the Heard murder case. The bullet was coated with Teflon. This material serves as a lubricant in order to provide a high degree of penetrability. As you know, these types of bullets are known as cop killers and—"

Yeomans knew that Beth would go on and on, so he went to the next message. A computerized voice stated, "Look for the killer through Uncle Sam's eyes."

Yeomans asked, "What the hell . . ."

He pushed the number 4 to hear the message again. "Look for the killer through Uncle Sam's eyes."

Forgetting that he took off his jacket, Yeomans patted his shirt for his notepad and pen. Finding the writing material, he jotted the cryptic message down. Then his phone rang.

"Yeomans here."

"It's me, Fordham. Trooper and Swoosh just got back in town from Detective Heard's funeral. I can't believe it's been a week already. They say that they are hungry and want to eat."

"Let's meet at The Beautiful restaurant on Cascade in 15. At this time of night, it's not that packed with people," said Yeomans who revved the engine of the car.

"Okie-Dokie."

Emerging from the car outside of The Beautiful restaurant, Yeomans could smell the soul food. Walking up to Trooper's car, he said, "Welcome back to the ATL. I think y'all will like this place."

As they followed Yeomans into the building, they felt the mist of rain in the air. Fordham said, "Y'all wait right here; let me go get the manager."

Trooper said, "Yeomans, what do you know about soul food?"

He winked his eye and said, "Don't let the skin fool you, partner."

Swoosh laughed and said, "That's what I've been telling her for years."

Fordham came back with a waitress who was wearing a long sleeve white shirt under a sleeveless orange tunic. Fordham said, "I got us a private section away from the other customers; and I have the laptop in my backpack."

The waitress escorted the group to a long table; then she pulled out her pad with a pen and said, "May I take your drink order?"

Swoosh said, "Sure, I'll take a Bud light—"

"Sorry sir, we don't serve beer here."

"Why not?"

"Well, this is a Christian establishment. See, The Beautiful restaurant name comes from the scripture about the lame man who was outside the temple at the Beautiful gate."

Trooper said, "I remember that miraculous story. The lame man ends up walking."

"Wow, I just learned something," said Yeomans. "I thought the name came from Ray Charles' song, "You are so beautiful."

The waitress laughed and said, "I seen you all on T.V. We are so sorry for the loss of that young police officer. We have been praying for your safety. Expect a miracle on your case."

"Thanks so much. Please bring us three pitchers of water for now," said Trooper.

Fordham started the computer and said, "The psychological profile came back on The Paradox as a mixed offender. He shows signs of planning and sophisticated modus operandi. However, the assault itself is frenzied or messy. This might indicate some control over deep seated and violent fantasies which is not good for Atlanta."

"So is this guy crazy or is he playing crazy?" asked Yeomans.

"Back at Little Five Points, The Paradox told me that he was ex-military. So, I suspect that he cannot be reliably rehabilitated," said Trooper.

"The Paradox gave me another clue today. Well at least I think it was him," said Yeomans.

"And what was the message?" asked Trooper.

"The person who called me used a voice modifier. The message was 'look for the killer through Uncle Sam's eyes,'" said Yeomans.

"Can we get something to eat?" asked Swoosh.

Fordham said, "It's a buffet. You have to go stand in that long line."

Everyone walked to the buffet line except for Fordham; and the waitress brought the pitchers of water to the table.

When they returned, Trooper said, "Fordham, you have got to get up from there and get you some food."

"I can't stop. I'll get something in a minute. While you guys were gone, I found something very interesting. Trooper, you told us that Captain Wicker said The Paradox used to be with a special governmental unit called RELLIK."

After chewing a bite of sweet potato soufflé, Trooper asked, "What's your point?"

Fordham said, "I ran the word RELLIK through a word scrambler program on the internet. You will not believe the word the program returned . . ."

"I know you aren't going to leave us hanging," said Swoosh.

"Killer is the word returned."

"Ummm, are you sure this isn't a coincidence?" asked Swoosh before he took a bite of the juicy baked chicken.

"Think," said Fordham who picked up a glass of water. "It says, 'Look for the killer through Uncle Sam's eyes.' We have the word 'killer' in 'RELLIK.' We have Uncle Sam, the government. Is he saying for us to look at him or to look at the government? Surely, the government doesn't have anything to do with this twisted game. Is this another damn paradox?"

"I'm not sure," said Trooper.

Fordham tapped on the computer keyboard. "I have an idea. I have to go through the back door of this governmental website."

"I didn't know you were a techie," said Swoosh who tasted a piece of fatback for the first time. He added, "This food is really good."

Yeomans said, "Don't let her fool you. She has security clearance on just about every governmental website."

Fordham said, "Listen, this says that team RELLIK was never created. They were born."

Yeomans asked, "What the hell does that mean?"

"Shhh!" said Fordham. "RELLIK is a special unit of 5 men and 1 woman. When you see one, you see them all."

"That doesn't match. The Paradox isn't travelling with 5 people that we know of," said Swoosh.

"Will you guys let me read the rest of the passage? RELLIK was inculcated to exist and not be seen. They are the shadows of the Navy SEALS. They work for no one but the hierarchy of the LOTO federal organization."

"Huh?" asked Trooper.

"Hold up. When RELLIK is unsuccessful at the completion of a mission, LOTO pays RELLIK a visit and not just one of them, but all 6 members are subject to be replaced."

Yeomans said, "This sounds like a riddle."

Fordham continued, "RELLIK's training took place at the Naval Amphibious Base Coronado. Their most notorious mission was in South Africa. If I press this button, I can get more information."

"Can you print this off for me to read? I will have to study it," said Trooper.

"Damn!" exclaimed Fordham.

"What is it?" asked Yeomans.

"It says that I'm unauthorized."

"Shall we tell them now Swoosh?" asked Trooper.

Swoosh winked at Trooper.

"Here Yeomans, this should help us," she said passing him a sheet of paper.

"Wow! Where did you get this?" he asked.

"What is it?" asked Fordham.

"It's the chess game with Michigan versus Curran in Philadelphia in 1876. Looking at these moves, they map to this case."

Yeomans said, "Wow, this is a goldmine. Where did you guys get it?"

Trooper said, "When Ronald died, the Washington D.C. Homicide Division went into overtime in working with the United States Chess Federation. No one wants Ronald to have died in vain."

The waitress came back with the check and said, "May I help you with anything else?"

Yeomans said, "I'm glad we came to Atlanta's 'Beautiful' gate because we have accomplished a lot today."

"Well, it gets better. The manager says that your dinner is free of charge and to tell you thanks for everything you do," said the waitress who walked away.

Fordham said, "Before we leave, I have one more thing to share. While y'all were in D.C., there was a kidnapping."

"Kidnapping isn't characteristic of The Paradox," said Trooper placing her fork on her plate.

"There is a connection, however. A Good Samaritan witnessed a woman being kidnapped and chased after the minivan. He said that his girlfriend was the one abducted. Are y'all ready for this?" asked Fordham.

Trooper leaned forward and placed her elbows on the table.

"This guy says that the woman abducted was Gail Que."

"What guy?" asked Trooper picking up her glass of water.

"His name is Tim Edmonds; however, he is using a Muslim name of Mustafa Muhammad. Tim Edmonds is Tracey "Goldfinger" Edmonds older brother who was recently released from prison on a ten year bid for murder."

Yeomans added, "I've been trying to nail Tracey Edmonds for years, but nothing will stick. For years, the Edmond brothers in southwest Atlanta have been drug rivals with the drug dealers in the Fourth Ward which is in northeast Atlanta. For the kidnapping, here is a possible theory. The Paradox is linked to the rival Fourth Ward drug cartel and snatched up the new queen of the Edmond family, Gail Que. This might be the real connection to The Paradox's chess game."

"Wouldn't this make Gail Que the king and not the queen in The Paradox's twisted chess game? If The Paradox has the king, does that mean the game is over?" asked Trooper.

"Yeah, but GQ is in New York with Teco; so she couldn't have been kidnapped. Right?" asked Fordham.

"Teco moved GQ to Philadelphia," said Trooper.

Yeomans asked, "Are you sure? We can't rule out anything. How do we know that Teco isn't back in Atlanta?"

Swoosh said, "Do you guys think that The Paradox is tied to a major east coast drug supply operation? After all, this would explain why The Paradox has moved to Atlanta from Washington D.C. and before that Philly. Maybe Gail Que's fashion business is a money laundering mechanism for the Edmond crew. Trooper, what do you think?"

Damn, I wonder if The Paradox was right about Teco and GQ still running a SB drug ring. Taking a sip of her water, Trooper did not respond to Swoosh.

Chapter 40

WHEN DETECTIVE YEOMANS walked into the conference room, Trooper was on her cell phone while Fordham read a police report. Suddenly, Yeomans dropped the files onto the conference table making a loud noise to get their attention. "Good morning guys."

"This better be good," said Swoosh.

"Better than Burger King this time in the morning," said Yeomans.

"I hope it's better than a good night's sleep as well," said Swoosh rubbing his eyes.

Walking over to the computer with a piece of paper in his hand, Yeomans asked, "What do you all know about RELLIK?"

Trooper reached out for the folders. *This down south detective has become very ingenious. Does he know more than me?*

"Where did you get this information from?" asked Swoosh.

"That's not important at the moment. We'll talk about that later." Pleased that Trooper was inquisitive about his findings, Yeomans added, "I also have something else for us." Trooper, Fordham and Swoosh turned to face Yeomans, who said, "I know someone who can lead us to The Paradox; and the person is right here in Atlanta."

"What!" exclaimed Trooper.

"I believe this individual was in the military with me. The best part is that he knows the members of the RELLIK unit. There's a place not far from here called Uncle Sam's Pub. A lot of vets hang out there, as do I from time to time. I'm sure we can get some help there. I know the owner, but one thing . . ."

"Alright, what's that?" asked Trooper.

"Our city, our shakedown," he said pointing to Fordham.

Trooper and Swoosh shrugged their shoulders. "Fine with us," said Swoosh.

"Do you think it will be open this early in the morning?" asked Trooper.

"Well, this is the only twenty-four hour pub in this area. Plus, the owner lives above the place."

Within the hour, they pulled up in front of Uncle Sam's Pub in midtown; and the crowd was starting to get thin.

"They'll be closing for one hour. It's the law. So, let's be quick."

Swoosh retrieved his inhaler from his left jacket pocket because the cigarette smoke met them at the door. International flags and pictures of vets from the past graced the walls. This collection of wall decor looked donated because nothing matched.

The men who were still inside wore field jackets and combat boots. Some looked lost while others appeared drunk. The few women who were inside didn't look as if they really belonged; rather, they looked like supportive companions. A couple of guys were in wheel chairs and others walked with a limp.

Yeomans approached the bald headed bartender, who was cleaning some glasses, and asked, "What's up this morning?"

The bartender asked, "Yeo, how's it going? It's too early and too late for you to be in here. What can I do for you?"

"As a matter of fact I do need your help," said Yeomans putting both elbows on the bar.

The bartender pulled out a frosted mug from a glass cooler and poured Yeomans a glass of draft beer, but Yeomans stopped him. "I'm on the clock; just give me a coke."

At this moment, Trooper noticed that the bartender was missing two fingers on his right hand and sported a tattoo of a Georgia bulldog on his left arm. The atmosphere was hospitable as "Hanging By a Moment" by Lifehouse boomed through the jukebox.

The bartender held up the soda tap and asked, "Coke for you guys as well?"

"No, nothing for me," Trooper said who was scanning the crowded bar area.

"Sure, I'll have a glass and so will he," said Detective Fordham pointing to Swoosh. Then she eyed a man leaving the bar.

"Yes, ma'am," said the bartender.

"Do you remember that jarhead that I had to break down a while back?" asked Yeomans.

"Are you talking about that guy who was bragging that he was with some unit called RELLIK? He thought he couldn't be beat."

"Yeah, that's the one," Yeomans said taking a sip of his cold soda.

The bartender pointed to a table where two people were sitting. "I haven't seen that guy since you put those quick hands on him." The bartender laughed lightly and added, "But one of his unit members was sitting right over there forty-five minutes ago. I overheard him telling another guy about his overseas stint. Check the head."

Yeomans hopped down off of the bar stool and went into the restroom with his hand on his 9mm.

Minutes later, Yeomans came out of the restroom and said, "We must have missed him. He probably was one of the guys who left just as we pulled up. Damn!" exclaimed Yeomans.

"So, what's this guy's name?" Swoosh asked taking a swig of his coke.

"Which guy?" asked the bartender.

"Let's start with the guy that Yeomans had the encounter with," said Trooper.

"Bernardo something . . . I remember him so well because he refused to pay his tab after Yeomans jacked him up. Here, let me look because I keep a record on all unpaid tabs." He thumbed through a Rolodex and pulled out a card. "Yep, that's him. Bernardo DeLuca." He slid the card across the counter; and Trooper picked up the card first.

"I see Mr. DeLuca ran a pretty large tab," said Trooper.

"So, what about the other guy that was here tonight?" asked Swoosh.

"You know; I don't know much about that guy. He just started coming around," said the bartender.

Trooper mentally recorded the name then gave the index card to Yeomans.

"Well, we're done here, thanks Jeff," said Yeomans who was contemplating about having to update the mayor later in the afternoon.

"Sure, Yeo," said the bartender.

On the way out to the car, Swoosh took two hits of his inhaler. "Now what?" he asked.

"We head over to the courthouse to retrieve a search warrant for Mr. DeLuca," said Fordham.

"Sounds good to me," said Swoosh.

Six hours later, the police force surrounded the brick 1928 single family house on Beecher Street. The law enforcement team totalled 16 and wore black uniforms with ski masks. They were ready for action.

The Humvee with the words "Fulton County Warrant Task Force" on the doors parked on the side of the house and blocked the driveway. This operation was not a normal take down because the occupant was a possible member of the RELLIK unit.

Four officers went up to the front door with the battering ram when Trooper's thoughts flashed back to the house raid in southeast D.C. She was hoping that this house would not explode upon entry; therefore, she lingered behind hesitant to rush into the house.

On the fifth stroke, the ram slammed into the door which came off its hinges. The team rushed in like a pack of wild dogs. "It's the Fulton County Warrant Task Force, get down! Get down!" They yelled moving from room to room. "Clear!"

When an officer reached the master bedroom, a man was in the bed with his hands up. "Don't you move!" exclaimed an officer who pointed the AR-15 right at the man's head while another officer came around to cuff him.

Fordham said, "Good to see you Mr. DeLuca."

When the squad stood the man up, he didn't match the height of The Paradox's description.

As they brought the person of interest out of the house, Trooper said, "That's not our perp."

"Where you see one, you see them all. Remember?" said Swoosh.

Within the hour, they took Mr. DeLuca back to City Hall East for questioning. Observing Mr. DeLuca through the two-way mirror, Trooper noticed that he seemed not to have a care in the world.

"Trooper, this isn't good," said Swoosh.

"Why you say that?"

"If they think DeLuca is going to lead us to The Paradox, the entire team is wrong. Military protect each other."

"So, what should we do now?" she asked.

"See if we can get a piece of his ass before he leaves."

"Look how calm he is. One thing I know. Criminals lie. Always have, always will. If they didn't, our jobs would be easy," said Trooper.

"Does that apply to Mr. Jackson as well?" asked Swoosh.

Trooper gave him a stern stare. However, Swoosh gave her a look to chill.

"He knows we're watching him," said Trooper.

"He's been highly trained to deal with situations such as this. We could take him through shock treatment; and he'll still hold his freaking ground."

"So, why did we pick him up?" asked Trooper.

"He's got to know something about Bobby Stephens. I bet he's expecting a mental fight. Let's act as if we're protecting him from somebody."

"So how do you propose that we trick him?" Trooper asked with her arms folded in a discombobulated manner."

"We will use the rule of expendability."

By this time, Mac from GBI walked into the observation room. Trooper turned to Mac and said, "Good afternoon."

"What do you think he'll give up, if anything?" asked Mac.

"I can't say until I feel him out," said Trooper. "Mac, that's a nice hair cut."

"Thanks," he said in a sexy tone which made Swoosh raise an eyebrow. "So, is this our guy?"

"The Paradox, no. A member of RELLIK, yep," said Trooper.

"I always believe the good cop/bad cop technique works the best," said Mac who left to go into the interview room.

"Do you think Mac has a priapic issue?" asked Swoosh.

"Hell no. You just think he's going to make a move on me," she said.

"Mr. DeLuca, I'm GBI Agent McLaughlin. We have us a very serious matter on our hands."

"Look man. I'm not who you think I am. Just tell me what you want with me because I have to pick up my wife from work," he said looking at his watch.

"Don't worry; we've already made arrangements for her to be picked up. Our compliments . . ."

"If you harm, my woman . . ."

"What!" shouted Mac getting all in his face. "One of your team members has done enough damage. He isn't caring about the families of the ones he has killed. So don't give me that shit!"

"I told you that I'm not who you think I am."

"Let me explain something to you. We have at least ten unsolved murders across the east coast that you're about to wear because of The Paradox. Are you harboring him? If so, that's called accessory to the crime. Guess what? All the other RELLIK team members have been classified as expendable. Know the term?"

"You don't know shit about RELLIK and neither do I."

Swoosh walked into the room and said, "Wait a minute Mac. Let me talk to him." Swoosh pulled up a chair to the table, turned it around, and sat down. "Mr. DeLuca, we have some Washington D.C. federal officers in that room." He turned and pointed to the two-way mirror. "They have no problem with taking you back to D.C.; and if they do that, we can't help you at all. Let me ask you a few questions on your whereabouts on these dates and times."

"Sure, I've got nothing to hide. I've told you that I'm not the guy you're looking for."

"Agent McLoughlin, do you mind leaving the room so I can speak with Mr. DeLuca?"

"Sure, but his ass is still going down for this," Mac said on his way out of the interview door.

Back in the observation room with Trooper, Mac said, "He claims that he's not Bernardo DeLuca. So when I go back in, I want you to come in ten minutes behind me. Also, we need to find his wife and bring her here."

"I already know where she is."

"Damn Trooper, you're fast."

"When we took him down, one of the neighbors offered the information about Mrs. DeLuca . . . something to the effect that she works at a hospital. Can you send someone to pick her up? I have a tactic in mind."

"Sure, but what will we tell her?"

"Tell her that her husband is helping us to solve The Paradox case."

"Where does she work and what's her name?"

"Her name is Sandra DeLuca; and she works at Grady Hospital."

The observation room door swung open and Yeomans said, "How are you guys doing? Thanks for making the arrest while I was updating the mayor and the Feds." Then Yeomans looked through the two-way mirror. "That's not Bernardo DeLuca."

"What!" exclaimed Trooper. "You gave us the address. I double checked the warrant."

"If it's not DeLuca, we're going to be in some deep shit," said Mac.

"I think it's too late for that," said Yeomans who stormed out of the observation room into the interrogation room.

Trooper reached for her cell phone to call Teco. The case was moving so quickly that she didn't have an opportunity to find out his whereabouts and determine what he was really up to in Philadelphia.

Chapter 41

"WHY DID YOU take this long way? I know you haven't forgotten the streets around Philly," said GQ.

"I wanted to see the city. It's been a while. Plus, stopping by Mr. G.'s house is like an old habit. After all, Fatboy was my best friend," said Teco as his phone vibrated in the glove box.

"I don't know if I can face Fatboy's father. You know that I was in the car the night Fatboy died. I didn't even go to the funeral. What will his parents think of me?"

"Well, Mr. G. is like a father to me. He'll understand."

Teco was silent for a few minutes before he spoke again. "I have a few things I need to accomplish while we're here in Philly."

"We've been here several days already. What do you mean?" she asked in a very concerned tone.

"When it's all done, you'll know. I promise."

The black Range Rover turned down the 7800 block of Fayette Avenue in Mount Airy. As Teco parked in an empty spot, he noticed that a few houses were repainted; otherwise, everything was the same.

Protectively, he scanned the block before he asked GQ to get out of the SUV. With his hand on his chrome Glock 40, Teco walked behind GQ as she knocked on the door.

Teco pulled the toothpick out of his mouth because he remembered that Mr. G. thought having a toothpick without food was simply gangster. Then the door came open; and Teco thought Mrs. Gordon was going to faint.

"Jean, who is it!" yelled Mr. G.

"It's me Mr. G., your prodigal son," said Teco with a sense of pride knowing that Mr. G. would be glad to see him.

Because Mrs. Gordon was caught off guard by the visit, Mr. G. turned to his wife to ensure that she was alright.

"Boy! How the hell are you?" asked Mr. G. as he grabbed Teco around the neck. "Teco, they killed my boy. They killed my boy," he said with tears in his eyes.

"I know Mr. G. I know. GQ told me all about it." Teco noticed that Mr. G.'s hair was completely gray.

Mr. G. said, "Gail, I almost didn't recognize you. What are you doing here?"

"Well, it's a long story. I must apologize that I left for Paris without saying goodbye," said GQ as Mrs. Gordon held GQ's hand tightly.

"Mr. G., let's go over here; we have a lot to talk about," said Teco gesturing in the direction of the cherry oak dining room table.

As Mrs. Gordon sat down on the sofa with GQ, Teco walked to the window to see if there was an old ride out back being restored.

"Son, I haven't worked on a car since they took my boy."

Teco noticed Mr. G.'s doleful face. *Damn, how am I going to break the news to Mr. G? I need to brace myself for his response.*

"About Fatboy's death . . ." said Teco.

"Son, I wish I could help you. We only know what the police told us, sad to say."

Teco stared at Mr. G. for a few seconds. "What if I told you that I'm working with the police who are trying to catch his killer?" He captured Mr. G's total attention. Teco added, "Please let me explain to you what the police have found out and what we're doing about it."

"I would love to bring closure to his death. I can't figure out how he was singled out."

"Mr. G., this information stays between you and me. The person of interest is from Philadelphia. He goes by the name of The Paradox."

"The Paradox! I've been hearing something about a paradox on CNN news."

"Well, the police believe that The Paradox is out to kill the entire Strictly Business crew. You know we called it SB."

"Son, you ain't back in the streets are you? I see that bulge on your waist. And what did Fatboy have to do with SB?"

"No, I'm not back on the streets. This fool is out to kill former SB members, to include me and GQ. I think Fatboy just got in the way while he was saving GQ's life."

"Teco, if I didn't know you, I'd most likely kill you and GQ myself for getting Fatboy tangled in this mess, but I know that neither of you did this to him."

Taking a big sigh of relief, Teco pulled a badge from his shirt pocket and put it on the table. As the sun peeked through the curtains, the badge sparkled.

"Jean! Come here. This boy's a cop or something."

Mrs. Gordon exclaimed, "GQ and I are looking through the family album!" Then they heard GQ laugh.

Teco smiled, "I'm not a cop. . . . God blessed me to be an armed bodyguard. That's why I have GQ with me. She is under my custody."

"Let me see what this badge says. I'll be . . . Concealed Weapons Permit.'"

"Mr. G., I need to make a run alone." Cutting an eye at GQ, Teco said, "Can you keep an eye on her for me?"

"Sure son, go do your thing and do it well for me in memory of Fatboy."

Teco looked at Mr. G knowing what he meant. Then Teco reached down to his ankle to get his 9mm automatic pistol. "Need this?" he asked holding the gun out to Mr. G.

Mr. G smiled. "Son, I've got one; and it's a lot bigger than that little boy's gun."

"Okay, fair enough." On the way to the front door, they gave each other some dap. "Oh yeah, GQ can make no phone calls," said Teco to Mr. G. Then he said to everyone, "I'll be right back. Would you guys like a cheese steak sub?"

GQ kicked off her shoes and said, "Sure, that would be nice. Thanks."

Mrs. Gordon said, "I'm not having it. You all are eating dinner with us tonight. Where are you both staying?"

GQ said, "We are at some dump on the outskirts of Philly."

"Well, you all are staying with us. That's final. We have plenty room in the basement. We've just finished it; thank God."

In the Range Rover, Teco put on his bulletproof vest because he knew that his next stop was critical to getting GQ and his life back in order. *I have to just step out there on faith and trust God.*

Once Teco pulled in front of Young Black Mafia's (YBM) crib, he noticed that there were not many cars on the block which was different from years gone by. When he was first put down with the SB crew, Teco came to this same house to get inducted by YBM.

He walked up to the door and noted that the steps were recently cemented and the peephole was actually a hidden camera.

"Who is it?" asked a tall slender dark skinned man who was wearing a Sean John polo shirt and crown embroidered jeans.

"It's Teco."

The lock tumblers turned. Then the door flew open; and there stood Basil Fiten, Bashi Fiten's brother. "Homicide!"

"No, it's Teco, not Homicide."

Basil was happy to see him. "Man, come in."

Once inside, Teco saw that the house was renovated in a lavish modern decor with thick white custom made drapes that accented the living room furniture. When Basil locked the door, Teco noticed a 5x5 security monitor by the door.

Basil had the nerve to ask, "Who is it?"

"What's up Homicide? Where the hell you been?"

Offering him a seat on the huge white leather sofa, Basil noticed a bulge under Teco's pant leg.

"You carrying?" Basil asked eyeing Teco's ankle.

"Yeah, I have to these days." Teco placed the gun on the glass coffee table beside a Jet Magazine and remembered that GQ's taste in furniture was similar, which was odd.

"Nice piece. What is it?" Basil reached for the pistol, but Teco stopped him by placing his hand over Basil's hand.

"It's a Smith & Wesson Sigma 9 millimeter."

"Homicide, I mean Teco, what can I do for you?" asked Basil crossing his legs like a true Don and pulling out a Romeo Y Julieta Reserva Real cigar from a small wooden humidor.

"I want to talk to you about who killed your brother."

"You know damn well who killed my brother."

"Wait Basil . . ." Teco sighed deeply. "GQ did not kill Bashi. She was vindicated. You know she's out."

Basil didn't seem too surprised and rolled the cigar on the tip of his lips. "Yeah, I heard; and we put a half million bounty on her head. Why, you want the hit?" asked Basil with a cynical smile.

With his head down, Teco shook it from side to side. Then there were footsteps near the foyer staircase. Basil smiled as if he won the lottery.

The woman gazed at Teco and batted her eyes twice. She was as beautiful as the first time Teco laid eyes on her years ago.

"Hello, long time no see," said Tina Campbell, Teco's ex-girlfriend.

The little girl that was with her ran over to Basil and asked, "Daddy, daddy, can I have some ice cream please?"

Quickly, Basil opened up the Jet Magazine to conceal the gun as he put his cigar down.

"What brings you here?" asked Tina.

Perplexed at the sight of seeing Tina, Teco was lost for words.

"Teco, are you okay?" she asked.

"Yes, I'm fine. I'm just a little confused." Then Teco looked back at Basil as he played with the little girl.

"Yes, Daddy's little girl can have some ice cream. What do you say?"

"Thank you daddy." After she kissed him on the cheek, Tina and the girl went into the kitchen.

Basil held out his chest with pride as if he won the prize trophy. However, the game was not over because Teco was protecting the queen.

"Teco, let me explain. When you left Philly, Trent, Tina's brother, came to me. Well, he came to YBM for some work. I remembered that he was a great runner when he worked for you. So, we put him down; and now he's running the block in Conshohocken. I guess you can say that he took your place," Basil said with a diabolical eye gesture. He added, "Trent introduced me to Tina. And how do they say it? The rest is history."

Knowing that Basil was trying to draw him back into the street game, Teco said, "Well, that's not my business. What is my business is GQ."

"Now, you talking Homicide. Let's drink to that."

"No, no, no, not like that. You have to remove that hit."

"What the hell are you talking about?"

Holding two crystal bowls, Tina and her daughter came back into the living room.

Waiting for the girls to get upstairs, Teco said, "GQ didn't kill Bashi." Teco took off his vest and pulled up his shirt to show Basil his wounds. When he did, Basil saw the scar from the bullet.

"What happened and who did it?" asked Basil.

"I believe the guy who killed Bashi shot me when I was working back in D.C. The person I'm looking for is Bobby Stephens from off the block in Conshohocken."

Basil said, "So tell me what's up with that badge?"

Teco was bewildered that Basil wasn't shocked when he mentioned Bobby's name. "Basil, I'm an armed bodyguard." He paused hoping that Basil would pick up on the fact that he was licensed to kill.

Teco added, "When I was hospitalized for the gunshot, the Feds found Bashi's SB ring with my personal property. They now believe that I had something to do with Bashi's murder. Basil, I'm protecting GQ, so that she can prove my innocence. You have to remove that bounty."

A scowl expression came over Basil's face. *How did Teco end up with my brother's SB ring?*

Basil said, "I'm sorry. It's a complicated matter, but I'll try."

Neither of them knew that Tina was standing at the foot of the steps. She wondered if she married the wrong man. Then she saw Teco stand and holster the Sigma 9mm.

"Basil, I believe my job is done here. Just know that GQ's safety is my top priority. How do they say it? . . . by any means necessary."

"Teco, one more thing before you leave . . ."

Teco turned and said, "Yeah what's up?"

Basil picked up his cigar, walked over to a box of matches on the marble fireplace mantel and lit the cigar. "Do you remember when my brother told you to leave Bobby alone; and let it go?"

"Yeah, what about it?"

"We knew that Bobby was in the military working on a drug task force," he said while opening up the liquor cabinet doors.

"I know that already."

"What you don't know is that the Feds were about to take YBM and SB down; and we needed them off our tracks. Do you also remember Candi? Bashi took her off the streets."

"Yeah, she was murdered in D.C."

Basil took a drag of the cigar and a sip of Hennessey Black cognac. "Well, back in the day, YBM plotted for Candi and Bobby to hook up. We knew that Candi would be able to rope Bobby into getting hooked on drugs. Candi was a dimepiece. What man could resist her?" Basil laughed softly.

"So . . . that's no motive for going after the SB crew."

"Because of his drug addiction, Bobby lost everything and any chance he might have had getting a job with any law enforcement agency fighting the so called war on drugs."

"What does that have to do with me?"

"We had Bobby under control until that beat down you gave him. If I were a betting man, I'd say that he's on a mission to prove that SB set him up. My brother is already gone; and that leaves the next SB boss . . . you or GQ. To him, SB still exists."

"Oh really . . . then that gives you even more reason to take that hit off of GQ."

"Not really. Life goes on my friend. If you're thinking about going after him you might want to be careful. You have to think like him."

"No, maybe I need to think like you." Teco put back on his jacket and revealed his huge sidearm. On the way out, Teco bumped into Tina by the stairwell. Because of the information he gathered, Teco knew that he had to come up with a better plan or get GQ out of Philly. The key was getting GQ to cooperate.

Chapter 42

THE NEXT DAY, TECO ENJOYED the beautiful afternoon as the lucent sun warmed his smooth skin. He leaned against the hood of the Range Rover while watching two northern oriole songbirds dancing in the air. Surveying the area around the home on Violet Street in Norristown, Pennsylvania, Teco noticed an unmarked blue Ford Crown Victoria drive by him twice. Then the blue Ford came to a complete stop facing away from the house.

Who in the hell is in that car? He swiftly moved toward the house and knocked on the door.

"Yes, may I help you young man?" asked GQ's grandmother in a feeble voice.

"Yes ma'am, I'm here for Gail."

GQ came from behind the eighty year old woman, opened the door wider and said, "Nana, he's with me." When GQ saw Teco's facial expression, she became gravely concerned.

"Look, we need to jet," he said peeking through the thick red and blue tapestry drapes.

In a soft whisper, GQ asked, "Teco, what's wrong?"

Sensing trouble, GQ's grandmother asked, "Son, are you alright?"

"Nana, he's fine. This is my bodyguard, Teco Jackson. Teco, this is my Nana, Ms. Que."

Teco simply glanced over his shoulder, smiled at the gray haired woman, and said, "Gail, we need to go. You are lucky that I agreed to let you come here in the first place. Now, there's an unmarked car at the corner."

Almost pushing Teco out of the way so that she could see the car, GQ asked, "Where?"

"See that blue car by the stop sign?" When he turned around, he was shocked that the inside was much larger than the outside of the home. The vintage furniture was made of oak wood. The blue velvet sofa and loveseat still sported the classic plastic covering for protection from dust. On the wall was a picture of John F. Kennedy and Dr. Martin Luther King, Jr.

Two burning candles were on the table; and behind the candles was a picture of Jesus Christ on the cross. Around the candles were a lot of pictures which Teco thought to be GQ's family. He bent over to have a closer look. On one of the photographs, there were two little girls playing on a seesaw; and they were identical.

As he reached to pick up the picture, GQ's grandmother said, "Young man, please don't touch my pictures. That's my anointed prayer table; no one touches that table but me. I have a question for you. Why are you with my grandchild? I know who you are, son. I was there at her court trial when you said those awful things about her. Don't you think you've done enough to hurt us?"

Teco quickly removed his hand as GQ said, "Nana! Be nice."

"Gail, are you sure you're okay honey?"

"Nana, I'm fine. I'll talk to you about it later. The past is behind me. Teco and I have forgiven each other; and I ask that you do the same."

"Well, God knows that I believe in the power of forgiveness; seventy times seven, you know."

"Yes Nana, I know."

"Who are the twin girls in the picture?" asked Teco.

"Gail didn't tell you? That's her twin sister, Gwen," said the grandmother with pride.

"What?" asked Teco looking at GQ.

"I didn't know how to tell you. I really need to see her before we leave Philly," said GQ.

"It's not going to happen on this visit. It's not safe," whispered Teco to GQ.

"Well Nana, I need to go. If you hear from Gwen call my office number right away. Okay, Nana?"

"Baby you sure you and your sister are okay?" she asked looking at Teco.

"Yes, Ma'am." GQ kissed her grandmother on the cheek.

On the way out of the door, Teco made sure no one saw him taking his heater out of its holster. Then he put the pistol inside the front of his pants. Once outside, he rushed GQ to the front passenger side. Then he ran around to the driver side. The SUV took off headed back to Philly. While they were on the back roads, GQ just gazed out of the window enjoying the beautiful landscape. Neither of them said a word to each other about Gwen until Teco turned the music down which was playing, "Who Can I Run To" by Xscape.

"Where do you think your sister is?" asked Teco.

"How in the hell am I supposed to know? You won't even let me go search for her."

"She's your sister, but you're my concern. Sorry to sound so harsh."

"Look Teco, if I knew where she was, don't you think I would have been over there by now?"

Teco tried his best not to get caught into the Broad Street mid-afternoon rush hour traffic, but it was too late. On top of that, he noticed that there was an accident up ahead of them which caused the traffic to move even slower.

As they were approaching Spring Garden Street, the gridlock started to undo itself, but then slowed down to a complete standstill leaving them in the middle of an intersection. GQ shifted in her seat and gripped her purse. *I need to find some way to get away from his ass and find my sister. It's time for me to take charge of my own moves while we're here in Philly.*

Teco rolled the window down and stuck his head out so that he could get a better view of what was the hold up. Before Teco could get his head back in the SUV, GQ quickly jumped out running towards the Southeastern Pennsylvania Transportation Agency (SEPTA) subway station.

"Gail wait! Shit!" Teco put the vehicle in park and snatched the key out of the ignition. Then he jumped out and slammed the door so hard that the window vibrated. In the process of chasing GQ, Teco almost fell when his right foot slipped into a pothole. As Teco stumbled to keep his balance, his cell phone came out of its cradle that was on his belt. The phone hit the ground and slid into a gutter.

Teco stopped in his tracks after he gained his balance and put his hands on his hips. "I'll be damned. Shit!" Then he gave chase after GQ. While he ran down the steps, he skipped a few and tripped over others. Making sure that the he kept his hand on the railing, Teco almost broke his ankle on the bottom step. As he limped to the turnstile, he jumped over it landing on his right foot to support his body. In a fast hopping pace, he rushed to the passenger platform. Looking around and turning in circles, there was no sign of GQ. While he watched the train depart, Teco said, "Shit! Shit! Shit!"

A lot of people were watching him as if he were crazy. Teco pulled out two dollars and gave the money to the attendant.

Even though Teco began to get upset, he was glad that his ankle wasn't as bad as he thought. When he reached ground level, he noticed that a blue Ford Crown Victoria car was behind his rental. *Oh great.*

The traffic cop was peeking inside of the Range Rover. As Teco approached the SUV, the cop said, "Is this your vehicle, sir?"

"Yes sir."

When Teco displayed his badge, the cop asked, "Are you an officer?"

"No, I'm a bodyguard. Let me get my credentials for you." With his right hand in full view, Teco reached into his pocket and handed his papers to the cop.

Then the cop said, "Mr. Jackson, would you follow me to the station. It's right down the street on 8th and Race Street."

"Sure."

While driving behind the blue police car, Teco contemplated a great deal of things; however, he was mostly ticked off with GQ because he didn't have plans to spend another day in the City of Brotherly Love.

Once he parked in the precinct parking lot, Teco placed his gun in a black bag under the driver seat. Then the traffic cop directed him into a side door that read "Prisoners Only" and up a flight of stairs to the main lobby.

"Mr. Jackson, you can have a seat over there," said the cop.

The building smelled of mildew. When Teco sat down with his legs wide open and his head bowed, he heard a voice say, "Mr. Jackson. I'm Officer Mortin with Internal Affairs. Detective Yeomans called and said that you might be in town. We have policies when conducting multi-jurisdiction operations." Officer Mortin cleared his throat. "You have to register your weapon with us as well."

"I'm not here on a job," said Teco.

"Are you carrying a weapon?" he asked making more of a statement than asking a question as he looked Teco up and down. "That's what I thought." Turning to the counter, Officer Mortin said, "Ms. Russo, please give Mr. Jackson the proper paperwork." Turning back to Teco, he said, "I see you are well connected with big people. Welcome home and be careful."

What the hell is he talking about, well connected? What does he know that I don't?

Ms. Russo passed Teco the papers and said, "You can have a seat over there and fill them out."

She doesn't even recognize me from years ago.

Ms. Russo checked out Teco's physique. *Nice ass. Damn, he looks very familiar.* She raised an eyebrow and proceeded to do her job.

Even though Teco was in a hurry to find GQ, filling out the paperwork took twenty minutes. As he walked up to the counter, Ms. Russo tapped a BIC ink pen on the wooden counter.

"Thank you sir. That will be all."

Teco stood there and Ms. Russo looked at him. "Is there something else I can do for you?"

"So Ms. Russo, how have you been?"

"Excuse me, but do I know you?"

"Well, not exactly. A few years ago you told me, 'When you get tired of playing with little girls, come back and you'll show me how a real woman hits it. Then I told you—"

"Your shoe size is a thirteen." They laughed. "Yeah, how could I forget that cute little scar under your eye? I remember you now. You dropped five thousand on the counter like it was candy."

Teco smiled.

"So now you're on our side of the fence? I'm very impressed."

"Well, a lot has transpired since then. I moved to Washington, D.C. Now, I'm in Atlanta, Georgia working as a consultant on a major case. I'm protecting a key witness," he said stretching the truth.

"Wow! I must say that's admirable of you."

Teco thought about GQ, pulled out his business card, gave it to Ms. Russo and said, "I need to run."

"How long are you in Philly?"

As he headed towards the door, he said, "Not long, I hope."

Chapter 43

TECO SAT in the precinct parking lot trying to think of where GQ could have possibly gone. *Did GQ go to find her sister? Did she go to Frontino Lefébvre's Philly office? I know where she went.* Then his plan to snatch up GQ unfolded.

Within the hour, Teco sat in the Range Rover while watching the dope fiends at the top of the hill in Conshohocken. Because the sun was setting, he knew that the runners would be calling it a day soon. This was the perfect location to stake-out the area in order to find GQ.

Then there was a tap on the car window. "Yo, I'll give you 5 dime bags if you let me rent your car for a few hours."

Teco turned; and thought he saw a ghost. Rolling down the car window, Teco asked, "What's up Trent?"

Trent didn't know if he should hug Teco or act as if it wasn't a big thing. However, Teco beat Trent to the punch and leaned over to give him a strong manly hug.

"Homicide, you're the last person I expected to see," said the young man with a gangster accent.

"Yeah, I know. I can tell by the look on your face." They both laughed as the night time stragglers watched the car under the street lights.

Then a female walked up to Trent.

"Homicide, hold up," said Trent who walked over to the cut to serve her some dope. Teco was torn between staying in Conshohocken to rescue Trent and leaving Philly to save GQ.

When Trent came back, he showed the brightest smile ever. Putting a wad of cash in his pocket like one of the big boys, Trent didn't look surprised that five rough guys were scoping him out.

Teco said, "Don't you think you've got too much money on you?"

Trent leaned on the window seal of the SUV, showed Teco the black automatic pistol on his hip and said, "I don't worry about that."

"I see. Is that supposed to protect you?"

Trent nodded towards, the boys behind him and said, "That's my protection." Teco was hoping that narcotic officers weren't in the black SUV down the street. Trent added, "So, what brings you back to the block?"

"I have some old business to take care of." Giving Trent the brotherly stare, Teco said, "When are you going to get out of the game? If you don't you'll find yourself—"

"Wait a minute, bro. I know you ain't trying to tell me about getting out of the game."

"Well, as a matter of fact, I am. Let me guess. You trying to get rich?" he asked motioning for Trent to join him inside the SUV.

Trent went to the front passenger's door, sat down, and said, "You the one who taught me the game."

"Yes I did; and I'm sorry for doing so."

"I'm not!" exclaimed Trent. "It pays quite well. As you used to say, 'It's Strictly Business.'"

"Man, I lost a good friend to the game."

"I know. My sister, Tina, married his brother, Basil. Look, I'm not Bashi. Speaking of SB, that's messed up that they let GQ go. Ain't it?"

"Well, that's why I'm here. Have you seen her around?"

"I wouldn't know her if I saw her, but I know some people who would like to meet her."

"Yeah, I know a lot of people who want to meet her too. Trent, get out of the game. It's for your own good. Save your sister the grief."

"When you got something better for me to do, call me."

"Now that's a good idea. I'm an armed bodyguard. When I get established I want you to join me. Bet?"

"Bet," said Trent who got out of the SUV and walked into the neighborhood bar.

Several minutes later, a taxi pulled up and turned off its lights just before Teco reached for the Range Rover visor. Then GQ emerged from the taxi cab wearing a short orange baby doll dress. Even though Teco was ready to snatch her up, he kept his composure. *I'll be damned.* Teco watched GQ as she spoke to the driver, got out of the cab, and walked into the bar.

Teco felt as if he were on a real stakeout and wished for some coffee and donuts. Within the hour, GQ walked out of the bar and got into the cab. The driver pulled off without asking her for a destination. GQ didn't say anything because he seemed to be headed in the right direction towards Philly. GQ felt slightly nervous. As she turned around, she observed a black SUV tailing the cab. She knocked on the dividing Plexiglas and said, "Cabie, turn right on the next block."

The driver kept going in the direction of Philly.

GQ hit the Plexiglas once more. "Did you hear me?"

The driver slid the window open and GQ came close to talk to him. Before she could say another word, the driver said, "Sit your ass back and chill out. You really think this shit is a game. Don't you?"

"What did you do with the cab driver?"

In a thuggish tone, he said, "What do you think? I killed him and put him in the trunk."

"You're crazy. Let me out of this damn cab," she said pulling on the door handles. However, the child safety lock was engaged.

"GQ calm down. He's behind us in the Range Rover. Do you understand that I'm trying to keep your ass alive and—"

"No you're not! Don't hand me that bullshit because you're trying to save your own ass while I'm trying to save my sister from the streets."

Teco slowed down the cab as he crossed over the Philadelphia city limits. Then he pulled onto the side of the road. Taking off a hat and a jacket, Teco passed it to the taxi driver and gave him $200. After opening the back door, Teco escorted GQ to the backseat of the Range Rover and engaged the child safety lock.

While they were riding down Germantown Avenue, a brown colored Honda Civic pulled up next to them as they were stopping for a red light. Teco glanced over at the driver, but the windows were tinted. When Teco pulled up to get a closer look, he knew that something was wrong.

"GQ, get down on the floor, now! Hurry! Hurry!" Teco exclaimed as he snatched out his Glock 40.

The SUV behind the Range Rover was mighty close on the bumper. Teco hoped the traffic light would change; and it did. The Honda Civic took off ahead and pulled in front of the Range Rover. Then Teco saw the Civic's brake lights.

As Teco rolled down the window, Teco and GQ felt a hard bump against the back which caused Teco's head to jerk.

"What's going on?" asked GQ concerned for their welfare.

"Just brace yourself!"

Teco watched as the Civic's reverse lights illuminated. He slammed the Range Rover into reverse, pushed the pedal to the floor, pointed his chrome Glock 40 out of the window, and fired down on the Honda Civic's back window. Simultaneously, a street thug on foot approached the passenger side of the Range Rover. There was a loud crashing sound mixed with the screeching of tires. A piece of glass sliced the right side of Teco's face. GQ yelled out loud while Teco aimed his 40 caliber pistol across his arm and returned fire. Pow! Pow! The last shot hit the guy on foot in the face causing blood to splatter.

While dodging the hail of bullets, the Honda Civic violently crashed into parked cars on the right side of the street. Teco put the Range Rover into drive; and smoke from the squealing tires filled the air. When Teco passed the Civic, the Range Rover clipped the front end of the Civic sending it into more parked cars on the right. Then the Germantown police came out of the police precinct parking lot rushing up to the scene with blue lights blazing and sirens blaring.

Continuing to drive towards the motel to get their luggage, neither Teco nor GQ said a word. Teco didn't park in the front of the motel because he didn't want anyone to see the damages to the Range Rover. So, he drove into the back entrance of the garage and parked the front end of the car to the wall.

Before they got out of the SUV, GQ said, "How did he find us?"

"GQ, I don't think that was The Paradox."

"Well, who the hell was it?" she asked dabbing at the cut on the side of her face.

Teco sighed. "I went to see Basil. He said that YBM has a hit out on you. I tried to tell him that you didn't murder Bashi, but that was useless."

"If you didn't go talk to him, he would have never known that I was here."

"You are the one who went back to the block which could have started this entire chain of events. You need to look at the fact that you are alive."

GQ didn't know what to say because she actually agreed with him. She was beginning to appreciate his powerful control over the situation. "Why are you so insecure?"

In disbelief he said, "You have got to be kidding me. I almost lost my life two, maybe three, times. Who knows how many times you almost lost yours. Now, let's go."

When they reached the second floor, Teco checked the corner of the ceiling and noticed that the mini cameras that he installed were gone. "Gail, get behind me," he said pulling out his gun.

"What now!"

"Just stay behind me." Every few steps they took, Teco glanced behind them. When they reached the end of the hall to their suite, the second camera Teco installed was also gone.

This is just more of Teco's bodyguard bull.

Once inside the two bedroom suite, Teco checked his laptop in the common area to view the video recording in order to see who removed the cameras. "Pack fast. We have to get out of Philly. I'll tell Mr. G. that we won't be staying with them."

GQ said, "I'm sick and tired of your controlling bullshit. If you haven't noticed, we're in this shit together."

"What are you talking about now?"

"Your bullshit . . . I can't go here or there without you."

"Okay, I tell you what. Go ahead and leave, but don't call me when your ass gets into trouble." Sitting down in front of his computer, he added, "And why are you taking off your earrings and necklace?"

"Don't let my looks fool you because I still got skills and can handle things myself."

"Yeah, just like you did when you were with my homie, Fatboy, right?" he asked with vexation.

"No the hell you didn't," she said acting as if she were about to square off with him.

"Who do you think I'm talking to?" he asked standing up.

"You think I've gotten soft, don't you?" she said walking towards him.

"You better not buck on me."

When GQ stepped into Teco's personal space, he lifted GQ by her waist, spun her around and pressed her back against the wall. He moved so fast that GQ didn't have time to react. She gasped passionately; and their lips locked in a very intense kiss as his hands caressed her tight breast.

As she let out a deep moan of enjoyable pleasure, GQ felt his bulge pressing against her inner right thigh. Flashes of Teco dancing on the stage of a male exotic dance club jolted through her mind. She reached down to feel him grow and loosened his belt.

After his pants dropped to the ground, Teco pulled up her baby doll dress. When he saw her black lace panties, his hands pulled her bottom closer to him. Then he slid her panties to the side, nibbled on her neck, and lifted her up.

Entering into her paradise, he couldn't believe how good she felt and smelled. They panted as her back went up and down the wall. When she began to shake in ecstasy, reality hit him and he exited her wonderland. Hoping this was a dream, Teco was afraid to open his eyes. When he did, GQ was still braced against the wall with her legs around his waist looking sexier than ever.

"I'm so sorry. I . . . I shouldn't have. I apologize if I went too far," he said wiping the sweet nectar of her kisses from his mouth.

GQ stood and straightened her dress and said, "I'm not, but you haven't changed. All you ever do is hit and run. I hate you Homicide." Then she ran into the adjourning bedroom and slammed the door. Bam!

Chapter 44

TECO STOOD in the common area of the motel suite with his hands raised. *Damn, what did I do wrong?* He paced the floor charging enough static electricity from the carpet to cause a surprising shock when he picked up his laptop. Jumping back, he exclaimed. "Shit!"

He knew that he needed to call Trooper and inform her about his romantic encounter with GQ. So, he rehearsed what he was going to say.

"Trooper baby, it happened like this. No, no, Trooper, I have something to tell you because I want to always be honest. No, no, no, Trooper, when GQ and I . . . Damn!" Teco's fist went down hard against the coffee table. Ready to make the call, he held the motel phone in his hand; but for some reason, his fingers would not dial her number.

As the phone rang, he looked at his time piece. At that moment, Teco realized the hour was one in the morning; and the crystal on his watch was cracked.

The man who answered the phone sounded disoriented. "Hello."

Teco paused when he heard a female's voice in the background say, "Baby, who is it?"

He started to hang up but thought otherwise. "Hello, Mr. G."

"Who is this?" asked Mr. G. trying to read the time on the digital clock.

"Mr. G., it's me Teco. I don't mean to bother you so late, but I need—"

"Son, are you alright? Are you in trouble?" he asked turning on the nightstand light.

"No sir, well not exactly," said Teco sitting down on the sofa chair.

"What do you mean?" Teco paused again not knowing where to start. "Teco, you still there?" Mr. G. sighed heavily. "Are you sure that you're alright?" he said sitting upright in the bed.

"Yes, yes, we're both fine." Teco walked Mr. G. through the excruciating details of the shootout. Pacing the floor and switching the phone from ear to ear, Teco rubbed his neck. "Mr. G., the Fiten brothers were my friends. Well, I thought they were. It's bothering me what the repercussions will be since I don't run the streets anymore."

"You're doing the right things and have changed for the betterment of society at large. Doing the right things don't always come easy, son."

"The police know that I'm in town because I had to register my gun. But tonight, I didn't follow police procedure. I should have given a statement; however, I just panicked like I used to do back in the day."

"You told me that you are a licensed armed bodyguard. Your first priority is the safety of GQ. In the morning, go down to the police station and give your statement. After all, you are working one of the most publicized murder cases since the OJ Simpson trial."

"Because of how I handled the situation tonight, does that make me like the Fiten posse? Have I really changed Mr. G?"

"Son, I can't answer that for you. Only you can."

Teco sighed with his hand on his forehead. "Damn, Mr. G. Excuse me," he said respecting the only father figure he knew. "How did I get caught back into the streets so fast? If this is tied to the hit on GQ; and I killed one of their boys, they'll want some get back."

At that moment, Teco could hear Bashi's voice from the grave. *SB for life.* These were the exact words Bashi said on the day that Teco was first put down.

Mr. G. said, "Son, know that it's a game between you and those brothers. What has happened can't be undone. After you make your police statement, I suggest that you leave Philly. It's okay to run in order to stay alive. If the Fiten boys find you, they will kill you or you will have to kill not just one brother, but all of them. Are you ready for that burden?"

Teco knew that Mr. G. was right. Only one choice remained and that was to handle his business. "Mr. G. thanks. I'm sorry for waking you. I will not be coming over to stay with you this trip."

"Son, remember this. Now that you have started a legitimate job, you must establish good work ethics. It's not always about the money. It's about making a difference in this world. Son?"

"Yes sir."

"It's not what you cop. It's what you keep. Make sense?"

"Yes sir."

"Things will be okay. I have to get back to bed; so that I'm not late for work in the morning. Son, continue to do the right thing."

"I will. I love you, Mr. G."

"I love you too, Teco."

As Teco put the phone on the receiver, he heard Bashi's voice again. *SB for Life.* Teco picked up his gun and knocked on GQ's door.

"Yes." She sounded half asleep.

"Pack your things. We're relocating. Be ready in 15 minutes," he said sternly. Then he remembered that his surveillance mini cameras were missing.

Within an hour, they were getting off of the motel elevator and walking towards the SUV. While Teco was putting their luggage in the back of the Range Rover, a black van pulled up and stopped directly in front of them. Two men jumped out. As Teco reached for his gun, one of the men pulled out a Saber Taser and stunned Teco who fell to the ground in a spasm.

GQ just stood there petrified.

Holding a gun to her head, one of the men said, "Ms Que, please get in the van or you'll end up like Mr. Jackson." After GQ got into the van, the two men picked up Teco's limp body and put him in the back of the van.

The man said, "This won't kill you, but if you don't drink it . . ." He engaged a bullet into the chamber. ". . . This will."

GQ took the cup and drank the strawberry flavored liquid.

Speaking to his partner, the man said, "I'll drive the van; you get the Range Rover and follow me."

THE VICE ADMIRAL, who was overseeing the mission of Team RELLIK, sat in his Washington, D.C. office waiting for a classified package. He hoped that the files were not intercepted or compromised by a team with higher authority such as the CIA.

There was a soft knock on the door; and he said, "About time." He wondered why his executive assistant didn't let him know that the Special Forces chief warrant officer (CWO) was here. Clearing his throat before he spoke, he said, "Come in."

When R-3, the only female in Team RELLIK, walked in empty handed, a dead look came upon his face. She said, "Sir, I mean not to bother you at such a late hour."

The CWO, his partner, walked in with a boldface smile knowing that the vice admiral would be agitated that R-3 disregarded the rule about unannounced visits. However, the vice admiral wondered if he should create his own file on her; but then again, he knew that she was just as good as he, if not better.

"Well since you are here, please have a seat," said the vice admiral who gestured his hand to plush black chairs in front of his mahogany desk.

"Thank you kindly," she said taking a seat on his left because she knew that was his weak side; everybody has one.

"So why am I so deeply honored by your visit?" asked the vice admiral.

"I'd like to speak with you about R-2 and R-4. We are the final three members of RELLIK. I'm here to understand why RELLIK members are vanishing into thin air. Have you heard from R-4?" she asked.

The vice admiral noticed that she rotated a signet ring in an upright position on her right ring finger. He said, "Let me address your first concern about the safety of RELLIK members. You and the others were informed of the risks before joining this elite group. R-2 is in Atlanta, Georgia on a military leave visiting his foster brothers. R-4, well how can I put this?"

"Is it true that R-4 is a suspect in the serial killings in Atlanta, Georgia?" she asked leaning forward.

"The local authorities have no tangible evidence or they would have arrested him by now."

With sincerity, she said, "He is capable of murder; you know."

"As you all are . . . R-4 contacted me a while back. I advised him to turn himself in."

"How can you be sure that he is acting alone since R-2 is also in Atlanta, Georgia?"

"R-4 admitted to me that he was responsible. I have no reason to believe that anyone else is involved."

"So, why won't you turn him in?" she asked crossing her legs.

"It's much too complicated. Besides, it was an off the record confession by a man who is a drug addict. I'd say that he was out of his mind . . . insane."

"I don't believe it. R-4 would never turn his back on the war on drugs. He was too passionate for the cause. Have you forgotten? He was convicted as a 20th Century Robin Hood because he was protecting foreign villages from the drug cartels."

"His methods were and still are unorthodox. Don't let your personal feelings get in the way of the facts."

The voice on the intercom broke the tension. "Sir, the package you've been waiting for has arrived."

"Thank you. Can you bring it in please?"

His executive assistant came in with the folders in a white envelope wrapped with a red band of tape.

The vice admiral loosened his tie and unbuttoned his top button on his white shirt. Pulling out a stainless steel letter opener, he read out the names on each file. "Hanae Troop, lieutenant of the Homicide Division from Washington D.C.; Gail Indigo Que, Fashion Designer from Atlanta, Georgia; and Teco Jackson, job unknown and current residence unknown." He threw the files on his desk. "What do these civilians have to do with this mission?"

The CWO didn't know how to answer him.

R-3 reached over to read the files herself. "Holy shit!" she exclaimed, "the instructions are as follows: 'Do not kill Teco Jackson. With this file is a set of Teco Jackson's transferrable finger prints. The Liquidator is to put the finger prints on a clean weapon before she terminates Federal Agents Rozier and Mullis. These two agents are sending classified information about Team RELLIK to authorities in Atlanta, Georgia. This multi-jurisdiction operation is too close in capturing R-4, who is capable of turning states evidence against the very people who trained him.'"

The vice admiral held a remote and pressed a button to get into his closet chamber behind him. He came out with a black cell phone.

"What are you doing?" she asked standing up while the CWO passed the vice admiral a number. She knew that the calls from the device were untraceable.

"My dear, the train has already left the station," said the vice admiral.

She said, "Your rank is commissioned by the President of the United States for Pete's sake. This can't be a Presidential order."

"Don't tell me how to do my job."

"Damn it! I'm not trying to tell you how to do your job. I'm the one that has the most to lose!"

"You listen to me and hear me damn good. We are no longer a RELLIK unit. RELLIK is no more because of a lack of governmental funding. So, I advise you to put it behind you. We are a part of a more classified operation; and that ring you are wearing signifies your commitment to a higher order."

Backing down a bit, she said, "I know; however, I have also pledged a vow to RELLIK."

The CWO turned to the vice admiral and said, "I told you so."

Pushing the last button, the vice admiral placed the phone to his right ear as she, now known as The Liquidator, looked at the photos of her next two targets.

Chapter 45

IN THE CONFERENCE ROOM at City Hall East, Trooper typed on the computer keyboard trying to ascertain the details about RELLIK's significance to the case. Then her cell phone rang.

"Hello."

The computer generated voice stated, "This is your last and final warning. Leave this case alone or you will have to face me; and I am nothing like the members of RELLIK. You are the one who can save Teco Jackson and Detective Marcus Brown. This is a good time to take a vacation." Then the line dropped.

Damn, who in the hell was that? Checking the caller-id on her cell phone, the number read "Unknown."

Swoosh, Fordham and Yeomans entered the room and took a seat around the conference table. Yeomans asked, "Any luck?"

"No, not yet. Oh wait. Look at this fax that just came in from Federal Agent Rozier," Trooper said.

RELLIK is the code name for the Key International Lead Littoral Elite Regimen. The primary mission of RELLIK is to (1) trace the illegal drug supply chain from the producers to the consumers and (2) report recommendations to the United Nations Office on Drugs and Crime on how to best eradicate the drug trade.

The RELLIK unit is a paradoxical project that appears to be operating contradictorily to international law but is in all actuality working within military parameters. RELLIK officials will never allow the mission to fail because it is aligned with the policies of the United Nations Commission on Narcotic Drugs.

"This isn't the same information, we received before," said Trooper.

"This is huge," said Yeomans.

"Damn right, it is. Y'all are from D.C., can't you contact the U.N. to find out what this really means?" asked Fordham pointing to Trooper and Swoosh.

"Wait a minute now," said Swoosh, "We have no control over the United Nations. We're not that plugged in."

"Have any of you worked with the United Nations Office on Drugs and Crime?"

"No, but it says right here that the United Nations Office on Drugs and Crime is a global leader in the fight against illicit drugs and international crime. Oh my . . ." said Trooper.

"What's that?" asked Fordham.

"The document goes on to say that the United Nations Office on Drugs and Crime works with countries to develop alternative, sustainable livelihoods for farmers and others involved in drug production. You know, we are so busy fighting crime in our own backyard that I never stopped to think about the beginning of the drug supply chain."

"I'll be damn. Why haven't I heard of this organization before?" asked Yeomans.

"Back in Little Five Points, The Paradox told me that he was fighting the war on drugs. If he is a part of RELLIK, this document has to be true," said Trooper taking a bite of her Snickers bar.

"Are you serious? You talk like The Paradox is doing an honorable thing," said Yeomans.

"I'm not saying that The Paradox is honorable. I'm saying that RELLIK's mission is honorable. How did things go so wrong?"

There was a knock on the glass door. A female mail carrier pushed an iron silver utility mail cart up to the threshold. Opening the door, she asked, "Is there a Lieutenant Troop here?"

"Yes, right here," she said reaching for the red, white and blue overnight package which showed no return address. "Has this been cleared?"

"Yes ma'am," said the mail carrier leaving the room.

After examining both sides of the envelope, Trooper pulled on the little red tab. She retrieved a picture and a note. "The Paradox has Gail Que as a hostage!" she exclaimed and read the note aloud.

Detective Troop,

In a chess game there are two queens. Now that I have Gail Que, you will have to decide if Gail Que is my chess piece or is she your chess piece? Nevertheless, I have her. The only thing left is for me to capture the king.

The Paradox

Trooper studied the photo of a woman bound with duct tape to a metal folding chair. *Where is Teco? Why hasn't he contacted me? Is he back in Atlanta?* Turning to Fordham, she said, "Let me see that kidnapping report."

"We don't have a lot of time. So, we need to act fast," said Yeomans who displayed an overlay of the chess game with a map of Atlanta on the overhead screen. Because Trooper was in a daze, he added, "Trooper! I need you right here with us. Teco might try to take down The Paradox on his own; and we can't allow that to happen. Now stay with us Trooper."

"You don't get it. Do you? Teco isn't answering any of my calls. It's extremely hard to concentrate, but continue; my head's in the game."

Fordham said, "We put a rush on the DNA lab results from the fabric that was found on top of the Front Page News building. It matches that of a man named Robert Edwards whose alias is Bobby Stephens. Trooper, your statement in the D.C. crime report says that you didn't get a good view of the suspect. Now, the only two people who can I.D. the suspect are Teco and Gail Que."

"That's not so," said Trooper with her hand up as if she were in high school.

With a puzzled expression, Fordham asked, "What do you mean?"

"Captain Wicker back in D.C. has a picture of Bobby Stephens, a.k.a. The Paradox, when Bobby was on drugs back in Philadelphia."

"Call Captain Wicker and get those photos ASAP," said Fordham.

Trooper said, "I already have them." Searching through her backpack, she added, "Here they are."

"Okay, now we have someone to I.D. Get this picture to metro-Atlanta law enforcement and all major news stations," Yeomans said to Fordham. He continued, "According to the chess game from the United States Chess Federation, in the 21st and 22nd move, the queen was taken. Now the next 2 moves are his queen to D-2 and our knight to D-4. On the map of Atlanta, that would put us in East Point."

"What the hell is East Point?" asked Swoosh who wondered why Trooper was still gazing at the photo.

"Well, that depends on what we're looking for. There's East Point Tower which is an old historical museum. Also, special events are held there. Then you have Fort McPherson."

"Isn't that a military base?" asked Swoosh.

"Yes, it is and we think that's where The Paradox will strike next. We need to pull a team together and—"

"I don't think that's our best move," said Trooper.

"Why is that?" asked Fordham.

"Well, let's take into account that we're talking about a man who is military. Going to Fort McPherson puts us at a disadvantage in playing his game."

"How so?" asked Fordham.

"When it comes to a crime being committed on a military base, one, it's a federal offense; and two, it will be investigated by a military crime unit; and three, we are outsiders or civilians. Since The Paradox knows this information, I don't think it is Fort McPherson."

"So what else is in East Point?" Swoosh asked Yeomans.

"See, that's it, he doesn't think that we'll figure out the 21st and 22nd move. What's another name for a museum?" asked Trooper. "Better yet, what is housed in museums?"

"Old antiques and jewels," stated Yeomans.

"Yes, you are right. What's another name for a historic item?" When no one answered, she added, "They are called relics. This can't be a coincidence. We must remember that things are paradoxical to this man. Most chess pieces are made out of wood, which fits the East Point Tower place."

"So, how do we know when he is going to East Point tower?" asked Fordham.

"That detective, I can't answer. How many moves are we away from the 21st or 22nd move?" asked Trooper.

"Well, let's see," said Detective Fordham. "According to the Atlanta grid, these moves have already been made. Besides, the photo proves that the queen has been taken . . . that's Gail Que."

"Today is the 23rd. That's it. How fast can we get a team over to East Point Tower?" asked Trooper.

"I can have a car over there in 20 minutes or so. Are you sure about this?" asked Yeomans.

"No, it's a gut feeling. Tell them to stand down until we arrive."

Later that morning, Yeomans made sure that the police squad was well covered because he didn't want to be too obvious that East Point Tower was being staked out. Waiting for 1 hour, nothing was going down. Then a coach bus pulled up to the East Point Tower building.

"All units, be alert. This may be a diversion."

"Copy that."

Trooper said, "Did anyone bring the photo of Bobby Stephens." Then she turned to Swoosh and whispered, "Today, I received confirmation that this case is a lot bigger then we know. I got a phone call from a computer generated voice that said to leave the case alone, but I'm not leaving until I have his ass. I don't think Bobby Stephens is going to show up today."

"You might be right."

An officer called on the radio and said, "We have a black minivan pulling into the lot."

Yeomans said, "All units stand down. I repeat; stand down."

Trooper and Swoosh reached for their binoculars.

"He's getting out on your side. Is this the target?" asked Yeomans.

"We can't tell yet," said Trooper who realized that the parking lot was full of cars. The passengers who were getting off of the bus seemed to be enjoying themselves as the sun did an incandescent staged appearance in and out of the beautiful white cumulus clouds. The entire stakeout team kept the black minivan in view from various positions and angles.

In the minivan, The Paradox tried to ignore the voice in his head which was getting the best of him. *Soulja, do you really think this will work? Why don't you just kill the po po and get it over with so we can move on? Why must you play these silly games?*

Trooper observed that their suspect was talking to someone. As he spoke, she tried to read his lips; however, he was not directly facing her. That's when Swoosh looked around not knowing if the suspect was accompanied by others. Trooper tapped on Swoosh's arm. When he turned around there was an East Point police cruiser pulling into the parking lot as if he were doing his routine rounds at this time in the early afternoon.

"Detective Yeomans, we may have a situation," said Swoosh.

"I'm already on it. Let's just hope that the police cruiser keeps moving. If not, we must move fast. Delta Charlie 1 and Delta Charlie 2, you're the closest to defuse the matter. Be ready. We have too many bystanders out here."

"Roger that sir." The entire law enforcement team watched as the police cruiser approached the black minivan.

Chapter 46

"SHIT TROOPER, THAT OFFICER IS pulling up to the van. Please, don't get out buddy," said Swoosh in a low tone.

"Oh Shit! He's getting out Swoosh!" Trooper reached for the door, but Swoosh grabbed her by the arm.

"Wait, let's see what happens." She wanted to rush The Paradox and catch him, but she knew that she needed to find out the whereabouts of Teco and GQ. With the minivan blocked in by the police cruiser, the first thing the officer did was place his right hand on the side of the minivan. This was a routine action when an officer is engaged in a traffic stop. When the officer tried to look inside the van, the driver closed the door.

The Paradox said, "Yes sir, may I help you?"

"I was checking the area because we received a few calls about a suspicious minivan in the area."

The Paradox scanned the parking lot because the officer said the word "we." That's when he noticed a number of unmarked cars at different angles.

"May I see your driver's license and registration card?" asked the police officer who didn't notice the telescopic steel baton that slid from the inside sleeve of The Paradox. Within a flash of light and one flicker of the wrist, the steel baton expanded to 21 inches. By the time the officer looked down at the black object, his timing was too late. The baton came across the officer's chest with great force, followed by a hard blow from a bayonet.

Rushing out of the car with her gun drawn, Trooper signalled for the other team members to follow. As the officer fell to the ground, The Paradox quickly retrieved the officer's gun and aimed it at Trooper.

The surveillance team surrounded the minivan as the bystanders scrabbled for cover. "Hold your fire! Hold your fire! We need to find out where Gail Que is located. Please hold your fire!" exclaimed Trooper. In the distance, the sound of sirens filled the air. The Paradox smiled.

"It's the police! Bobby, put the gun down. We've lost enough people already. I don't know how long I can hold them off."

With fiery eyes, he looked at Trooper. Then The Paradox saw the wounded officer who was trying to inchworm his way to safety. "I told you we would meet in due time." Without warning, The Paradox shot the wounded officer in the head. Intentionally avoiding Trooper, he fired at the surveillance team as he used the front of the minivan as a shield. People ran and screamed for their lives as multiple bullets invaded the area. The undercover officers ducked behind their vehicles as they fired back at the crazed gunman who escaped behind the East Point Tower building.

Trooper and Yeomans ran after him. Behind a mail truck at the end of the plaza, The Paradox heard Trooper say, "Hold your fire! I repeat hold your fire!"

Standing up against the back of the postal truck, The Paradox felt his heart trying to escape out of his chest. He wanted to run back to his van which housed his ammunition. After assessing his options, he said, "One, two, three . . ." Like a bat out of hell, he approached a catering truck which was full of food for the day's events at the East Point Tower.

The Paradox was relieved that there were no police following him. The driver of the catering truck dropped a cake as The Paradox held a gun to the driver's face.

"Where are the keys?" asked The Paradox.

"There in the truck," he said shaking with intense fear. "Please don't kill me." The Paradox slapped the driver in the face with the stolen 9mm pistol. As The Paradox used the man as a shield, he hopped into the truck and put the gear shift in reverse. The driver of the catering truck moved out of the way just in time.

The Paradox wondered why the police cars were not behind him. Heading toward the highway, The Paradox thought his way was clear until he heard the whirling blades of the helicopter above.

Detective Yeomans, this is Air Support 7254, we have the stolen vehicle in sight, copy."

"Air Support 7254, we copy. Keep us posted. We need to find out where he's holding a possible hostage. SWAT is ready to move."

"The suspect is moving on I-285."

"Copy that 7254," said Yeomans as officers on location at the East Point Tower surveyed the damages. When EMT placed a sheet over the dead officer, Trooper held her head down as if she were carrying the weight of the world on her shoulders.

GBI Agent McLoughlin arrived on the scene and said, "Lieutenants, I have some good news and bad news. Which do you want first?"

"You tell me. It's all news," said Swoosh taking out his inhaler.

"Well, Bobby Stephens was spotted going into a hotel off of I-285." Trooper jumped up as if she were commanded to come to attention. Mac said, "Slow down Trooper. We called off the police chase as The Paradox exited this scene. We will be handing over the case to the Feds once they arrive. Sorry guys."

Trooper was overly excited to get to the hotel. She walked to her car and opened the door. Yeomans stopped her and said, "And where do you think you're going? You don't even know where he's at. Plus, we need your help here. Do you know how much evidence could be in that minivan?"

"You don't get it do you?"

"I get the fact that you are not acting like a team player."

"Back in D.C., I'm the one in charge. There are too many cooks in the kitchen in this city."

"Okay, okay, I know where The Paradox is. Together Trooper, together, if we can get to him first, we might be able to gain the ups on finding Gail Que."

"I'm listening," said Trooper.

"We here in the Dirty South don't like when things are taken from us. This is why we gave you such a hard time when you first got here. But now, you are one of us."

Yeomans walked over to speak with Mac before getting into an unmarked vehicle with Trooper, Swoosh and Fordham. They left East Point Towers at high speeds with lights flashing.

Trooper asked, "What did Mac say?"

"Well, he said not to let him down in nabbing this guy. We don't have much time before the Feds get here."

Fordham said, "We're not dealing with some thug from the streets. This guy has single-handedly killed in other states; and now he's using our city as a freaking chess board. You damn right; I want a piece of his ass first."

Swoosh said, "You'll get the chance. Don't we always get our man?"

Within an hour, the unmarked car pulled up to the Perimeter Westin Hotel.

"Damn, this is the hotel where we're staying," said Swoosh.

"Has he been staking us out?" asked Trooper who felt uneasy.

Detective Yeomans got out of the car to speak with two other officers who were already on the scene.

Fordham said, "Trooper, can you get in contact with that reporter you know?"

"Who? Christa Hall from CNN?"

"Yeah, that's her."

"I'm not sure. I haven't talked to her lately."

"I've been thinking. Since the Feds are taking over our case, I want to get the jump on them with the media. We need to put our spin on this case; after all, we were the ones to corner The Paradox."

"I'll try to reach her," said Trooper reaching for her cell phone.

Yeomans said, "Swoosh, can you come with me? We need to talk with the hotel manager so we can figure out what floor this nut case is on."

As Trooper walked away from the Westin Hotel building to get a better cell phone reception, Christa Hall from CNN answered the call. After Trooper briefed Christa on the latest events, Trooper looked up towards the clear blue sky and said, "Oh my word."

"What Lieutenant Troop? Are you alright?" asked Christa.

"Yes, I'm fine. I'm looking at these two blue glass buildings. It's making sense to me now. Are those crowns on the top of those buildings?"

"Are you talking about the king and queen towers? The square crown is the king and the round crown is the queen. They are office buildings . . . Hello, Hello Lieutenant Troop?"

Pulling herself out of the hypnotic state, Trooper shook her head from side to side and said, "Christa, just hurry to the Perimeter Westin Hotel if you want an exclusive interview."

Trooper closed the cell phone, walked over to Detective Fordham and said, "Can we talk for a second?"

"Sure," she said as she led Trooper to the edge of the hotel's entrance.

"Why didn't you tell me that those buildings over there were called the king and queen towers?" asked Trooper.

Fordham stood there looking into the sky as if she were struck by a bolt of lightning. Then she realized that Trooper was walking towards the king and queen buildings. Fordham rushed to catch up with her and asked. "Why do you think this building has something to do with our perp?"

"Well, I have a hypothesis. He is using these buildings to signify that we are at the end of his deadly game of chess."

"Could be."

"In Little Five Points, that robot, TRASH, was headed in the northeast direction. What is the location of these towers?

Trooper always amazed Fordham with her encyclopedic memory. *How in the hell does she remember all of these tiny details?*

"Well?" asked Trooper.

Fordham said, "I'd say that they are on the northeastern corner of I-285 and Georgia 400. Why?"

"This all can't be a coincidence . . . the northeast direction and buildings that look like chess pieces."

They walked into the queen tower and advanced towards the security desk. Trooper said, "Excuse me sir, have you seen this guy or this guy around here?"

The security officer squinted as he looked at the two pictures. "Ma'am I've seen a lot of people come and go. I don't recall seeing them at all."

"So what businesses are in these two big buildings?"

"Well cutie, we have 34 stories of offices. There are a few empty offices if you'd like to lease one. I can give you a personal tour," he said licking his bottom lip.

"You know that I can take that as sexual harassment," she said pulling out her detective badge. ". . . And you will be out of a job."

Embarrassment consumed the security officer's face; and he said, "To answer your question lieutenant, there are too many businesses here to name. If you want, you can take this directory guide." He handed the booklet to Trooper as if it were a peace offering.

Seeing a SWAT car and a Sandy Plains police cruiser pass by, Fordham said, "They're here."

Turning to the security guard, Trooper said, "Sir, may I keep this book?"

"Sure ma'am, I have several."

When they walked out of the queen tower, Trooper came to the conclusion that Gail Que was the police department's chess piece; and she was determined that their next move would be to capture The Paradox's king.

Chapter 47

WHEN FORDHAM AND TROOPER EXITED the building, the security guard was curious why the detective said, "They're here." Coming from behind the desk to see what was going on, he knew that their purpose was very important because a lot of law enforcement vehicles were pulling up to the hotel as guests were coming out in droves.

Just as Trooper reached the hotel parking lot, Swoosh turned to Trooper and said, "Yeomans has confirmed that a room is currently occupied by someone who does fit the profile of The Paradox. The Atlanta PD is waiting for all floors to be evacuated."

Trooper walked to the trunk of her car and pulled out her SWAT Airsoft protective vest.

Swoosh asked, "What are you doing?"

"What does it look like? I'm getting suited. I think you should be doing the same," said Trooper as she put her right arm through the sleeveless vest.

Grabbing her by the arm, Swoosh said, "Trooper this is not our show."

Snatching her arm away from his grasp and pulling her hair back to put on her multicolored scarf, she said, "As long as my partner is involved, I will be a part of this show." With haste she unzipped the black Homeland Security assault rife case. Retrieving the AR-15 rifle, she attached the carbine stock and threw the rifle over her right shoulder.

"Hanae, I'm your partner; and I'm right here with you. I was there when this fool killed Ronald, not Teco Jackson. It was me damn it!"

In that moment, she put her hand in her pocket to feel Ronald's red D20 die. "You know, right now I don't know who to trust because I was brought back in on this case for someone else's political gain. There's a great deal of underhanded shit going on in D.C. So, my mission is to find Teco . . . for my own personal gain." Turning to look Swoosh square in the eyes, she added, "Swoosh, are you with me? If not, move out of my way!"

He looked at Trooper as if she were crazy. "You can't go in there with them. The SWAT team is about to make the call to the suspect's suite now."

Trooper took out two 30 round Zytel magazines. Then she said, "Whatever happened to the multi-jurisdiction operation we had going on?" When Swoosh gave her a blank stare, she continued, "Yeah, that's what I thought."

The SWAT team went into the building while covering all of the emergency exits. When everyone was in place, the SWAT commander made the call in order to be patched through to the 6 SWAT team members who stood on both sides of suite 841. They were ready to barge into the room.

Covered from head to toe with black tactical gear while wearing their Kevlar helmets with clear protective shields, the SWAT team's eyes were the only visible body part to be seen.

The SWAT team leader to the left of the door held up 2 fingers, then 1 finger, and finally closed his hand into a tight fist. The SWAT breacher took the key card and swiped the glimmering brass lock. When the LED light turned to green, the same officer cracked the door and threw in a 4 inch high hexagonal pyramid wireless camera which rolled over to the middle of the room and landed in an upright position. The SWAT breacher on the right held a Sony GVD-800 micro-monitor in order to view the suite which appeared to be empty.

"Clear!" yelled the SWAT breacher with the monitor.

The other men held their Bushmaster A3 rifles in a firing position ready to enter into the suite. At the count of three, the SWAT team rushed into the room; however, none of them noticed the tan colored government issued trip wire attached to the bottom of the door which ran under the plush carpet.

One SWAT scout went into the large bedroom and exclaimed, "We have a hostage!"

Another SWAT scout rushed into the dinette area to search under the cabinets and said, "Clear!"

"Sierra one to the command post," said the SWAT breacher with the monitor.

Standing at the command post, Trooper and Swoosh heard the SWAT commander say, "Sierra one, go ahead with your traffic."

"We have a hostage duct taped to a chair. The female is conscious, but barely. Sir, she looks like Gail Que, our kidnapped victim."

Passing by a concealed camera which was sticking out of a flower pot full of white, pink, yellow and red geraniums, the officers were not prepared for what happened next. Out of nowhere, there was a bright flash of light which blinded everyone. As they took cover, the television exploded. Ka-boom!

The entire suite was on fire; and the explosion knocked the complete outside wall of the hotel onto the patio furniture below. SWAT team members were instantly killed on impact including the female hostage.

"Sierra one! Come in! I repeat. Sierra one, come in!" When the SWAT command post never received a response, the fire marshal yelled, "Secure the area. Secure the area and get a team in there with EMT fast! Hurry! Hurry damn it!"

While the fire and rescue team stormed into the hotel, there was pandemonium all around. Trooper found this as her opportunity to make a quick move. So, she eased her way to the back of the building.

A firefighter said, "Excuse me ma'am. The fire marshal is not allowing anyone into the building until the upstairs fire is contained."

Trooper flashed her badge and said, "I need to check for additional hostages in this area of the building. Can you get clearance for me to enter?"

Getting impatient, Trooper sensed that The Paradox was close by because she heard the confirmation over the radio that The Paradox was not seen leaving the building from the security video film.

The firefighter said, "Ma'am, the fire marshal said that I should go in the building with you."

"Look," Trooper said viewing his name tag, "Wilson, this killer may be armed with a weapon. You are not equipped to rescue these hostages; and I can't risk you getting killed."

Firefighter Wilson gave Trooper's comment some thought and said, "Okay, you can enter, but radio us back if you see any signs of smoke."

As Trooper went into the hotel's north side exit, the back door was slightly opened. With her back to the wall she opened the door completely. The bright sunlight flashed into the dark hallway making the area visible from the distance.

The hall lights flickered on and off. Moving slowly down the hallway, the exit door slammed shut behind Trooper. The loud sound caused her to involuntarily jump. Now the area was dark; however, she was able to maneuver her way to the first door to the right. She turned the knob and the door opened. This room was full of storage boxes. Thinking that she heard something, Trooper spun around quickly, but there was no one behind her. For some reason, she was feeling very nervous.

Damn, I need to find Teco.

At the moment she was about to exit the room, she heard light footsteps coming her way. When she stepped out with Sunshine raised in the air, she put the barrel in the person's face and said, "It's the police. Don't move or I will shoot." When Trooper saw the familiar face, she said, "Girl, I almost shot you."

"I almost shot you too," said Detective Fordham trying to look around the area with a Maglite flashlight. "Why is it so dark down here?"

Raising her Maglite flashlight at the emergency light box, Trooper said, "I guess the lights went out during the explosion, but the strange thing is that the emergency lights never came on."

"Yeah, that is strange. We shouldn't be down here without backup."

Trooper asked, "What are you doing down here anyways?"

"I saw you come around to the back. Why are you—"

"I wanted to see if there were any other hostages before this guy gets away. Teco has to be close by. Remember that the chess game isn't over yet."

"Will it ever be over?" asked Fordham as she tried to focus on Trooper who was moving to the next door. Since Trooper didn't reply, Fordham continued, "We'll search for The Paradox together. Maybe, he'll lead us to Teco."

They moved from door to door in search of hostages. Halfway down the dark hallway of the laundry area, The Paradox plunged from the ventilation duct and snatched Fordham around the neck with a knife to her throat. All forms of trepidation entered her mind for what this man would do to her. When Trooper spun around, she feared the worst as she heard Fordham's gun fall to the floor.

Fordham said, "Trooper, help me," but her voice was faint.

"Bobby! Let her go." Then Trooper pushed her chin on to the microphone on her shoulder and said, "This is Detective Troop. I have the suspect on the bottom level north side laundry area."

The radio screeched and Swoosh responded, "Copy that Trooper. We're 10-24!"

Soulja, don't play any games. Kill Detective Troop. Do this and I'll bring you in for another mission.

"Shut up and let me handle this!" exclaimed The Paradox.

Trooper wondered was The Paradox talking to her. She wanted to turn around and see if there were others down the hallway; however, she knew from past experience not to take her eyes off of him.

"That was a stupid move Detective Troop, but we meet again at last. Yesss!" exclaimed The Paradox.

"Trooper, please don't let him kill me," Fordham cried out.

Seeing the same fear in Fordham's eyes that Trooper once had years ago in that dark alley back in D.C., Trooper said, "Bobby, why are you on this suicide mission? Just let her go. We have—"

"This isn't suicide. It's called having leverage over a situation. To you it would be murder." The door behind them swung open and a gust of lucid sunlight brightened the hallway; and the ray's resplendency blinded Trooper's vision.

Pulling out a hand grenade with his free hand, The Paradox made Fordham bite down on the pin with her teeth. "Don't move; or I'll jerk her head back to pull the pin out right now!" exclaimed The Paradox.

Outside of the hotel's north side exit, the lead SWAT officer held up his fist and all the rest of them behind him stopped in their tracks.

Into the microphone, Trooper said, "SWAT team, please exit the building. He has Detective Fordham in a chokehold with a knife to her neck and a live grenade in her mouth."

Screaming, The Paradox said, "I encourage you to do as she says!"

Without warning, The Paradox released the hand grenade away from Fordham who tried to squirm from under his grasp; however, his grip was too tight.

"Bobby, where is Teco Jackson? And don't move your left hand."

"Detective Troop, what are you going to do this time? Since you know me so well, why don't you know the reason for my mission? I'm not the one who's killing without a cause. You people are committing genocide and calling it government funding for war on drugs."

"Bobby, Robert, whatever the hell your name is, let her go. I'm who you want. Your game is with me, not her. Where is Teco Jackson in this building?"

The Paradox let out a diabolical laugh that scared Fordham even more.

"Let her go or I'll kill you, you sick son of a bitch." Then it dawned on Trooper that GQ might be dead. The Paradox could see tears rolling down Trooper's face as the lights flickered.

Unexpectedly, Fordham elbowed The Paradox in the ribs; and then she gave him a head shot to his chin which stupefied The Paradox. Fordham rushed towards Trooper who knew that a decision had to be made. If The Paradox was killed, she might never find Teco.

The Paradox swayed backwards from Fordham's blow. Trooper took aim and fired once grazing him in the left wrist. Trooper grabbed Fordham and rushed into another room and took cover behind a metal filing cabinet.

The Paradox burst in behind them as the hand grenade dropped to the floor. Expecting a big boom, the room was still. When Trooper saw The Paradox reaching for the grenade pin, she shot him again but this time grazing him in the other hand. She said, "Don't make me kill you. Where is Teco Jackson?" she asked while walking over to him as he dropped to the floor. She put her right foot on top of his wounded left wrist.

"AARRGH!" vociferated The Paradox. Looking up at Trooper he asked, "Is that supposed to make me tell you something?"

Swoosh came into the half lit room with his weapon raised. When he saw Trooper's gun against The Paradox's temple, Swoosh said, "No, don't do it. If you shoot him, we will never get the information we need."

Finding it difficult to keep her composure, Trooper asked, "Where is Teco Jackson?" As she pressed the barrel harder to his head, she repeated, "Where is Teco Jackson?"

Chapter 48

UNDER POLICE CUSTODY, Bobby Stephens, a.k.a. The Paradox, came from the hospital to the City Hall East interrogation room with his wrists all bandaged up. He constantly complained that the handcuffs caused him great pain; however, for three long hours Yeomans kept asking The Paradox about the whereabouts of Teco Jackson. However, The Paradox didn't give him a single clue.

Coming out of the interrogation room, Yeomans looked at Trooper and Swoosh and said, "This prick is hard as a rock. Good luck."

Lieutenant Troop did not hesitate to enter into the room first. The Paradox's eyes lit up; and he smiled. Swoosh came into the room and took a seat by the door as if he were blocking it from anyone else entering.

Trooper paced the floor in front of him. Suddenly the sound of ka-pow filled the air and The Paradox's neck snapped back.

Trooper said, "That's for shooting me in D.C."

Rushing into the interrogation room from the observation room, Yeomans asked, "What the hell are you doing slapping the suspect?"

The Paradox said, "I'm not complaining. I like it rough before I stick it to her."

Swoosh said, "Show some respect." Then he lunged for The Paradox; and Yeomans had to hold Swoosh back.

"I've got this. I've got this," said Trooper. "Paul, this I know for sure. Mr. Stephens tried to kill me. Why don't you go get us some hot coffee."

As Yeomans left the room, Trooper stood behind The Paradox, bent over to his ear and said, "I have two words for you, check mate."

The Paradox smiled and then laughed, "Ummm . . . that feels good. Why didn't you tell me that your lips were so soft?"

Moving to his right side, Trooper drew back her fist punching The Paradox square on the jaw. Pow! This time he spit out blood.

"No fair, when do I get to tap you on that ass?" asked The Paradox.

Swoosh said, "You have one more time to be disrespectful."

"If she is not engaged in S&M, I'd call this police brutality."

"Let me be clear. That punch was for Ronald Heard," said Trooper. "There is no next move for you Bobby Stephens, so tell me the location of Teco Jackson." Pulling out a syringe and a small vial from her black briefcase, Trooper put these items on the table. "There's only one other thing for me to do."

Soulja, Detective Troop thinks you have Teco Jackson. What a crock of bullshit. Don't fall for it.

When The Paradox didn't answer Trooper, Swoosh stepped forward, picked up the vial and said, "Look man; let me tell you something. In this tiny bottle is 1000 cc's of sodium pentothal."

"Truth serum?" asked The Paradox.

"Yep, she's never used this stuff before, but we do know that it works. The problem is that if Detective Troop uses too much, the drug can be lethal; and you'll rapidly go into an induced coma. Then ten to fifteen minutes later you're dead," said Swoosh shaking his head from side to side.

Tired of playing games, Trooper rolled up The Paradox's sleeves and started to tie a medical rubber band around The Paradox's upper arm.

"Detective Troop wait! Bobby, are you with a unit called RELLIK?" asked Swoosh.

The Paradox looked at Swoosh and asked, "What do you know about RELLIK, lieutenant?"

Swoosh said, "Not much, I was hoping that you'd help me to understand the team's mission. I think I can talk Detective Troop out of killing you."

In a rage, The Paradox lashed out and said, "See, that's it. You don't know shit about the mission of RELLIK. You didn't see the things I've seen that our own government did to people abroad. You have no idea about the real war or the risk of casualties when your livelihood is taken from you. You become a chess pawn for their cause—"

"I'm not buying it. Who is the LOTO group that runs the RELLIK mission?" asked Swoosh.

"Lieutenant Brown, the clues are all around you; and you and Detective Troop haven't figured this shit out yet." The Paradox looked at Trooper and continued, "You out of all people I thought would have figured this out. To answer your question Detective Brown, I'd have to kill you because it's top secret; however, I might just enjoy that."

Swoosh was ready to take a few swings at The Paradox; however, he said, "I bet you would."

Trooper picked up the syringe and put the tip into the vial. "This is your last chance. Where is Teco Jackson and who is the head of the LOTO group that runs the RELLIK operation?"

When The Paradox didn't answer, Trooper drew 50 cc's from the vial.

Just as Swoosh looked out the small square door window, he said, "We've got unwanted company." When Swoosh grabbed The Paradox's right hand, The Paradox let out an anguished cry of pain. Swoosh asked, "Who is running LOTO?"

At the sound of the door knob turning, Swoosh and Trooper spun around.

"You don't have to answer that. I'm FBI Special Agent Fairchild Vargus," he said in a foreign accent. "This is my prisoner now."

Trooper rushed over to Agent Vargus, snatched him by his lapel, slammed his back into the wall and said, "I don't give a damn who you are. You're not taking him any place until he gives us the information we need."

Agent Vargus said, "If you don't take your hands off of me, I promise that you won't have a job when you get back to Washington, D.C. nor will you have a license to operate your P.I. business."

Trooper was caught off guard that this FBI Agent knew so much about her. When she released her grip, he straightened his black jacket.

"As I was saying, this prisoner is now in federal custody." Reaching in his jacket, Agent Vargus pulled out some papers. "Here are the orders from Washington, D.C."

Trooper stormed out of the door to find Yeomans. However, she was stopped by Mac from GBI, who said, "Lieutenant Troop, this is out of our control. You have done a superb job of helping us to catch this serial killer. You and Detective Yeomans will receive the Presidential Medal for Merit award for your commendable service in the most successful multi-jurisdiction operation between Philadelphia, Washington, D.C. and Atlanta in United States history. Government officials are talking of expanding this success to a wider base."

As Agent Vargus escorted The Paradox out of the room with shackles, The Paradox turned to Trooper and said, "Detective Troop, check the game. I believe you moved the wrong piece."

Even though Trooper heard Mac, she was in deep thought about what The Paradox said and ran down the hallway and yelled, "Wait, Agent Vargus!"

He asked, "What is it Lieutenant Troop?"

"Can we at least find out if there are other hostages hidden by your crazy psycho prisoner?"

"Lieutenant Troop, that's not a federal issue." Turning to The Paradox, Agent Vargus added, "He is."

"That's a bunch of government bullshit."

"I'll tell you what. When we get Robert Edwards, a.k.a. Bobby Stephens, to a high security federal prison, we'll contact you on the location."

Trooper said, "Wait, I have one more question."

"What's that?" asked Agent Vargus.

"How do I find out information about the LOTO group and the RELLIK operation?"

"Lieutenant Troop, that's highly classified information. You don't have the proper security clearances."

As the elevator door was closing, The Paradox mouthed, "Ignorance is strength."

Trooper stood there looking at the elevator door with her interlocked hands resting on her head. Then she pulled the multicolored scarf from her head to her neck. She needed to get some air, so she pressed the elevator button. This should have been a very victorious moment for her after she was told by Mac that she was going to receive the highest United States police decoration; however, she didn't know how to celebrate until Teco was found.

As Trooper took the elevator down to the lobby floor, she slammed her fist against the elevator wall. "Shit!" She wanted so badly to rip someone's head off; and the only person in mind was Captain Wicker for hauling her back into the field. She was doing just fine running her own business as a P.I. Her thoughts turned to Gail Que.

Why did GQ have to die? She was doing so well in becoming a productive citizen and role model after leaving the Strictly Business crew in Philadelphia. Who will take over the Indigo Signature Collection now that GQ is gone?

When Trooper reached the lobby level, she thought about sitting on the same bench where Teco sat just a few days ago; however, the bench was occupied by a man who looked to be an attorney. He wore a blue pinned striped suit with a light blue dress shirt. In his hands were a stack of manila folders and his silver monogram cuff links were shining.

Then Trooper looked outside the front door and saw a flock of news reporters trying to get into the building. Cameras were flashing as she passed by, so she turned around to go out the back exit. She needed seclusion.

"She's going out the back door . . . west end of the building," said the man speaking into a microphone at the end of his sleeve. This was the same person Trooper saw sitting on the bench.

"We are in position and ready. Get out of there," said the voice in a British accent to the man on the bench.

When Trooper opened the exit door, she paused thinking that an alarm should have gone off. She tried to leave the door cracked; however, it closed. *Damn!*

Suddenly, a black Escalade Extended SUV Vehicle (ESV) pulled up and two blond haired men wearing black suits and dark shades jumped out of the side passenger doors. Trooper reached for Sunshine; however, the man to the left with the British accent said, "Lieutenant Troop, we suggest that you not do that."

"Who the hell are you?" asked Trooper.

"That's not important right now," said the man to the right with the southern accent.

The men just looked at her dubiously when she placed her right hand on her weapon. "We need you to come with us, please," said the man to the left.

"Who are you? FBI?" asked Trooper.

"No ma'am," said the man to the right who now displayed a Sabre stun gun in his hand.

"Oh hell no, I'm not going anywhere with you," said Trooper.

"Suit yourself," said the man who raised the stun gun.

"What the fu—" asked Trooper as her body went limp. Before she met the ground, the British man caught her while the southern man swooped up her legs. Together, they put her into the SUV.

"Go! Go! Go!" said the southern man to the driver.

By the time the SUV hit Martin Luther King Boulevard, Trooper's feet and mouth were bound with duct tape. Within minutes, the black van drove into an undisclosed hanger at the Charlie Brown Airport where they boarded a black Gulfstream Micro Jet.

On the side of the private jet was a red thick stripe with a logo of a white shield. A dragon was on each side of the shield. On top of the shield was a royal crown; and in the center of the shield was a phoenix with its head turned to the right.

After the door of the aircraft closed, the British man said to the pilot, "We have her and are ready to go."

To be continued in *The Street Life Series: Is It Power or Envy?*

If you wish to contact the author, Kevin M. Weeks,
the email address is *info@thestreetlifeseries.com*.
He looks forward to corresponding with you.

SOURCES

The following citations were used as sources of information in writing this novel.

Harris, Clifford. "No Matter What." Paper Trail. Atlantic, 2008.

"History of Chess." eSSORTMENT. 20 September 2008.
<http://www.essortment.com/all/chesshistory_rmct.htm>

"History Civil War." World Book. 1996 ed.

"Icosahedron." Wikipedia. 13 June 2009.
<http://en.wikipedia.org/wiki/Icosahedron>

Lyle, D. P. HowDunit — Forensics. Ohio: Writer Digest Books, 2008.

Polgar, Laszlo and Bruce Pandolfini. Chess: 5334 Problems, Combinations and Games. New York: Black Dog & Leventhal Publishers, 2006.

Stevens, Serita, Ann Bannon. HowDunit — The Book of Poisons. Ohio: Writer Digest Books, 2007.

"SWAT." Hollywood Police Department. 6 June 2009.
<http://www.hollywoodpolice.org/special_units/swatteam.htm>

U.S. Chess Federation. <u>United States Chess Federation's Official Rules of Chess, Fifth Edition.</u> New York: Random House Puzzles & Games, 2003.

Waton, John. <u>Mastering the Chess Openings: Unlocking the Mysteries of the Modern Chess Openings, Volume 1</u>. London: Gambit Publications, 2006.

Wizards of the Coast. <u>Dungeons & Dragons</u>. Rhode Island: Hasbro, 2000.